RUSH

BRIDGET L. ROSE

First Edition – 2022

Editing: Bridget L. Rose Books Inc.

Cover Design: Bridget L. Rose Books Inc.

Formatting: Bridget L. Rose Books Inc.

Illustrations: @emilyxvrs

Pitstop Series

Team Names

Velocità Rossa

Alfa Adrenalina

GRENZENLOS

Hawke

Tempête Racing

zeitgeist racing

CK

Klein Racing

Spark Racing

Carousel

Racing

Aerodinámica

This book is dedicated to all the girls and women out there with a dream. Never give up on your dream, even if it feels like your dream is giving up on you. And if you have already, start dreaming again. The world needs you to be the change.

Trigger Warnings

The ***trigger warnings list includes***: working through grief, topics of loss and fear of loss, child abandonment, sexism, emotional and (the mention of) physical abuse, dealing with trauma and trying to work through.

Author's note

Hello, my dear reader,

Thank you so much for wanting to read Rush: Part One & Two. Before you dive into the book, I just wanted to say a few things about this story. For one, this is the first book in Valentina and Gabriel's story. There will be two books, so please don't expect a happily ever after just yet, that will only come later. This book is about Formula One and a woman's journey into F1, but it is also about love and relationships and healing. It's about Valentina and Gabriel as they find their way to each other. This is a book about two friends who have known each other for a while and have developed feelings, so you will see them already having feelings for each other.

This book is less about the before of a relationship and more about two people trying to figure out how to be together after all of their pain, grief, and loss as well as fears of abandonment. While there is still some slow burn, it is more because of them not knowing how to give into their feelings without their fears getting in the way. Most of this book, therefore, is about Val and Gabriel figuring out how to be in a relationship, so they will be together for most of this. If that sounds like something you will **NOT** enjoy, please don't read this book.

Because this book was originally published as two books, it is on the longer side. There are a lot of chapters, but that's because my chapters are quite short, so don't let the number scare you. However, if you do not enjoy longer books, you probably won't like this one either.

There is also a lot of talk about grief, so I just wanted to tell you all that if you've ever lost anyone you've loved and found light in the darkness, I'm so proud of you. I know it never really gets easier—that's something the movies tell you, but it most certainly isn't true, especially not for everyone—so I'm proud of you for finding any light to hold onto. And if you haven't found light yet, that's more than okay, too. Take your time. Grieve however you need to grieve. Don't let anyone tell you that you have to feel a certain way about your loss. Gabriel and Valentina both have lost so many people, and they grieve in different ways even if some of them are similar. Adrian grieves in an entirely different way, too. I hope my characters can show you and allow you to see that happiness isn't found in the absence of pain. Happiness is found everywhere, even in the midst of pain.

Take care of yourselves. I'm so proud of all of you.

All my love,

Bridget.

RUSH

Part One

A. ROMANA
V ROMANA

Chapter 1

Valentina

Spending fourteen hours on a flight with my brother while he snores into my ear is *not* fun. Adrian usually doesn't snore, but, for some reason, he became a professional at it last night. His head hung back against his seat on the plane, his mouth hanging wide open. That means I haven't had a wink of sleep in the past twenty-four hours.

If that wasn't enough to make me cranky, Mr. Bigfoot stepped on my toes as we got off the plane without realizing it, so I shoved him off with several curse words falling from my lips and my middle finger raised high to flip him off.

I love my brother. He's my favorite person in the entire world, but when I don't get sleep, no one should be around me. Especially not the person who prevented me from getting my eight hours in. As an aspiring Formula One racer who works out almost every single day, I need rest to let my muscles rejuvenate.

Adrian's been walking behind me for a while now, keeping his distance, asking why the hell I'm limping. I don't dignify his question with an answer, merely continue making my way out of the airport so we can go... *home*.

After a couple more minutes of me silently walking ahead, I take a deep breath and turn around only to realize he's disappeared.

"Adrian!" I hiss, hoping he will hear me. He appears in front of me with a smug smile on his face moments after I first called out his name and probably made a fool of myself spinning in circles to find him.

"You look like a lost child," my brother says, laughing at his joke.

"Where the hell were you?" He cocks an amused brow at me, smiling like he always does before he says something that'll make me want to punch him in the arm.

"I told you I had to pee, but you were too busy pouting to notice. I'm pretty sure the whole airport knew where I was, except for you, Ms. I'm-limping-for-no-apparent-reason." The smirk that follows his words only intensifies my irritation with him.

I need to get some sleep, and *soon*.

"Ten, nine, eight, seven..." I count down, enunciating each number and probably spitting in his face. When I finally reach "one," I take a deep breath. "Taxi?" I ask with the fakest smile and a chipper tone.

Adrian wipes my saliva from his face with an unimpressed look but follows me toward the taxi line outside the airport.

"Grandpa's house isn't too far from here," he informs me for the third time today after telling the driver where to go. I know exactly where the house is, but he's nervous, and when Adrian's nervous, he repeats himself and points out obvious things.

I nod absentmindedly, closing my eyes and only opening them once we're in Monaco, my attention drifting out of the window. The Mediterranean Sea is captivating. The landscape is just as breathtaking as I remember it, sending guilt through me for not coming back sooner. Guilt for being unable to work past my grief enough to come back.

I never thought I would return to Monaco after everything that happened. It was my home for so long, but when I was ripped from it when everyone I ever loved here was ripped from me too, I couldn't imagine living here ever again.

But not even my grief is strong enough to get rid of the homesick feeling that's been camping out in my stomach for the years I lived in L.A. Not even my grief was strong enough to make me stay with my aunt.

My heart is here, in the old yet highly valuable buildings. In the harbor filled with yachts and other boats. In the cafés and restaurants that serve overpriced food because Monaco is one of the most expensive countries in the world. In the people who have always been so kind and adventurous here. I belong here, to the roads I walked with my grandfather when I was a kid. I belong to the streets where he taught me everything I know. I belong to the place where my heart and soul feel at home.

I close my eyes again when tears shoot into them, hoping it'll help keep my emotions at bay. Nostalgia combined with grief makes breathing almost impossible.

When we pull into my grandfather's driveway, I suck in a sharp breath without meaning to. This house represents family. My family. Adrian and I spent most of our childhood here, learning our manners, how to read and write, take care of ourselves, excel at racing, and who we are.

"Valentina."

Adrian's voice brings me back to reality, but his hand waving in front of my face doesn't. I slap it away and glare at him, but he reaches it out again and, suddenly, there's a compassionate look on his face. My brother wipes away my involuntary tears and forces a smile.

"I know. I miss them, too," he admits, leaning toward me and placing a swift kiss against my temple, hugging me to his chest to give me comfort and take some from me, too.

Grandfather's house seems bigger than I remember it. The white columns at the front of it, including the stone facade, are still the same ones my grandparents had used to build the house. What people consider the backyard is actually next to the driveway of the house. The only thing separating them is a carefully crafted barrier of stone that reaches my hips. There's a gate that needs to be opened to drive into the driveway too, ensuring no one can come in without permission.

The veranda leads to a grass area and the pool, and as I study it all, taking in the house that always felt more like a home than my father's place, I feel my heart drop from the overwhelming pain that always comes with my grief.

Grandfather left us his home five years ago when he died of lung cancer. Until now, Adrian and I haven't been able to come back, but six months ago, we decided to renovate it and move in.

The familiar smell of roses and freshly watered plants hits my nose. The sun burns my skin. I take off my flip-flops before I step onto the grass near the veranda and let the feeling of the slightly wet, cold grass envelop my feet. They carry me toward the large front door, which Adrian and the taxi driver patiently wait for me to unlock.

We carry the luggage inside and put it in the foyer, handing the taxi driver the money before he leaves again.

The antique chandelier hanging from the high ceiling catches my attention, reminding me of the day my grandfather explained to me what a "chandelier" is.

"Val, are you okay?" Adrian asks when I don't move or talk. I nod and feel his hand on my shoulder before he squeezes it comfortingly. My eyes move to the glass doors leading to the kitchen, the living room, and the dining room.

"Are *you* okay?" I ask him when he studies our house in the same way I am.

"Yes, I'm just feeling a little nostalgic, I guess," he admits as he runs his hand through his curly, dirty blonde hair with a nervous laugh.

Adrian and I look a lot alike, too much alike for siblings with a four-year age gap. Our hair is the same color; our eyes are the same combination of green, blue, and a little bit of brown. He and I have the same set of straight teeth, round lips, and small ears. However, I'm pretty short and curvy while Adrian is the complete opposite.

Many people think he's too tall to drive in a Formula One car, but he proves them wrong with every race he wins. Adrian is a young championship contender at merely twenty-three years of age, but he's a fantastic racer, just like our father and grandfather were.

When I first asked my grandfather what Formula One was, he said, "It's a fast-paced racing sport with twenty drivers competing in the championship. The cars race around unique tracks at a speed of over three hundred kilometers per hour. A specific number of laps have to be completed within a two-hour window for each track, and whoever crosses the finish line first wins. The race weekends are held from Friday to Sunday, with press events and fan meet and greets on Thursdays. The main event is the race, the Grand Prix, on Sunday. The sport was founded in the UK, and more than half of the races take place in Europe, making it very Eurocentric."

It was so technical, my four-year-old brain only understood a few words, but he kept repeating it, kept saying the same thing over and over until I understood not just the words, but what they meant put together that way.

He helped me study the team names too. There are ten teams in total: Spark Racing, Grenzenlos, Hawke Racing, Aerodinámica, Carousel Racing, Tempête Racing, Zeitgeist Racing, Klein Racing, and Velocità Rossa. I haven't forgotten any names since he told me.

"Want to go out with me tonight? I'm meeting up with some of the other drivers," Adrian offers, and I smile.

As competitive as all of them are, the drivers still make up a tight-knit community.

"Who is coming?" I ask, trying to hide the curiosity I feel spreading across my face.

"James, Leonard, Cameron, and Gabriel."

Gabriel Biancheri...

My heart beats faster against my ribcage, but I hide my excitement. Gabriel Biancheri is the goofiest, most compassionate, and most gorgeous guy I've ever seen. For more than two years, I've had the biggest crush on the Monegasque. He is kind, intelligent, and an incredible racing driver. We've been friends since we met a little over two years ago at a dinner party Adrian invited me to. It was to help me make connections in the Formula One world, to get my name out there.

As soon as I saw Gabriel across the room, I couldn't look away anymore. He was just so... breathtaking. Mesmerizing.

"Okay, what time?" I ask, trying to stop my heart from racing from excitement.

"Seven o'clock," he replies and follows me into the kitchen.

The kitchen has a modern electric stove in the middle connected to an island, which has three brown leather chairs standing against it. There are brown, wooden cabinets all over the walls, and an oven and a microwave on the left. My eyes drift to the clock by the oven to see it's only two in the afternoon.

"What do you think we should do?" he asks, so I look up at my brother.

"It may be better to go grocery shopping since we both haven't eaten much in the past twenty-four hours," I tell Adrian as my stomach growls, and he winks knowingly at me. A grin spreads over his face, so I furrow my brows, unsure what the look is for.

"Excited to see the cars?"

Realization washes over me before I almost jump up and down in excitement. Adrian leads me toward the garage before opening the door and letting me step through it first.

My heart explodes into a million pieces at the sight in front of us. A black 1955 Chevrolet Bel Air stands at the front of the garage, followed by a blue 1973 Ford Mustang. However, Grandfather possessed more than just classic cars. He also bought a white 2014 Audi Q7 and a gray 2014 BMW X6 before he died. I love those cars, both classic and new, although nothing will ever come close to the adrenaline rush I feel when I see an F1 car.

"Which one?" Adrian asks. I point at the Mustang without hesitating.

With a simple smile, he gets the key and throws it to me. Thanks to years of reflex training in preparation for racing in Formula One, I catch them with ease. Without wasting any time, I get into the baby blue car. My fingers run over the black leather steering wheel, and I sigh when my eyes drift to the air refresher hanging from the inside mirror. It was the first one my grandfather had ever gotten. He always kept it there as a good luck charm, even after the scent faded.

My heart is pounding, and my right knee shakes as I turn on the engine of the first car I ever drove.

After our trip to the grocery store, I head upstairs and unpack my things. The walls in my old bedroom are a soothing, light blue color. My curtains are thick and dark, and my golden brown wooden bed stands in the middle of the left wall.

I finish unpacking within an hour, making sure to put all my pictures on my nightstand and sitting down at the foot of my bed to study the art Grandfather chose not too long ago. The painting of the last Formula One car Dad drove, a much smaller version of Adrian's Velocità Rossa this year, stares back at me, and my mind drifts to him.

A memory I have been suppressing since the day he died appears in my head, and I let it consume me.

"Daddy, how fast can you go?" I look up at my father, a bright smile appearing on his face. We're walking past tall people who wear all different kinds of colors. I see blue, yellow, and green. My dad says all teams have a different color, but my favorite is the one he is wearing: red.

"Very fast. At our fastest, almost three hundred kilometers per hour," Daddy explains, and I stare at him, completely mesmerized. My daddy stops walking when someone starts talking to him.

I wait impatiently for the woman to leave him alone so I can ask my next question.

"Can I drive one?" He only shakes his head. His blonde hair hides underneath a hat, which has a picture of a black horse on it. Dad calls it the Velocità Rossa symbol, but I call it "Champion," like my daddy.

"It's too dangerous for children. When you're older and become the strong woman I know you will be, you can drive one," he assures me, but I pout anyway. I want to drive one right now.

My dad leads me to the bright red car. He allows me to touch it. My tiny fingers run over the smooth metal, and I jump when I feel how cold it is. I lift my eyes to look at Dad again, but he is talking to a different person. Even though it's really cold, I leave my hand on the car and tilt my head to the side. It's much bigger than the one I sit in when Grandpa takes me karting. It has a long, pointy nose with a mustache at the front, reminding me a bit of my grandpa. It gets bigger where the cockpit is. Adrian calls it the belly, but I like the word "cockpit" better because my daddy and all his friends at work use it. Another word I like is "wing," and it's behind the cockpit. It is the tallest part of the car, a lot taller than me.

I pull on my daddy's arm.

"Not now, Valentina," he scolds, and I frown. He does this to me a lot.

My eyes go back to the car, and I smile. It's very loud here. I barely heard my dad yell at me before. People run from one side to the other, screaming at each other. Almost everyone has a serious expression on their face. They look like Adrian when he concentrates really hard on coloring inside the lines. I always tell him he can't do it, and I'm always right. I don't think he likes my coloring books very much.

I bring my eyes back to the car. It must be a lot of fun to sit in it, but I'm never allowed. Dad doesn't want me to break anything, which is why I'm only allowed to touch the nose and mustache. I'm not sure what it's actually called. My dad's best friend stands next to me, so I poke his leg to get his attention.

"What is that thing?" I point at the mustache. At first, he seems confused, but then he gives me that same weird smile many adults give me.

"That is called a front wing. It makes sure the airflow is redirected so the car can go faster. With the shape of the car and its light weight, it needs a–" He stops, and I blink cluelessly at him. "Uhm, how can I explain it to you? The air goes... swoosh.*" I nod, although I still don't get it. My eyes stay on the car.*

"I'm going to drive you one day," I whisper right before my dad pulls me away.

Chapter 2

Valentina

"Valentina Romana," Adalene Beaumont says, pulling me out of my memory.

"Madame Beaumont," I say and stand up to hug her tightly.

I contacted Mrs. Beaumont a couple of months ago, hoping she would take her old job back, but my efforts were unsuccessful. She didn't email me back, and I didn't think I'd see her again until this very second, until her arms wrap around me in a comforting hug.

"How are you?" I ask in my mother tongue because I remember she only speaks French and Spanish. Even though I'm fluent in both, I prefer to speak French.

We fall into a casual conversation, one that makes me realize how much I've missed her. The small woman in front of me was Grandfather's housekeeper until the day he died, but she was always a part of the family.

"I heard you're going to dinner tonight," she states, bringing a shy smile to my lips. "Adrian said Monsieur Biancheri will be there. He's a very polite man. I've known him since he was this big." She holds her hand three feet above the ground. I can't help but grin at the visual.

"I didn't know that," I reply, hoping the heat I feel creeping into my cheeks doesn't paint them a deep red.

Whenever I think about Gabriel, when someone mentions him, I blush. I don't know why. It's an involuntary bodily reaction to the image of his dimpled smile appearing in my head, at the sound of his laughter filling my ears.

"Shall we do your hair and makeup?" Mrs. Beaumont asks sweetly, leading me to my closet before I have a chance to respond.

"Thank you, madame." Before I can get emotional, she *shoos* me into the bathroom, ordering me to take a shower.

The warm water relieves all of the tension in my body. I don't remember a day I've not been sore from training, when none of my muscles ached from me pushing myself harder and harder every single time.

Because that's what women like me, trying to make it in the field of motorsport, have to do. We have to do *more*, *be* more.

When I walk into my room again, Mrs. Beaumont has laid out a stunning outfit for me to wear. The top half of the dress is decorated with lace, and the bottom is a simple cream color. There are white wedge heels next to it and some silver jewelry. My fingers run over the fabric for a moment, more nostalgia filling me at the memory of her laying out my outfits for me when I was a kid.

I put the dress, heels, and accessories on before sitting down in the chair in front of the vanity. Mrs. Beaumont curls my hair so it falls down my shoulders in waves and draws a simple line of white eyeliner on my lid. She adds mascara and puts a pink, matte lipstick on my lips.

Usually, I would do all of this myself, but she's always told me how happy it makes her to help me. Mrs. Beaumont doesn't have any children, so this is the only time she gets to dress up her "daughter." It's a win-win because she likes doing it, and I end up looking beautiful, just like today.

"You've grown to be a stunning woman, Valentina, inside and out," she tells me when I admire myself in the mirror. "And I missed you. You and Adrian. I'm sorry I didn't email you before, but I had every intention of coming back," she says, making tears shoot into my eyes.

Speaking French with her makes me feel truly at home.

I shift my eyes to her face and see a single tear falling down her cheek.

"Oh, look at me, getting all emotional." Mrs. Beaumont laughs and wipes the tear away. "I should get back home. Early day on Monday, lots to take care of here," she says with a wink and disappears from my room.

I'm still processing that information when my brother's voice fills my ears.

"You are not wearing that," Adrian snaps when he walks through my door.

He put on white shorts and a cream dress shirt. He looks handsome, but it does bother me that we are matching.

How does this always happen?

"We are not going out in matching outfits." He shakes his head and, even though I know he is serious, I don't care what he says.

"Then go change," I tell Adrian and grab my purse from the dresser. He simply shakes his head at my determined facial expression.

"Fine, we'll go matching, but don't get upset when everybody calls you a copycat because I wear these colors so much better than you," he teases, so I shove an elbow into his ribs, making him let out an *oof* sound.

"Ready?" is all I say.

The drive is silent because neither one of us is in the mood to talk. We don't have to though. Silence between my brother and I is never uncomfortable. It's quite the opposite actually, which is probably why I love spending time with him.

I enjoy being behind the wheel of the Mustang, hearing its roar and feeling how smoothly it drives.

My heart races when I think about seeing Gabriel for the first time in weeks. We arrive at *Les Perles de Monte-Carlo* where I park my car at the valet booth. Adrian gets out, and I adjust my hair while waiting to give my keys to the valet. To my surprise, Adrian opens my door and holds his hand out. A smile takes over my entire face.

"When did you become so chivalrous?" I ask. He rolls his eyes but doesn't hide his amused smile. His attention drops to my feet, a wicked grin appearing on his lips. "What's with the face?" I ask.

"Well, I'm just surprised to see you wearing heels, you know, considering you were limping this morning," he replies before imitating what he perceives I looked like after he stepped on my foot. I attempt to kick his ass, but he dodges the attack of my vengeful foot. "I knew you were being dramatic." I glare at him and cross my arms in front of my chest.

"How about I get an elephant to step on *your* foot, and then we'll talk," I retort, and his mouth falls open.

"Bring it on." He presents his foot to me, inviting me to step on it. Naturally, as soon as I try to, he moves it away and lets me stumble forward.

"That's it!" I yell and manage to jump on his back. "Go, donkey, go," I tell him, pointing toward the restaurant.

"So, what am I? A donkey or an elephant?" I can't help but laugh.

"You're a donkey with elephant feet. Now, go!" I slam my knees into his sides to get him to move already. I should be embarrassed that this is happening in front of such an expensive restaurant, but my brother and I are too busy laughing to care.

Adrian gently drops me back onto the ground before we walk inside to where Leonard, James, Cameron, and Gabriel are already sitting at a table.

When my eyes focus on Gabriel, I giggle a little. He's playing thumb wars with Cameron and making grimaces to distract his friend. As Cameron presses his thumb on Gabriel's, the Monageasque makes a screeching noise so loud, that it throws his opponent completely off-guard, earning him the win. People at the surrounding tables frown at his childlike behavior, but I burst into laughter.

If only they knew who he was.

CHAPTER 3

Gabriel

THE SOUND OF VALENTINA's laughter fills my ears, calling my attention to where she and Adrian are walking toward us. She takes my breath away. She always does. We've been friends for years, but something has changed recently in my heart, something that absolutely terrifies me. When I look at her now, when I see those light eyes of hers sparkle with amusement and love—she has so much love for a world that's been so cruel to her—I get a little weak in the knees.

Valentina is wearing a dress that was designed to bring stronger men than me to their knees. It hugs all of her curves in ways I want to study. I long to cup her cheeks, trail my fingers over them, and watch them turn pink. The way she blushes will never fail to mesmerize me.

But I can't. I can't let her get closer. I can't risk it all because of my stupid feelings when she probably doesn't even feel the same.

"Adrian," Leonard says, getting up to hug his friend. I watch him give Valentina a curt nod, and she smiles at him in response. She told me once she thinks he doesn't like her, but I know better. Leonard is reserved with most people.

James fucking Landon, her friend for most of her life, walks over to Val, and she smiles at the tall twenty-two-year-old. I hate him, hate everything about him. I hate it even more that it's so painfully obvious how in love he is with Valentina, but she doesn't want to see it, so she doesn't.

"Hey, gorgeous," he greets her before wrapping his arms around her. "You look lovely," the Englishman adds, and when she leans away again, I notice the blush on her cheeks.

She nudges his arm a little, but he kisses her cheek once, in a way I've seen him do a million times, before turning to his best friend.

"I see you're embracing the Californian culture of casual wear for any occasion," James jokes, and everyone laughs, excluding me. I'd still very much like to punch him in the face for just being who he is.

"VAL!" Cameron Kion, my best friend of almost four years, calls out and picks Val off the ground. The sound of her giggle fills my ears until I'm grinning at her because, fuck, I love her laugh. I love her joy.

Cameron is the nicest guy I've ever met. He was Adrian's first teammate in Formula One, so he and the Romanas have bonded over the years and become good friends, too. He's slim and short, but he's also surprisingly strong for someone who hates training arms and chest. He thrives on leg day.

Finally, Valentina's eyes shift to me again, and I'm suddenly very aware of my appearance. My tousled hair that I can't quite get under control. My black pants and white dress shirt that I feel ridiculous in. My facial hair that I desperately have to shave.

But when she smiles? Fuck, none of it matters. Nothing matters at all except for watching her walk toward me with a twinkle of joy in her eyes.

"Hey, Gabriel," she says, but I hug her to my chest before my name is completely out of her mouth.

She smells like watermelon, fresh and sweet, and I know that scent comes from her perfume and from whatever she painted her lips with. As I pull back, my lips brush her cheek, something I've never done before. If I didn't know better, I'd think she shivers at the touch of my lips, that she lingers a little to enjoy my kiss, but I do know better.

"You look incredible," I say, incapable of holding the words back or stopping myself from taking a strand of her hair between my fingers and playing with it.

"So do you," she says, narrowing her eyes a little at me.

She gives me a strange look as I tuck it behind her ear. It wakes me up, reminding me I can't be touching her like this. Giving her casual affection isn't something we've done as friends, especially when the intentions behind me playing with her hair aren't platonic. I clear my throat and sit down, mumbling an apology. Valentina steps away from me, even more confused now, but she doesn't linger. Instead, she sits down beside her brother, James taking the spot next to her and across from me. Because of course he fucking does.

Anything to irritate me.

"How have you been?" he asks as he hands her a menu. I try not to listen, to give them their privacy, but Adrian and Cameron are lost in their menus and Leonard doesn't speak a lot anyway.

"Good now that I've finally graduated." Valentina laughs, James joining in as he leans a little toward her, his smile brightening his blue eyes.

I remember her telling me that she had to repeat a grade when she moved to L.A. because the school system was so different from the one in Monaco. She also told me how much she hated school because all she wanted to do was race. I understood that, sympathized because I was the same way. Racing was all that mattered to me for many, many years. Apart from my family, of course.

"How about you? How do you feel about your new contract with Hawke?" Valentina asks, and he sucks in a sharp breath.

Every driver signs a contract with a team, depending on salary, duration, and additional benefits. We then race for that team for however long our contracts last. James recently switched from Spark to Hawke Racing. I started in Klein Racing, one of the lower-ranking teams, and then got a seat at Velocità Rossa, a championship-winning team, because they were impressed with my performance over the last few seasons.

"Great, I'm really excited." A nervous laugh escapes him as he runs his hand through his blonde hair. He's nervous about starting the season, that much is obvious, and he should be because I'm going to crush him like a bug. "Any plans for this year since we last spoke?"

"Not really. I'm going to keep training for now and see what opportunities present themselves," Valentina replies, making James nod.

His eyes focus on hers, and his hand inches closer to where her arm lies on the table. She cocks a confused brow at him, so he quickly retracts his hand while a blush settles on his face. Have I mentioned I hate him? Because I really do. I want him as far away from the beautiful woman across from me as the universe allows, and I'm not even allowed to feel this way because Valentina and I are just *friends*.

Her eyes drift to me, so I stop scowling at James long enough to force a smile on my face to prevent her from noticing how much James' affection toward her bothers me. I don't think I'm successful.

"Val?" Adrian asks, making her break eye contact with me to give him her attention. The waiter stands next to them now, taking her order before moving on to ask James what he'd like.

The ambiance of the restaurant is pleasant. It's not too loud, and the instrumental music is slow and soothing. All of us listen to Leonard, Cameron, and Adrian talk about the brutal workout regimes they're going through every day in preparation for the start of the season. And they are brutal. I didn't even know my body could ache in so many different places all at once. But Val is smiling to herself because she does the same routines as us but probably doesn't find them as painful. I can't help but smile a little at her, but it's soon wiped away when James turns to talk to her again.

"Have you thought any more about coming with us when the season starts?" His question catches me by surprise. "As I've said before," he continues, "you could focus a little on yourself, keep training, and you'll have a better chance to find opportunities," he adds with an excited smile.

Valentina is an aspiring Formula One driver, who has been looking for an opportunity to make it into Formula One for years. It doesn't surprise me that she's considering traveling the world with Adrian in hopes of making connections and potentially meeting someone who believes in her. But it does surprise me that she doesn't seem caught off-guard by his question, which means they must have discussed it before. She does, however, seem unsure.

She told me that watching Formula One is her favorite thing to do, besides actually racing, and I get it. The atmosphere on track is an entirely different world. The thrill is overwhelming, with the fans in the stands cheering throughout the weekend and our, the drivers', passion for the sport.

"It's a great idea, and if you want to, you know I'll make it happen," Adrian, my teammate for the first season ever, chimes in.

"I still need to think about it," she states, and Adrian nods, taking her hand in his and squeezing it.

The thought of Valentina coming to every race this season sends a strange combination of excitement and panic through me. Valentina. At every race. In close proximity. Where my feelings will be able to grow like flowers that have been watered, fertilized, and placed in the sun.

More panic sweeps through me until I find myself pushing away from the table and rushing outside to get away from this overwhelming pressure building in my chest. Once I'm outside, I take a deep breath, trying to slow my racing heart. Stay away from Valentina. That's all I have to do to keep my heart safe. To prevent our friendship from breaking. I can't lose her. She means too much to me, always has, and no matter what I feel, I will not risk everything for something that might not even work.

Even if I keep asking myself how it wouldn't work when I know how right I could be for her. When she could be so right for me.

"Gabriel," she says, her voice soft and gentle, like she's scared to startle me. But it's the way she says my name that hits me right in the chest, with so much fondness and adoration that I know I don't deserve.

"Please, go back inside, Valentina," I reply, watching her cock a brow at me. When she doesn't move, I find myself drawn to her, my frustration bubbling over. "Just leave me alone, please. I don't want to talk right now." *I can't tell you why I'm like this because if you knew, you'd never look at me the same way again.*

"Whatever it is that you're struggling with, I want you to know I'm here for you. Always." She places a comforting hand on my chest but right as I reach for it to wrap mine around hers, she steps away and disappears inside again, the warmth of her touch lingering on my chest.

Chapter 4

Valentina

We all finish our food while Cameron tells everyone how thrilled he is to start the new season in three weeks. Leonard chimes in and agrees as Adrian sits back in his chair, watching everyone closely. Gabriel's eyes are on me when I glance at him, and I wish I knew what he was thinking. He looks guilty, the way his eyes are pleading with me, and his lips are slightly parted as if he wants to say something. But he doesn't. Neither one of us speaks again for the rest of the night.

Adrian and I leave the restaurant around midnight. I let my brother drive since I'm too tired and want to give my mind a break, to let it roam free.

"About you coming with me—" Adrian starts, and my head flips in his direction. "I'll be flying back and forth a lot, and sometimes, I will be staying in one place longer than in another." He pauses, then frowns. "I would love for you to travel the world with me. The past four years, every time I left, I wanted to take you with me."

I understand what he means. Adrian and I have been through a lot. We are each other's most important people. Yet, there is a war going on inside my head. One side tells me I have a better chance of realizing my dream if I travel with him. The other thinks I should stay in one place and keep training here while also finding a job to make some money. It's challenging to make a decision when I don't know what the right choice is. However, I know that my chances are pretty low either way, and I want to spend as much time with my brother as possible.

"Get ready for months of greatness then because I'm going with you," I tell him, causing the biggest smile to appear on his face.

"Alright," he replies just as giddily.

Adrian taps his fingers on the steering wheel as I get back to my thoughts. *Back to Gabriel*, my subconscious reminds me, and I roll my eyes. I don't understand what is wrong with me, why I've spent years crushing on a guy who is not interested in me. We're friends. Good friends. The kind of friends who can talk to each other about their grief and understand the pain the other has gone through.

My thoughts drift to the day we met. I think about how awkward it was, how I held his hand for a little longer than necessary without shaking it because I was too mesmerized by him to do anything but stare. How he laughed and then pressed a kiss to the back of my hand like I was royalty, calling me "Lady Valentina" to lighten the mood. My cheeks were probably as red as fire, but it's a memory I hold close to my heart now.

Then, I think about the time he visited Adrian in L.A. and we ended up spending the whole night talking about the people we lost. How he lost his grandparents one by one before his mother had a brain aneurysm and passed away too. His father died shortly after, so the only family he had left were his aunts and his brother. He listened to me as I spoke about my own family. How my grandparents died. How my father drove his car into the middle of our living room while drunk, killing himself on impact. How my mother abandoned Adrian and me when we were young children.

It's always been so easy to talk to Gabriel.

Maybe that's why I'm having such a hard time getting over my feelings for him.

I lie in bed and stare at the ceiling, feeling beyond weird sleeping in Grandfather's house without him here. After half an hour of struggling, I get out of bed and walk down the hall to Adrian's room. I knock twice before he tells me to come in. He sits up in the bed that is way too big for him, and I stand awkwardly in the doorframe, scratching at the door frame.

"What's wrong, Val?" he asks with a frown on his face.

"I can't sleep. I feel... weird," I mumble, and he pats the side of the bed next to his. I walk over, and he holds the blanket up for me.

"I get it. It feels like he's here, but he's not," Adrian admits. "Well, you can sleep here until that feeling goes away."

I nod and close my eyes, relieved my brother is always there for me when I need him most.

"Just remember, we are going to have months filled with excitement, traveling, and, most importantly, winning ahead of us. I'm so happy you're coming with me." He squeezes my shoulder before dramatically falling backward onto his pillow, making me laugh.

"Goodnight. Love you," I say as my eyelids get heavy.

"I love you, too," he replies and turns the other way.

Chapter 5

Valentina

"You know, Valentina, if you want to achieve your dream, you have to stay in the best physical shape you can be," Grandfather informs me as I watch him closely.

His gray hair stands up at the sides because he's been running his hands through it too often.

"When you sit in that fast car, the limits of your body are tested. You have to be mentally, emotionally, and physically ready. The first step in succeeding is understanding they are all interconnected."

Grandpa stops to pull out a piece of paper while I shift impatiently in my seat. Adrian is absentmindedly listening as he plays with his Nintendo, but my full attention is on Grandpa. I want to hear everything he has to teach me.

Grandpa writes the three criteria on the paper, and I watch him draw arrows to connect them.

"If you are out of balance in one, you will have an imbalance in all. Do you understand?" I nod, but Grandfather's thin lips form a frown. "Do you understand me?"

"Yes," I reply. "But why do I have to be in control of all three?" A smile replaces his frown. Grandpa likes it when I ask questions.

"If you're not in control of your emotions, they will lead to mistakes. You can't be too aggressive. You have to be mentally strong to focus entirely on the track ahead of you. You need to be aware of the other drivers, identify the track conditions, adapt, and monitor your vehicle. Lastly, you have to be physically strong to drive for a very long time. Your body will be exhausted after each race."

I stare at him in awe. I want to be that strong.

He pauses for a brief moment, clearly contemplating his following words.

"I don't want to scare you, but there is a lot at stake. When you sit in the cockpit and compete for the win, there are risks involved. Your body has to be prepared for any case, even

if it is a crash into the barriers or one with another driver. Your muscles can help you take the force of the hit."

His words are a lot to process and not something I can take lightheartedly. Racing is risky, but I love it more than anything. It will be different when I train and learn how to do it properly. As long as I'm careful and prepared, I will be on top.

It's my dream.

"Can we start today?" I ask, and Grandfather nods.

"Yes. We will start by going for a slow, short run," he tells me, so I get up from my seat.

"Adrian, are you coming?" My brother looks at me and then at our grandfather before bringing his attention back to his toy.

"No, not today," he simply responds.

"Ready?" Grandfather asks me instead. I nod.

I'm ready to be just like him.

It's only six in the morning when I wake up. Adrian is sound asleep, just like I should be after the dinner we had. My body probably won't run well on four hours of sleep, but there's nothing I can do about it now. A small groan leaves my throat as I aggressively remove the blanket to get out of bed.

A hot bath will help my muscles catch up with my mind.

When I walk downstairs to meet Adrian in the kitchen a few hours later, I almost choke on my breath. Gabriel is sitting at the island, drinking coffee with my brother.

"Morning, Adrian," I say, giving him a brief hug. "Morning, Gabriel," I go on but move over to the fridge without giving him more of a greeting.

"Val," Gabriel says, his voice soft. I take a sip of my orange juice before turning to him.

As always, his hair is tousled, a green shirt sits on his muscular body, and simple blue jeans hang from his hips. Gabriel's sunglasses dangle from his neckline, and the single necklace he always wears is under his shirt. His eyes scan my body in a way they never have before as he stops at my breasts three seconds too long. I look down and remember that I didn't put on a bra, blushing at the sight of my pebbled nipples pressing against the thin fabric. I cross my arms but can't stop the smile from spreading across my face. *What is wrong with me?* I should be embarrassed.

Instead, I feel good about catching his attention.

"I'm so sorry about yesterday," Gabriel starts. "I had no right to be so rude to you because I was upset over—" He breaks off but doesn't give me more of an explanation. "All that matters is I am truly sorry. I hate pushing you away." The way he pouts and pokes my cheek with his index finger makes a grin spread over my lips. I was never upset with him for not wanting to speak to me.

"You didn't have to apologize," I assure him, but he shakes his head in disagreement.

"Yes, I did." His proximity confuses my senses, so I move away from him, toward the cupboard with the glasses, to get rid of this longing to wrap my arms around him and let him comfort me with a hug.

"You want some orange juice?" I ask to change the subject.

"I actually have to go. Jean needs some help building a bookshelf he bought yesterday," he says, and I smile at the mention of his brother. Gabriel steps in front of me again, placing a hand on my shoulder until warmth spreads through me. "Again, I'm really sorry," he says before wrapping his arms around me.

His mahogany scent makes my head spin. The way he guides me against his chest is familiar yet excites every cell in my body. One of his hands trails down my spine leaving shivers in his wake.

Right as I'm about to ask what he's doing, if he meant to make me melt into him this way, he steps out of the hug.

"Bye," he mumbles and smiles, flashing me his handsome dimples before disappearing.

After minutes of mindlessly sipping on my juice, I cook breakfast for Adrian and me. I make some eggs, banana pancakes, and cut up some more fruit before calling my lazy brother into the kitchen.

"How did you sleep?" I ask as I turn to Adrian, who just put the biggest chunk of pineapple into his mouth.

With a full mouth, he smiles and shrugs before he attempts to answer. All I hear is gibberish as juice starts dripping down his chin.

"Never mind." I laugh and shake my head. "Also, next time we have a visitor, please let me know so I can put on a bra," I beg, and he chokes on his coffee. His laughter fills the kitchen. I nudge him in the ribs, and he catches himself.

"That's why he was walking so weirdly," Adrian says, making my mouth drop. "Yeah, wide legs and all." I swat his arm, but he seems to enjoy his joke too much to stop laughing at the top of his lungs.

"Did I miss something?" Gabriel asks from behind us, curiosity in his voice. I shoot up in my seat, panic gripping my chest.

"No!" I reply and glare at my brother.

"I forgot my phone," Gabriel explains as he walks over to it.

An annoyed expression appears on his face as he reads something on his screen. My curiosity vanishes when my eyes focus on his three-day stubble, and I get lost in his handsome features.

"Well, apparently, I'm free today after all. Jean just canceled on me. Mind if I join you?" he asks me specifically.

"Sure, but Adrian and I are going for a run soon," I tell both men, and Adrian's eyes go wide right before they plead with me. I've always been more serious about the workout routine. When his trainer isn't around, I make sure to push him, as I do myself.

"Great, I'll join." Gabriel sits down while I get up to bring him a plate. "I'm not hungry, chérie." My heart skips a beat at this new nickname, one he's never called me before. I fight every muscle in my body to keep from turning around, from revealing my pink cheeks or the way my heart is racing.

"You need to eat a good breakfast," I say instead of acknowledging him calling me "chérie." If I ignore it, maybe he didn't say it. If he didn't say it, I don't have to pretend I don't love it. "We have a lot of training to do."

Again, Adrian's eyes plead with me, but I ignore him and put my plate in the dishwasher. I am rushing to go upstairs and put on some workout attire.

"You guys are having a party without me? That's not cool," a voice with a heavy English accent calls out, and I shake my head.

How do they keep getting into my house?

James appears in the kitchen seconds later with a single sunflower in his right hand. His eyes focus on mine before they drop to my body, but he swiftly looks away when he notices my bra-less chest.

It's a bad day to decide not to wear a bra.

"Good morning, beautiful," he says and hugs me tightly. "This is for you." He hands me the flower, a shy smile playing on his lips.

"Thank you," I reply, and James winks at me. He is probably the only other person apart from Grandpa and Adrian who knows that sunflowers are my favorite.

My eyes shift to Gabriel, his expression unreadable as he looks at James.

"What are you doing here?" Gabriel asks James, so I give him a confused look. His gaze momentarily meets mine but shifts it back to James almost instantly. The testosterone stinks up the whole room. I think about opening a window to let some of it out, but there's no use. Instead, I simply go upstairs, change into some sportswear, and pack a bikini for later.

Once I'm dressed, I sit down on the edge of my bed and take three deep breaths to calm myself. I would prefer it if Adrian and I were alone, but I also know it's good for Gabriel and him to spend time together. After all, they are teammates this season. Velocità Rossa acquired two strong drivers for their team this year, but I can already predict the chaos that is to come. While the drivers compete for the same team, they also individually fight for the Drivers' Championship. Adrian and Gabriel are both very competitive and eager to be first-time champions.

Twenty minutes later, it is time for me to face the trio again. To my surprise, they are all ready to go for a run, both guests clad in my brother's clothes. I smile when I see Gabriel doesn't fit in them since he's much shorter. He catches me grinning at his outfit and tugs the shirt into the pants before tightening the waistband to make himself look even more ridiculous. I shake my head as I laugh.

We start running soon after. The guys are trying to keep up with me as I lead them down the path Grandfather started taking me on when I was eight years old. That's why running is second nature to me. My whole life, I trained harder than everyone else because I had a dream. A dream, which was crushed over and over when the people in charge decided I wasn't good enough.

Gabriel runs past me in a sprint, smirking at me over his shoulder. I try to keep up but have to slow down earlier than him. He sticks out his tongue at me, so I run into him on purpose. Sadly, he catches me and spins us around before wrapping his arms around my upper body. Laughter escapes his throat, so contagious I can't help but join in because I love how playful this moment feels.

"You still have more practice to do if you want to beat me, chérie." I push away and scowl at him. His dimples are deep as he smiles brightly.

"Yes, either I get better or grow taller. Your legs are twice as long as mine," I complain, the smile on his face starting to annoy me.

"Stop making excuses," he teases, his accent thicker than I have ever heard it. Gabriel has the typical Monegasque accent. He chooses to speak in English with me because it's good practice for him. The Formula One press conferences and interviews are primarily in English, which is why it's so crucial for him to learn.

A warm breeze runs down my spine, and I lean my head back to let the sun shine onto my face. When I look at Gabriel again, he's staring fondly at me, studying me like he's never been more fascinated by a person.

"Why are you looking at me like that?" I ask, the curiosity threatening to eat me alive.

"Why are you as red as a tomato right now?" he asks in return, making me burst into laughter.

"Okay, no need to attack," I reply and place my hands on my stomach to imitate being stabbed. Gabriel laughs at my dramatic reaction before we grin at each other. Our gazes lock, the whole world around us vanishing as we share this happy moment.

Pressure builds in my chest as the longing I always feel around him returns stronger than before, so I break eye contact and look over my shoulder at James and Adrian, who have *finally* caught up to us. They are both out of breath and seem exhausted already. *Slackers.*

I convince them to work out for half an hour longer. When we finish, we are all beyond exhausted. Our tired expressions remind me of something my grandfather used to say to me every time I wanted to quit.

"You can give up if you want, you can throw it all away and pretend your dream never existed, but if you clench your teeth, scream at the top of your lungs, and go through with it, you will end up more than happy with yourself."

There were many times in my life when I wanted to give up on my dream, but I didn't. *I haven't.* I haven't become who I want to be yet, and I'm not giving up. Not now, not ever.

"What do you want to do now?" Adrian asks the group and the other two shrug.

"Well, I'm going to the beach," I inform them and grab my backpack before changing into my flip-flops. "I'll see you at home." I look at my brother, and he swiftly nods to acknowledge my words.

I turn around and start walking toward the beach.

"Do you mind if I come with you, love?" James yells after me, causing me to stop dead in my tracks.

I don't know what to tell him. On one hand, all the time we've spent alone together has always been platonic and comfortable, but he has been acting strangely toward me these past twenty-four hours. Then again, he's my friend, and I love hanging out with him.

"Sure." I never want to hurt James by pushing him away. He's my oldest friend. He's the person who's helped me up after every single fall. He's one of the very few people I've let into my heart.

"So, how are you feeling?" James asks after I've changed into my bikini. I give him a confused look, so he decides to elaborate. "About the move? About being back in Monaco? About living in your grandpa's house? It can't be easy, darling," he says, hitting the nail on the head.

"I'm managing." That makes him frown.

We sit down on our towels close to the ocean, silence stretching between us as I gather the courage to say what's weighing on me.

"After everything, I'm just glad to be home."

My eyes drift to the trees near the beach and then to the nearby restaurants. I'm trying to avoid eye contact with James because I know I will break down if he looks at me. I will cry because I don't want to be in Grandfather's house without him, and being back in Monaco reminds me of everything I've lost.

"Tell me how *you're* feeling," I say after another moment of absolute silence. "You're taking a big step driving for Hawke." Although we've already talked about this, I need to change the topic.

James looks down and picks a single, small rock out of the sand before twisting it between his fingers. "Well, today is my last day of relaxation before I have to take everything more seriously again," he admits, a nervous laugh escaping him.

James flicks the rock from his fingers, his arm muscles flexing with the motion. He has gained a lot of muscle over the winter break, but he's done his best to stay lean because of his job.

Formula One drivers need to be slim to fit in the car.

"But it's fine. I'm fine," he mumbles, a childhood habit of his. When he says "fine" twice in under ten seconds, it means he is freaking out.

I smile.

"All right. Well, since it's your last day, let's forget all about work, help you take your mind off all the pressure." He nods eagerly. This will be good for him, and it'll be good for me, too.

"Bring it on, gorgeous!" he says as he sprints toward the water with me running after him.

A while after first getting into the water, James and I end up on our separate towels, talking about everything and nothing at the same time. When a period of silence stretches between us, I bring up the one thing he's been avoiding talking about for a few months now.

"Can I ask you something?" James turns his head so he can look at me, smiling brightly.

It's easy to understand why James has hundreds of fan accounts. He's gorgeous, sweet, talented, and kind. His smile alone could make anyone fall in love with him within a second.

"Anything," he replies and puts his hands under his head.

"Why did you really break up with Katie? It's been four months, and I thought maybe you're ready to tell me the truth." His expression never changes, but his body language does. He goes from lying openly to rolling onto his side to look at me, almost like he's closing himself off.

"I was in love with someone else; I *am* in love with someone else. There, is that honest enough for you?" A smile grows on my lips, and suddenly, I am so much more curious.

"Who is she?" I ask, scooting closer toward him.

"I will not tell you her name, but I can tell you this: She's beautiful, the most beautiful girl I've ever seen, and I've known her for a while. I love her smile, her sense of humor, her eyes, and how they sparkle when the sun hits them; her determination; her fascination with the tiniest things; and the way she always fights for what she wants."

He pauses briefly.

"Actually, I love everything about her. I have for a while, too. If I had to guess why my relationships never work, it would be because I never had the chance to fall in love with someone else while being in love with her. I told Katie from the beginning about the girl, and she was very understanding until she started to want more, which I couldn't give her. Katie was good for me for a little, but this other girl, she has me all kinds of messed up," he admits, so I grin. I love hearing him talk about her.

"Have you told her how you feel?" James' eyes drift from my face as he sighs.

"She doesn't feel the same way, trust me. I wish she did, but she only has eyes for another guy," he explains and shrugs.

"You're an amazing guy. I'm already sure she doesn't deserve you. You're way too good for everyone, trust me on this, I know. I don't even deserve you as a friend." He shakes his head and puts his fingers on the back of my hand.

"What a silly thing to say," he replies, so I flick a bit of sand his way.

"I mean it. You've always done everything for me, for as long as I can remember. I—I love you, James." I try not to linger on the fact I just admitted this out loud. I've never told anyone who isn't part of my family I love them, but it feels really good to say it to James.

"I love you," he says, turning back over to pick up the book I handed him.

James loves to read, which is something I've always loved about him. When we were younger, he read all those great classic novels and then gave me the ones he enjoyed. James waited patiently for me to finish the books before we discussed them. This time, however, I gave him my favorite book.

I gave him a copy of *Die For Me*. He's been reading it since we got to the beach and I handed it to him, and I love his facial expressions.

"By the way, this back and forth between them is killing me, Val," he complains, and I smile.

"But that's the best part. Their love story isn't easy. They don't just fall in love and live happily ever after. They fight to be together," I tell him, making him nod. "Also, when they finally do get together, it's beautiful." He puts on a dramatic shocked expression.

"They end up together? Jesus, Val, you just spoiled the ending," he jokes.

"I'm so sorry," I say and push my bottom lip forward teasingly. James glares at me but then smiles and shakes his head.

I didn't know how much I needed to spend the day with my best friend until this very second.

Chapter 6

Gabriel

"Do you think it's a good idea to spend more time with her if you're trying to keep your distance?" my little brother asks as I grab my keys on my way out the door.

Jean and Val became friends around the same time she and I did. My younger brother went through a difficult time when she met him. He lashed out because he couldn't deal with his grief and with all of the pain he was feeling. I couldn't blame him then, nor can I now, because I've felt hopeless, devastated, and *broken* more often than not.

Jean is the only one who had the courage to say, "I'm not okay, please help me." And we did. Adrian took him to therapy, I took him to the most beautiful places around the world, and Val simply spent a lot of time talking to him on the phone, helping him work through his feelings.

After a couple of months, he seemed much better, and now he's happier.

"Adrian invited me to go karting to have a friendly competition before the season starts. Valentina is going to be there. What am I supposed to do?"

While I may have known Adrian for over two years now, we're not exactly close. For two racers who will be spending an entire season competing side by side, fighting each other and together at the same time, it's best if we get to know each other better. Build a bond, or whatever the fuck Hector, my performance coach, meant by telling me to spend more time with Adrian before the season restarts.

"You're only going to make it worse. You have feelings for her that won't go away with proximity, Gabriel." Jean picks up my wallet to hand it to me, giving me a comforting smile.

"Thanks, Jean, that advice really helped," I say, and my brother's face lights up.

"Really?" There's a childlike excitement to his features now even though he's only three years younger than me.

"No, of course not." He attempts to smack me up the backside of my head, but I dodge his hand and give him a warning glare.

"You can be a real asshole, do you know that?"

"I'm your older brother. That's my job," I tease and nudge his side before mumbling a goodbye and leaving our house.

Jean is right. The more time I spend with Valentina, the harder it gets to ignore whatever is happening in my chest. A few days ago, when we went for our run and Val and I shared yet another moment of joy, I felt the rush of adrenaline and fear someone experiences right before jumping out of a plane. Hell, before I get into my Formula One car. It's not fear of falling or fear of racing itself. It's the fear of crashing. Of dying upon impact. That's how I feel whenever I'm around Valentina and we have a moment when it's just the two of us. When she directs that smile of hers toward me the entire world disappears around us.

Ever since I lost my parents, my grandparents, Maxime—my best friend—I've done my best to shield my heart. I've been good at it too, until something shifted. I want to know what that something is, why I'm so drawn to Valentina, but I'm scared if I acknowledge it, it'll only make things worse too.

I can't fall in love, can't open myself up for more heartbreak. If I lose someone else, if I allow myself to feel everything I want to feel and then lose *her*, I don't think I could survive it.

That thought lingers in my head as I arrive at the karting track. Valentina is leaning against her baby blue Mustang, sunglasses resting on her nose as she laughs at something Adrian said. James is watching her with his fucking heart in his eyes, *again*, and the urge to shake the beautiful woman standing with him, to point at his fucking face and say "Look!" is almost overwhelming.

How she doesn't notice it is beyond me, but she also doesn't seem to notice my growing feelings for her, and I'm having a shit time trying to hide them.

"Gabriel," Adrian says with one of his typical sunshine smiles. He hugs me before I have a chance to process his words. "I hope you're ready to get your ass kicked," he says, and Valentina snorts in response.

"Are you?" she asks her brother with a cocky smile. I grin at her confident expression because I'm fully aware of how talented of a racer Valentina is.

She's been racing in karts since she was a kid. As she got older, she fought for a seat in Formula Four, Formula Three, and Formula Two. She made it into Formula Three and raced like no one I'd ever seen before. She won races, fought for the championship, and after coming in third place in her first year, she got kicked off the team.

When I asked her why, she said, "The only explanation I have for being kicked off the team is because I'm a girl. I followed all the rules, showed nothing but respect, and was rewarded with the opposite. They don't want women in this sport, no matter how much they claim the opposite. They're threatened by what girls and women are capable of after they told the world how incapable we were for decades. If I or any other girl starts proving otherwise, they have to shut it down immediately."

There was no arguing about how right she was, and I felt a little stupid for even asking why she got kicked off the team in the first place. I've watched her races, seen what kind of driver Valentina is, and there's no doubt she belongs in a team right there with us.

"Well, I'm ready to lose. Shall we get this show on the road?" James chimes in, bumping his shoulder against Val's before wrapping an arm around her.

I grind my molars at the sight as jealousy pours through me, and Adrian furrows his brows at me, almost like he's challenging me to say something, but I don't. With my lips pressed shut, I walk past my chuckling teammate.

"Fuck off," I mumble under my breath, so he starts laughing wholeheartedly, placing a hand on my shoulder and giving it a reassuring squeeze.

"Don't worry, James pisses me off a lot, too," he says, and while I know he's joking, I appreciate the way he takes the tension out of the moment.

A typical Adrian thing to do.

"Yeah? Do you want to punch him in the face during those times too, or is it just me?" Another laugh. This time, I join in.

"Sometimes," he says. He gives my shoulder one more squeeze before we all split up to arrange for our karts and helmets.

A few fans approach James, Adrian, and me to take some pictures and get autographs. My eyes shift to Valentina during the interaction, and the longing in her eyes as she takes in this moment, longing to experience the same love and support from fans, hits me in the chest like a steel truck. When she catches me staring, she blinks the tears away and forces a smile I know she doesn't mean.

She walks away a second before I can find a way to comfort her, wrap my arms around her, and promise her I'd do anything to make her dream happen. Because I would. I would fight the entire world to get her a seat, and not just because of my feelings for her, not just because she's my friend. It's because she deserves it more than anyone else I've ever met. The other two reasons simply add to the lengths I would go to for her.

"How many laps are we doing?" Val asks as soon as all of us are standing next to our karts. We're at a private track in France, not too far from Monaco, and they let us book an entire hour just for the four of us to race.

"Ten?" Adrian suggests, and we all give an agreeing nod.

Anticipation rolls through me just like it does before every race, whether it's a friendly one like this or the real thing. The only difference is I'm not even a little nervous. I want to win, of course I do, but I'm not nearly as competitive as the Romanas, and I always find it incredibly entertaining to watch the two of them in any competition.

Once, when we were playing a German game called *Mensch Ärgere Dich Nicht*, Adrian got so upset with Val for continuously kicking his characters off the board—which is the entire point of the game—he ended up breaking the board in his rage. Not on purpose, at least that's what he claims, but how easily does something like that really break? The funniest part is, it happened as we were putting the board back in its box, too, and the shock on his face was hilarious.

"Will you even make it ten laps? It's been a while since you sat in a kart," Val teases, making Adrian glare at her.

"Wanna make this more interesting?" he asks with a quirk of his brow, challenging her.

"Obviously. What did you have in mind?" God, they're so competitive. I can't help but grin.

"Loser has to pay for the next five group dinners," Adrian suggests, holding out his hand for his sister. She shakes it without hesitation, James and I shaking both of their hands. "Last one across the finish line is the loser," is the last thing Adrian says before slipping his helmet on and settling down in his kart.

"Good luck, boys. You'll need it," Val adds, smiling at both of us before shoving her helmet over her hair.

She pulled it into a braid that rests at the side of her head, so once the helmet is on, it sticks out, falling to the top of her breast. She has such long hair, hair I want to run my fingers through, hair I want to tug on as I kiss her neck and make my way up to her mouth.

I shake my head to get rid of the visual, taking a deep breath and letting it out through gritted teeth before placing the helmet on my head too. James is the last one in his kart, and I'm going to make sure the asshole comes last in this race too. Even if I have to fight dirty, I don't care. This is not a Formula One racetrack where I have to behave. Here, on this karting track that I've raced on since I was a kid, I can misbehave a little.

Nostalgia fills me with the memory of my mother and father taking me karting. Maxime teaching me how to race, how to win. Jean crying and complaining because he wanted to go home and play with his toys. All the hours I put in so I could win the Karting Championship, work my way up until I reached Formula One.

A wave of grief floods my system, but I push past it, refocus on this moment with my friends—and James—to take some of the weight off my chest. When Valentina turns her head in her brother's direction to show him her middle finger, I burst into laughter, the heavy feeling inside of me lightening at the sight.

One of the workers at the track counts down for us, and as he reaches one, I already see Val shifting her feet to get a better start. She's always been remarkable at them, quicker than all of her competitors. This time is no different. As the man waves the green flag to signal the start of the race, Val shoots ahead. She makes her way into the first corner with Adrian cursing so loudly, I can hear him from my kart, through my helmet padding. I shoot past James, not afraid to nudge his kart with mine, making him hit the brakes to avoid crashing into the barriers on the left of us. I knew he was a lot of things, but I didn't think he was a coward.

Makes sense, though. If he really is in love with Valentina and hasn't told her in all of the years they've known each other, he must be.

Then again, when it comes to feelings, so am I.

My teammate and I go into the first corner side by side, chasing down the badass woman who's left us in her rearview like we're children who haven't raced a single day in our lives. The thought makes me chuckle as I overtake Adrian, making my way around the track to get to her. While Adrian and James fight it out at the back, I attempt to close the gap between Val and me.

There's no use. I come close during the last two laps, but Valentina is an aggressive racer. She takes corners hard, and doesn't slow down as much as I do. She drives riskily, but she does it beautifully.

She wins with ease, and I just stare at her as she brings her kart to a stop again, jumping out and ripping her helmet off to show the joyful expression that's taken over her face.

Her curly hair is all over the place, the braid barely holding it together at this point. Sweat drips down her forehead as she bounces on her heel, waiting for all of us to take off our helmets too to stick her win in our faces.

All I can think about is just how gorgeous and incredible she is, not giving a fuck who came last.

All that matters is Valentina and her joy.

And the fact that I get to share it with her.

Chapter 7

Valentina

It's been two days since I've seen anyone but my brother. To be honest, I'm enjoying the peace and quiet. Since I got back, I have been trying to find somewhere to buy clothes, but I've been unsuccessful. For the third day in a row, I'm strolling past cafés and restaurants when I spot a single boutique between two coffee shops named *Rush*. The place has an antique style, piquing my interest. It's charming with the light-red-colored bricks building up the tiny clothing store.

There are three mannequins in the window display. The first one is wearing a simple blue skirt with a white tank top and a matching blazer. The second mannequin is wearing black jeans, a green blouse, and black high heels. The last outfit, however, is the one that catches my attention the most. It's a long red dress covered in white flowers.

My feet move before my mind catches up.

The inside of the store is just as elegant as the outside. The same bricks decorate the walls, racks of clothing neatly placed around the room.

"Bonjour," a short woman says from behind me, so I turn to look at her.

She must be in her seventies and has long, gray hair and crystal blue eyes. The woman is breathtaking, and the smile on her lips is welcoming.

"Can I help you?" she asks, continuing to speak in French.

"Yes, please," I reply, adding the same level of warmth to my smile. "How much is the red dress from the mannequin in the window?" A knowing smile appears on her face

"Fifty euros," she says. "There are more sizes on the far left."

I find a medium and go into the small changing room to try it on. The silky fabric feels smooth against my skin, and the dress highlights my curvy body in a sexy yet classy way.

"How was it?" she asks when I walk out of the changing rooms with a grin on my face.

"I love it. I'm going to buy it," I say, pulling out the card Adrian gave me for our joint bank account. It holds all the money Grandfather and Dad left us both.

She nods, the same, kind smile as earlier spreading over her face.

"Do you mind if I keep looking?"

"Not at all. Take your time, mademoiselle." Her French is flawless, and so are her clothes. I go through the racks and find seven more items, all of them exactly what I've been looking for. "Are you from here?" the sweet lady asks me a few minutes later.

"Oui, madame," I reply.

"I thought so. I can hear it in your French." I am glad I don't sound like a foreigner, which is why my smile brightens.

"How long have you had this store for?" I inquire, wanting to make conversation.

"My husband bought it for me after he won his first Formula One championship." I almost drop the clothes I'm holding as I spin around to face her.

"My brother is an F1 driver!" Her eyes go wide as well.

From there on, we talk for a while about her husband, whom I then find out is Carlos Klein, the youngest driver to ever win a race and a championship, and the man who has a Formula One team named after him. She tells me about his first race and his last one. Part of me would love to tell her my racing story too, how I'm trying to make my way into the world of Formula One, but every time I attempt to form the words, they die on my tongue like a lost thought. I'm too embarrassed. After all, she is married to a Formula One legend.

"How did you two meet? If I may ask," I say, hoping I'm not prying. She and I have more in common than I would have ever expected at first glance, and the sense of comfort her presence provides is so unfamiliar, I can't help wanting to know more about her.

"In school. We were paired together for a project. We had math together. It took months for us to become more than friends."

She lets out a small laugh, and I love the way her cheeks blush a bright red and her eyes sparkle as she talks about her husband.

"I thought his career would take him far away from me, and I didn't want to fall for him, but I had no choice. Luckily, he didn't have one either and fell at my feet. It's something for the books, I tell you." Her index finger waves around in front of me, making the smile on my face permanent. "But enough about me. Is there anyone special in your life?"

I think about Gabriel. Gabriel is not only an incredible race car driver but also an amazing artist. I think about him telling me that he's been drawing since he was seven years old, him showing me some of his sketches. I think about his big, beautiful heart that's been broken one too many times. I think about his face and his kindness, and everything else that makes him the wonderful man I now know.

"I used to have a boyfriend, his name was Luke, but he was not good for me. I broke up with him and never looked back. There's been someone else on my mind for a very long time."

"Does the other person know about your feelings?" I blow raspberries but recover quickly when she cocks an eyebrow.

"No, madame. We're good friends, and I wouldn't want to ruin that. Not to mention, he is friends and teammates with my brother, which complicates the situation even further." Her eyes narrow slightly.

"You never know. Maybe he has feelings for you, too."

"Maybe, but I can't take the risk. He means too much to me." She nods, and we move to the small, wooden table at the front, where the cash register is. "It was really nice talking to you. I hope I can see you again," I tell her, and she nods in agreement.

"That would be lovely. My store is always open, dear. I'm here Monday to Saturday, ten to six." I hand her my card so she can swipe it on the machine. "Whenever you need someone to talk to."

"I will take you up on that offer," I reply as she hands me my card back. "I never got your name," I say.

"My name is Evangelin." She holds out her hand for me.

"Valentina. It is a pleasure to have met you." Evangelin hands me the bag with clothes and grins.

"Likewise. And here, take this, dear." She hands me a black leather jacket, making me gasp. "Please, don't tell me you cannot accept it. You bought so much, and I know you will look stunning in this," she adds with a crooked smile.

"Merci." Evangelin walks around the table and squeezes my arm ever so gently.

"Good luck, Valentina." My cheeks flush, and I nod, hiding the embarrassed expression on my face with a polite smile.

We exchange goodbyes before I make my way home.

Adrian, James, and Gabriel are at work, which means I have the whole house to myself without possible interruptions. I go upstairs to the training room. There is a racing simulator, weights, a treadmill, and bands for neck exercises... *Those are the worst* yet most important ones.

I start by doing some cardio before moving on to the weights and then going through the pain of strengthening my neck. The last part is the simulator. Adrian used to call it a fancy video game, but for me, it has always been a way to stay connected to the sport. To stay fit to race. To learn everything there is to know about the tracks all around the world.

I put on the helmet I bought when I first started training with the simulator in L.A. and sit down in the seat, which looks exactly like those in a Formula One car. It's a bit uncomfortable because it's fitted for Adrian's body, but he lets me use it whenever I want.

The screens in front of me are bright, and as always, excitement courses through me. I choose the Singapore track since part of it drives through the city and part on the permanent race track. In real life, it's one of my favorites because of how beautiful Singapore is. And because it's a night race. Those are my favorite races.

Once I've selected the track, I close my eyes and take a deep breath. All of my senses heighten while I feel the adrenaline rush through my veins. This is as close as I can get to racing in a Formula One car, and it's always a thrill, even if it's only a simulation.

When I open my eyes again, I wait for the lights to go out and push down on the gas pedal, pressing the right buttons simultaneously.

I could stay in the simulator for hours, but unfortunately, it's exhausting, and my body gets tired quickly. By the time I get out of the seat again, I'm smiling like a happy child, satisfied with my performance. Adrian arrives at home minutes after I finish showering and getting dressed. He comes to my room to let me know he will wash and be right down to have dinner with me.

As I place the lasagna between our plates, Adrian reappears with a big grin on his face and a towel in his hand. He rubs it over his wet hair, and within seconds, it's dry.

"How was your day?" I ask, and he shrugs as he places some food on my plate.

"It was good. Daniel and I got a lot of work done." Daniel is Adrian's performance coach, supporting him in his mental and physical training daily.

It's almost like the performance coaches shadow the drivers, and, during the race weekend, I often compare them to parents, carrying everything the driver might need in their bags. They are in charge of warm-up exercises, muscle regeneration after the races, and countless other things.

Daniel and Adrian are very close like many drivers are with their coaches.

"I'm getting ready to get back in the car. I'm also getting more nervous every day, Val. So fucking nervous," he says, a nervous laugh bubbling out of him. "How was your day?" He takes a bite of the lasagna, a happy groan escaping him. "This is *so* good." He's speaking faster than usual as if he is running out of time, but instead of pointing it out to him, I go along with it. I don't want to make him feel worse by telling him how on edge he seems now that the start of the season is so close.

"I had a good day. I met a very kind woman. Her name is Evangelin, and she's so sweet. And you won't believe who her husband is!" Adrian waits patiently, and I smile brightly. "Carlos Klein!" He drops his fork, and it makes a loud *clink* with the porcelain plate. Carlos Klein has been Adrian's hero ever since he was five years old.

"You have to introduce me to him. Valentina Esmèe Cèlia Romana, you *have to* introduce me to him. *Please*, please, please," he begs.

"Okay, relax. I haven't even met Carlos, and I only met Evangelin today. *If* I ever meet him, I will let him know how big of a fan you are, and he may do what he wants with that information. Maybe, and only if you're nice, I'll ask him if you could meet him." Even though I'm giving him a lot of hypotheticals, he smiles like a child in a candy store. "Anyway," I go on, so he focuses on my face once again. "I bought a really nice dress for the pre-season dinner with the team tomorrow, and Evangelin gifted me a leather jacket."

Once I've finished telling him about my day, I take a bite of my food and listen to all of the changes Adrian has to figure out how to work with this season. Driving for a new team is challenging, especially when the cars are ever-developing. It's impressive to hear about the technological advances the team has engineered.

After Adrian is done speaking, we eat in silence for a while until he starts a conversation about Gabriel. I only listen to half of it because my mind battles with whether or not it's time to share how I feel. My mouth is quicker than my restraints can hold me back. It felt good talking to Evangelin today, and I know I'll feel even better after sharing this part of my life with Adrian.

"I have feelings for Gabriel," I blurt out.

Adrian doesn't seem surprised by this new information. I don't know whether he's mad at me or just speechless. *Why isn't he reacting? This is huge!* I expected some kind of response. It doesn't matter if it's good or bad, *just something!*

"I know, Val," he finally says, making my mouth slightly drop. "I've known for a long time."

"Oh," is all I say. "I know it's stupid because we're just friends, but I don't know what to do." He puts his fork down again and takes a deep breath. His expression is serious, but he also seems pleased in a way.

"I don't know either," he admits and crosses his arms as he leans back. His eyes never leave mine as I wait impatiently for him to continue. "What I do know is that he doesn't deserve you in the slightest. Yes, I'm biased because you're my favorite person on the planet, but you deserve someone open about their feelings, who isn't scared to love. Gabriel is not that person." He takes another brief break, chewing on his bottom lip as he considers his next words. "But I'm here for you whenever you want to talk about your feelings."

I get up and walk over to him before wrapping my arms around his shoulders and pressing a kiss to the top of his head.

"*Thank God*, you finally admitted it. I was making secret bets with myself."

"What? I'm getting very worried about you," I say and laugh a little, feeling lighter now that I have no more secrets from my brother.

Well, except for one, but I'll never tell him what happened when we were living in LA, not if I can help it.

Chapter 8

Gabriel

I HATE THESE EVENTS. I'm supposed to love them. As a Velocità Rossa Formula One driver, or a Formula One driver in general, it's these events the team relies on to wow their investors and promise them a season they will never forget. But it gets tiring when they happen so often. Just a few weeks ago, Adrian and I had to be the most charming men, wooing investors for an entire evening when the new F1 model was revealed. It's exhausting. It's a part of my job that I don't enjoy, but if it were up to me, I'd spend all of my time in my car, racing until my body was too tired to do so. It's the only place in the world I can escape the constant pain in my chest.

Well, somewhat.

"I'm honored you invited me to be your date," Cameron says, ripping a laugh out of me.

"I didn't. I told you I didn't want to come, and you insisted on joining me to lighten my mood," I point out and smooth a hand down my black tie.

"Exactly. See what an amazing friend I am? I could be at home, moping over the man I have feelings for who doesn't feel the same, but instead, I'm supporting you," he says, taking a glass of champagne off a waiter's tray and sipping from it a second later.

"You haven't told him how you feel, Cameron, how would you know he doesn't have feelings for you too?" I ask, turning to stand in front of him. His blue eyes find my face, scanning it as he thinks about his next words.

"The same way you know Valentina doesn't have feelings for you. Because you don't even want to allow yourself to hope in case she doesn't feel the same way and it breaks your heart all over again. That's how I feel about Elijah. I'm scared to let myself hope and even more terrified to find out he doesn't." Fair enough.

"What a pair we are," I mumble, taking the glass of champagne from his hands to down it in one swig.

"Yeah, a pair of losers. God, are we pathetic or does it just feel that way?"

"No, we're definitely pathetic. That's why we only talk to each other about this shit." This earns me a wholehearted laugh from my best friend. I'm about to join in when my eyes drift to something over his shoulder.

My heart stops, tumbles all over itself at the sight of Valentina stepping into the room on Adrian's arm. She's wearing a long red dress with white flowers painted all over it. The fabric clings to her curves in a way that makes me want to study her forever. Her curly hair isn't styled like it was when we had dinner together on her first day back in Monaco. Today, she embraced her natural hair, letting it fall down her back in perfect curls. She's wearing a simple makeup look, but her lips are painted a bright, bold red. I want to kiss them, let her smear the color all over me.

"Careful, mate, you're drooling," Cameron says, but I can't bring myself to care when Valentina smiles at the man approaching her and Adrian, shaking his head and saying something that makes the man laugh with her.

"Sometimes, I can't quite believe she's real," I blurt out, not meaning to tell Cameron my thoughts but also wanting to share how I feel.

"What do you mean?"

"How can someone so smart, talented, beautiful, and big-hearted exist? It shouldn't be possible, so, sometimes when I look at her, I think I'm dreaming." Cameron gives me a smug smile.

"I hope you know how wrapped around her finger you are," he says and takes another glass of champagne. He takes a sip, turning away from me.

I roll my eyes at the back of his head, and, almost as if he feels it, he laughs again. The sound is so loud, it catches Valentina's attention from across the room. When she spots us, her eyes light up and she excuses herself to walk over to us. I watch her the entire time, incapable of looking away when the way she moves has me in a trance. The way her dress moves with her and her eyes sparkle with confidence. She's always been so fucking confident, and I love that about her. I love how the entire room seems mesmerized by her, but she's almost running to get to Cameron and me so she can wrap her arms around my best friend.

"Hi," she says right before he wraps her up in a hug.

"You look beautiful," Cameron replies, kissing the top of her head. She leans away to compliment him back before turning to me and smiling.

"You look very handsome, Gabriel." A blush creeps onto her face as I slide an arm around her waist to drag her against my chest. Valentina giggles as she wraps her arms around my neck to return my gesture.

"You, chérie, look like a dream." She pulls away to show me her cheeks are an even deeper red than they were a second ago.

"You flatter me, Monsieur Biancheri," she says and takes another step back to create some space between us. Her gaze shifts between Cameron and me, a shy smile stretching her red lips wide.

I find myself drawn to her all over again, moving toward her even though I should turn the other way and run.

"Ladies and gentlemen, please have a seat," someone says from the stage area of this banquet hall.

Valentina moves first, Cameron and I following behind her like two bodyguards. The way I glare at every man who smiles appreciatively at her, I might as well be. Adrian decides to join us again, but he only hesitantly leaves the waitress he was flirting with. We sit down at the same table, listening to the investor who made tonight happen, introduce himself.

Then follows a mind-numbingly boring three hours of more speeches, people approaching our table to make conversation, and Adrian continuing to flirt with the same waitress until she slips him a piece of paper. He smirks at her until she blushes, the poor woman unable to resist my teammate's charm.

"What did she write on the paper?" Cameron asks as he leans forward on the table to get closer to Adrian.

"She wrote down where I'm supposed to meet her after this thing ends." He leans back in his chair and takes a sip of his water, smiling to himself.

"I can go home with Gabriel, then you can have the car," Valentina says, and I turn my head to look at her. She meets my gaze, tilting her head a little at whatever she reads on my face. "You don't mind, do you? Your house is a three-minute drive from mine, otherwise, I'd take a taxi."

"I'll take you," I assure her.

She gives me a grateful smile before handing Adrian the keys to her car and refocusing on the stage in front of her. My eyes drop to where one of her hands moves to her lower abdomen, her face pulling into a grimace a second later.

"Chérie, are you okay?" I ask, wrapping my fingers around her elbow. She brings a smile to her lips and drops her hand from her stomach.

"Yeah, just fine."

Chapter 9

Valentina

I'm, in fact, not exactly fine. Cramps have taken over my body, and I can hardly breathe past the pain. The dress is too tight. I want to rip it off, to cry because of how much pain I'm in from my period, but I'm in public. Women and people with uteruses aren't allowed to fall apart in public when they get their period. Especially not during a work dinner where I'm trying to impress people.

So, I take several shallow breaths to help me manage the pain. It doesn't work, it never does, but I'll only have to go through this for a little longer until Gabriel is taking me home.

"What's wrong, Val? Talk to me," Gabriel tries again when tears flood my eyes. My brother has left the table already to meet with the woman he was flirting with, so I can't ask him for help.

Gabriel's hand covers mine on the table and the wave of hormones hitting me has the tears rolling down my cheeks. "Val."

His voice is soft as if he's pleading with me to tell him what's wrong, but I'm out of my chair and on my way to the bathroom before I can tell him everything's fine.

More pain floods through me, and I drop onto one of the benches outside of the bathroom when my legs don't want to carry me any further.

"Fuck," I mumble under my breath, trying my best to keep more tears from falling down my cheeks. I bend over at the waist, trying to find an angle that helps relieve the pain.

"Alright, Valentina, tell me what to do."

His voice fills my ears and as much as I want to look up at him, to reassure him I'll be fine in a minute, only a sob escapes my lips.

"Please, chérie, I need you to tell me what to do. Tell me how I can help." His hand slips onto my thigh, lighting my skin on fire.

"I got my period. It hurts," I croak out. "So fucking much," I add with a watery laugh.

"Wait here, don't go anywhere." I frown at him, and he gives me an apologetic smile. "You know what I mean."

When he returns minutes later, he pulls me into an upright position and wipes the sweat off my forehead with a small towel. He hands me a glass of water and two painkillers. I take them gladly, and he removes the glass from my hand when I'm done.

"Do you think you can stand up?" I nod, and he wraps his hands around my forearms to help me. "I'll take you home. Lean on me, and no one has to know anything's wrong." Another wave of emotions hit me so hard, tears jump back into my eyes.

"Thank you."

Gabriel leads me out of the room, holding onto my hand where it rests on his bicep. I'm clinging to him, breathing deeply to get through the cramps. As soon as I'm in the car, I let my walls down. I curse several times. My head is pounding. Every limb hurts. I'm crying for no reason.

"Almost home," Gabriel assures me.

"I hope you know that I hate you a little right now," I say, and he turns his head to show me his confused expression.

"Why?"

"Because you don't have to experience this," I say and laugh, trying to lighten the mood.

"I'm sorry, chérie." His hand slips onto my thigh, squeezing it comfortingly once before moving back onto the steering wheel of his Velocità Rossa sports car.

I try not to overthink that little touch, try not to read into what it means, but he only confuses me more when he parks his car in front of my house, gets out, opens my door, and lifts me into his arms to carry me all the way inside my house.

"What are you doing?" I ask, my arms flinging around his neck.

"I'm taking care of you."

He carries me all the way upstairs, gently placing me on my bed. With a careful, soft stroke of his thumb over my cheek, he disappears again, leaving me to change into something more comfortable. Right as I'm about to drop back onto bed, Gabriel strolls into my room with a hot water bottle and some chocolate.

"I didn't know if you were craving something sweet, so I brought something just in case," he says in French, placing the food on my nightstand and handing me the hot water bottle. I press it to my lower abdomen, sighing at the heat.

"Thank you, Gabriel, for everything." I reach out to take his hand, and he meets me halfway, probably so I don't have to sit up.

"You don't have to thank me." He settles down on the bed in front of me, still holding onto my hand. "Is there anything else I can do for you?"

"Stay with me." The words are out before I can overthink them. Gabriel is my friend. This isn't a weird thing to ask of a friend, right?

"Of course," he says, pulling his suit jacket off, followed by his tie. He kicks off his shoes before lying down on my bed, facing me.

My eyes close as my brows furrow when another round of cramps hits me. Gabriel's hand lifts to smooth out the crinkles in my forehead before dropping to my arm where he starts running his fingers up and down.

"It hurts," I whisper after a moment of silence.

His thumb wipes away the tears that continue to stream from the corners of my eyes. His skin on mine feels heavenly. His hand moves to my arm again, rubbing it over my tired muscles to comfort me.

"Make it stop." Pain flashes in his eyes.

"I would give anything to make it stop, chérie, *anything*." His voice is so soft. "I can't begin to describe how much it pains me to see you like this. Maybe it's because you mean so much to me, or maybe it's because there is nothing I can do to help you. Either way—I guess what I'm trying to say is—"

He cuts off before he finishes his sentence, but I sense he isn't done speaking.

"You're so very strong," he adds, making my head spin.

The mahogany scent coming off him, his smooth accent, his handsome face, all of it clouds my senses until there's nothing left but him.

"Stronger and more beautiful than anyone I have ever met." I must be imagining his words because they don't make any sense to me. *He's drunk,* I tell myself. He must be intoxicated because Gabriel wouldn't say this to me. We're just friends.

"I don't understand." He smiles at me, his dimples appearing on his cheeks.

"Neither do I. You've turned everything upside down for me." He strokes his thumb over my cheek, watching me as my eyes flutter shut from his touch.

"Gabriel, what are you saying?" He runs his finger over my bottom lip before retracting his hand and sliding it under his head, never looking away from me.

"Nothing, Val. Nothing at all." That's all he gives me as he continues to look at me like he can't bring himself to look away.

"You're confusing." That makes him smile.

"I know. I'm sorry."

We lie on the bed in complete silence for a while, my eyes fluttering shut every few seconds because now that the painkillers are working enough to make the pain bearable, I'm exhausted.

"Do you have something for me to take your makeup off? Wipes?" Gabriel asks when my eyes have been closed for a while.

"Mhmm," is all I manage to get out. The mattress moves as he stands up, and I watch him through half-opened eyes as he walks into my bathroom. My makeup wipes rest in his hand as he walks back to me.

I sit up a little as he settles back down on my bed, looking ridiculously hot in his black button-up and black slacks. His hands are gentle as one of them cups my jaw and the other glides the wipe over my face to take off my makeup. We sit in silence as he does it because I'm too tired and he doesn't seem to have anything to say.

One gentle stroke after another, he wipes over my face until no hint of makeup remains. I stare at him the whole time, trying not to smile at the way he presses his lips together in concentration until his dimples appear.

"Thank you," I say when he's finished, still watching him as he throws the wipe into the small trash can I keep next to my bed.

"You're welcome."

His gaze meets mine, uncertainty lingering in his eyes as he studies me. I lie back down in my bed, but he stands up to lift my blanket and help me get under it. My hand reaches out to hold onto his as he attempts to move away.

"Gabriel, can you—" I cut off, too unsure if what I'm saying is taking things too far.

"Can I do what, chérie?" he asks gently.

"Don't leave."

"I'll stay until you're asleep, I promise," he says and settles back down beside me, resting his head on my spare pillow and keeping his distance from me even though every part of me wants him to come closer, to wrap me up in his arms. His eyes shift to my ceiling as he chews on his bottom lip. "Do you ever feel lost, Val? Like there's something you desperately want, but you can't bring yourself to go after it because you're scared?" he asks as my eyes fall shut.

"I feel lost all the time, but not because of that. When there's something I want, I go after it. I won't stop fighting until I've achieved whatever it is I want." I pause, then add, "Unless you're talking about feelings for people because then I'm terrified." I open my eyes just in time to see him tilting his head my way.

"How are we supposed to open our hearts to more people after we lost so many?" he asks, and I reach out to take his hand in mine.

"I don't know. It's something I struggle with all the time," I admit while he laces his fingers through mine. Electricity shoots through me from this simple touch until everything inside of me heats. "But I think we're not supposed to close ourselves off from heartbreak either. It's part of life. Pain and grief. They're something everyone needs to experience. Some more, some less, but either way, it's part of life. It's our job to find joy and love and the sense of success in the midst of all of it and make sure we hold on tight because those are our lifelines." I don't know if I'm making any sense, but Gabriel nods anyway, so mesmerized by my words, he can't stop staring at my lips.

"I'm not as strong as you, Valentina," he mumbles after a while.

My eyelids flutter shut again as I say, "That's okay. You can take some of my strength whenever you need it and give it back when you've found more within yourself."

Chapter 10

Valentina

The following day, I wake up early without Gabriel beside me and decide to go for a run. I leave a note for Adrian on the fridge to let him know where I am, grab some water, and start running the same track the guys and I followed almost a week ago. Training usually helps me clear my head and focus on what's important: my career.

But today, I can't seem to turn off my thoughts like I normally do.

The events of last night come crashing back when I sprint down the same path where Gabriel and I raced last time. The way he took care of me and called me "strong" more than once. The way he touched me and took off my makeup. The way we lay in bed and had another one of our deep talks. My heart keeps growing more attached to Gabriel with every moment we spend together, and not in a way friends are supposed to feel attached to their friends.

By the time I come to a stop, I'm out of breath, my mind is running wild, and the cramps return to my lower abdomen.

The sound of the steady waves as they crash onto the shore relaxes me. The smell of saltwater fills my nose, as well as the sweet scent of chocolate from a crêpe stand not far from where I'm sitting.

For years, I wanted to hear Gabriel speak to me the way he did yesterday. He told me I've flipped his whole world upside down, which isn't exactly a thing friends do either.

Does that mean he has feelings for me? Was I the person he was talking about when he asked me how he could open his heart to anyone again?

Frustration has me running again, even though I have no idea where I'm going.

A gasp slips out of me when I arrive at Evangelin's store. It's crowded, a complete contrast to how empty it was the last time I was there, and she looks overwhelmed. My feet move before my brain has a chance to catch up.

"Bonjour," I say, making her face light up at the sight of me.

Evangelin is holding thirty different articles of clothing, and the look of panic is even more evident on her face up close.

"Can I help you?" I ask. She nods as I glance at the lineup at the cash register.

I readjust my ponytail to try and make myself look more presentable, putting on a smile to prepare myself for speaking to the customers. Evangelin follows me and gives me a brief introduction to her system. Once I understand, I start cashing people out.

After another hour of absolute stress, the store clears up, and only a handful of people are left.

"Thank you so much," is the first thing she says to me when we finally have a second to breathe. "Danielle quit this morning, and my other employee has the flu. They left me to take care of the store all by myself on a Saturday!" The petite woman throws her hands into the air and shakes her head.

"Don't worry, I don't mind helping you at all. Here is my phone number. Whenever you need me, and I'm in Monaco, I'll come in and help out." I say and hand her a piece of paper with my number. Her small eyes study me, and a warm smile appears on her face.

"Thank you. I will, of course, pay you," she assures me, but I shake my head.

"No, please don't pay me."

"Okay, at least let me repay the favor someday," she says, making me smile at her.

Evangelin shows me everything I need to know about the clothes, prices, sales, and so on. I pay close attention, hoping I will remember everything when more people come into the store again. I also notify Adrian where I am so he doesn't worry about me.

At lunchtime, she disappears for a little while but holds up takeout in her right hand and coffee in her left when she returns. We eat and talk a little more about the store. Evangelin even offers me some clothes to change into, and I gladly accept. I don't want to scare off any customers because of my sweaty workout attire.

"What is it you usually do when you're not helping elderly women in their stores?" Evangelin asks before biting off a piece of her sandwich.

"I'm a racecar driver," I blurt out before I can stop myself. "At least, I want to be one. I've trained my whole life. Just waiting for an opportunity," I add, hating the way my cheeks heat as I rant to get the words out.

"That's amazing, Valentina!" she says, excitement lighting up her eyes. "We need more women fighting for their place in this sport," Evangelin adds, so I refrain from telling her that I already had a spot before I got kicked out. That every opportunity I had was taken from me.

So the only thing I say is, "I agree."

We fall back into silence before she broaches another complicated topic.

"How are things with the person you like?" I barely bite back a nervous laugh.

"We're just friends. Nothing more. Neither one of us is capable of opening ourselves up to love when love has given us so much pain already." After my conversation with him yesterday, that has become abundantly clear.

Even though I'm not completely sure if I feel the same way when my feelings for Gabriel are something I've never felt before. Something I don't ever want to let go of.

"Nowadays, love is something rare, as if it's something that only happens to people who understand what it takes. You can't give up on someone you love after one fight, and you can't give up when you drift apart in the slightest bit. If you truly love someone, you have to fight to make it work because these days, it's so rare to find the person that makes you want to breathe forever. Pain comes and goes, but real love? That doesn't ever go away, not even in death."

Her words make me speechless. I never looked at the world from her perspective, but I'm glad she gave me something to think about.

"But what is real love?"

"Real love can be anything, Valentina. Real love is the kind of love you share with your brother, unbreakable. The kind of love you can have with a best friend or a partner, or any member of your family. Real love doesn't fade. It may change over the years, but it can never disappear. That's what it is." I tear off a piece of my bread, playing with it as I consider her words.

I think about my brother, the one person I love most in the world who I know loves me and will protect me forever.

I think about James, my best friend, who has done nothing but love me for as long as I can remember.

I think about my grandfather, who protected me and fought for me until the moment he died.

I think about my grandmother, who, even though she didn't agree with me on my wish to become something so "unfeminine" in her words, still loved me and raised me until she passed away, too.

"Can real love even exist if it's not reciprocated?"

Evangelin smiles at me then.

"Some people can be so blind when it comes to figuring out how the other person feels." She cocks a brow, obviously meaning me. "Communication is crucial. People tend to forget this. So, I am reminding you: tell him how you feel. The only way to find out if it's reciprocated or not is to hear how the other person feels."

***

A few hours later, I make my way back home, exhausted and in pain. As soon as I'm home, I shower, take something for my cramps, and then fall onto the sofa to read countless emails of rejection. It's nothing new, hearing back from driver academies or other training programs that are currently "not accepting new recruits." It's a bullshit excuse, one I've gotten ninety-five percent of the time when a few weeks later, these same places announce new drivers they've taken in.

Every time I try, I get another rejection from people who see my name, see my gender identity, and turn me away because of it. If I wasn't so damn tired of it, so angry, I'd cry over the rejections I received today. I'd cry for the lost opportunities that are blowing away in the wind. I'd cry for my dream as it slips further away from me, as it rejects me again and again.

But I am tired. And angry.

A combination that has me falling asleep on the couch without meaning to.

I don't know how much time passes, how long I've been sleeping when, all of a sudden, it feels like a hand runs over my cheek, gently dropping to my jaw to trace it.

The softness of the touch reminds me of Gabriel's, but I must be imagining the way his index finger runs over my cheek again, the way it drops to my neck and makes goosebumps spread over my entire body. His name leaves my lips, a sound entirely out of my control.

I want this to be real.

I want his skin on mine.

I want him.

His name leaves me for the second time, but I still don't know if I'm dreaming or actually saying it out loud.

"Chérie." Gabriel's voice fills my ears, causing me to shoot up on the couch. "I'm sorry, I didn't mean to scare you," he says, placing a hand on my arm to steady me. I wipe my eyes, hoping I'm not hallucinating.

"What are you doing here?" I ask him when I finally find my voice. My eyes focus on his handsome face, trailing down to study the black long-sleeved shirt and jeans he's wearing. His hair is messy yet sexy at the same time, as always, and his lips seem fuller and pinker than ever before.

"I wanted to check on you. Adrian let me in, and I found you sleeping on the couch." I nod, but it doesn't explain why he touched me, why he ran his fingers over my face. "You were saying my name in your sleep," he whispers. I blush instantly. Embarrassment washes over me until I remember why I said his name.

"Why were you touching me?" I counter, putting him on the spot instead. He leans back and looks directly into my eyes, swallowing once like he's not entirely sure what to say.

"I tried to wake you gently," he explains, but by the way he grinds his teeth and a muscle in his jaw flexes, I'm not entirely certain that's the whole truth. "How are you feeling?" he asks, clearly wanting to change the subject.

"I'm fine," I say.

"That's good," he replies, looking down at the ground between us. "I wanted to apologize," he adds after a moment of silence.

"Uh oh, what did you do?" I ask, smiling at him to take some of the tension out of this moment, but when his gaze meets mine again, there's a battle reflected in his eyes. My smile fades as soon as I take it in.

"I left you last night. After you fell asleep, I left and I hated myself as soon as I was out your door," he explains, running a hand down the length of his face as he lets out a humorless laugh.

"I'm not following, Gabriel. I was expecting you to leave. You told me you would. There's nothing to apologize for," I assure him, placing a hand on his shoulder. He leans against it, twisting his head until his lips rest against my skin. My breath catches in my throat.

"But there is. I left, but what if you had needed me? What if your cramps had gotten worse again? I left for selfish reasons. I left because I got scared and—" He cuts off, his eyes flitting back to mine to show me the surprise in them. He hadn't meant to tell me that.

"I'm a grown woman, Gabriel, one who's been having painful periods for almost nine years. I know how to take care of myself." He nods several times, acknowledging my words with that simple motion instead of words. "Why did you get scared?" My heart is racing. It's been racing since he came here.

"Because lying next to you, falling asleep in a bed with you, scared me. It scared me how right it felt." Scratch that. My heart isn't racing anymore. It isn't beating at all, too scared that if it makes a sudden move, Gabriel will startle and leave.

"I'm sorry?" I say with a laugh that's more emotional and shaky than anything else. Gabriel lets out the same sound.

"Do not apologize for my fucked up way of thinking and feeling," he replies, taking my hand from where it's resting on his shoulder. He studies the ring Adrian gave me a while ago, a circle of infinity signs with crystals between each one before he lets go of me to stand up.

"Where are you going?" I ask, wanting more answers. Wanting to know if he has feelings for me too, if that's why it felt right. If that's what scared him.

"I should go, Val. I've already said too much," he says and when he leans down to press a kiss to my cheek, I twist my head so his lips are only a centimeter away from mine without thinking.

My eyes are on him.

Time seems to stand still.

I can hear his heart racing, feel mine begging him to give in, to close the space between us.

"Kiss me," I say, feeling him close the distance just enough to press his nose to mine. A shaky breath escapes him, hitting my lips.

"We can't," he whispers and rushes out of my home.

Chapter 11
Gabriel

I AM STUPID. THERE'S no other way to phrase it. She asked me to kiss her, and I fucking ran. Things got too real, and I rushed out of her house like she'd just asked me to commit a crime, not kiss her and get what I've wanted for a while now.

What's wrong with me?

Why is it so hard for me to open myself up to her?

Why do I push her away when I want to pull her close instead?

I'm a mess. I'm all over the place.

I want her, yet I can't bring myself to voice those thoughts without risking that she'll never look at me the same way again. That she didn't mean that she wanted me to kiss her. That she'll change her mind as soon as my lips are on her.

Kiss me.

There hasn't been anything I wanted so desperately in a long time, nothing but becoming a Formula One World Champion. So, why the hell didn't I kiss her?

The scent of her still lingers in my nose, haunting me as I walk home. The feel of her skin on mine has me burning up. The taste of her was so close, almost in reach, it lingers as if I'd kissed her instead of being a coward.

If I could, I'd go back. I'd apologize to her for confusing her, for denying us what we both want, but every time I even think of doing so, I get nauseous. My heart fights my intention to do so, reminding me I'm not ready to lose her.

I'll never be ready to lose her.

CHAPTER 12

Valentina

I FEEL FOOLISH, *SO INCREDIBLY foolish*. My legs refuse to help me walk. Embarrassment has taken over my whole body, and my mind is allowing every question and feeling about Gabriel to enter. I shake my head repeatedly to let go of the thoughts and emotions.

Why did I have to say something?

Why couldn't I leave it alone?

Why was he being so affectionate and telling me sleeping beside me would have felt right if he didn't want to kiss me?

Anger settles in my chest, all of it directed at Gabriel. I'm mad at him for confusing me, for making me speak before thinking. I'm mad at him because how am I not supposed to have feelings for him when he's such a caring person, when he takes care of the people that mean something to him? When I'm one of those people.

Adrian walks into the living room, my brother's presence forcing tears to start streaming down my cheeks. "What the fuck did he do?" he asks and sits down on the couch next to me, wrapping his arms around me.

I tell him what happened while Adrian holds me close, comforting me.

"Dickhead," he whispers, making me laugh. "Say the word, and I'll beat him up, no questions asked." I sit up and look at my brother.

"No, I don't want you to do that. I'm sorry for crying. I just had to let it out." Adrian wipes away my tears and nods. The last thing either of us needs is for him and Gabriel not to get along. After all, they are going to have to work together for at least a year, if not longer.

"Don't apologize for sharing your emotions with me. I love you, and I would do anything for you," he reminds me and presses a kiss to the top of my head. "I have to go to sleep, lots of packing to do tomorrow." Adrian gets up but stops halfway to the stairs.

"By the way, Gabriel is taking the same flight as us on Monday. So..." He trails off, pulling his lips into a thin line.

"Does that mean we have to go to the airport with him?" I ask, and Adrian chuckles.

"Yes, we're practically neighbors. Taking two cars wouldn't make sense, Val." I groan and lean back on the couch. "Don't worry, it will be okay," he assures me, but I cock an unconvinced brow.

"Yeah, sure. That's really easy for you to say, isn't it, Mr. I-Never-Get-Into-Relatio-nships-To-Avoid-What-You're-Going-Through-Right-Now."

"You said it, not me." Adrian grins, then shrugs before he leaves me to my thoughts.

My phone vibrates, and I look down to see a message from James, asking me if I want to meet him tomorrow after I finish packing.

I let him know when to come over.

Something inside me doesn't want to get out of bed when I wake up the next morning. My body is tired from only getting five hours of sleep and from the events of last night. Instead of dwelling on them and getting angry all over again, I pull the blanket off my body and saunter into my bathroom.

James walks onto my veranda with yet another sunflower exactly when I told him to be here. I laugh, but he simply smiles brightly at me.

"Hey, darling," he greets me and holds out the flower. I take it from him with a genuine grin on my face.

"Thank you." He winks at me and leans down to press a kiss on my cheek. James always smells amazing: minty and woody, a combination I never thought would smell good. For as long as I can remember, I associate his smell with safety and comfort.

"What do you want to do today?" he asks after I put the flower in the same glass as the first one he brought me a week ago. To my surprise, it's still alive and blooming. I shrug and look at James again. "Feel like boxing?"

A smile spreads over my face before I go upstairs to get the gloves and focus pads.

James puts on the focus pads first as we move to the garden. The sun is hot, yet the grass is still wet. We're both barefoot. I'm hitting hard against the pads, and James is clearly having difficulty not asking what's bothering me. Eventually, he does open his mouth but just to make casual conversation. He asks me how I'm feeling about flying out tomorrow and how I am doing in general. We switch, and James starts to hit the pads.

"I talked to my team principal about your career situation yesterday," he says out of nowhere.

"What?" I ask and lower my hands, not realizing James would keep hitting. His hand reaches forward, and he punches the left side of my throat. I gasp for air immediately before ripping off the pads so I can wrap my hand around the ache.

"Oh my God, Val. I'm so sorry."

He gets closer to me, but I hold up one of my hands, still gasping for air. The area burns with pain, and it starts throbbing almost immediately. It takes me a while to breathe evenly again, trying to stop tears of pain from falling. James wraps a bag of ice around my throat, pressing it to the area I'm clutching like it'll make the throbbing go away.

"I'm so sorry, darling, I'm so fucking sorry." There is pain in his eyes, revealing that hurting me brings him more agony than the physical one I am feeling.

"Don't worry, I'm going to be fine." My voice cracks a little, making him flinch. "You were telling me something," I say to distract him. James shakes his head, his expression still filled with worry.

"Never mind, love. Can I bring you anything else?" He reaches his hand out and runs the back of his fingers over my cheek.

"No, I'm fine, really," I assure him, so he takes his hand back, leaving the skin there tingling a little. "Please, tell me what your team principal said," I say.

"He said that Formula One is too stuck in its way to let a woman race anytime soon. He said women don't belong in the cars either. In other words, he's a fucking asshole who has no clue what the hell he's talking about."

It doesn't surprise me to hear that. Many people in motorsport share that same mind-set. They think women aren't as strong as men, as talented, and, therefore, they can't race as well as them. But he's wrong. Women belong in the cars. And Formula One isn't that stuck in its ways anymore. This is the time for change.

I'll be the change.

After a little while of complete silence, James' phone lights up on the table. His manager is calling him, but he completely ignores it, still studying my injury.

"Go answer your phone," I croak and press the device into his hand. He hesitates, so I glare at him. James lifts his hand and excuses himself to take the call. When he returns, an upset expression lingers on his face. "What's wrong?"

"Nothing," he lies and sits down next to me again.

"If you have to leave, go. I'll be fine, I promise," I assure him, but he frowns.

"I'm not leaving you, especially not after I hurt you," he says with frustration in his voice.

"We both know when your manager calls, you drop everything and go. So, I'm kicking you out of my house, and you better see what she wants," I command, but he hesitates again. "I'm alright. Go." He gives me a swift kiss on the cheek, gathers his stuff, and leaves, but not before looking over his shoulder one more time.

My throat is burning. The ice eventually numbs my entire neck, so I put it down. Luckily, the pain and throbbing stop, but I wince when I look in the mirror. The mark is big and a flaming red color. It runs from the middle of the left side of my throat to my collarbone. I shake my head, regretting the motion immediately.

"Val?" Adrian screams through the house. He sounds concerned, which makes me worry.

"In my room," I call back. Within seconds, he's in my door frame and running toward my bed.

"James told me what happened. Are you okay? Let me see," he says and almost rips the ice pack from my throat. When I cry out, he mumbles, "Sorry," and gently removes it. "Fuck, that's bad," he points out. I frown at him.

"Oh, is it? I hadn't noticed."

"I'm sorry," he mumbles once again. "Is there anything I can do?" Adrian is still examining my throat, but I shake my head. His arms wrap around me before he presses a kiss to the crown of my head. "I was so worried about you." His words are barely audible, but I hear them anyway.

More, I feel the worry wafting off him in waves.

"You should have seen the other guy," I tease, making my brother burst into laughter. "He better have two black eyes."

"Of course," I reply like it's the most natural thing. Adrian snorts before leaning back and taking my face in his hands to squish my cheeks together.

"I taught you well, my child." I burst into laughter.

Chapter 13

Valentina

"Passport? Plane tickets? Backpack?" Adrian sounds nervous, which brings a smile to my face.

"Got it. Got it. Got it," I promise, but he doesn't seem to process my words. He's running around the house, searching for who-knows-what, and never even stops to think about what he's doing. "Adrian, we've got everything. Relax," I say with a firm tone, so he stops to look at me.

He nods and picks up his backpack before squeezing my arm. His hand reaches out to touch my throat, and he gently tilts my head to the side to inspect my bruise.

"It looks awful, Val," he tells me. I roll my eyes right before I zip up my jacket and put my hood over my head.

"There, nothing to see anymore." Adrian frowns but doesn't argue with me.

Today, we're flying out to Melbourne for the first race of the season. The circuit is located around Albert Park. Adrian has told me many times how bumpy the track is but also how much fun he has in the corners.

Our trip to Australia will take a day, and I don't look forward to sitting for that long. I wasn't made to sit for that long.

The taxi arrives at the same time as Gabriel. He's wearing black sweatpants, sneakers, and a simple, white shirt. As soon as he sees me, he stops walking, but I simply grab Adrian's arm to let him know he's going to be my barrier for the moment. I don't want to talk to Gabriel right now. I don't want us to have the same, useless conversation that we did yesterday, the one that cleared up absolutely nothing for me.

"Valentina," Gabriel says, stepping toward me.

"Back off, mate. If she wants to talk to you, she will." Gabriel's eyes narrow, but when he sees my pain-filled expression, he drops it. Usually, I wouldn't hide behind Adrian, but I'm still a little angry about yesterday, and embarrassed.

When we get into the taxi, Gabriel sits in the front, and I sit behind him. The drive is primarily silent, except for a few things Adrian and Gabriel discuss. Involuntarily, my eyes shift to the outside mirror of the car, finding Gabriel's eyes on me already. He looks away when I catch him, taking a deep breath that has his shoulders rising in the seat.

My phone vibrates, and I look down to see a text from Evangelin, wishing me a safe trip.

For so long, I've had bad luck meeting people I could connect with in the same way I have with Evangelin. She listens to me, understands me, lets me vent, and I love hearing about her life. I haven't felt this sort of connection since my grandparents were alive.

I can't help my thoughts shifting to my grandmother, who died when I was very young, leaving my grandfather devastated. He hid it well, but Adrian and I knew he was heartbroken. It took him years to be able to smile when Grandma's name was mentioned. Now, he's with her again, probably talking about who ate the last barbajuan. Every Sunday, they would have the same conversation, arguing over who was the culprit. To this day, neither of them knew it was either Adrian or me who ate it. Or, at least, they'd never let us think that they knew it was us.

Adrian, Gabriel, and I walk through the airport, check in our luggage, and find the security check. I make sure no one notices the bruise, and as soon as I'm through security, I pull my hood over my head again. We sit down on the seats near our gate, and Adrian excuses himself to go to the bathroom. Like the mature adult I am, I put on my headphones and turn up the volume, too afraid Gabriel wants to talk to me.

A couple of minutes pass when all of a sudden, Gabriel holds up a piece of paper.

Can we talk?

I shake my head and pull my feet onto the chair. There is a sad expression on his face, but he looks down at the paper again and starts writing.

Please, Val. I'm so sorry.

Once again, I shake my head. It's not that he rejected me, but this whole chaos threatens our friendship. I'm scared that whatever conversation he and I are going to have will end up with us no longer being able to look at each other.

Valentina Esmèe Cèlia Romana, you know we have to talk.

He is right; we do need to speak, but not now.

Adrian comes back, looks at Gabriel and me, then glares at his new teammate. I close my eyes when my favorite song starts playing through my headphones. My fingers fumble with the string from my hood absentmindedly, and I think about what to do. Naturally, I come to no conclusion.

They call our flight for boarding, so we make our way onto the plane. I sit down in my seat, and Adrian attempts to take the one next to me, but Gabriel appears behind him and whispers something into his ear. I don't know what it is, but it makes my brother move away and sit down in a different one.

"I'm a coward," he says as soon as he sits down.

"What?" is the only thing I'm able to croak out.

"I'm a fucking coward. I wanted to kiss you yesterday, but, instead, I ran," he clarifies, flashing me his wonderful dimples as a sad smile covers his face. "I care a lot about you, chérie, and I hope what happened yesterday won't stand in the way of our friendship."

There it is, the reason I didn't want to have this conversation.

"We both know the uncomfortable situation from yesterday will always be embarrassing for me. I put myself out there, waited for you to kiss me, no, I *asked* you to kiss me, and you let me think you were going for it..." I pause and take a deep breath before I can continue. "How do you expect us to go back to just being friends? We're screwed, Gabriel, because I can't go back."

I've been waiting years to tell him this, years of staring after him. Gabriel leans back and pulls his bottom lip between his teeth, thinking about what to say.

"Val, I'm terrified of my feelings for you. I won't deny them, but I also can't address them without risking everything between us. You're one of my best friends, compassionate and open, and I know I can always count on you. If things go wrong between us, I will lose you forever, and I can't," he rants so quickly, I have trouble keeping up with him.

Once his words have registered in my brain, and I understand his fear, I can finally speak.

"I get it, Gabriel, but how do you expect me to keep on suppressing how I feel?" I ask, turning him speechless.

When he doesn't say anything for a few moments, I get nervous, but I don't push him. It wouldn't be fair of me to expect him to have an answer ready for something like this. I simply put my headphones back on and play some random songs.

My eyes drift to the window, but I feel his hand reach for my hood to turn my face back to look at him. I attempt to smack his hand away, but my hood falls before I have the chance to.

"What is this?" he asks, concern laced in his voice. I have no idea what he's talking about for a moment.

"It's nothing," I snap. The last thing I want is for him to get mad at James. They seem to have enough problems with one another as is.

"Valentina, tell me who did this to you." I choose to ignore him, and he groans beside me. "Why are you so stubborn?" My blood boils, although I know the only reason why he called me that is because he's worried about me. And because I *am* being stubborn.

"Why am *I* stubborn? Why are *you* so confusing? Why do you act like you have feelings for me and then decide that 'we can't'? Why do you have to be the only guy I've ever—" I stop myself and flinch. *Great job, Valentina, really fucking smart.*

"What?" His lips part, shock covering his face.

"Never mind," I say and attempt to pull my hood back up, but he takes my hand and stops me from doing so.

"Does it hurt?" he asks me, his concern stronger than his surprise.

"Yes, but you hurt me more." Gabriel lets go of my hand, and I'm finally able to put my hood back on to hide from the world. To attempt to hide from my feelings.

Ten hours go by without Gabriel speaking to me; ten hours of listening to music and trying to sleep. Eventually, I give up and pull out my favorite book, *Die For Me*. I get lost in Vincent and Kate's love story.

They don't have it easy either, I tell myself, *but they also have the supernatural to deal with.*

Gabriel and I don't.

We only have to deal with the fact that Gabriel can't decide what he wants. When I get to my favorite part of the book, I swallow the lump in my throat. I look over at Gabriel, but he's fast asleep.

He told me he couldn't lose me, but I am prioritizing my crush over our friendship. People have been dying, leaving, and disappearing out of our lives, and I don't have the heart to break both of ours.

I poke his arm, forcing his eyes to shoot open. Ten hours gave me enough time to think and make a decision I am probably going to regret. Gabriel removes his headphones and looks at me, confusion on his face.

"What's wrong, chérie?" His hand reaches out, and I take his in mine.

"I'm sorry about earlier. If you give me a little time, I can go back to being friends. I promise, I just need time." Gabriel studies my features. There is a short pause. No one says anything, neither of us moves, but I can see the conflict in Gabriel's eyes.

"I don't want this to be as painful for you as it is for me," he says firmly, and I suck in a sharp breath.

"The alternative is not speaking at all. Would you prefer that?" His eyes reveal his indecisiveness.

"Of course not, but you'll suffer with me constantly being around you. Trust me, *I know*," he points out, making me realize he's right. That's the problem with having feelings for one of your closest friends. You'll always *long*. Long for more. Long for them to feel the same. Long for them to open their eyes and see you in the same light you see them.

"Don't flatter yourself," I try to tease, but this whole conversation is dreadful. I'm embarrassed, whether or not he admitted he has feelings for me too. I should be excited knowing he does, but instead, we're having one of the most confusing and draining conversations I've ever had.

"I can't be the only guy you ever *dot dot dot*. You need to be with someone who isn't as broken as me, chérie. Someone who isn't scared to love, and I can't give that to you," he admits with shame, and instead of trying to understand him, I get angry.

"Okay, then leave, Gabriel. If you want me to move on, you have to leave because there is no getting over you if you're constantly around me. Please switch seats with my brother and don't speak to me again for the rest of the trip."

I place my headphones back on my ears and turn away from him. This was, by far, the worst way I could have reacted, but he's the only one with defense mechanisms in place. He isn't the only one with walls and barriers built by pain and grief. I push people away. It's wrong, and it hurts him, but it protects me.

Adrian is next to me a moment later, his hand wrapping around mine. I tell him nothing but that I am tired and probably going to sleep for the next two hours until we have to catch our second flight. He nods before I rest my head against his shoulder, drowning out the rest of the world as my brother comforts me.

Chapter 14

Gabriel

Cameron loves golfing. I'm horrible at it, but it entertains him to watch me fail at his second favorite sport, so he brings me along anyway. Especially when he gets to tell me how fucking stupid I am for what happened between Valentina and me.

"She asked you to kiss her and you *didn't*?" he asks after we've played three holes. I get behind the wheel of the golf cart, waiting for him to join me so I can drive us to the next teeing area.

"Yes. I tried to explain to her that I have feelings for her that I'm scared of, and when she said she'd go back to being friends, I freaked out all over again. Then, she basically told me to fuck myself and not speak to her again, only in nicer words."

Cameron's mouth hangs wide open as he listens to me, so I reach over to close it for him, but he slaps my hand away before I have a chance to.

"Alright, stop the cart. We've been tiptoeing around this for too long, but I'll have no more of it. You're going to listen to something I have to say, whether you're going to like it or not," my best friend says, pointing to where he wants me to drive the cart to stop. I do as I'm told, even though I'm a little scared of what's going to come out of his mouth.

"Is there an option not to hear whatever it is you have to say?" I ask with a small laugh, but Cameron shakes his head, his serious expression hardening his already chiseled features.

"I love Valentina. And I love you. There is no getting out of what I have to say to you," he says, and just to annoy him, I step on the gas again, racing toward the next hole. "Gabriel!" Cameron barks before bursting into laughter and clinging to the cart when I turn right a little too aggressively.

If it weren't for his quick reflexes, I'm pretty sure he would have flown out of the cart, so I slow down again, giving him an apologetic look. But my best friend is still laughing, wiping under his eyes to get rid of the tears that have jumped free.

"Okay, say whatever it is you want to say." I tilt my head as I speak, watching him shake his head with a smile.

"You are *not* broken, Gabriel." All amusement leaves his face as he turns to look at me. "At least not in the way you think you are. I know you've lost a lot of people, and I know you've grieved more losses than a man your age should have at this point in his life, but it doesn't make you any less capable of falling in love, of being everything your partner needs you to be. To close yourself off and stop living is not the right path, Gabriel."

Cameron looks down at my heart for a moment before bringing his gaze back up to mine.

"I know your real fear isn't losing her if this goes wrong because you know it would be magic with her. Your real fear is not being good enough for someone. You're scared you won't be what she needs, so you push her away before you hurt her, but you don't realize just how good of a person you are, Gabriel. You're a good man with a big heart and so much love to give. Don't hoard it all out of fear it isn't the right love."

Having a heart-to-heart with Cameron is nothing new for me. Ever since we met years ago, he has made a point to get me to talk about everything I'm feeling instead of bottling things up the way I've done in the past. It's why I've tried my best to open up more with him, talk through what bothers me and what has me lying awake at night staring at my ceiling. Cameron's made me a better man, but I'm not sure that means I'm the *right* man for Valentina.

"I fucked up, Cameron. I pushed her away. She's probably moving on as we speak, and it'll be my fault. All mine, no one else's, because I told her I was too scared to be with her! Who fucking does that? Who hides from the person they have feelings for because they're... scared?" I ask, throwing my hands up in frustration and almost accidentally slapping myself in the face.

Cameron presses his lips together at the sight to keep from laughing but doesn't comment on it.

"A lot of people, my friend. A lot of them. Now ask me how happy I think they are," he says, so I turn my head to look at the greenery ahead of us, all mowed down grass and areas of sand that I specialize in shooting my golf ball into.

"Probably as unhappy as I am," I mumble, so Cameron clasps a hand over my shoulder, an expression of awe spreading over his face.

"Wow, I'm impressed. Is that the first time in your life you got an answer about your feelings right?" I nudge his arm, starting the cart back up to continue driving to our next destination.

"You know how I'm going to get you back for that comment?" I ask, smiling at him before refocusing on the road in front of us.

"Sure as fuck not in this golf game. Even if you got hole-in-ones for the rest of the game, you're not gonna win this anymore," he says, so I hit the brakes particularly hard as we arrive at the next hole.

"No, I'm going to win the Drivers' Championship this year. Then, I'm going to shove the trophy in your face and say, 'Fuck you!'" Cameron bursts into laughter at that, bending over at the waist. I join in because it's hard not to laugh when he's laughing.

"Not if you drive anything like the way you just drove that cart." As much as I try not to laugh even harder, I can't help myself. "But I'm honored you'd dedicate your win of the *championship* to me."

I almost fall to the floor laughing.

Chapter 15

Valentina

When I was seventeen years old, James found out my aunt was abusing me. He found out that she hit me whenever I didn't do as she wanted. He found out that I'd been keeping that a secret to keep my brother from having to give up his career to raise me. The day James saw the slap mark on my face, he confronted my aunt.

He said to her, "If you ever hurt her again, if I ever find out that you hit her again, I will call the police, and I will have them arrest you. Then, I'm going to make sure you lose your house, all of your money, and any good reputation you might have. If I ever hear anything about you abusing Valentina again, I will destroy your life."

Afterward, my aunt avoided me. Knowing the influence James Landon had in the world, even at that time in my life, she couldn't risk him following through on that threat. In a house where I never felt safe before, I suddenly found myself breathing a little easier. I felt as safe as someone could while living with their emotionally and physically abusive guardian.

Maybe that's why I run into his arms when I see him at the place where Adrian and I are having dinner today. Maybe that's why I hold him tight. Maybe that's why he's my best friend, well one of the reasons why.

"Hi, darling," he says, kissing the top of my head as he hugs me back.

"Hi," I reply, leaning back to watch a smile break out across his face. "What are you doing here?"

"Having dinner with my teammate, Eduardo. We're trying to get to know each other a bit better before the season officially restarts," he explains, pointing to the man standing next to Adrian.

My brother waves me over with a smile.

"Val, this is Eduardo. Eduardo, this is my sister Valentina," Adrian introduces us, and I smile at the handsome man.

He has full lips, light brown eyes, a clean-cut beard, long lashes, and a bronze skin tone. He's lean and muscular, and when he smiles, I see his slightly crooked set of white teeth. His brown hair fits his thick, well-shaped, dark brown eyebrows. I've seen him on television before, but I've never met him in person because, until this year, Adrian and James didn't have much to do with him.

"It's a pleasure to meet you," he says and holds out his hand for me. I shake it politely as I return his smile. It feels forced like I'm not supposed to give him a flirtatious look, but I try to ignore that feeling.

"The pleasure is all mine."

James invites us to join them for dinner where Eduardo and I start talking. He's twenty-six, from Spain, has three sisters, and it's his sixth year in Formula One. Eduardo is kind and open, and he asks me lots of questions too. I tell him about my plans to travel the world with my brother this season. Talking to him is easy, although we don't seem to have much in common. Luckily, my love and passion for racing make having a conversation with any of the drivers very natural.

"Valentina is a stunning name," Eduardo compliments with his enchanting Spanish accent. I enjoy listening to him talk, hearing him pronounce words in such a unique way. "You and your brother look a lot alike." James and Adrian are deep in conversation, but I look at my brother anyway.

"So I've been told my whole life," I reply and let out a nervous laugh. Eduardo also laughs, a deep, sexy sound that, to my surprise, warms my insides. Not in the same way they do when Gabriel smiles at me, but something's better than nothing. "So, did you bring any family members this weekend to support you?"

"My sister Angelina," he replies as my eyes shift to my glass, watching the condensed water run down the sides.

When I look at him again, he's smirking at me, half of his bottom lip between his teeth. My eyes linger on his mouth, even as he leans forward on the table.

"Has anyone ever told you how beautiful you are?" I roll my eyes at his cliché question. "Can I take you out on Thursday? On a proper date, not a dinner with your brother." He chuckles, but I'm too surprised by his question to respond right away.

"Eduardo," James warns, but when he sees me flash him a glare, he holds up his hands and backs off. I turn to the handsome man in front of me and smile. I want to decline politely, but I'm not sure why.

No, I know why. Gabriel is why.

"What time?" I ask him, the smile on his face growing.

"I'm working until seven. So, seven-thirty?" I nod as his rough hand wraps around mine. Eduardo lifts them to his mouth and presses the smallest of kisses to the back of mine. "Good night, hermosa."

"Buenas noches," I reply, earning a smile from him. Eduardo leaves, and both of the other boys scoot closer to me.

"You're going out with Eduardo? How come?" Adrian asks, and I know what he means. A day ago, I was crying over Gabriel, and now, I'm agreeing to go on a date with a guy I only met a couple of hours ago. It's very unlike me, but that is precisely why I am doing it.

"He's a nice guy and incredibly easy on the eyes," I swoon, and both boys scrunch their noses.

"All right, Val, we don't need to know what gets you going," Adrian complains, making me laugh. "We should go too. Long day tomorrow."

Chapter 16

Valentina

Adrian and Dad stand in front of me, the picture of a Formula One car in Dad's hands. They have been quizzing me on the names of the parts for the past week. It's surprisingly easy for me, even though I'm only nine years old and some of the words are difficult to pronounce. Dad starts to point at the different parts, and I name them quickly.

"Front wing, rear wing, engine intake," I say as he continues to move his finger over the page. "Suspension, disc brake, also engine intake, brake cooling intake," I go on, and a proud smile appears on his face.

"That's correct," Adrian tells me, but I need Dad to reassure me. He knows more than my brother.

"You're absolutely right. The mechanics who work on the car would be very pleased with you. Maybe if you can't become a driver, you can be a mechanic," he says, but I frown.

"Why wouldn't I be able to become a driver?" I ask, confused. Dad always tells me he believes in me.

"Because it's difficult to become a Formula One driver. If it were easy, everyone would do it, but they can't. There are many factors involved, and, sadly, talent is not the main one. However, I strongly believe you have what it takes to live your dream. Just like I believe in your brother." He stops and puts his hand on my shoulder. "I'm so proud of you."

This is one of the rare moments he ever shows affection. When he does, he makes sure I will never forget it. I hug him as fiercely as I can.

"I love you, Daddy," I say, and he hugs me back.

"I love you, too, little champion."

Adrian takes me with him to work this Thursday morning. Today is an autograph session and press conference. I haven't spoken to Gabriel or seen him in two days, but I'm not sure what I'd say to him either. He's made it abundantly clear that he doesn't want us to be friends because it's too painful for both of us yet he doesn't want us to be more either because he's scared.

Avoiding him and any thoughts of him will be a fun task for me to try and accomplish today.

James briefly greets me before I get into the car with him, Adrian, and Daniel. We arrive at the track and walk toward the paddock. I smile brightly as I take in my surroundings. Here is where I'm meant to be, where I want to spend my life. Looking at the track and feeling it underneath my fingertips as I bend down has always been my highlight of the race weekend. This is all my grandfather and I have wanted, and yet only Adrian gets to live his dream.

As soon as we step into Adrian's garage, my eyes land on Chloe Barbosa, his race engineer. Excitement blooms through me at the sight of her, so I hurry over to where she's standing with some of the mechanics. I chose the world of racing, the world of Formula One. I chose to make it my life, but that means that often I feel very alone as a woman.

Chloe makes me feel less alone.

As soon as she sees me, she turns my way to open her arms for me, the usual scowl on her face. I don't think I've ever seen this woman smile in the four years I've known her. Adrian always says it's her grumpy nature that makes sure no one fucks with my brother.

"How are you?" I ask after stepping out of the hug and smiling at her. Chloe places a hand on my cheek, her brown eyes full of warmth. She has long brown hair she usually keeps in a single braid that falls down her back. She has a light brown skin tone, full lips, and curves to die for. Chloe is very beautiful.

"Better now that I see you. These men were giving me a migraine larger than Mount fucking Everest," she says, her accent thick.

Chloe is from Brazil and is fluent in English, Portuguese, and Spanish. Sometimes, she slips into Portuguese when she speaks to me because she knows I can partially understand her.

"Any updates?" she asks, clearly meaning my career, but I shake my head as a sad feeling spreads through me.

"No, none so far. I've been reaching out, training, but I don't have good news for you," I say with a laugh that I don't mean to lighten the mood.

"Yet. You don't have good news for me *yet*, but your time will come. You'll see," she assures me.

"Hopefully," I reply with a forced smile. "How's your wife?"

Chloe urges me to follow her as she says, "Talia is good. Looking after our fur baby while I'm here. He just turned four months old," she says, holding up a picture of their cat.

"He's adorable," I say right as she stops in front of a row of screens.

"Are you ready to learn? I've got some new things I would like to show you, but they're a bit complicated," she explains as she gestures toward a matching set of headphones for us to put on and drown out the loud noises the mechanics create as they work on Adrian's car.

Chloe has been teaching me about racing strategy, what a race engineer does, and some procedures of the race weekend whenever Adrian invites me to be at a race with him. Now, I'll get to learn more, and spend more time with Chloe as she teaches me more about the world that I fell in love with when I was a child.

"I'm ready," I reply, grabbing a pair of headphones and slipping them onto my head. I smile at Chloe as I do so, watching her shake her head at me.

"I've never seen anyone so excited to learn about complicated analyses and boring race procedures," she says after putting on her headphones too.

"Well, I'm not just anyone. I'm Valentina Romana, and I'll be the first woman to be a permanent championship contender. And I'll only get there by learning these things from people like you," I reply, giving her the easiest smile I can manage.

"Then, let's focus. This is going to be a long day."

And there's no better way to spend it.

Chapter 17

Valentina

Today is one of the most important days of my life, and my nerves prove it. Adrian used his connections to get me a special test drive for some of the driver academies. Usually, they recruit drivers based on their karting results and points they have collected, but since my case is quite different, they made an exception. I get to set a time to see if I can compete with the drivers who are already part of the academy.

Adrian flew me out to Barcelona for this because a lot of testing for Formula One is done here. James and Gabriel decided to come with us and are impatiently waiting at the sidelines. My oldest friend being here isn't a surprise, but Gabriel coming to support me was a big shock. We're good friends, but I didn't think he would travel to Spain for me. I can't help but like him more for it.

My eyes scan all three men, and I can tell how nerve-racking this is for them, especially Adrian and James. Since I was kicked out of Formula Three, all they've done is help me make it back into the racing world.

It all seemed hopeless until today.

"Ready?" my brother asks me once I'm seated in the familiar F3 car. It's been a while since I've sat in one, but I've been training, studying every single track and footage I can to prepare myself for an opportunity like this.

"I'm ready," I assure him, but my heart is racing in my chest, and my palms are sweating under the gloves. The helmet is snug on my head, and the racing suit is tight, making it difficult to breathe properly.

"You've got this," Adrian assures me. I nod.

I can barely hear him, and my mind is preoccupied with calming my body. My lap time has to be outstanding for me to get a spot in the driver academy. I've waited two years for another opportunity, and today is the day of my second chance.

I'm given the green light and make my way out of the garage. After I familiarize myself with the track for a couple of laps, I'm ready to set a time and grab my opportunity by the horns. Once the starting line is in my sight, I speed up and race down the track as quickly as possible.

The force of the turns is strong, but I lean into them as I have done countless times. Adrenaline runs through my veins, and suddenly, I feel completely calm. This is where I'm meant to be, and I will do anything to prove it to the people watching me. With every bumpy turn and curb I take, my smile gets bigger. I calculate the different angles I have to take to speed down the perfect racing line, something I could never do in my day-to-day life but is second nature to me in the race car.

By the time I reach the finish line, I feel sweat dripping down my back. That was exhilarating, and my time was better than any I've ever set before. I'm told to do a slow, cool-down lap and then return to the pitlane.

James, Gabriel, and Adrian each give me a thumbs up, pride replacing anxiety inside of me. Once I'm out of the car, I remove my helmet and balaclava. My hair clings to my forehead, but I don't mind it one bit. It takes me back to the races, and so does the exhaustion my body experiences post-driving.

"That was bloody fantastic," James congratulates me before picking me up from the ground to spin me around. I feel like crying out of happiness.

"I'm sweaty," I remind him, but he hugs me tighter.

"Good, that's how you're supposed to be." I laugh.

"That was phenomenal," Adrian says next, but when I go to hug him, he holds me back. "Just because James is okay with your sweat doesn't mean I am," he says, and when my mouth falls open, he pulls me into a hug and chuckles. "Have you lost your sense of humor today?" he asks before I push him back and smack his stomach, making him lean forward and cough dramatically. "She has wounded me, mortally wounded me," Adrian almost screams, and I shush him.

I'm smiling so brightly, my face hurts.

Gabriel is the last one to come up to me.

"Did I make your trip worthwhile?" I ask in an attempt to make him smile, which he does.

"Seeing you already made it worth it. Watching that lap was the cherry on top," he says so calmly, it knocks the breath out of me. Gabriel hugs me as well, and I grin against his shoulder.

Then comes a long wait.

Adrian, James, Gabriel, and I are led to a room while the people from the driver academies decide my fate. Adrian hands me electrolytes and something to eat to keep my energy from dropping drastically. I thank him with a smile, and Gabriel and James sit down at a table with me. James repeatedly informs me how proud he is, but my leg bounces up and down anyway.

This was all a test, and there are people now judging me.

I feel nauseous.

"I compared your times to the other drivers in the academies, and you were second fastest. If they don't take you, then I don't know what their problem is," Adrian states, but I'm not sure who he's addressing. It could be me, but it could also very much be himself. Gabriel takes my hand in his, grabbing my full attention.

"There is no driver out there like you, Val. Your determination is priceless, and if they can't see that, they're fools," he says so sincerely, warmth spreads through my chest.

The moment is soon interrupted when the door swings open, and the recruiters from the three different academies walk into the room. They all have serious expressions on their faces. Whatever they have to tell me will not be pretty.

"After analyzing every category, we've all concluded that Miss Romana would not make a good fit in our academies." My heart sinks into my stomach as tears shoot into my eyes.

I didn't need all of them to take me.

One would have been more than enough.

I only needed one.

"What, why?" Adrian blurts out, and as much as I'd love to talk, I'm devastated and speechless. "She's one of the fastest drivers you've ever seen!" My brother is angry then, maybe too angry to have a rational conversation with the people who are denying me the opportunity to live my dream. I'm about to get up to hold Adrian back when Gabriel places his hand on my brother's shoulder to calm him.

"We have to consider more than her lap time," says a man with gray hair and blue eyes. Gabriel tenses visibly.

"Okay, then consider the other categories. Talent: she has more than just talent. Money: it's not an issue. Time: this is her dream; she'll do anything to make it happen. Fitness: Valentina works out every single day and is in the best shape she could possibly be. There are your categories, and she's perfect in every one of them. Tell us, how do you justify turning her away?" Gabriel's words surprise all of us, especially me.

He came here to support me, but I would have never expected him to fight while I try to compose myself.

"We don't have to justify ourselves. We simply don't think she'd be a good fit for any of our academies." Those three men can really stand there and say those words without hearing the problem behind them. Well, not on my watch. I'm so sick and tired of getting turned down because of who I am.

"So, your justification for not giving me a chance is because I'm a girl, correct?" Everyone turns to me. Gabriel and Adrian move out of the way to let me speak to the three men whose eyes have widened.

"Now, young lady, how dare you accuse us of—" I interrupt the middle-aged man with a beard then.

"I'm not accusing you of anything. If you take offense to my question, it only proves me right. You have not given me a single reason why I don't belong in your academies, simply that I am not a 'good fit.' If you cannot come up with any other reason except my gender, how can I see it differently?" For a moment, there is absolute silence. They look at each other, but none of them seem to have an answer that will make them look less sexist.

"You were already kicked from a team once. Doesn't that speak for itself?" The other man, who hadn't addressed me before, points out, and I nod in agreement.

"I was kicked out for the same reason you are refusing me now." My tears have long dried, and I'm starting to feel numb.

"We cannot take a risk on you. I'm sorry, Ms. Romana. We did this as a favor to Mr. Romana, but it didn't work out." They're about to leave when I stop them dead in their tracks.

"Then tell me what I can improve on!" I demand, and the man with blue eyes turns to me one last time.

"Improve your ability to let it go. You'll never reach Formula One." They all leave as Adrian wraps his arms around me to hold me up.

I'll never score enough points in a junior league like Formula Three or Two. I'll never get the Super License every Formula One driver is required to have. I will never meet all of the criteria to fulfill my dream. Everything my grandfather and I have worked toward is moving further away with each step I take forward.

"You'll never reach Formula One."

Well, it sure is starting to feel that way...

As the memory replays in my head, keeping me awake at night, a tear drips down my cheek. This was the most recent in-person rejection I received, a wound that has not yet healed properly.

A wound that keeps me up at night.

Chapter 18

Gabriel

There's a pre-race press conference every Thursday of a race weekend. The FIA chooses ten out of the twenty drivers to answer the media's questions. Five of them will be interviewed per session, so there are two sessions in total. It always changes with different drivers getting picked every week. This week, Cameron, Adrian, James, Leonard, and I were chosen for one of the sessions. My teammate is smiling at the rows over rows of reporters. My best friend is proudly wearing a baseball cap with the Australian flag on it. The guy I hate with a fucking passion is leaning back on the couch and waiting for the first question. The only multiple-time World Champion is scowling at all of the reporters, unhappy to be here. I share that sentiment. I also don't want to be here while I know Valentina is going on a date with Eduardo tonight.

Adrian told me what time they were going out with a pointed look that obviously meant, "If you want to do something about it, do it soon."

I don't know if he knows I have feelings for her, but sometimes, when he does things like that, I'm convinced he sees right through me with those detective eyes of his. He knows more than he's letting on, but he's too smart for his own good and pretends he knows nothing when asked about it.

"Good afternoon, everyone. The drivers are ready for your questions now," someone tells the reporters, and I tilt my head to stare into two dozen different faces, all of them dark because of the spotlights that are on the five of us.

"I'd like to start off with a question for each of the drivers to answer," Gillian Fender of *Griffin Sports* starts, standing up so we can look at him as he asks the question. "Can you describe how you're feeling now that the season is restarting after the many changes made to the teams and their drivers?"

James sits up a little and leans forward to answer the question first, but Leonard beats him to it. I almost smile at the way James deflates back in his seat.

"Drivers changing teams is important, but what's a lot more important is how much the cars have improved. We'll only be able to truly answer that question once this weekend is done and we've seen how all the drivers have fared in their new cars, with the new updates."

I love it when Leonard answers these questions. After over a decade of racing, he's getting tired of them, especially when the reporters ask things we don't know how to answer yet.

"Well, I'm excited. I like that we'll all be a bit more challenged. Keeps things interesting," Adrian says as he leans back in his seat and smiles. I watch his PR manager, Fatima, shake her head at his answer, but I'm grinning because I feel the same way he does. But I understand her too because Adrian can be a PR nightmare.

"Next question is for Cameron. Do you think Spark will be fast enough this weekend to finally get you your first win in your home country?" another reporter asks, this time one from *Specter Sports*.

"Well, that's the dream, but I doubt the improvements so far will allow us to catch up to the big three teams yet." The reporter seems satisfied with that answer, so she sits back down again.

"I have a question for Adrian and Gabriel. This is your first season as teammates, but you've stated in the past that you are friends. Do you think that connection will help you become better teammates or become an obstacle in your fight for the championship?" the next reporter asks.

I turn to Adrian to see if he will answer, and he gives me a curt nod in response.

"I will not hesitate to do whatever it takes to win the championship. Whether I'm racing against Gabriel or even if I'd be racing against my own sister, as long as it's safe and clean racing, I'm doing it. I came here to win, not to be given a medal for being a good friend or brother. Although, I deserve those anyway if you ask me," Adrian says, making the entire room snicker. He nudges my knee, signaling for me to say something too.

"I'll definitely be doing everything I can to prevent Adrian from outperforming me, especially because he's my friend," I tease and he flashes me a mean smile, a promise in that simple expression.

He's going to try to kick my ass this season, but I won't let him. This is my season. I will claim it, win it, and go down in history as one of the youngest world champions the world has ever seen. At twenty-one, I'll be the second youngest, right after Carlos Klein.

"Next question is for James. How do you feel now that you're in one of the top teams?" The Brit leans forward in his seat again, happy to answer the question.

"I'm very excited. Racing for Hawke is an honor. I'm hoping we'll present a real challenge for Velocità Rossa and Grenzenlos this season, maybe even compete for the Constructors' and Drivers' Championship," James replies. I don't mean to snort, I really don't, but I do it anyway. The thought of him stealing the championship from right under me is too ridiculous for my mind to process.

The room goes quiet, everyone looking at me until my cheeks heat from embarrassment. Well, at least until Adrian bursts into laughter, smacking his knee as he falls backward against the couch. The reporters join him, and even Cameron starts chuckling beside me. James flashes me a glare that would probably kill me if looks had that ability, but I'm smirking in response.

"I second that sound," Adrian says as he wipes under his eyes and recomposes himself. "No one's taking the championship from Velocità Rossa. Watch and see," my cocky teammate says, placing a hand on my shoulder.

I offer him a grateful smile before refocusing on the press conference to answer the next question.

Chapter 19

Valentina

I scan all of the clothes I brought, hoping something will stand out and make my choice easy. I'm nervous, *really nervous.* This is my first proper date since I've broken up with Luke. My fingers trail over the same three dresses, but I can't decide. Eventually, I give up and sit down on my bed, the towel from my shower still clinging to my chest.

A knock on my door startles me, and when I look through the peephole, my heart stutters. I open the door despite being barely dressed, but his eyes only focus on my face.

"Hi," he says with a sad smile. I cock a brow.

"What do you want, Gabriel?" He starts to shift uncomfortably from one foot to the other. His hands are behind his back.

"I wanted to talk," he admits, sucking in a sharp breath. He stares down at the ground before bringing his gaze back to me, pain in his eyes. "I can't give you what you need, what you *deserve*." He's way too calm about something so heavy.

"Oh my god, you are ridiculous. Telling someone who has feelings for you something like that doesn't make the feelings suddenly disappear."

It hurts them, breaks their heart, it can even destroy them. Lucky for me, I don't give him such power over me.

"I just want what's best for you," he explains.

"Okay, then why can't you be what's best for me?" I challenge, watching him study me like he wishes he had a simple answer for me.

"All I do is upset you," he replies, shame laced in his words. His face falls, and I lift my hands to his cheeks to force his eyes to meet mine. Gabriel never shies away from being vulnerable with me, which is one of the things I admire most about him.

"Because you push me away, and you don't need to," I whisper, and his hands wrap around my wrists.

"Yeah, I do. I'm not good enough for you. Not yet." I retract my hands, shaking my head as he reaches for me again. He drops his hand, his eyes never leaving me.

"Then what are you doing here, Gabriel? You already told me that, so there was no need to come here and repeat yourself," I say, trying my best not to linger on the "not yet" he mumbled.

"Oh yeah, sorry," he replies nervously, his eyes drifting to the floor. "I got you something." He fishes around in his pocket before retrieving a small box. "It's for you to wear on your date," he states, both of my eyebrows lifting in surprise. "I know, it's very unlike me to do something like this." Gabriel lets out a sad laugh, and I open the top to reveal a claw hair clip in the shape of a sunflower. I gasp, catching his attention. "If you don't like it, I can return it," he promises, but I shake my head.

"It's stunning, but I don't understand why you bought me a gift," I reply. Gabriel only shrugs.

"I saw it and thought of you. Maybe it'll complete your outfit," he suggests, but I'm still confused.

"It might, once I figure out what I'm going to wear," I tell him with a small laugh. His eyes focus on mine once more.

"If you want, I can help you choose something," he offers, but I can't hold back my following words.

"Okay, what is going on with you? Why do you want to help me choose an outfit for a date with another guy?"

"To be completely honest, chérie, I just miss you as my friend. I don't want to lose you for good." I lean against the door for support and study the man in front of me.

With all of my strength, I try to understand him. Gabriel said he has feelings for me, but at the same time, doesn't think he deserves me. As much as I try to convince him otherwise, he's not ready to listen. But he wants to be my friend, and if I'm moving on, then why wouldn't I want him to be my friend too?

"Well, I do have three options, but I don't know which to choose," I reply, and, finally, a sincere smile appears on his face.

Gabriel helps me pick out my green maxi dress combined with black heels and a matching purse. I add the hair clip, and he gives me an approving grin when I've finished my subtle makeup. His eyes then shift back to the floor, so I let out a long sigh.

"Now, what will I wear tomorrow?" I walk back over to my clothes while he watches my every move.

"I'm not sure what you mean, chérie," he answers sweetly, and I wish for the millionth time we weren't in this situation.

"For our 'friend date.' It's been a while since it was just the two of us," I explain, and Gabriel jumps up from the bed, excitement evident on his face.

"That would be great. I'll arrange it!" He kisses my cheek and leaves my room before I can say another word.

I can't tell if this is going to be good for us or a complete disaster. I guess I'll have to find out the hard way.

Eduardo takes me to the track where he set up a table for us to eat at. I smile brightly when I take in the rest of the scenery. The lighting is dim but still bright enough so we can have a clear view of everything. There are two plates filled with food, and candles stand between them. It's cheesy and very cliché, but also thoughtful and romantic. Eduardo pulls out a chair for me, making me roll my eyes while a grin plays on my lips.

The dinner goes by faster than I would like, but I'm enjoying myself a lot. Eduardo has a great sense of humor, likes to make me laugh, I can tell that much, and he's charming. He shares stories about his childhood, and I listen closely.

We continue our conversation, and he tells me about his experiences in Formula One. I share stories about growing up with Adrian and about my life in Monaco. It's easy to share a connection with someone who has lived a similar lifestyle in another European country. We then talk about the most random things, and I laugh harder than I have in a while.

Eduardo and I drive back to my hotel hours after he first picked me up. The drive is silent, but his hand feels comforting in both of mine. There might not be a tingle, an ache, or anything that Gabriel ignites inside of me, but it's pleasant. I enjoy holding Eduardo's hand, feeling the butterflies in my stomach.

"Are you ready for tomorrow?" His head moves to the side so he can look at me.

"Yes. It's only free practice, after all," he assures me and gently squeezes my hand. I nod as his eyes drift back to the road. His thumb caresses the back of my left hand in a steady motion, and I smile.

Eduardo gets in the elevator with me and walks me back to my hotel room. We stop in front of my door, and I face Eduardo with a big grin on my face.

"Do you think I can kiss you without getting a black eye from your brother?" I laugh at his question.

"Yes. My brother will only attack on my command." Eduardo nods and smiles at me.

His lips meet mine a second later.

Another second passes, and I realize how wrong this feels. Because it does. It feels like I'm cheating on my feelings, betraying them with this single kiss. All the butterflies in the world won't be enough to make me feel like this is the right thing, not when my head is screaming for me to step away.

Because Eduardo is not Gabriel, he never will be, and I'll never be able to pretend my heart doesn't belong to the man who thinks he isn't good enough for me.

"I'll see you tomorrow," I say after breaking the kiss, barely refraining from putting my hand to my lips to wipe his kiss away. Instead, I offer him one more smile before I slip into my hotel room and sink down against the door.

Chapter 20

Valentina

Today was the first two free practice sessions of the season. During those, the drivers can familiarize themselves with the track and weather conditions while driving their cars. They can also try different strategies and tires, and set lap times to compare with the other teams. Gabriel and James did well, but Adrian struggled visibly today. He'll have another chance to improve in the third practice tomorrow, and, hopefully, it will allow him to set a good time during Qualifying.

Thousands of fans were already in the stands today, supporting their favorite drivers by cheering them on, wearing their teams' colors, and holding up posters and flags. This is something that always warms my heart. The excitement of the fans every time the cars race by them is unlike anything else, in my opinion. I barely had fans when I was racing for Formula Three, but the few who supported me meant the world to me.

Chloe kept me close to her the whole day, teaching me more about the track and discussing parts of the strategy she's thinking about for Adrian's race on Sunday. She's not exactly supposed to talk to me about this stuff, but she knows I won't do anything that could ruin my brother's race, let alone share information that could help another team and driver.

As much as I tried not to think about Gabriel and our "friend date," my mind kept drifting to it the entire day, up until now, while I'm standing in the shower, letting the warmth of the water calm me.

There is no reason for me to be nervous, but I get out of the shower to stand in front of my suitcase. Water is dripping down my back from my hair as I'm looking through my things once more. A knock on the door startles me, and I shake my head at Gabriel when I open it.

"Do you get an inner alarm every single time I'm in a towel?" He shrugs with a naughty smile.

"No, but I most certainly wouldn't mind having it," he jokes, and I step out of the way so he can come in. "I brought you something else," he informs me. I frown at him.

"Stop bringing me things," I complain, but Gabriel only grins as he holds out a Velocità Rossa team shirt.

"It's important for where I'm taking you," he simply replies, and I tilt my head to the side ever so slightly, hoping he'll elaborate. "Come on, Lady Valentina, we have somewhere to be," he teases me, my cheeks heating at the nickname.

"You haven't called me that in years," I mumble, overwhelmed by the sudden wave of nostalgia and happiness.

After all of the chaos between us, I'm glad to see our friendship isn't ruined. Gabriel tells me to get ready, probably to give us both a break from the emotional tension between us.

The shirt fits me snugly around the top, and when I inhale, I realize it's Gabriel's. Not just the number painted across the chest area, but the scent, his mahogany scent, tells me it's one of the ones he's worn in the past.

Wearing it gives me a strange feeling of belonging and comfort. I add a pair of shorts and the hair clip he gave me before putting on my sneakers and following Gabriel to his rental car. He stays quiet the whole drive to the track while I wonder what we could be doing there at this hour.

Not knowing what he has planned is slowly making me more and more impatient.

"Can you give me a hint, at least?" I beg, but he only laughs.

"We're almost there, chérie. You'll see soon enough," Gabriel promises.

For the first time tonight, I study his outfit. He's wearing a white dress shirt and simple blue jeans. I feel underdressed next to him, but my outfit was his choice, so if I am, I'll just blame it on him.

Once the car is parked, he turns to me with a sincere smile.

"Now, the question is, do you trust me enough to let me blindfold you?" he asks, and I furrow both of my eyebrows in response.

"I think we had different ideas about what tonight would look like," I joke, but Gabriel's cheeks turn a bright red.

"Jesus, Valentina, get your head out of the gutter," he laughs. "No, I don't want to blindfold you for that reason," he adds, but the way he looks at me tells me he wouldn't be opposed to blindfolding me in the way I was suggesting either.

"Okay, then you may blindfold me," I say, my heart racing and his fingers carefully tie the fabric of one of his bandanas, the ones I've seen him wear quite a few times in the past, around my head to take my vision away.

Gabriel does a good job not bumping me into things, *for the most part*, but it takes a while to get to wherever we're going. Eventually, he stops me from going any further, and I hear him speak to someone else about whether or not everything is ready.

That only makes me more impatient.

"Okay, finally. I had to pull a lot of strings for this, but it will be so worth it," he says before pulling the bandana from my eyes and revealing his Formula One car. "I know your dream is to race in one, but for now, you can sit in mine."

This wouldn't seem like a big deal to anyone else, but to me, it means the world. I've only ever been allowed near the car, never in it. One of my biggest dreams has always been to know what it feels like to sit in one.

I stare at Gabriel in disbelief, and he smiles brightly.

"You did this for me?" During a race weekend, this should be impossible. The car and driver are the most protected components because, without them, there is no race.

"Of course. It's long overdue." His green-brown eyes stare into mine, and I wonder how someone can remain so pure after losing so many people. "Go, sit," he pulls me from my moment of awe and helps me into his car.

The seat is tight at the sides and incredibly uncomfortable at the back, but that's because it's made to fit Gabriel perfectly, not me. It would be different if this were my seat.

I look straight ahead at the halo, one of the most important additions they've recently made to the car. It's a safety measure in the shape of its name that sits over where the driver's head is. It has saved the drivers' lives many times when they crashed.

The thought almost makes me shiver.

Formula One is not to be underestimated.

My eyes focus on where the steering wheel usually is, and I stretch out my arms to imitate a driver's body position during a race.

"How do you feel?" Gabriel asks after a while of me admiring the car.

"Like one of my fantasies has just become a reality," I admit, he cheers in victory.

"So, you're happy?" he goes on, and I nod.

Tears have been threatening to leave my eyes since I've sat down, and when he celebrates my joy, I let them fall.

Gabriel allows me to stay in the car for a bit longer. He even takes a few pictures of me in it to capture this moment.

"You know, the first time I sat in one, I was so nervous, I kept pressing the off switch instead of on. But, at first, I didn't realize that, so I started complaining. 'Why is this stupid car not turning on? Something's not working. It's fucking broken.' Eventually, someone came up to me and had to remind me what the right button was. Val, I almost died from shame," he tells me, and I burst into uncontrollable laughter.

"No, you didn't," I reply, still too amused by his story to keep from laughing at him.

"It was so embarrassing," he admits, and I finally catch myself. The smile on my lips remains, but at least I'm calm enough now to see his shy grin and red cheeks.

It's not fair that his outside is just as beautiful as his inside.

"Will you share more stories?" I ask.

Gabriel squats down next to the car to tug a loose strand of hair behind my ear. I stop breathing until he retracts his hand and runs it over his stubble with a thoughtful expression on his face.

"Would you like to hear about the time I almost pissed myself in the car or the time I was incapable of putting my balaclava on?"

"Both!"

Adrian and I sit on Grandfather's couch as we stare at the television. Our dad didn't want to bring us to his race, which is a normal thing now. Grandfather has been making sure we aren't too excluded, but it doesn't make it hurt any less. Our father has abandoned us for his career.

However, Grandfather is doing his best to raise us. Adrian and my dreams are his priority, and my brother has been taking racing more seriously the last couple of months. Not as serious as me, but still.

"Look, the safety car is out," Adrian informs me, and I bring my attention back to the television.

The safety car is a sports car and usually comes when the conditions on the track are unsafe. The rest of the drivers are instructed to follow behind it at a much slower speed. The safety car comes out when there has been a crash of any type, engine failure leading to a car standing in the middle of the track, or numerous other reasons.

"What happened?" I ask because I didn't pay attention to the screen.

"Silver drove into the wall because they didn't properly screw on his tire. He's fine. They just need the safety car because his car is in a dangerous position for the other drivers," Adrian says.

My eyebrows lift, and I gasp. Patrick Silver is my father's biggest rival and the only one who was in his way of winning the championship.

My daddy is going to win the championship!

I jump up from my seat to run into the kitchen where my grandfather is to tell him what just happened. Excitement overwhelms me.

If I am this happy for my father, how happy will I be when I win?

Well, I guess I will have to find out.

CHAPTER 21

Gabriel

TODAY IS THE FIRST Qualifying of the season, which determines the starting positions for us drivers on the grid for the race the following day. I'm beyond nervous. I feel it as I walk, in my lack of communication, my body language, and especially how I keep checking the time. I'm still operating, but inhumanly so.

This is important for me.

The first race is always the most nerve-racking.

Today, everything is amplified because it's my first Qualifying with Velocità Rossa. They are one of the top three teams in the sport, and in the last five years, they have been attempting to eliminate Grenzenlos' dominance. Although Grenzenlos has won the Constructors' Championship three years in a row, Velocità Rossa has always been a close second. Winning that championship means the team has collected the most points over the season.

A driver can secure up to twenty-five points for their team with every race, depending on their position at the end. The points from both drivers are totaled into one sum for the Constructors' Championship. Those points also count to the Drivers' Championship where each of us competes for the title individually.

This year, Velocità Rossa has younger, more motivated engineers and Adrian and I are eager to prove our worth.

My eyes scan the Velocità Rossa garages, but I can't find Valentina anywhere.

"Focus," Hector, my performance coach, says as he approaches me.

"I'm focused," I reply, but I see blonde curls bouncing in my peripheral vision.

Valentina smiles at Adrian's race engineer, Chloe, as the other woman speaks to her. I let my eyes linger on her, on the way her jumpsuit makes her look as elegant as always but also hugs her curves in a way that has my self-control slowly slipping away. Her smile is breathtaking, lighting up the entire room. I watch her as she disappears again, my heart hammering a little harder now than it did before.

"You're definitely not focused," Hector complains, standing next to me with a scowl painted across his face. "You can longingly stare after Valentina once Qualifying is done and you've gotten pole. Until then, eyes off her." I hate how easily the people closest to me see through my feelings.

I hate it even more because since yesterday since we went on our friend date, all of my feelings have been amplified. Like I can't properly breathe when I don't see her. Like all of my thoughts run wild until her presence silences them. Like she's my motivation, determination, and drive. Seeing her smile yesterday when she sat in my car and I made one of her dreams come true was one of the best moments of my life.

"Let's go warm up. Maybe that'll help," he says, waving his hand to signal for me to follow him.

We spent the next half hour warming up my muscles to get ready for Qualifying. I jump rope and stretch, making sure my body is awake and prepared to take the toll of racing. It's a draining job because all of our muscles are constantly working as soon as we sit in the car. Our minds cannot drift, under any circumstance. We can't get distracted unless we want to cause an accident. Adrenaline floods through us, and when that wears off again, it leaves our bodies exhausted.

And yet, the most tiring thing I've ever put myself through is trying to keep my feelings for Valentina at bay.

Hector hands me my helmet, balaclava, and gloves before urging me back inside my garage where I'm supposed to get into my car for the start of Qualifying. My eyes drift over to where Adrian is slipping into his car, Valentina taking his hand and mumbling something to him that has him nodding.

I slip into my car, going into the proper headspace, the one where I drown everything out. Where I delete the world around me to focus entirely on my job.

The image of Valentina's smile slips into my head one last time, motivating me.

Then, I wait for the go-ahead before starting the first lap of the first Qualifying session of the season.

Chapter 22

Valentina

When Qualifying starts, I'm tempted to bite my nails as I look at the small TVs inside the garage. James gets a good lap in and so does Cameron, but I'm waiting to see how Adrian and Gabriel do.

By the time Q1 is done, Gabriel completed the fastest lap, Adrian had the second best, and then the Grenzenlos team occupied the third and fourth positions. Five drivers are out in Q1, and Q2 is set to start soon.

In Q1, the drivers who place anywhere between sixteenth and twentieth are eliminated from the next Qualifying round. That means their positions are set for the Grand Prix on Sunday. They have eighteen minutes to complete as many laps as the team deems necessary without using their regulated amount of tires.

In Q2, the same principle applies, except the session is only fifteen minutes long, and any position after the tenth is eliminated.

In Q3, the remaining ten drivers race for twelve minutes for pole position, which is the first position, and anywhere between two and ten, depending on their lap time.

James, Eduardo, Adrian, and Gabriel all make it to Q3, and my heart is racing in my chest. Cameron is positioned in eleventh place, Leonard occupies thirteenth, and the Grenzenlos drivers, Jonathan Kent and Kyle Hughes are also in Q3.

I constantly switch between standing and sitting, depending on how nervous I am. The time starts counting down on the clock for the third time today, so I jump out of my seat to get back to standing near one of the screens not too far from Chloe.

All of the mechanics in the garage follow my lead and are probably as anxious to see the results as I am.

These twelve minutes feel like the longest of my life, but when the Qualifying finally ends, I can't believe my eyes. Adrian gained pole position, Jonathan takes second place,

Gabriel is third, while James and Kyle occupy the fourth and fifth positions. My eyes scan the leaderboard for Eduardo's name, and I notice that he came in seventh.

I'm jumping up and down and clapping my hands together in joy. I feel overwhelming pride for Adrian as he snatches the first pole of the season.

After what feels like forever, I finally get to hug my sweaty brother, who picks me up and squeezes me tightly.

"Congratulations! I'm so proud of you!" I say before he puts me back on the ground. "I can't believe you did it." Adrian has gotten poles before, he's also won races, but I'm still surprised he got the first pole of the year.

"You don't have to sound so shocked," he says and smiles at the same time, nudging my chin with his index finger. "I gotta go, but I'll see you back at the hotel tonight. Love you," he adds, kisses the top of my head, and jogs out of the room.

A couple of hours go by while I talk to Fatima, Adrian's press officer, and we have a great time discussing the strategy for Adrian's Formula One future. Fatima leaves me in the conference room, and I pull my phone out of my pocket to check my messages. I enjoy the brief moment of solitude because I know it probably won't last very long.

"Hola, hermosa," Eduardo says from behind me and lightly presses his fingers to my elbow. I turn around and almost immediately feel his lips on my cheek.

"You're not satisfied with seventh place, are you?" He shakes his head and tugs one of my curls behind my ear.

His hand cups my face, his thumb caressing my cheek. I want to lean away. I want to put distance between us because his touch doesn't light my skin on fire. It doesn't make me shiver with need.

"Although, I'm happy because I get to look at you now," he says.

"Eduardo," I start, and, sensing something's wrong, he steps away. "I enjoyed our date, but I'm sorry, I'm not interested in having a relationship with you. I have feelings for someone else that just don't seem to go away," I admit, hoping the truth is the right route to go.

"Are you fucking serious?" he asks, taking another step away from me. "Then why the hell did you lead me on?" I furrow my brows at his reaction, a little irritated with his angry behavior.

"We went on one date, Eduardo. I didn't agree to be your girlfriend or even insinuated that's what I was looking to be. I'm not going to date someone I don't feel a connection with," I say, but he just shakes his head several times, like he can't believe me.

"Whatever. I can do better than some woman who thinks she can make it into Formula One. You're pathetic, Valentina, so give up on that stupid dream and try to spend more time on not letting people believe one thing and then telling them another."

He storms out of the room before I have a chance to process his words. So, I let out a breath and almost burst into laughter. Some men really can't handle rejection, and it's a horrifying and sad sight to see them lash out in response.

"Is he treating you right?" Gabriel's familiar voice drowns into my ears, and I turn around to look at him.

He's casually leaning against the wall, but I can tell something's bothering him.

"It bothers you to see me with him," I state because it's obvious. Gabriel's eyes lift to my face, and his lips part in an attempt to speak, but he closes his mouth without saying a single word. "Why does it bother you?" I challenge, and he looks away. I want to tell him what just happened between Eduardo and me, but I want his answer first.

"It bothers me that I can't be him." That wasn't the response I was expecting. "Eduardo has always had a picture-perfect fucking life. No one's ever left him; no one's ever truly hurt him. He can deal with emotions better than someone like me." He pushes off the wall and takes three steps closer, making my heart beat rapidly in my chest.

"As a matter of fact, he just yelled at me and called me pathetic for my dream to become an F1 driver because I rejected him. I doubt that qualifies as being able to handle his emotions better than you," I point out, watching anger cross Gabriel's face.

"I'll destroy him for that," he says, his eyes shifting to the door Eduardo walked out of. I take Gabriel's face in my hands, cupping his cheeks to bring his attention back to me.

"Why not just let me go? Why not ignore your feelings if they're such an inconvenience for you? Why have feelings for me when you're not going to do anything about them?" I ask, trying to remind him that this isn't about Eduardo.

It's about him and me.

"They're not an inconvenience, Valentina. They're my weakness," he says, wrapping his fingers around my wrists. "Chérie, you are the most incredible woman anyone could ever ask for. You're so kind and, at the same time, a complete badass."

I chuckle at his word choice.

"You're not afraid to speak your mind, and I love how forward you are," he says, a sad smile tugging at the corners of his mouth.

"Okay, if you love that about me, then here it is: stop trying to fight what's happening between us. I understand how terrified you are, but we're both suffering from your fears when we don't have to be. You want me," I state, and he nods. "You make me happy, Gabriel, can't you see that?"

He shakes his head, so I take a step toward him.

"Think of yesterday, would you?"

Gabriel puts his hands in his pockets, closing himself off from me. I reach out to touch him, and to my surprise, he lets me. My hand rests on his cheek again as I see the hurting boy inside of him, the one living with the grief he never quite learned how to deal with. Gabriel allows himself to be vulnerable with me, and I love how close it makes me feel to him.

"Stop pushing me away," I almost whisper, his eyes fixating on mine.

"I'm sorry, chérie," he replies, fighting back his tears.

His apology is so sincere, so full of pain, and I can feel how lost Gabriel is. Nothing makes sense to him, just like it doesn't for me.

"I know you are, Gabriel." I take a step toward him, lifting my other hand to his other cheek. "And it's okay. I'm also scared. Very, very scared of how deeply my feelings for you run, for how long they have been. To this day, I don't really understand them either. Maybe one day I will. Until then—" I cut off, stepping onto my tiptoes and bringing my lips toward his. "I'll let them do whatever they want to do," I add as he places his forehead against mine.

"Kiss me," he whispers, his mouth almost on mine.

And I give in.

I kiss him.

I press my lips to his, feeling his hands slip onto my hips to drag me closer. His lips melt against mine. Shivers run down my spine as heat takes over my body. My heart explodes into a million pieces before they put themselves back together as Gabriel moves his lips over mine.

He tastes like fresh mint, sunny days, and home all at once.

I can't help sliding my hands into his hair while he crushes my chest against his and explores my mouth in the same feverish way as I explore his. Whatever I taste like for him, whatever I *feel* like, he can't get enough either. His tongue slips through my parted lips before he groans into my mouth, his fingers digging into my hips as he brings me even closer. I tug on his curls, our mouths moving in perfect harmony as if I've always been meant to kiss this man and no one else.

It's easy to lose myself in this kiss, to forget how terrified he is and that neither one of us really knows what we're doing because this is the first time we've felt this way, but I can't let this go on. I step back, pressing a hand to his chest as reality comes crashing back in. His hand covers mine, desperation in his eyes. I can tell he's scared of what I'm about to say, but there's no avoiding this.

"Figure out what's stronger, Gabriel. Your feelings for me or your fear of them." I put more distance between us, my heart still racing from that kiss. From how perfect it was. "I won't rush you to figure it out, but I won't wait around either. I have a life to live, a career to chase. You just have to decide how you want to fit into my life. As a friend or as more."

I walk out of the room, leaving a piece of my heart with him and hoping he'll carefully hold on to it.

CHAPTER 23

Valentina

ADRIAN IS SITTING IN his Formula Three car right before his first race in it. My heart races in my chest, and my breathing is uneven. I'm nervous for him.

Grandpa stands next to me and waits for a chance to talk to Adrian.

"Breathe, race, and win, as long as it doesn't cost you a limb," Grandpa states slowly, and I look at him.

These are the only English words he ever says to us because he likes how they rhyme. Grandfather gives me a brief smile, revealing how happy he is. There is nothing more important in this world to him than us. We are his life and his pride. He gives us the affection, respect, and attention that our father has long found unnecessary.

Winning is important to Grandpa, but our health and happiness are even more so. Succeeding has nothing to do with winning for him.

"I will give it my all," Adrian assures both our grandfather and me. I smile proudly at him.

Adrian is one of the youngest drivers in Formula Three, but he's also one of the most talented. Grandfather takes my hand and leads me away from the car, which is much smaller than an F1 car.

"Don't worry, little champion, your day will come," he promises me as I chew on the inside of my cheek.

He adopted my father's nickname for me a few years ago. In his words, it will help me reach my potential. It will give me confidence and faith. I never doubt myself because I know I want this more than anyone else.

I want to be the first female championship contender in Formula One.

Staring at the small screens, I can't calm the anxious feeling turning my stomach upside down. There are so many things that could go wrong, and I can't bring myself to look when the lights go out and the cars start to race.

"Don't be scared. Adrian is doing well," Grandfather informs me, and I remove my hands from my eyes.

Adrian is indeed doing well. He's in the sixth position, which is excellent considering he started tenth.

"Go, Adrian," I cheer and clap my hands together with excitement.

I am filled with pride.

The loud noises around me have become familiar and pleasant. It would be odd not to hear them anymore. It would be strange if I didn't see people running around and having heated arguments. It would be unusual not to see the mechanics with helmets on, staring at the screens as I do too. I have grown used to all those things, giving me a sense of belonging. I understand more of the language spoken here now, and I can even ask Grandfather questions to expand my knowledge.

He always has patience as he explains new aspects of the sport to me.

Today, I ask him about the different penalties drivers can receive. He tells me about time penalties, grid penalties, and drive-through penalties. For time penalties, additional seconds would be added to the gap between the different drivers, which might result in the loss of positions for the person who received the penalty. A grid penalty means the driver has to start certain places behind what he qualified. The drive-through penalty requires the driver to go through the pit lane once. Since it is the only part of the track with a speed limit, they usually lose a lot of time and even a certain number of places, depending on how far ahead they are. This decision is made by the FIA, which is in charge of enforcing the rules.

"Thank you for teaching me," I say to the person I look up to the most.

"I will do so until there is nothing left to teach you. I promise."

"Are you ready?" I ask Adrian, and he nods his head too quickly for me to believe him.

"Breathe, race, and win, as long as it doesn't cost you a limb," we say in perfect harmony.

Grandpa used to say it to Dad before his races and then to Adrian and me before ours. It's a tradition to say because it brings good luck.

Adrian gives me a quick hug and then joins everyone to listen to the Australian anthem.

All twenty drivers stand in a line as they respectfully listen to the anthem sung by a young woman. Fans are quiet in the stands but soon cheer when it's over.

The drivers then move on to have a group picture taken. The nervous feeling in my chest is overwhelming as they move back to the cars on the starting grid. The crew works hard to warm the tires with tire blankets and make any final adjustments to the car. All the fans get more impatient, including me, as the time runs down to the start of the race.

I see Gabriel smiling at his performance coach on the monitors right before putting on his balaclava and helmet. My mind briefly drifts to our kiss last night, but I push those thoughts aside to focus on my brother.

Once all the drivers are in their cars, they take one lap called the formation lap to heat their tires, allowing for better grip on the track, and charging their batteries. They do that by swerving from left to right.

After they return to their designated places, I wait for the lights to go out. This is always the most nerve-racking part for me because the cars are so close together, and it's all about the drivers' reaction times.

I'm at the edge of my seat, watching the screens, and when the lights go out, I nervously bite down on my bottom lip.

Adrian gets away well and stays ahead; Gabriel overtakes Jonathan and moves into second place; Kyle overtakes James for a brief second, but then James moves back ahead.

So much is going on, and I have no idea where to look.

I bite on my fingernails as I watch the race.

After the first couple of laps, I start to worry less as Adrian creates a time gap between himself and Gabriel to ensure he stays in first place. But when it's time for the pitstop to change the tires, I hold my breath.

Adrian's stop is incredibly slow, closing the gap he worked so hard to achieve. Gabriel is merely two seconds behind him since he already stopped to change his tires a lap earlier. Everyone in my brother's garage seems to stop breathing, and so do I.

Toward the end, Adrian and Gabriel are still one and two, fighting for first place. Gabriel comes closer and closer until he overtakes my brother a lap before the end of the race. It's a head-to-head battle until the very last second, but Gabriel manages to snatch the win from Adrian.

Kyle comes in third place, James is fourth, Jonathan is fifth, Eduardo comes in eighth, Cameron is tenth, and Leonard Tick's car never makes it over the finish line.

The whole Velocità Rossa paddock celebrates as the two drivers get first and second place finishes, and I do so with them.

When the three guys stand on the podium, I am at the bottom, mouthing the words to the anthem of my home country. The trophies are distributed, and Adrian is forcing a happy expression. I know my brother well enough to know he isn't happy. This isn't how he wanted the season to start. But the smile on Gabriel's face makes me smile, too.

Chapter 24

Gabriel

For as long as I can remember, I've had a passion for drawing. I don't know what it is about putting a pencil to empty paper and drawing line after line until I've created a sketch or a painting I'm happy with. It calms me, makes me feel connected to a piece of my past in a way, even though no one in my family knows how to draw. Maybe someone from my family I never met knew how. Or maybe I was an artist in a past life, one who sold his art and made it his career. In this life, I only do it as a hobby.

I sit down with my brother as he refreshes the admission portal of the International University of Monaco, his dream university. He applied a few months ago, wanting to go there to study business but also be close to home and our family.

For a while, I don't say anything. I watch him sit in front of the screen while starting to draw in my sketchbook. Line after line until I'm staring at yet another drawing of Valentina. It's been months since I've drawn anything that isn't related to her or just simply her. It's frustrating, but I find myself trying to perfect it anyway. Trying to make it anything even remotely as beautiful as the woman is in real life.

"No matter how many times you refresh the page, it's not going to change that they haven't updated your application yet," I say, smiling at my brother as he slams his laptop shut only to drop his forehead on it.

"I hate you," he replies, groaning before lifting his head again. "I hate you for never having to experience this anxiety and simply becoming a millionaire."

"They're going to accept you, Jean. You're one of the smartest people on the planet, and your transcript shows that." I try to reassure him, but he merely glares at me.

"You don't know that! A lot of brilliant people apply to this university. They might not accept me." I give him a pointed look, so he drops his head back onto his laptop. "I hate this," he mumbles. I close my sketchbook and place it on the table as I turn completely to him.

"What do you need? Want to go for a drive? Clear your head?" I ask, but he merely groans again.

"No, let me wallow in my misery," he says, so I let out another laugh and go back to sketching.

Once I'm happy with the piece, I flip onto another page and start writing a letter to Valentina.

I can't stop thinking about that kiss. About her. The way she felt, the way she tasted. I can't stop thinking how right it felt when I pulled her body flush against mine. She won't leave my head. Even as I raced last weekend, as I fought my way to first place and won the first race of the season, all I could think about afterward, and a little during, was Valentina. How desperately I wanted to share that win with her. I wanted to kiss her again as she smiled against my lips and congratulated me on my win. And there was no fear in that. There was no panic. It was just a feeling I let myself have without thinking about all of the consequences it would bring.

She asked me what was stronger. My fear or my feelings for her.

"I wish I could talk to Mom," I blurt out, not meaning to say the words to my brother but wanting to talk about it anyway.

"About Valentina?" Jean asks, lifting his head once more to show me the red line on his forehead.

"Yeah," I admit, scratching an itch on my left arm with the pencil I'm holding.

"You know what she'd tell you to do, Gabriel," Jean says, leaning his elbows on the table as he talks to me. I wait for him to say more, so when he doesn't, I almost roll my eyes.

"What would she say?" Sometimes, I have to pull things out of his nose.

"She'd say that your fear of loss shouldn't be the reason you lose more. She'd tell you that all the fears your mind is harboring can only determine what you do in your life if you let them. And she'd tell you that Valentina is the kind of woman you hold onto, not push away, because there's only one like her."

"What would she say about me feeling like I'm not good enough for her because of that very reason?"

My brother thinks about my question for a moment, then smiles.

"She'd tell you that you can only be good enough for someone if you give yourself a chance to be," he says, but I narrow my eyes at him.

"No, she'd tell me I'm more than good enough. You're telling me to give myself a chance to be good enough for her." Jean chuckles to himself.

"Same thing. She raised me to be a mini version of her, after all," he adds with a grin.

"Go back to refreshing the website. I liked you better when you were the wreck instead of me."

We burst into laughter at the same time, my brother flipping me off as he reopens his laptop to do exactly as I said. I, on the other hand, go back to writing my letter for Valentina, ripping out the piece of paper I wrote it on along with the drawing I made of her.

I go upstairs, grab an envelope, and then walk all the way to her house to drop it into their mailbox.

Chapter 25

Valentina

"What are you doing?" My grandfather asks, and I look up from my paper to answer his question politely. He has taught me that when somebody speaks to you, you should give them the respect of making eye contact.

"I'm drawing my dream helmet," I inform him.

He sits down next to me, his light eyes scanning the drawing. I asked Adrian to print out a plain helmet, and I've spent the past two hours drawing on it.

"Looks lovely." I am not terrible at art, especially not at drawing flowers, and since a significant part of my design includes them, it looks stunning. At least to me. "How come you wrote the number nine on it?"

I stare at the helmet and shrug.

"I'm not sure. I think the number picked me," I say, embarrassed, but Grandfather puts his hand on my shoulder.

"Then it's your number."

He walks away, leaving me to finish my design.

"Come on, Val, push," Adrian yells, but I'm too exhausted. "The final corner, come on," he reminds me, and I force my body to cooperate.

This is the longest I've ever been in the simulator, and every single muscle of mine feels it. Although I have no sense of how much time has passed, I know I've never made it this long. It makes me smile.

"Yes, come on!" Adrian cheers when I pass the finish line and can finally relax. I take deep breaths to calm my heart, and my brother gives me a soft smack on the helmet. "How do you feel?" he asks as he helps me out of the simulator.

"Like a champion," I reply, and he grabs my helmet, shaking my head in excitement.

"As you should! Today you've truly worked out harder than I ever could."

This morning, I went for a slow run that he didn't want to join me on, then we went on to do weights and our routine neck exercises, and lastly, the simulator.

My phone rings in Adrian's pocket, and I frown when he pulls it out.

"Oh, sorry, I thought it was mine," he says innocently, so I reach out to feel his other pocket where his phone is. Adrian gives me an apologetic smile. "Oops?" I grab my phone out of his hand and laugh at my brother while answering the persistent caller.

"Hello?" I say as soon as I pick up.

"Hello, Ms. Romana? This is Colin Reiner. I am the head of the Velocità Rossa driver academy," he states, and I feel my heart skipping a beat.

"Yes, Mr. Reiner, thank you for getting back to me," I reply, and Adrian whispers that I should put the call on speaker.

We fight over it for a brief moment before he glares at me, and I cave in. Two days ago, when we returned from Australia, Adrian and I emailed Mr. Reiner because the Velocità Rossa Driver Academy was the only one we had not contacted yet.

"I'm afraid I don't have the news you were hoping for." I want to punch a wall. Then again, I didn't expect anything else. "We see great potential in you, but unfortunately, we are unable to take in new drivers at the moment. As soon as a spot becomes available, we will call you," he assures me, but I only nod.

"Okay, thank you, I appreciate your call."

We hang up, and Adrian squeezes my shoulder.

"They're not going to call again, are they?" He simply shrugs.

"I don't know, but let's not give up hope yet." I can't help but be disappointed.

They have put me on a waitlist, but who is to say they won't "forget" about me? Plus, I'm almost nineteen, most likely making me the oldest candidate. And I'm a woman. "It's not over yet," Adrian reminds me, but when tears stream down my cheeks, he wraps his arms around me.

As much as I love my brother, I can't help the anger I feel toward him at this very moment. He never struggled as I have. It was easy for him. He did his two years in a junior league, scored enough points, and was recruited by Alfa Adrenalina to race in Formula One. Adrian was never turned away. Instead, he got sponsored and pushed toward success.

The complete opposite happened to me, and I've worked twice as hard as him, something even he admits. Before I push him away, I remind myself that it's not his fault, so I wrap my arms around him for comfort.

"What can I do to make you feel better?" he asks, kissing the top of my head.

"Will you cook dinner for once?" I say, and he chuckles while pulling out of the hug to look at me.

"I think it'd be safer if we order takeout or go out for dinner," he suggests, and I agree with a small laugh. He's absolutely right. If we want to eat tonight, Adrian cannot be the one cooking. Even James would be a safer choice, and he's set the kitchen on fire twice in my presence.

At the reminder of my best friend, my eyes skip over to where the miniature helmet he got me for my eighteenth birthday sits next to a row of Adrian's full-sized ones. My helmet, the size of a small melon, is the design I drew when I was twelve years old. The flowers run from left to right, and the blue and red colors harmonize perfectly. The number nine is written on the sides, and a yin and yang symbol is in the center of the back. It's my most prized possession because it reminds me every day of what I'm working towards.

A full-size one.

The helmet I'll win my first championship with.

Adrian falls asleep ten minutes into our movie, but I can't sit still. My body is exhausted, but the news from earlier prevents me from relaxing. It's still early, and I write a quick note for Adrian to let him know I will be at James'. My friend is already waiting for me with open arms when I arrive at his house. I happily walk into them and sigh against his chest.

"Hard day?" he asks, and I let out a sarcastic laugh.

"Hard fucking decade," I reply, and we both burst into laughter.

James leads me inside where he hands me a cup of tea along with a piece of chocolate. I take both with a smile before sharing the news I received earlier. Obviously unsure whether or not it's good information, James leans forward on the counter to grab my hand.

"I have a good feeling about this. Be patient, and I'm sure something will open up," he assures me, and for the first time tonight, I feel a bit of hope, too. James is not often optimistic, and I'm glad he is this time.

"What should we do?" I ask after a while of silence. A small smile creeps onto his lips.

"Something that'll cheer you up," he replies, and I almost jump up and down in excitement. There is no way he'll do this with me to make me feel better. "Oh yeah," he promises, and I smile brightly.

"Yes! It's been forever," I cheer, and James leads me into the living room where he gets everything ready before handing me a microphone and letting me pick a song.

Neither of us is great at singing, but it's not about our skill level. Karaoke is something I've always enjoyed very much, but Adrian and James have never cared for it. James, however, will occasionally, especially when I'm upset, pull out the karaoke machine he bought for me to cheer me up.

James' voice cracks and hits all the wrong notes, but we end up laughing so much, my stomach hurts. I choose one last song, but he, on purpose, sings even worse, and I can't even manage to pick up my microphone to join him.

It was a good decision to go to James' house. I already feel ten times better, and finally, my body feels tired enough to sleep.

"You better stay here, darling. I don't want you driving when you're tired," he says, but I'm already texting Adrian to let him know I'm sleeping here.

Chapter 26

Valentina

"This one, or that one?" Adrian holds up a white dress shirt and a dark blue one. He's shifting his weight from one leg to the other, his arms are shaking a little.

We're having dinner with Evangelin and Carlos tonight, and Adrian is, to put it lightly, sweatingly *nervous.*

"You'll look good in either," I assure him absentmindedly. I'm looking through my clothes to find an outfit to wear to dinner, but Adrian pulls me out of my closet and sits me down on the bed. He holds the two shirts up again, and I laugh. "The blue one," I say, and he frowns at the shirt.

"I'm not sure," he mumbles, so I throw myself back onto the bed.

"Good God, just wear something. As long as you don't show up naked, you'll be fine." My hands are in the air as I wait for him to pull me back up. He ignores me as he walks out of my room again, clearly upset with me for not helping him.

Laughing, I get up and walk back into my closet. I decide on a yellow dress which reaches just above my knee. It's tight around my breasts, just like every other dress, and falls loosely from thereon. My curly hair is tied into a ponytail, but a few strands hang around the sides of my face. After putting on some makeup, I go downstairs to pack the dessert I prepared. The tiramisu looks mouthwatering as I cover the top with some cling wrap.

Adrian walks into the kitchen, wearing a completely different shirt, and hands me the box.

"Are you sure you want to wear that?" His eyes go wide, and he starts to fumble with the hem of his black dress shirt. "I'm kidding. You look handsome," I say, and Adrian lets go of his shirt.

"Thank you, you look beautiful as always," he replies, and I smack his arm when he stares at me, tears flooding his eyes. "Sorry, sorry, it's just difficult for me to believe that you're all grown up sometimes. You don't need me as much anymore, and it scares me a little." Adrian is a very emotional person, and he's never been ashamed of showing his feelings to me.

I admire that about him.

"I'm always going to need you more than I need anyone else. You're my family, Adrian, and you will *always* be the most important person in my life. Now, stop crying because if you cry, you're only going to get your shirt wet, and then you'll have to change it for the thirtieth time," I scold teasingly, and he laughs.

We make our way to my favorite car, the baby blue Mustang, and Adrian holds onto the tiramisu while I drive.

When we arrive, my lips part in surprise. Their house is much smaller than I expected. It's a two-story house with a single garage door and a small yard.

Adrian fixes his appearance three times, looking in the small mirror on his side of the car, and then gives me a small smile before opening the door. I shake my head and chuckle. I can't even begin to imagine how nervous Adrian must be.

We walk the small stone path toward the wooden door before I ring the bell once. I can hear Adrian swear nervously next to me and squeeze his arm to comfort him. As soon as Evangelin opens the door, everyone starts to greet each other.

"I apologize, Carlos is preparing dinner, but he will join us shortly," she assures us and leads us inside the house, which is just as simple as the outside.

There are no fancy furniture pieces, no chandeliers hanging from the ceilings, only simple white furniture, and a few paintings.

"The tiramisu looks delicious, Valentina," Evangelin says.

"I hope it tastes as good as it looks. We better put it in the fridge." She nods.

Evangelin hurries into the kitchen and returns a minute later with Carlos Klein. The famous man isn't much taller than his wife, very slim, has thin white hair, and an inviting smile, which he uses to greet us.

"Valentina," he says and reaches out so he can shake my hand. "My wife has told me many great things about you. It's a pleasure to meet you, dear," he informs me in the most perfect French I've ever heard anyone speak. It's hard for me to believe his mother tongue is Spanish. "And Adrian, yes? I've heard you are a fan of mine."

He's not cocky or arrogant; he's merely stating a fact. He faces my brother with the sweetest smile.

"It's very nice to meet you, too." They shake hands, but Adrian is completely speechless. He looks at Carlos with the utmost admiration, and if I didn't know better, I'd think he is about to cry.

"I'm so sorry, sir, I've always wanted to meet you," Adrian stutters, but Carlos isn't annoyed by him.

He simply starts talking to Adrian about Formula One and that he has been watching him for years. The way my brother's eyes light up makes my heart ache. The way joy fills him from that simple sentence sends some through me too.

Evangelin and I fall into a conversation as Carlos serves dinner. I notice my brother following his every step closely, like a lost puppy that just met its new pack leader.

"So, Valentina, what is your goal for the future?" Carlos asks while we eat the delicious gnocchi with seafood he cooked.

"Oh, I'm taking a gap year to try and figure that out," I lie because I don't want to make things uncomfortable.

"Actually, Valentina has been training her whole life to become a Formula One driver, but no one has given her a proper chance so far," Adrian chimes in, and I drop my spoon.

Carlos and Evangelin both look at me, but I simply blush and look away.

"She was the best in every race as a kid. When she turned fourteen, she got a chance to drive in Formula Three, but a year later, they dropped her. Nobody wanted to sponsor her anymore. Valentina fights harder than I ever did, but no one wants to help her reach her potential for some unknown reason."

I don't know why my brother is sharing this sad, terrible story with them, but I also can't tell him to stop. His big mouth seems to have gotten the better of him in the presence of the great Carlos Klein.

"I'm sorry, Valentina," Evangelin replies, but I just force a smile. "That must have been horrible. I'm so sorry, my dear." Her hand reaches forward on the table, and she squeezes mine tightly.

"That's terrible, Valentina," Carlos says with a frown. "There haven't been many women who were allowed or 'fast enough' to race in a Grand Prix, and sadly, it's not always because they weren't talented. I'm not surprised to hear you're a gifted driver. You seem like a remarkable young woman." The forced smile on my face turns into a real one.

"Never give up, Valentina. We're all rooting for you," Evangelin adds, sending tears to my eyes.

"I won't. I promise."

The rest of the evening goes by in a blur, and I realize Evangelin and Carlos are genuine and down to earth. They talk about their marriage and share stories from their life together, and Adrian and I listen attentively. We also share a little bit more about our past, even though we're both so reserved when it comes to talking about our family.

We leave their house around midnight, and I let my brother drive to give myself some time to think. I should be mad at Adrian for telling my personal story, but I know what he would say if I complained.

"To move on, you have to speak about certain things. The more you address them, the easier it will get every single time. Why do you think it's so much easier to talk about Mom?"

This is precisely what Adrian would say to me, and he would be right.

I'm not giving up yet. I'm still training, and as hopeless as it seems, I'll keep trying. This is my dream, and I'm not done fighting for it.

We arrive home minutes later, and my feet bring me upstairs to my room. I spot two envelopes on my nightstand where Adrian usually leaves my mail for me when he goes to the mailbox.

I recognize the handwriting immediately. *Gabriel.*

I tear open the first envelope and take out the hand-drawn picture of... me. It's a sketch of me in Gabriel's Formula One car. I find a note attached to the back.

Chérie,

I wanted you to have this. I know I make your life difficult, and I'm deeply sorry for it. Please, never lose sight of what is most important: your dream.

Yours only,
Gabriel

The next envelope holds a drawing of me sitting on a chair in the waiting area of an airport. I'm reading a book, biting my lip, and my legs are crossed. It's breathtaking.

There's a note stuck to the back as well.

Chérie,

My fear could never compare to my feelings for you. It took me a while to realize it, and for that, I'm so sorry. I'm so sorry I ever made you think that there was even any doubt that my feelings didn't outweigh my fears.

I know I've made a mess of everything, but I hope you can forgive me because I've not been able to stop thinking about you. About your lips on mine. About how right it felt to hold you and be with you.

No one compares to you. You're Valentina Romana, future Formula One champion. How could I not be, without a shadow of a doubt, wrapped around your finger?

I want to be with you, and I'm so sorry it took me this long to figure myself out. But I want to be better for you. I want to be the kind of man you deserve, and I won't stop until I become him. You have so much patience for me, and I can't begin to describe how much that means to me. I know you're just as scared as me, so let's be scared together, chérie.

Only yours,
Gabriel

I drop onto my bed, holding onto the drawings and notes as my heart stumbles all over itself.

And I have no idea what the fuck I'm supposed to do about it.

Chapter 27

Valentina

I haven't spoken to Gabriel since I opened his letters, but he hasn't reached out again either. He admitted his feelings are stronger, admitted that he wants to be with me, but I've been so overwhelmed with everything that's been happening, I haven't taken a moment to really let that sink in. To understand what that could mean for us. Then again, I'm also actively avoiding dealing with that to keep my heart safe, which is a lot easier when I'm with my brother since he continues to find ways to keep me busy.

Adrian and I flew to Bahrain for the second race of the season a few days ago, and he's made sure I spent every minute with either him or Chloe doing what I love most: learning more about racing.

Today is Qualifying. I'm sitting and waiting impatiently for Q3 to finally be over.

Gabriel takes pole, Adrian comes in third, James fourth, Cameron in eighth, and Leonard is in tenth.

Adrian brings me back to the track after we were already at the hotel. He doesn't tell me why or what's happening, but I don't ask too many questions either. He covers my eyes with his hands, finally making me impatient.

"Why are you being so secretive?" Adrian leaves his hands on my face, and I follow him down a path.

When he uncovers my eyes again, I'm standing in front of a Velocità Rossa 75S. Adrian holds out a helmet for me, and a confused expression settles on my face.

"You're going to drive this baby around the track," he tells me, and I barely keep my mouth from dropping. "I've arranged everything. All you have to do is try not to crash the car. After all, there is a race here tomorrow," he says and chuckles.

I can't believe he did this for me.

I take the helmet from him, put it on my head, and get into the car. Adrian gets into the passenger seat and puts his seatbelt and helmet on as well. He gives me some quick instructions and then lets me take over.

I feel the car under my control as I let my fingers run over the steering wheel and the rest of the gear. The helmet is tight on my head, but it feels secure.

My foot barely presses down on the gas pedal, and I try to get a feel of the car during the first lap. The track is lit up so I have a clear vision of everything. When I arrive at the starting line, I come to a complete stop. Adrian counts down for me, and I get ready for a good start.

When he says go, I rev the engine and make the car speed down the track with a cheer of excitement.

Whenever I race, I feel free. Adrenaline shoots through me, and I feel more alive than ever. Like nothing can hurt me anymore. Like I found the one place I belong in a world that has made me feel so lost.

This is why I started racing in the first place.

A scream of joy escapes me, and I hear Adrian laugh next to me. He trusts my driving enough not to be afraid.

Moments later, I'm driving back over the finish line and bringing the car to a much slower pace. My heart is pounding, and the level of happiness I feel is overwhelming. Every corner of this track is so familiar because of the training I do in the simulator. At the same time, being here is an entirely different feeling, and I prefer this over sitting in my room.

"Thank you," I say, and Adrian takes my hand in his.

"We'll find a way to get you into a Formula One car. I don't want to be the only one who gets to do what they love, especially when your time is better than mine," he informs me and holds up a stopwatch. "I was half a second slower than you in this car." Adrian shrugs and pulls back the stopwatch. "It's everything, by the way. That smile on your face." Naturally, the smile only gets bigger, and I have to look away.

He's going to make me cry if he continues.

I thank him repeatedly for letting me drive the car on the track. I pull the helmet off my head and hand it back to him. My brother disappears into his garage, and I wait outside, staring up into the night sky filled with stars and a full moon tonight. It's breathtaking.

"You're one of the best drivers I've ever had the pleasure of watching," Gabriel's familiar voice appears from beside me, so I tilt my head to grin at him.

"Likewise," I reply, and he smiles from ear to ear.

"One day, you'll sit in a Formula One car, and the only thing the other drivers and I will see is your dust on our visors," he says, and I let my mind wander to the image.

"Wouldn't that be something?" I mumble.

Gabriel's eyes stare into mine for a moment, a million unspoken words dancing between us. That longing in my chest, longing for *him*, is still there, reminding me that no matter what happened, he's the only person I want to be with.

I break eye contact first, looking back up to admire the sky again while Gabriel's eyes remain on me as if I'm more beautiful than any painting created by the night.

There is no way.

Anger courses through my whole body as I watch Adrian get stuck in the gravel because Kyle pushed him off the track. I'm furious by the rookie mistake Kyle makes, especially when Adrian has to bear the consequences. My brother's race is now over because of that move.

On the monitors, I watch Adrian get out of his red car and kick the ground out of frustration. I understand him because I want to kick the ground, too. I also want to kick Kyle, but then again, Adrian probably imagines Kyle's face on the gravel.

Minutes later, Adrian is back with Chloe, discussing something he will probably tell me about later. For now, I have to be patient and continue to watch the race, trying not to constantly wish something would go wrong during Kyle's pitstop to cost him ten places.

Unfortunately, the Grenzenlos team is one of the fastest and most consistent in pit stops. The FIA eventually gives Kyle a ten-second penalty for pushing another driver off the track and causing a collision. That penalty will either be added at the end or, should Kyle do another pitstop, the pit crew will have to wait ten seconds before they are allowed to change the tires.

The race is a complete mess.

Jonathan's car has to retire because of an engine failure, Eduardo crashes into Gabriel, but luckily, both of them stay in the race. I'm not sure what happened between those two, but I also can't find more information.

The best thing about this chaotic race is that James goes ahead and finishes in first place. Excitement shoots through my whole body, and I rush outside with the rest of the team just in time to see him get out of his car and hug the people on his side.

It's only his second win in Formula One, which is why I am so incredibly proud of him. He deserves this, even if it was mostly luck that got him into first place. My excitement is dulled a little by the fact that Gabriel only came in fifth and that Adrian didn't cross the finish line at all.

Putting his own feelings aside, Adrian comes with me so we can celebrate our friend's victory.

We go to a restaurant where James' team set up a congratulatory party for him.

"Well done," I tell James yet again, and he wraps his arm around my shoulder before he presses a kiss to my temple.

"Thank you, my love. Thank you for being here and celebrating with me," he says, and I smile.

James takes a sip of his beer as he continues to hold me close to him for most of the night.

Sooner than I would like, the party is over, and Adrian and I go back to our hotel. We have separate rooms this time, which is why I can take my time showering. I lie down in bed, my stomach starting to cramp.

Without looking at a calendar, I already know what time it is. I groan and curl up into a ball on my bed.

Chapter 28

Gabriel

The race was an absolute shit show. I'm still fuming over Eduardo driving into me, but part of my anger might come from the fact that he went on a date with Valentina. The only thing that kept me from going to him after the race to punch him in his fucking face was knowing she rejected him.

I'm still pissed, though, especially because James Landon won the goddamn race too.

With my sketchbook in my hand and my hair still dripping from my shower, I settle down on my hotel bed to wind down after my long day. Another drawing of Valentina comes to life on the page without my permission, but I'm interrupted by a knock on the door.

I open it to reveal a crying Valentina, panic settling in my stomach at the sight of her.

"What's wrong, chérie?" I ask, but her attention drifts from my face to my body, which is only covered by my boxers.

She lingers on my bulge for a moment before her gaze drops to the floor, her cheeks turning pinker even though tears are still streaming down her face.

"Chérie?" I try again, my hands reaching toward her to cup her cheeks and wipe her tears away. Seeing her cry is by far one of the most painful sights for me.

"I didn't want to come here because I'm not entirely sure what's happening between us anymore, but I also wanted to see you because—" More tears fall as she rubs a hand over her lower abdomen.

"Are you in pain?" When she nods, so do I, several times to process that information and figure out how I can help her. "Okay, baby," I say, watching the way her heart jumps into her eyes at this new pet name. I grab her hand and pull her into my room.

"What are you doing?" she asks, but I don't answer. Instead, I lead her to my bed where I pull back the covers and wait for her to crawl under the blanket.

"I'm going to go down to the lobby and see if the reception has a hot water bottle, okay?" Her hand slips onto my arm to stop me from leaving, shaking her head as she does it. "It's okay. I'll be right back," I promise. I press the swiftest of kisses to her forehead before putting on some clothes and slipping out of the room to hunt down everything she needs.

I return carrying a bottle of water, painkillers, and a hot water bottle.

"Sorry it took so long, chérie, but I went to the store and got you the hot water bottle."

I pull back the sheets and place the bottle onto her stomach before handing her some water and painkillers. She takes them from me, her cold fingers brushing mine. A frown takes over my face.

"You're cold," I point out before grabbing my long-sleeved shirt from my bag. "Here." I hand it to Valentina, watching her slip it over her tank top. This is the second time she's ever worn a shirt of mine, and I can't help the feeling of happiness spreading through me.

"Why are you doing all of this for me?" she asks as I run the back of my fingers over her cheek, watching her eyes flutter shut at the simple touch. A touch I've been so desperate to give her because I haven't quite managed to control the urge to trace her features with my fingers when she allows me to.

"Is that a rhetorical question?"

Another tear flows down her cheek, so I wipe it away and caress the skin there for a moment. She takes my hand in hers, guiding it to her mouth and pressing a kiss to the back of it. If I wasn't sitting down, I'd drop to my knees because of that, because of the affection she's offering me when it's all I've been craving for longer than I've realized.

"This shit hurts," she says as she takes a deep breath, her brows scrunching together as she probably experiences another wave of pain.

"You know, I read that having an orgasm helps with cramps," I whisper, loving the little, naughty smile tugging at the corner of her mouth. She stares at my naked chest for a moment, her fingers reaching out so her nails can run down my torso. My body responds immediately to that touch, to the way she drops her fingers lower and lower and lower.

"Maybe another time," she replies right as she removes her hand again.

My index finger runs over her bottom lip so carefully, one might think I would break her if I pressed harder. But I know better. There's no one as strong as her, and even if she sometimes is forced to bend, Valentina Romana never breaks.

"Lie down," she says after a while of silence, making me smile.

Biting the inside of my cheek, I fight the urge to lean down and kiss her and make my way to the other side of the bed instead. She turns to face me as soon as I'm lying beside her, that perfect smile of hers on her lips as she watches me. It fades as she reaches out to place a hand on my torso.

"I'm really sorry about today. I know you must be mad about the result," she says, her hand pressed against the area above my heart.

"You're right, I was mad, but I'll never stop pushing. I will never give up because that's not the kind of person I am. This championship will be mine. It has to be. I'll fight however long it takes to make it mine," I say, but I know as I stare into her eyes, she can see that I'll never stop fighting for her too.

Not unless she's done with me.

"I don't know what we are or what we're doing, Gabriel," she admits, her hand on my chest pressing down a little, probably to feel how quickly my heart is racing.

"What do you want us to be?" I ask, moving to lie on my side and face her completely.

"I don't know. I just know that things are nowhere near easy with us," she admits but inches closer to me anyway.

"We don't have to label it. We can just see where things take us if you want," I offer so she comes even closer.

"Cuddle with me?" I pull her against my chest before turning her around so I can place my chin in the crook of her neck and my arm under her breasts. A small sigh escapes me while she runs her fingers over my arm.

"Good night, Gabriel." I kiss her neck, smiling against the skin there as I revel in the feel of her in my arms.

"Night, baby," I say, kissing her neck once more before falling asleep wrapped around the woman I'll never be able to run away from again, not without my heart staying behind with her.

Chapter 29

Valentina

Gabriel's arms are still wrapped around my body when I wake up the following day. Somehow, I feel worse than yesterday, but also better. Worse because the cramps are more painful, but better because his arms around me feel amazing.

I turn around, holding back the groan of pain threatening to leave my throat, and sigh when I'm finally facing him. It's difficult for me to comprehend how attractive he still looks, even when he's sleeping. His lips are slightly parted, but he's not snoring, nor is he drooling. *How's he doing that? If my mouth were open, I would do both in my sleep.*

I shake my head and focus on his face again. His long lashes almost rest on his cheeks, and his curly hair is all over the place. He still smells like mahogany, just like he always does, and I can't help but place my hands on his muscular chest. His skin is smooth, and my curiosity is overpowering my self-control. I run my fingertips over his nipples, then his stomach, over the small line of hair leading from his belly button to his boxers. I study all of his birthmarks and freckles, tracing a line from one to another.

Over and over.

Until his eyes shoot open and he looks down at me.

"You're getting me all worked up," he says with a husky voice and sinful smile that make my insides turn. His hand reaches out to cup my cheek, and goosebumps spread down my arms. "You're so beautiful in the mornings," he mumbles, his nose brushing over mine as my breath hitches. "Can I kiss you?"

There isn't a moment of hesitation before my answer spills out of me.

"Yes," I reply, making him grin sweetly.

His thumb moves onto my bottom lip, pulling it down right before he releases it again and presses his mouth to mine. My lips part, his tongue entering smoothly, kissing me like I'm the only thing that makes him feel alive. Like I'm everything he's ever going to need.

His morning wood rubs against my stomach as he comes closer to deepen the kiss, his moan vibrating through me. A small moan escapes me when he rubs against me again, his tongue playing with mine.

"Gabriel," I say when he kisses my jaw, nuzzling his face into my neck again as he tries to catch his breath.

Mine is just as uneven, my heart racing in the same way his is.

"How are you feeling?" His hand runs over my stomach, and I smile.

"Good," I lie. "But I really have to go." I attempt to make my way out of bed, but he guides me back down and wraps his arms around me.

"No, you have to stay here so I can take care of you," he replies plainly and kisses my cheek. "Please, chérie, I don't want you to leave." His arms tighten around me, and I try to wiggle free, unsuccessfully. I giggle and lean my head back against his shoulder.

"Gabriel, I have to go back to my room," I repeat, but he shakes his head.

"No, you can stay here. You don't have to leave," Gabriel mumbles, and I laugh.

"Gabriel, you don't understand. I *have* to leave," I try to tell him without having to say it out loud.

"Why? Why do you *have* to leave?" He says the "have" in the same way I did.

"I have to change my pad unless you want me to bleed all over the bed." He slowly loosens his grip.

"Oh," is all he says before he lets go of me entirely. "Sorry." I turn around to find him rubbing his nape with his hand and shake my head, laughing. "Will you come back?" he asks and finds my hand on the bed.

"No, but you can take me out for breakfast if you want. I'm starving," I complain, and Gabriel flashes me his perfect smile.

"What do you want to eat? Eggs? Pancakes? A whole buffet?" He starts laughing at his joke, and I join him. I can't not when he starts laughing his pure, genuine laugh that makes my heart melt.

"You know, your laugh is funnier than your jokes," I say, and his jaw drops dramatically. "I'll wait for you in my room."

"Maybe I won't take you to breakfast anymore. You're too mean," he complains, so I roll my eyes at him when he covers his face with his hands and makes crying sounds.

Gabriel might be the most dramatic person I've ever met. I sit back down on the bed and put my hands on his, going along with his joke. When I remove them, he's smirking at me and pulling me down on the bed again before he kisses me again, this time moving from my lips to my neck to nip playfully at the skin there.

"Gabriel," I say and burst into giggles.

He lets go of me but quickly presses his lips to mine.

I take a shower and get ready. I put effort into my appearance, a little bit of makeup, and a beautiful black dress, and even let my curls fall down my back instead of tying them into a ponytail.

There's a knock on my door.

Gabriel is leaning against the door frame, a piece of paper in his hand and a grin on his lips. He hands me the drawing, and I stare at a perfect sunflower, then back at his face.

"What are you doing?" I ask, and he raises a brow.

"It would have been a waste to get you an actual flower since we're flying back home today," he says and smiles. "This one is forever. I thought you'd like that," he mumbles, and I watch him for a moment, dumbfounded.

"I love it," I reply before placing the drawing on my backpack to make sure I won't forget it.

When I'm in front of him again, I fling my arms around him and kiss him passionately because I feel an indescribable need to be as close to him as possible.

"Thank you." Gabriel kisses me once more before holding out his hand. My fingers lace through his, but he quickly holds up our hands to kiss the back of mine.

"So, where are you taking me?" I ask, and he grabs my hand more tightly.

"To the hotel buffet, just in case you don't feel well so we can go back to your room whenever you need it."

We get out of the elevator once we reach the lobby, and he pulls me toward the breakfast area where he grabs two plates. He flashes me his dimpled smile, happiness all over his face.

"I'll hold, you dish up," he instructs, making me giggle a little when he puts on a stern expression.

"Sir, yes, sir." He bursts into laughter, shaking his head at me but also looking at me with those green-brown eyes full of adoration. No one has ever looked at me the way Gabriel does, and I'm sure I'll never get sick of it.

Once we've both stopped laughing, he stands in front of me, waiting for me to put whatever I want on my plate. Gabriel tells me what he wants, and I put everything in a large amount, making him smile. I know how much he eats better than anyone else.

We sit down at an empty table and start eating our food.

"Tell me, are you still taking me to *Les Misérables* in August? Or do I have to make other plans?" A smile spreads over my lips as I think about the theater tickets he gifted me for my eighteenth birthday almost a year ago.

"You know, I've never been in your bedroom, I've never met your aunt or her wife, I've never watched you draw. There's so much I want to know, Gabriel, so much I would like for us to do," I admit because before I can even think about where we'll be in August, I have to know how we'll work in the present.

"As soon as we get back to Monaco, I'll do all of that with you," he promises me. His hand lifts to my face where he runs his thumb over my bottom lip. "Whatever you want, I'll give it to you, chérie." He retracts his hand from my face, and I almost whimper at the loss of his touch.

"I'd like that." Without thinking about it, I lean forward again, not caring who can see us as I wait for him to kiss me.

He doesn't hesitate, merely brings his hand to my cheek to cup it, then kisses me for everyone here to see.

Chapter 30

Valentina

Adrian and I check out of our rooms, and when I turn around, I find Gabriel sitting on a couch in the lobby, smiling at me. A blush settles on my cheeks, and an involuntary grin spreads over my lips.

Gabriel gets up from the couch, making my mouth water. His dark gray sweatpants hang snugly on his hips, his white shirt is almost see-through, and his white sneakers fit the rest of his outfit well. He turns around for a second to pick up his backpack, and as he leans down, the sight of his round ass makes my body ache.

He makes his way over to where I am standing, but I smile and spin around, focusing on something inside my purse so he doesn't see me drooling. But Adrian turns around at the same time and throws my purse on the ground.

"Shit, sorry, Val," he says as we both bent over to get it.

"My, my, Romana, that's an impressive view," Gabriel says from behind us with a low whistle, and my eyes go wide.

"Thank you, I do a lot of squats," Adrian replies, and I laugh.

Gabriel winks at my brother as soon as we're both upright again, making Adrian fan air to his face with his hand. He walks away a second later to call for a taxi, leaving Gabriel and me alone.

"You know, I expected him not to react so playfully," I tell Gabriel, but he seems amused by what I'm saying.

"Oh, no, I'm sorry, baby, I did mean your brother," he says, so I swat his arm teasingly. "Your ass doesn't create an impressive view; it creates a *heavenly* view," he adds, slipping his hands onto my elbows and dragging me against him. My heart stutters when he drops his lips to my ear. "I'll sit with you on the plane," he assures me, but I can only nod as his hands trail over my hips. He steps away, leaving me wanting more. Leaving my lips tingling with the need to kiss him. I push past that desire, focusing on my brother where he's waving Gabriel and me over to him.

I have no idea how he's going to make that happen, but I know somehow he will. Gabriel touches my neck at the same place James punched me about two weeks ago, and I can tell he is glad about how well the bruise has healed. It's barely visible anymore, and it doesn't hurt either.

The drive to the airport is quiet. Gabriel is sitting in the front passenger seat, I'm in the back on the left side, James is in the middle, and Adrian is on the right. It's hard for me to comprehend why we're all sharing a single taxi, but it's better for the environment, which I appreciate. Except for James and I, who exchange a few sentences, no one talks. Gabriel turns his head every now and then to smile at me, but that's the only interaction between us.

James catches it and gives Gabriel a weird look in return, but the Monegasque doesn't even acknowledge James' presence in the car.

I don't know why they hate each other so much.

Halfway to our terminal, two guys and a girl come up to Gabriel, excitement written all over their young features. They ask him for an autograph and a selfie, and Gabriel asks me to wait for him before we continue on our way.

It's unbelievable that Gabriel ends up sitting next to me, but he lets me take his window seat. Once I'm seated and organized, I turn to the handsome man, who is already watching me. The smile on his face brings one to my own.

"You know, you're starting to worry me. You've been smiling an awful lot recently," I state, and he lets out a sweet laugh.

"You can only blame yourself for that. Ever since you kissed me, I can't seem to stop. Now, after last night, every time I look at you, I remember how it felt when you were in my arms, snoring peacefully." I swat his arm playfully.

"I do not snore," I reply firmly, but Gabriel chuckles.

He has beautiful eyes. A combination of green and brown that I've never seen on a person before, with thick black lashes that frame his eyes perfectly. Yet, the thing that makes his eyes the most beautiful is the sparkle in them, the one I know comes from happiness. When I realize I'm part of the reason why he's happy, I place my hand around his and pull it onto my lap. He gives me a confused look but doesn't remove it.

"Okay, you may not snore, but you did drool a lot," he tells me, embarrassment immediately heating my cheeks. My hand leaves his so I can cover my face with both of mine. "No, chérie, I'm kidding." He laughs a little and removes my hands from my face. "Valentina, I'm just joking, but even if I wasn't, what does it matter?" I look at him again.

"It's embarrassing," I point out, and he smiles at me.

"You know, if we were dating, I don't think it would be so embarrassing for you." He laughs, and I lace my fingers through his again.

"I think it's best if we stay friends, no matter how badly we want each other," I tell him, trying to tease him, but since I'm watching his lips more than his eyes, he notices my lie.

"Oh, really?" His hand moves from my cheek to my collarbone, stopping above my breast. "You don't want me?" he whispers. My eyes close involuntarily, but I force them open again. "You don't want me to touch you like this?" He moves his finger from my collarbone to my cleavage and runs it down.

"I do, but I don't think now is the right time for us," I lie and grin, and he smiles even more brightly. Gabriel removes his hand, giving me a moment to try and calm my aching body.

I want him to continue to touch me, to never stop.

"And you don't want to touch me either?"

He takes my hand in his and brings it underneath his shirt. My hand is flat on his abs, and I have to use all of my self-control not to pull his head down and kiss him.

"Not like this?"

He brings my hand down to his pants, and my finger runs along the waistband without him having to do anything.

"You don't want me?" he asks again, lifting my hand back onto his stomach.

I'm speechless, and all I want is to continue feeling his hard muscles underneath my fingertips. I started this game, but now I'm the one losing.

"Because I really want to know what it feels like to undress you, to run my hands all over your beautiful body, to slip inside of you and make you see heaven," he whispers, his voice rough and low so the other passengers don't hear.

My insides turn upside down, need coiling in my stomach from his words. I cross my legs to soothe the persistent aching between them. Gabriel notices that too, allowing a victorious smile to spread over his full lips.

"You want to know what it would feel like, too, don't you?"

Before I can think, I nod. My fingers run over the hot skin underneath his shirt, and he leans back, making my hand lose contact with his body.

"Too bad we're just friends."

He puts his headphones on, and it takes me a minute to get back to reality. My hands reach out to remove his headphones and pull his head down so I can press my lips against his. Gabriel puts one hand on my cheek, but I lean away sooner than either of us wants.

"We are friends, friends who do this," I tell him. He licks his lips and grins.

"Okay, friends who will have phenomenal sex," he says, and I shake my head, smiling.

Gabriel plants his lips on mine one more time before taking out his sketchbook and pencil. I place one earpiece into his ear and the other into mine, playing some of the songs we both like. My eyes don't leave the page while he sketches a Formula One car on it. I'm confused until he draws the number nine on it, making tears shoot into my eyes.

"One day," he promises as he hands the paper to me. My eyes meet his, and a small smile covers my lips.

"One day," I mumble, my feelings for Gabriel Matteo Biancheri wonderfully out of my control, growing and flourishing with every moment between us.

CHAPTER 31

Valentina

"VALENTINA! COULD YOU BRING me the yellow dress with the floral print in a medium?" Evangelin asks while I'm cashing out the people waiting in line.

"Yes, give me one moment," I say, handing the last customer their receipt and bag before hurrying toward Evangelin.

It's surprising how much I enjoy working in this small boutique. I would have never thought fashion would interest me this much, but it does, especially whenever Evangelin sits down with me before we choose the items she will order and stock.

As always, Evangelin connects naturally with her customers to find clothes she can suggest to them. I watch her run around the store for items to present to the tall lady who walked in a couple of minutes ago, and I hurry over to her to make sure she doesn't need any help. Evangelin tells me I can start closing the shop, so I do as I'm told.

By the time I'm done, the customer ends up not buying anything and leaving. Evangelin rolls her eyes and strolls over to where I'm standing.

"Some people," she complains with annoyance in her voice. "Who is that?" she asks me after a while and points outside.

Shock covers her face, so I bring a hand to her arm as worry makes me turn around to follow her finger. The person she's referring to is holding a bouquet of sunflowers, smiling his perfect dimpled smile. I can't keep the smile off my face. I haven't seen him in days, but I've missed him. So much.

After that day on the plane, I told him to give me a few days to get my life in order. But I never expected him to show up at *Rush*.

"Gabriel Biancheri," I reply and turn to look at Evangelin. She's smiling too, but there is also something else on her face, something I can't quite identify. "What is it?" I ask, bringing her attention back to me.

"Nothing, dear, he just reminds me of someone, that's all. Now, go, have a good evening," she tells me, still smiling that forced smile.

I grab my purse from the chair and give her a kiss on the cheek before walking out of the store toward Gabriel. When he spots me, the corners of his mouth lift, and he lowers the bouquet so I can wrap my arms around his neck. His mahogany scent fills my nose, and I almost let out a small sigh.

"I've missed you," I admit as he wraps his arms around my body.

"I've missed you more, chérie, which is why I couldn't stay away anymore. I hope that five days were enough," he mumbles.

Gabriel hands me the flowers, his lips meeting mine right as I attempt to thank him. It's brief and leaves me wanting more, but it's also sweet and makes my body tingle.

"Well, I could have used a couple more days of break from you, but seeing as you're already here, we might as well hang out." He chuckles, tickling me until I giggle an apology.

Gabriel and I walk home, talking about the simulators we've been training with. I look at him feeling so proud he's working hard to improve, but when I notice the redness in his eyes and the dark circles underneath them, I get worried.

Ever since I met him, and probably for most of his life, Gabriel has had this tendency to get completely caught up in doing something to the point where he forgets to eat, sleep, or drink. Right now, he's hellbent on improving his results. His priority is to get faster times and win more races.

My hand tightens its grip on his, and he gives me a confused grin before continuing to talk about all the different things he has to prepare for next week.

I tell Gabriel about work, and he listens attentively, asking me lots of questions about it. The way he's genuinely interested in my life makes my heart flutter, it always does. He leads me to my house but then pulls me past it and down the road to where I know his home is.

"Domi and Nicolette aren't home this week. They are on vacation, but Jean is home, and I finally want to show you where I live. If you would like that," Gabriel says and smiles at me.

"I would love that," I assure him, so we continue to make our way down the street to his house.

Gabriel's home is small, a two-story house with a simple beige façade and a few columns at the entrance. The front garden is fenced and well-kept. Flowers are growing on the left side, and I remember Nicolette likes gardening, which is why Gabriel gifted her lots of supplies last Christmas.

He brings me inside his house, and a delicious scent hits my nose. It smells like tomato sauce. Of course Gabriel made food for me, I'd be surprised if he hadn't.

I sit down at the wooden table in the kitchen and put my chin on one of my hands, watching Gabriel closely.

"What's with the swooning expression?" he asks when he catches me staring. He puts down the kitchen towel he was holding and walks over to me slowly. "You look happy," he states and squats down in front of me. I place my hand on his cheek, feeling his stubble underneath my fingertips and tracing his features.

"I am happy," I admit, and Gabriel smiles. His eyes sparkle with joy, and the dimples make my breathing catch.

"Come with me." Gabriel leads me up the stairs, and before we enter his room, he covers my eyes with his hands. I'm about to complain, but he says, "Don't ruin it, just go along with it." I grin because he knows me so well.

When he finally reveals his room to me, I gasp. There are ten bouquets of sunflowers spread all over his room, his bed is made and there isn't a speck of dust anywhere, and the blinds are letting in the fading light of the setting sun.

"I can't believe you did this for me," I whisper as Gabriel's arms wrap around me from behind.

"Can't you? You know how I feel about you. This can't be a surprise," he replies before he presses a kiss on my shoulder.

My feet bring me to the bookcase on the very left side of his room so I can read the covers. He has classic novels, science fiction novels, romance novels, and more. I take one book out and open it, spotting notes written on the pages. The book is worn out, making me wonder how old it is. I also wonder who wrote inside of it because the handwriting is not Gabriel's.

"What are these?" I ask and turn to face him. Gabriel is sitting on the bed, watching me closely.

"All of them are second-hand. I like buying books that have notes written in them. In fact, I make sure the previous owner took notes. Reading a book and then reading it from another perspective helps me see things I may have never considered," he explains, and somehow, my feelings for him run even deeper. I would have never expected Gabriel to collect something so beautiful.

I put the book back on the shelf and walk over to where he is.

"Why haven't you ever told me about this?" I join him on the bed and look around his room some more.

He has two large windows next to his bed and two more that lead to what I assume is a balcony. His curtains are a light beige color, almost the same as his walls. Gabriel's room is empty with only a bed, a nightstand, and the bookshelf filling the space. There is nothing else, but I understand. Gabriel is hardly ever home, and when he is, he doesn't want too much to tie him to one place.

I do the same thing.

"I've never shown anyone my books," he admits and lets out a nervous laugh. He's embarrassed about them, which doesn't make any sense to me.

"I think it's beautiful, Gabriel," I say, and he lifts his head so he can look into my eyes again. I don't know if he's trying to figure out if I mean it or not, but he can search my face as much as he wants. I mean every word.

He shakes his head ever so slightly before he reaches up to take my face between his hands.

"This is why I showed you. I knew you would never make me feel bad about it, that you'd think this is something special. You understand me in a way no one else does, Valentina, and I never want to lose the way I feel with you."

Before I can respond, he presses his lips to mine, sending shivers down my spine. My hands rest on his thighs for a while until he pulls back.

"Which book is your favorite?" Gabriel takes a strand of my curly hair between his fingers, and a genuine smile spreads over his face.

"I don't have one. There is one series I've read many times, though. It's called *Die For Me*," Gabriel informs me, and my mouth drops.

"Are you serious?" He puts his hand flatly on my collarbone.

"Yes, it's an excellent book. The idea alone, I don't know how Amy Plum came up with it. Also, it plays in France, which I like." I shake my head in disbelief, and Gabriel smirks. "What?"

"I have read Amy Plum's *Revenant* books at least ten times," I tell him.

Gabriel walks over to his bookshelf, takes one of the books into his hand, and gives it to me. It's a worn-out copy of my favorite book.

"Read the comments the previous owner wrote inside. It will surprise you what they saw, I promise." I smile at him and place the book back on the shelf, planning on taking it home with me tomorrow. Gabriel drops down on the bed again, his eyes meeting mine. "Are you hungry?"

"No," I tell him, and his hand reaches out to touch my thigh.

"Do you want to watch a movie?" he asks me, and my heart skips a beat when his hand reaches further back and touches my butt. I nod to answer his question, and he gets up from the bed. My feet bring me to where he's standing, and I fling my arms around his neck, hugging him tightly. He hesitates for a moment, but soon enough, his arms wrap around my body too. "Are you okay, chérie?" he asks me as I step out of the hug.

"Yes," I reply in all honesty. I'm beyond okay. I'm really happy. "Although, I am getting a little hungry now. Maybe I can have some of your delicious-smelling food." Gabriel chuckles and places his hands on each side of my face.

"Sure," he replies bending down to give me a quick kiss.

After dinner, we move to his couch and start watching a movie. Gabriel is sitting on the right side, and I sit down on the left. Something inside me wants to see what he will do, whether he will come closer or stay on his side. After a few minutes, I find Gabriel fiddling with the hem of his sweatshirt. He's looking at me, and I cock an eyebrow, waiting for him to say what's on his mind.

But he doesn't say anything.

Gabriel simply pats the space next to him on the couch, telling me to come closer. I look away, not moving an inch. A small smile spreads over my lips as he gets up from the couch. He pulls me into the air and sits down so I'm between his legs, making a surprised laugh burst out of me. His jaw rests in the crook of my neck, his stubble tickling my skin.

I turn around in his arms, studying his stomach where his sweatshirt isn't covering him anymore. I spot black writing on his hip bone for the first time, but it's mostly covered by his pants. Confused, I reach out and pull a little on the waistband, exposing seven different tattoos. They're small and close to each other, and when I lean forward to get a better look, I see they're dates.

Seven different dates.

"My mom, my dad, my grandparents, and my best friend Maxime, who I lost a couple of years ago. Those are the dates on which they died," he tells me, and I can't help the tear that rolls down my cheek. "I've never told anyone this. No one ever cared enough to ask." Gabriel wipes away the tear and wraps his hand around mine, the one that's pulling down his underwear so I can look at his inked hip.

"Is the reason you chose number seven for your car because you lost seven people?" Every Formula One driver gets a number for their car; some get to decide, others don't, which is why I wonder if he chose it himself or if it's a coincidence.

"Yes," he simply replies, and I nod. "But it's more than that. Both my parents were born on the seventh of the month. So, seven just means the most to me," he explains. "It's also a nice coincidence that I met you on the seventeenth of March," he says and laughs a little.

"You remember the day we met?" Gabriel's eyes move from mine to my lips and then back up to my eyes.

"How could I not? I started questioning everything the day I met you. It's kind of hard to forget."

I lift my hand to touch his cheek. Gabriel closes his eyes at the contact of my skin against his.

"You are everything I could have ever imagined, and the best part is, I didn't even have to look for you. You simply walked into my life without any warning, and I wouldn't have had it any other way."

My eyes are searching his face, but I can't find anything that could prove he doesn't mean what he's saying. Panic settles in my chest. Suddenly, I'm feeling too many emotions, and I can't share any of them with him without admitting how much I truly care for him. Instead of overthinking things, I pull his hand to my mouth and press a kiss to the back of it.

"Any other tattoos I don't know about?" I ask him, trying to lighten the mood. An embarrassed blush spreads over his face, and I look at him, waiting impatiently.

"I have a tattoo of the moon on my left ass cheek," he admits, and my mouth drops. "Yeah, I was drunk, and Cameron thought it would be funny to get a moon on... well, on my moon."

The laughter that leaves me is out of my control. I can imagine Cameron drunk and saying this to Gabriel, and I can also imagine Gabriel just going along with it.

As soon as my laughter dies out, we fall into silence. My ear is pressed over where his heart is, listening to the unsteady and fast beat of it. Mine mimics that rhythm without hesitation.

Chapter 32

Valentina

I shoot up in bed, trying to figure out where I am. My eyes scan the room, and I find the now-familiar bookshelf, the sun shining through the tall windows, and finally, Gabriel, sleeping peacefully next to me. My heart rate slows, and I lie back in bed.

He must have carried me up here after I fell asleep on the couch.

Gabriel lets out a painful sigh. He's still fast asleep, but his eyelids are fluttering, and there is an odd expression on his face. I'm convinced he's having a nightmare, but I also don't want to wake him. Gabriel needs to rest to get rid of the dark circles under his eyes. I can't stand to see him as exhausted as he was yesterday.

I slip out of bed as quietly as I can, walking down the stairs to get to the kitchen to make breakfast for the sleeping man upstairs and myself.

"Valentina?" I hear someone ask, and I turn to find Jean standing behind me. There is a knowing smile on his lips, making a blush settle on my cheek. "Finally. Gabriel has been moping over you for *months*," he blurts out and sits down at the kitchen table.

"Oh no, we're not..." We haven't put a title on what we are yet, but we're not nothing, so I have no idea what to tell him.

"You're something, which gets you a step closer to becoming everything." Jean smiles at me, and I shake my head.

"You want breakfast?" He frowns and gets up from his seat.

"Yes, but you're not making it. You're the guest, and I will make breakfast for you." I recall the last time Jean tried to make a meal and flinch.

Luckily, I convince him to make it together.

"Chérie," a voice says right after Jean finishes telling me he got accepted to his dream university here in Monaco. I look up to see a half-naked Gabriel rubbing his eyes. "You weren't there when I woke up," he mutters, and I realize he must have woken up and run downstairs when he couldn't find me. "I thought you left."

Gabriel rubs his left arm as I close the distance between us. The left side of his face has marks all over it, probably from his pillow, and I can't help but grin at the sleepy man.

"Nope. Jean and I were just making breakfast," I assure him, and he takes my face between his hands. There is a concerned look on his face, worrying me. "What's wrong?"

Gabriel shakes his head, his lips finding mine before he even answers my question.

"I just had a horrible dream," he explains, and I nod. I had a feeling.

"Well, I'm here, and breakfast is ready," I inform him, and he places one more kiss on my lips before we walk over to the table and sit down.

Jean cut some fruits, and I made the pancakes. Both guys assure me they taste "incroyable."

After we finish breakfast, Gabriel and Jean clean up the table, not allowing me to move an inch. When they're done, Gabriel walks over to me and reaches his hand out. I place mine in his, letting him pull me against his body.

"Take a shower with me," he whispers, causing shivers to run down my spine.

Gabriel grins at me when I nod slowly.

We walk into his large bathroom, and for the first time, I really look at it. The shower is oversized and has glass doors, and his bathtub is enormous. Everything is white and beige, and I'm too mesmerized by how beautiful it is to realize Gabriel got naked, but once I do, I can't tear my eyes away. It's as if his body is calling out, and I'm the only one who can hear. His back is turned to me, which is why I finally get to see the infamous moon tattoo. It may have been a joke, but it looks... well, to be honest, it looks terrific on his trained ass.

The sound of my phone ringing tears me out of my ogling trance.

"Give me a moment, Gabriel. I have to check if it's Adrian." I rush out of the room, worry grabbing a hold of my chest.

Adrian doesn't call me unless something's wrong, and if it's not my brother, it might be the Velocità Rossa Driver Academy with an update. The last one is less likely, but my heart still races at the possibility of either of those scenarios.

Relief and disappointment flood through me at the sight of James' name.

"Hey, James, do you think I could call you back later? I'm a little busy," I say right as Gabriel walks out of his bathroom with a towel slung around his waist. He leans against the doorframe, crossing his arms and studying me with a serious look on his face.

"Yeah, of course. I just needed to talk to you, but maybe I can swing by your place later?" he asks, something sounding off in his voice.

"Sure. I'll text you when I'm home later." We hang up a second later and Gabriel lets his head hang for a moment, shaking it and letting out a humorless laugh.

"You know he's in love with you, right?" he asks, pushing off the wall and taking several steps toward me.

"James?" I ask, waiting for Gabriel to nod before I burst into laughter. "No, he's not. He's my oldest and best friend. That's all." The man in front of me rolls his lips together for a moment, stopping as he stands in front of me where I'm sitting on the bed.

"For you, maybe that's all he is. But he's in love with you, chérie. He's been in love with you since you were kids, from what I've gathered. He stares after you longingly, his touches linger. He wants to be with you, and everyone but you seems to have noticed that," he points out, not angry but gently trying to make me aware of something I'm not sure I can accept just because he said it.

"And he wouldn't have told me about his feelings for all of those years why?" I challenge, trying to make him see the flaw in his logic.

"Because you see him as a friend and only a friend. If he told you, it would ruin everything." He squats down in front of me, his hands slipping onto my thighs. "With us, it was different because there was a mutual pull between us, dragging us closer. For James, he gets pulled toward you, but you continue to walk in the opposite direction. Why would he ever confess he has feelings for you?" Tears sting my eyes at the possibility that what Gabriel is saying is true.

"Why are you telling me this, Gabriel? Is the point to make me feel bad because it's working," I say, but Gabriel immediately shakes his head.

"No, chérie, I don't want to make you feel bad. That's the last thing I want. I just thought you should know."

"And because you hate him and don't want him near me," I add, feeling a bit angry now.

"I do hate him, and, if it were up to me, James Landon would never come close to you again. But he's your best friend, and I don't want you to lose him." I stand up and step away from him.

"Then what do you want? What am I supposed to do with this information?" I ask, pointing around the room in my frustration.

"Talk to him. Maybe I'm wrong, but you deserve to know," he says, taking a step toward me right as there is a loud banging on the bedroom door, making both of us jump.

"Gabriel, Hector is here, and he is not happy," Jean calls out from the other side of the door.

"I'm sorry, chérie, I have to go deal with this. Just give me a few minutes, and I'll be right back." I nod several times, letting him kiss my cheek even though I'm mad, even though I don't know what the hell I'm supposed to do now. "I'm sorry," he repeats, squeezing my hand and leaving me to call James to tell him to meet me at my place.

Now.

James arrives at my house precisely fifteen minutes later. He's standing on my doorstep with one sunflower, smiling brightly. Gabriel's words paint this action in a completely different light now.

"What? What's wrong?" he asks, clearly sensing something's not right by looking at my face.

"You are an incredible friend. Ever since I can remember, you have always cared for me, and I can't tell you how much that means. I never want to lose you."

The words fall off my lips more easily than they would have a month ago. I realized a long time ago that once you let someone in, you have to make sure they always remember how much they mean to you. If you don't, and they get taken away from you, you will regret not reminding them for the rest of your life.

But, right now, I'm not saying it to remind him. I'm saying it so what comes next isn't as bad as I think it'll be.

"Do you have feelings for me?" James' face reveals how surprised he is to hear those words from my lips.

"Why would you ask me that?" he says, attempting to take my hand in his, but I step back to give us both space to breathe during this conversation.

"Because Gabriel—" He cuts me off before I have a chance to finish that sentence.

"You must be joking, Valentina. I know you have feelings for him, which, by the way, he'll probably never return, but not everything that comes out of his mouth is true." He looks irritated now.

"I don't understand why you're lashing out. I'm sorry if the question was uncomfortable, but you haven't even answered it yet. I don't believe him over you when it comes to *your* feelings. But you have to tell me, James." My voice is gentle, careful, knowing if I start getting annoyed with him he's only going to get more upset with me.

"This is ridiculous, Val," he says and shakes his head.

"Why can't you say it then? If I'm being ridiculous?"

I think about our conversation at the beach a month ago. I think about him describing the girl he's in love with. The way he looked at me while he told me about her. My heart sinks into my stomach.

"I can't believe you'd let Gabriel do this to us," he says and shakes his head.

"Am I her or not, James? Am I the girl you were talking about at the beach? The one who isn't interested in you because she has feelings for someone else?" I ask, a nauseous feeling spreading through me because I *know*. I know the answer.

"No," he says, looking away from me as he says the word, his tell that he's lying.

"Don't lie to me, James! You have to tell me if it's true. You have to—" He cuts me off again.

"Yes! You're her."

My body is overwhelmed by all the emotions flooding through me at once. Because of three little words. It begs me to breathe, but I've forgotten how.

"Fuck. Are you happy now? Is that what you wanted to hear? Because it's not going to help anything! It's just going to ruin things," he says, running his hands over his face. "I knew Gabriel ruined things, that he was an arsehole, but I didn't think that he'd do this to us."

"No, James, this isn't on Gabriel. I should have seen it before, we should have addressed it."

"I don't want to talk about it, Valentina! That's why I didn't tell you." He stares at the sunflower where he dropped it on the floor, biting his bottom lip as he thinks. "You know what? I can't do this."

He storms out of my house, leaving me to drop to the floor because my weak knees can no longer hold me up. Gabriel was right. James has feelings for me.

The wave of emotion hitting me right after has nothing to do with either of those men and everything to do with all of the suppressed pain that has been lingering inside of me. Getting rejected by the driver academies. Getting waitlisted by the Velocità Rossa Driver

Academy, which probably means they'll never reach out to me again. Losing so many people I've loved with my whole heart. Getting into a fight with Gabriel, in a way. James probably hating me now.

I start crying without meaning to, so overwhelmed by the world that breathing becomes impossible.

So, I do what I do best when I feel this way. I grab my running shoes and sprint down the trail the guys and I followed not long ago.

Grandpa always warned me about letting my emotions control me.

"You're an athlete. Your body is only as strong as your mind. If you let emotion consume you, you betray your body."

I wonder what he would say to me now. I've been training but haven't gotten far, haven't reached my dream. I haven't done anything he hoped I would by now.

My feet bring me to a halt at the spot where Grandfather stopped me the first time we went for a run.

"Your determination and dedication will make you a champion," he'd told me.

I bring my hands to my lips and cover my mouth as I scream as loudly as I can.

For the first time in over five years, I make my way to the one place I hate the most. I haven't been able to return because of the pain it brings me every single time I read my grandfather's name on the gravestone, but it's time. Grandfather deserves a visit from me, no matter how painful it will be.

I come to a complete stop once I'm in front of the stone Adrian and I had to choose. I wipe the dirt off the top and kneel in front of the grave while I let tears flow from my cheeks. My heart aches in my chest, and I have a difficult time breathing properly. I wrap my arms around myself and rock back and forth while the same words fall from my lips.

"I'm so sorry." I repeat them over and over, ashamed of my actions and inability to make our dream come true. "I really tried, but I'm not good enough," I explain when I've calmed down enough to form a proper sentence. "I wish you were here. I love you and miss you so much," I go on, sending a wave of pain through my chest. "You must be so disappointed in me," I cry while I run my fingers over his name: *Josue Beau Romana*. "I just want to live my dream and make you proud, but I can't. I don't know what I'm supposed to do anymore."

All of the pain and anger fade for a moment when my phone rings, and I read Colin Reiner's name on my lock screen. My eyes drift to Grandfather's gravestone before I compose myself and answer the call.

"Hello, Mr. Reiner?" I ask, my heart thumping rapidly against my ribcage.

"Good afternoon, Ms. Romana. I'm sorry to bother you, but I have some news. A spot has opened up at our academy, and we would be delighted to have you join us. Are you still interested?"

My eyes fixate on the gravestone again while goosebumps spread over my entire body.

Thank you, Grandfather.

RUSH

Part Two

Chapter 33

Valentina

"You've been training for two years to get to this moment, little champion. How do you feel?" Grandfather asks as I settle down in my kart.

If I win today, I will become the champion of this year's karting league.

"I'm very nervous," I admit while he helps me get comfortable in my seat and readjusts my helmet to make sure the clasp is closed.

Adrian takes my hand and gives it a reassuring squeeze. Meanwhile, James is walking around my kart to check if everything is in order.

"I know, but you've got this, Valentina. There is no one like you, and you'll show them that today," Grandfather says before stepping back and nodding at my brother to let him know it's time to go.

"Go kick those boys' asses," Adrian adds in English, earning himself a frown from our grandfather.

"Adrian, watch your foul mouth," he warns, making my brother lift his hands in surrender. Grandpa leans down then so I'm the only one to hear his next words. "Go kick their asses," he whispers, going against his strict rule of solely speaking French to us, and I let out a little laugh. It relieves some of the tension and pressure on my shoulders.

"Breathe, race, and win, as long as it doesn't cost you a limb," Adrian, James, and Grandpa say in unison.

They stand in front of me for a moment before offering me one last nod and, involuntarily, the sadness of my father not being here creeps into my chest. Then they walk away, leaving me to enter my high-concentration mode. I shut everything out, focusing entirely on the task at hand: proving everyone who is doubting me wrong and winning the championship.

The race starts soon, and I manage to stay ahead for most of it. By the time the last few laps come around, my rival Christian Crovetto is right beside me, almost pushing me off track to get past.

I hold my ground, only giving in and letting him pass by so he doesn't force me to crash into the barriers. Then, at the next corner, I overtake him again, my kart touching his briefly before I'm ahead.

We race for one more lap, but I'm the one who makes it over the finish line first. Despite him playing dirty tricks, I win.

I drive my kart toward the little podium area where my family is waiting for me with big smiles. They clap and cheer the entire time while happiness fills my soul.

This is where I belong.

This feeling is what I long for every single day of my life.

It has taken a lot of disappointment to get here, but it was worth it.

I'm a karting league champion, and, one day, I will be one of Formula One.

The wind around me becomes more chilly with every minute I remain in front of Grandfather's grave. My fingertips feel like ice, but I can't bring myself to move yet. The thoughts in my head spiral, sometimes in a good way when I think about getting accepted into the Velocità Rossa Driver Academy an hour ago. Other times, they fixate on the disaster between James and me.

For now, I revel in my success in getting what I've wanted since I was a little kid. My fingers brush over my grandfather's name on the marble stone once more. *Josue Beau Romana*. I hope he would be proud of me, despite the chaos in my life. After all those years of teaching me about balance, I've never been further away from it than I am right now.

I wipe the dirt off the top of the stone and place the flowers in the holder next to it, whispering "I love you" before standing up. My hands straighten out my clothes while I turn around to see my brother a few meters behind me.

A smile dances onto my lips at the sight of him, and he opens his arms for me. I run toward him, excitement acting like adrenaline in my veins.

"I made it, Adrian. The Velocità Rossa Academy offered me a spot," I say as soon as he envelops me in a hug.

He steps away, joy and surprise all over his face.

"Are you serious?" I nod with enthusiasm, and he jumps up and down. A few people around us glare at him for it, and he stops immediately. "Sorry," he apologizes, guiding me out of the cemetery to continue his cheerful behavior. "When? How?" Adrian asks and takes my hand to squeeze it. I've never seen him this giddy before.

"Mr. Reiner called me a few hours ago and told me a spot has opened up. I took it. The first training camp starts the week after the third Grand Prix," I explain, my cheeks burning from the smile I can't keep off my lips.

"Fuck yeah! My sister has finally got her chance to become a World Champion!" Adrian yells for everyone around us to hear. I try to shush him, but he's too excited. "Oh man, I'm going to be the brother of the first female champion. Now that's a fucking honor, holy crap," he says and wraps his arm around my shoulder to pull me close while we walk toward his car.

Tears sting my eyes at the thought, but I swallow them down. There has been enough crying for today.

"Thank you for never leaving my side during this difficult and frustrating process." Adrian presses a kiss to the side of my head and opens the door of his Velocità Rossa for me.

"I will never leave you, Val, no matter how hard times get." My eyes shift to the ground as the thought of my fight with James resurfaces.

I sit down in the passenger seat, and Adrian settles down in the driver's, letting the engine roar to life with a simple press of a button.

"What's up? Why do you look upset?" he asks on our way to a restaurant where he wants to celebrate my news. "Please, tell me I don't have to kill someone." This makes me let out an awkward laugh.

"There is something we should talk about," I admit, and he cocks a curious eyebrow. "James told me he has feelings for me and we ended up in a fight..." I trail off before adding, "And I got into a small fight with Gabriel because he told me James had feelings for me and I didn't believe him." Adrian tilts his head my way, and I realize he knew too. He knew about James' feelings, and he didn't say anything.

"It wasn't my place," he says when he watches the realization dawn on me.

"I know." I let out a string of curse words before turning to my brother again. "I have no idea how to fix any of it. What am I supposed to do about James having feelings for me?" I ask, my eyes shifting to the Casino de Monte-Carlo as we drive by it.

"James is our best friend. He's been there since we were kids, and, no matter what, we will never be able to let go of him. Deep down, you know you'd do anything to save your friendship because he's family. A little bit more complicated family now, but still. He's been there for us for every important event in our lives. Yes, he has feelings for you, but he's James. We're always going to need him, and he's always going to need us," Adrian says, once again reminding me of the admiration I hold for my brother.

His willingness to speak about emotional things with me is why he's my favorite person in the whole world. Well, it's one of the reasons.

"I'll talk to him," I reply, but the words are so quiet, it makes me realize they are meant for myself and no one else. "For tonight, I just want to celebrate." Adrian briefly looks at me to reveal his smile.

"Anything for a future Formula One World Champion," he tells me with a wink before focusing on the road in front of us again.

Chapter 34
Gabriel

I'm losing my fucking mind.

Valentina has disappeared, no note, text, or anything letting me know where she has gone. I've tried calling her, but she's not answering her phone. I thought she'd stay and wait for me to be done dealing with Hector so we could keep talking, so I could apologize again.

But she's gone.

She left while still upset with me, and now she's ignoring my messages.

"Jean!" I call out because worry has consumed every part of me.

Thoughts of what could have happened to her take over, and I panic. Despite my rational brain trying to assure me she's alright, that she just needs a minute, but the trauma of all the people I lost has me spiraling into worst-case scenarios.

"Jean!" I scream louder this time, and my brother appears in front of me downstairs, a confused look on his face.

"Why the hell are you screaming?" he complains, his French sloppier than usual. It irritates me, but I can't focus on scolding him right now. He might know where Valentina is.

"Did Val tell you where she was going?" I ask.

If Hector hadn't acted like it was the end of the world that I didn't go to one training session, I would have never left for so long.

"No, but try calling Adrian or James. They might know."

I dial James' number first because I remember her saying she'd meet him when she got home today.

The phone rings a few times before he answers.

"I'm not in the bloody mood, Gabriel. Leave me alone," he slurs into the phone, and I cock an eyebrow.

"Is Val with you?" I ask and hear him sniffle.

"No, mate, and she probably never will be again."

He hangs up before I can ask him what the hell that means.

My thumbs fly over my screen, searching for Adrian's number. I hate being like this, but I just need something, anything, to slow my racing thoughts. The fact that she didn't tell me she left bothers me. I need to make sure she's somewhere safe.

My heart is racing while I wait for Adrian to respond, but he doesn't. I'm about to have a panic attack when my screen lights up from an incoming text message.

Chapter 35

Valentina

My focus has been on the countless yachts in the harbor for most of the meal. The water barely moves, except for the occasional seagull that disturbs the peace as it collects some food. Gabriel has been trying to reach me, but I'm ignoring his texts. We need to speak in person, not over the phone.

"Can I bring you both something else? Maybe a little dessert?" our waitress asks, tearing me from my thoughts.

Her attention is on Adrian, a challenging look on her face. They've been flirting since we've sat down, which is why I can't keep the smile off my face. My gaze shifts to my brother, who gives her an easy smirk that turns her cheeks a deep red color.

"Depends. What are you offering?" he asks, and I roll my eyes when she slips him a note.

"Would that be of interest to you?" she replies, making me feel the urge to cover my ears. I don't want to know what she wrote on that paper.

"How could I say no to someone as beautiful as you?"

I smack my forehead, earning me a kick to the shin from him. It's not hard, just enough to serve as a "stop that." A laugh slips from my lips before I can contain it.

"Do you want to walk home?" he asks, so I cover my mouth with my hand.

He turns back to the patiently waiting waitress, Julia.

"I get off in ten minutes," she informs him, and Adrian smiles at her.

"If we follow the instructions on your note, yes, you will," he assures her, making another blush settle on her cheeks.

I suppress the urge to make a hurling sound but let it out when Julia leaves our table to get the check Adrian asked for.

I text Gabriel to meet me at my house. I don't want to torture him any longer nor do I want our fight to remain unresolved.

"Give me the keys, please. I can't stay and watch more of that," I say and point at him. Adrian grins as he hands me the keys to his car.

"I'll be home later," he assures me, and I roll my eyes for the second time before standing up.

"You know, relationships aren't as bad as you think. They might be worth a shot." Adrian frowns in an instant.

"No, thank you. I've gotten hurt enough times in my life," he replies, and I bend down to press a kiss to the top of his head.

"Someday, a wonderful person is going to step into your life, and you won't be able to turn away from them, no matter our past. Trust me, *I know*." Adrian squeezes my side, acknowledging my words without responding.

If I were smarter, I'd adapt his mindset to shield myself from further pain, but Gabriel is under my skin now. He's the reason why my walls have turned to dust.

By the time I finally get home, he's sitting on my porch, his head between his arms, and his phone in his hand. When he looks up and sees me, relief washes over his face.

"Thank God, you're okay! I was worried sick about you," he says as he tries to close the distance between us. I hold up my hands to stop him, which he does at once.

"You were right," I admit, and his eyebrows twitch from uncertainty.

"About James?" I would have expected him to be angry with me for avoiding him, for getting mad at him earlier during our fight, but he's genuinely trying to make sense of how I feel instead.

"Yes." His eyes go wide, and the confusion vanishes from his face. "I confronted him, and he admitted to it."

Gabriel nods, his lips pressed into a thin line. It makes the dimples on his cheeks stand out. I take a step toward him, and he takes on toward me.

"You deserved to know," he says, and I nod again. It's good that I know now because James and I will be able to talk about this. We will be able to put up more boundaries to protect his feelings, make sure he doesn't resent me for them being unrequited.

"He and I got into a fight," I say next, watching sadness spread over his face.

"I'm so sorry, baby." I move even closer until my hands rest on each side of his neck, pulling his face down to mine.

"I'm also sorry. You can always talk to me, especially when it's something like this, and I'm sorry if I made you feel like it was the wrong thing to do," I say as he leans his forehead against mine.

Our breaths intertwine, and his fingers slip onto my hips to guide me against his body. Electricity courses through me, making the blood in my veins hum to Gabriel's melody.

"I know. You're the most understanding person I've ever met. I'm sorry we fought, chérie," he replies, the sincerity in his voice clear as day.

"So am I."

Gabriel nods before leaning down and pressing a soft kiss to my neck. A wave of goosebumps spreads over my arms as my skin lights on fire.

"How can I make things up to you?" he asks, his lips moving to my jaw and then cheek. The affection clouds my mind for a moment, but I refocus quickly.

"Be happy for me when I tell you I got a spot in the Velocità Rossa Driver Academy," I blurt out because, more than anything right now, I want to share this success with him.

Gabriel lets go of me to step back and stare into my eyes. A bright smile lights up my face, showing him I'm not joking.

This is real.

"You did it! Oh my God, you fucking did it, mon tournesol," he cheers and kisses me all over the face.

My mind is stuck on this new nickname, "my sunflower," but I'm also giggling as he attacks my face with love.

"I'm so proud of you! And happy for you. This is the best news I've ever heard in my life."

Gabriel's lips envelop mine then, and I almost sigh against them. It feels like it's been days since we last kissed, even if it's only been hours. His tongue slips into my mouth, making a little moan escape me. My knees go weak as he bites down on my bottom lip, but he holds me up, not ready for the kiss to end yet, and neither am I. Unfortunately, we're interrupted by the ringing of his phone.

"I swear, if it's Hector again, I'll fire him," Gabriel complains in French, causing a chuckle to escape me.

He rips his phone out of his pocket and cocks an eyebrow at the name before answering.

"Adrian? What can I do for you?" he asks, confusing me. I watch Gabriel, trying to figure out what my brother could possibly want right now. "I'll let her know. Yeah, okay. Bye," Gabriel says and laughs as he hangs up. "You forgot your phone at the restaurant, and he wanted to let you know he won't be back until tomorrow."

A yawn leaves me as I attempt to reply, and Gabriel brings his thumb to my bottom lip after.

"Let's go to bed, chérie, you must be exhausted." That's an understatement. It's been a long day.

He brings his lips to mine one more time before we go upstairs, and I take a shower. I give Gabriel an extra toothbrush so he can get ready too. We're in bed soon, and as tired as I am, I can't help but ogle Gabriel as he lies next to me without a shirt and pants on. The ink on his left hip bone stands out just above the waistband of his boxers, and I reach for it, like the first time I saw it. My fingers trace it for a brief moment, smiling because only I know about his tattoos.

Gabriel and I are facing each other on the bed, but we're too far apart for my liking. I inch a bit closer, desperate to feel his body pressed against mine.

"Are you hot?" I ask him after a while of silence, but he shakes his head and leans it back to study my face.

I'm only wearing a shirt, but it's so warm in my room, I'm jealous of him being half-naked. Frustrated because I want to cuddle, I sit up in bed, let out a heavy breath, and pull my shirt over my head. I feel like my skin can breathe again. Gabriel is watching my body with a toe-curling intensity, but there is also an amused smirk on his face.

"It's too hot," I complain, and he chuckles, his index finger reaching out to touch my cheek. It runs down from there to my neck and then to my breasts, leaving goosebumps in its wake.

"This is going to be a real problem," he says and pulls his bottom lip between his teeth. A blush settles on my cheeks, making me wish my body wasn't exhausted.

"What happened with Hector?" I ask, trying to distract myself and get him to stop touching my sensitive areas.

His green-brown eyes lock onto mine, and his full, round lips pull into a thin line. He's upset about whatever dragged him away from me this morning but doing his best to hide it from me. His gaze is on mine, a smile warming up his features when I give him a wiggle of my eyebrows.

"Don't worry about it, chérie, all that matters is I'm here with you now and we're okay." Gabriel's grin makes my heart weak.

It's ridiculous to me how much I love him and that, after three years, I finally got what I wanted. Gabriel is lying in my bed and he has feelings for me. I've been offered a position at the Velocità Rossa Driver Academy so I can work toward my dream of becoming an F1 driver. Everything is slowly falling into place.

Now, I only have to figure out what the hell I'm going to do about James.

Chapter 36

Valentina

My eyes flutter open, and, like yesterday morning, I'm awake before Gabriel. A smile stretches across my face as I inch closer, and he wraps his arms around me in his sleep. My fingers trail across his naked torso, studying every birthmark and little scar they can find.

His heartbeat is steady, I can hear it perfectly with my ear flat against his chest. Gabriel's hand drops from my back to my ass, and I look up to see if he's still asleep. His eyes are closed, but there is a hint of a smile on his lips now.

Two can play this game.

I reach for his morning wood but don't touch him. All I do is swiftly graze it, as if by accident, and then shove my hands between my legs. Gabriel squeezes my ass, bringing a smile to my face. My fingers move back to his chest, and I lean forward to press a kiss on his hard nipple.

Almost instantly, he pushes my ass toward him, my aching clit pressing against his groin. A low moan leaves me, my needy body happy because of the pressure against my most sensitive area.

I lift my head to see his eyes are open now, his lips are parted, and lust is all over his face.

"Good morning," I whisper, and the sweetest grin appears on his lips. His dimples seem to be everything I want to see at this point along with his stubble and green-brown eyes because my heart does a happy somersault at the sight.

"Bonjour," he replies, his mouth brushing over mine.

My body lights on fire when he rubs against me, every part of me vibrating with need.

"Touch me," I beg and command at the same time, bringing a sexy smirk to his full lips.

His hand slips inside my panties without hesitation, running over my swollen clit before his index and middle fingers slowly slide inside of me. They curl at the perfect spot, making a loud gasp escape me.

"You're so wet for me, chérie, this early in the morning," he whispers into my ear, his voice husky and rough from just waking up.

He moves his fingers back out before he glides them in again, this time a little faster than before. Fire spreads through my stomach and chest, my eyes rolling into the back of my head at the same time.

"Look at me," he says, but I don't listen. "Eyes on me or I'll stop," he demands, and I smile as I obey.

He's so bossy... *I love it.*

His thumb rubs over my clit, tracing perfect circles. My moans are quiet, but they are also coming out fast and breathless. Gabriel brings his lips to mine and lets his tongue slip into my mouth to massage mine with his. Pleasure grabs hold of every cell in my body, coursing through me in waves.

My eyes close in response, but he stops his movements.

"Eyes on me, baby," he reminds me, so I force them open again.

Gabriel keeps going before lifting his free hand to grab my chin between his fingers, tilting my head to face him completely.

"That's my girl," he praises, picking up speed and bringing back the familiar tension in my body.

"Can I touch your cock, Gabriel? I want to make you come too," I say, the need to make him orgasm at the same time as me taking over.

"Touch me, baby. Make me come," he says before pressing his lips back on mine and kissing me hard.

I bring my hand up to our mouths, interrupting our kiss long enough to lick my hand and slip it inside his boxers.

"Shit, Val," he moans as soon as my hand glides down his long, thick cock. My eyes stay on him but his are closed now as he enjoys the pleasure of my touch.

A wicked grin dances onto my face before I say, "Keep looking at *me*, Gabriel, or *I* will stop."

He half-chuckles, half-moans before obeying, his gaze revealing how good I make him feel. I rub faster, putting a little more pressure when he groans my name. It's so hot, I keep going to hear it over and over again. Every little sound from him pushes me further toward my release, toward paradise.

"God, baby." He kisses me, his fingers thrusting in and out of me faster, eager to push me off the edge with him.

I feel his legs go stiff before his high takes over and his body starts to tremble. He rolls his hips forward to fuck my hand, riding out his pleasure for as long as he can.

Gabriel's lips crash onto mine a moment before my own orgasm pumps through my veins, releasing my entire body from the build-up he was responsible for. I cover my mouth to muffle my scream and grind myself against his hand to enjoy the orgasm and all of its effects.

"Fuck," I breathe and roll onto my back, trying to calm my accelerated heartbeat, which is useless, at least until he removes his hand from my panties and I manage to find my way back into my body.

Gabriel disappears into my bathroom, but he returns soon, wearing his sweatpants from yesterday and smiling brightly at me. I'm still out of breath, and my mind is in a trance.

"Can we wake up like this every morning?" I joke, but Gabriel's expression is dead-serious.

"Say the word, I'll move in tomorrow." I shake my head, the smile on my face never fading. He cocks a brow but grins too. That beautiful, handsome grin of his. "Fine, I guess we can just pretend we don't belong together for a bit longer if that's what you need."

He makes everything sound so easy as if we could run away together into a fairytale land where problems don't exist and we could live happily ever after. Just trying to put myself in a mindset like that is absurd. Worlds like this don't exist, but mine is pretty good, even if I have to push through things.

"What do you want to do today?" Gabriel asks me after a while of silence, and I take his hand in mine.

"I have to go make things right between James and me. I don't want this painful feeling in my stomach to be permanent," I explain, and Gabriel nods.

"I'm here for whatever you need, chérie," Gabriel agrees.

I place my hand on his foot and tickle him, making him jerk his feet toward his body.

"What are you trying to do?" he asks, a big grin on his face.

"I'm trying to be cute," I reply, and he chuckles.

Gabriel pulls me toward him by my wrists and starts tickling my stomach. I don't know if he knows my feet aren't ticklish, or if he just wanted more surface to attack, but I start screaming and laughing until eventually, he just pins me to the bed.

"You don't have to try to be cute. It comes naturally to you."

He gives me a swift kiss on the lips before he gets off me.

My hand has been in the same position, a few centimeters away from James' door, for about five minutes now. I can't make my fist connect with the wood. I want to talk to him, I *need* to, but, somehow, my body is refusing to take the first step in the right direction.

It's been twenty-four hours since the fight started, and I don't know if it's the best idea to talk to him already. Maybe I'm too much of a chicken to find out what it means for our friendship now that I know he's in love with me.

His feelings will change everything.

Won't they?

I don't know anymore, which is why I finally bring myself to knock on the door. Uncertainty is scarier than anything James could ever tell me.

When nobody answers, I walk around the side of the house and open the gate leading to his garden. James is sitting on one of the lounge chairs in front of his pool, his head between his arms and empty bottles of beer scattered around him.

He must have slept out here.

"James?" His head snaps up, and I can see his red, puffy eyes and the dark circles underneath them. "Good God," I say and walk over to him. I wrap my arms around his head, ignoring the stench of alcohol coming off his clothes. "What the hell are you doing?" I step back, letting my eyes scan his sad face.

"I'm so sorry," is the first thing slipping out of his mouth. He's not drunk anymore, I'm sure of it, but he's exhausted.

His blue eyes seem lighter because the white part has turned blood-red, and his blonde hair is all over the place.

"I know, I'm sorry too. We should have talked yesterday."

James probably spent the whole night hating himself, trying to forget about everything by consuming too much alcohol and putting himself in a dreadful head space.

"Let's talk," I tell him, and he nods.

"I was in love with you for years, pretty much from when we were kids."

My heart is racing in my chest, and I feel like throwing up.

"Since you moved back to Monaco, I've realized we aren't supposed to be together. I am supposed to protect you, love you, care for you, and always be there for you in a brotherly kind of way. You need me as a friend, and I need you, which is why I never want to do anything to ruin that, even if I already did."

Tears are rolling down his cheeks, which bring some to my own eyes. We are two people who love each other too much for their own good.

"Once I realized what we both need, it was a lot easier to let go of my feelings. I even met someone a couple of weeks ago, and she and I have been getting along well."

He rubs his face with his hands before he takes mine again.

"I should have always put protecting you first, and I'm sorry I let a ridiculous fantasy cloud my judgment. You deserve better, my love."

His hand slips out of mine, but I take it back and lift it to my cheek. It lies flat against my skin, and I take a deep, calming breath. This is a lot to take in all at once, but at least I finally understand him. I can make sense of his feelings, which is all I've ever wanted.

"I'm sorry for all the pain I have caused you over the years. It must have taken everything out of you to give me advice and listen when I talked to you about Luke and Gabriel, or every time I friend-zoned you," I say and laugh a little.

"Yeah," he mumbles, his thumb caressing my cheek.

"I'm so sorry something like this happened," I tell him, my voice cracking.

He's about to talk when I cover his mouth to stop him.

"You had your turn, now it's mine," I scold, and he grins at me. There it is, this is all I wanted to see. "There is nothing you could ever do that would make me hate you." He shakes his head, shame in his features. I let out a strained breath. "I love you." James pulls me into a tight embrace.

"I love you so much, Valentina."

We hug for what feels like an eternity before I pull back to look at him. The smile on his face warms my insides because I'm glad to see happiness has taken over again.

"Now, tell me, what's been going on?"

A small, nervous laugh escapes me before I tell him about my spot at the Velocità Rossa Driver Academy.

"Shut up, love!" he says, shaking me out of excitement. "It finally happened! Soon, you'll be kicking all of our arses," he cheers, and I cover my face to hide the blush on my cheeks.

Soon...

Chapter 37

Gabriel

My fingers run over the soft skin of her cheek, tracing her features to memorize the feel of them. Valentina fell asleep as soon as she came home from James' house. I've been watching her like a creep for the past half an hour, but I can't help it. She's everything to me and admiring her face is the only thing I want to do while she's asleep beside me.

Val lets out a little, tired groan, her dream creasing the skin between her eyebrows. I smile at her, brushing her nose with mine as I inch closer. Just as my eyes are about to shut, a crashing noise shudders through the house.

"Hmmm?" Val says, raising her head, but she's still mostly asleep.

"I'll go see, chérie," I whisper, and she falls back onto her pillow, trusting me to check on Adrian.

He's on his knees downstairs, picking up the shards of the vase he broke.

"Are you okay?" I ask when he doesn't acknowledge my presence in the foyer.

His gaze shifts to my face, revealing that something is bothering him by the redness around his eyes.

"Is Val sleeping?" he says, and I nod to assure him it's just him and me. I help him pick up the pieces, waiting for an explanation. "I'm having a bad night," he explains, but I already knew that. Adrian is more transparent than he thinks.

"You can talk to me about it, if you want," I offer, and he drops backward until he's on his ass, tears falling down his cheeks.

This is the first time since I've met him that he's felt comfortable enough around me to cry, and I'm not sure what to do.

"Do you ever have those nights when you get lost in your head, thinking about everyone you've lost and picturing the pain they felt when they left this world?" he asks, so I sit down too.

"All the time," I admit, doing my best to calm my racing heart.

He wipes his tears, wrapping his arms around his legs and leaning back to look more casual than he's feeling.

"I can't get my dad out of my head. The day he crashed into our living room, drunk out of his mind. A small part of me died with him as I watched the paramedics drag his lifeless body from the car. For some reason, I can't get the image out of my head tonight, and it's ripping open old wounds," he says, allowing me to envision what he had to go through as a child.

Chills cover my whole body.

"I'm sorry, I can't imagine how traumatic that must have been. I was only told what happened to my mom, but, every now and then, I see an image in my head of her dropping to the ground in the grocery store. I didn't have to be there for it to haunt me, so I understand," I reply, and he gives me a compassionate smile.

"It feels surreal when I replay the memory, like a bad dream I had, or a nightmare that's consuming me." I nod, moving forward to pick up the shard I've been focusing on. "Why can't my head let it go? Why does it have to show me what happened over and over?" he asks, pulling on his dirty blonde hair as more tears fall.

"You miss him, Adrian, and, unfortunately, that's the last memory you have of him. It's the most recent and traumatic, so your brain latched onto it. It's difficult to forget, if not impossible."

His eyes shift to my face, studying me with an intensity that tells me he needs a distraction, to focus on something else to let go of what pains him.

"Come on," I say and stand up before holding out my hand to help him off the ground.

"Where are we going?" he asks, letting me pull him up. I place my hand on his shoulder, squeezing it to comfort him.

"You're going to show me where you keep the broom so I can clean up the shards. I don't want Val to kill us tomorrow for leaving pieces of porcelain on the ground," I start, and he chuckles at my words.

"She *is* really bossy," he complains with a smile, and I return it.

"Yes, she is, and rightfully so with us," I add and follow Adrian to the cupboard where the cleaning tools are.

"I'll take care of my mess," he says when he grabs the broom, but I snatch it out of his grasp.

"No, you're going to set everything up for a card game of your choosing so I can kick your ass," I reply and make my way back to the broken vase.

By the time I've finished cleaning, Adrian is already at the table on the veranda, staring at the full moon in the sky.

"Are you praying to God to help you win? I think that's a hopeless case," I tease, and Adrian lets out a small laugh.

"No, I haven't prayed since I was a child. I don't even know if I believe in God anymore, or something like Him. I don't know." I was not expecting a serious response from him, but it's interesting how alike we think.

"I feel the same way, but what I'm sure of is that the people we've lost are watching over us, caring for us," I say as I settle down in the seat across from him. Adrian's eyes, the ones that remind me of the woman I love, stare into mine.

"I don't like how close we're growing, Gabriel. I think I need a break from you," he points out, and I burst into laughter.

There is the Adrian I know.

"You can try, but I'll still be here, at your house, bugging you with my presence because Val wants me here," I reply, picking up the cards to see what I'm working with this round.

"I really don't know what she sees in you. Your good looks? Your kind heart? *Pfft*," Adrian says, and my jaw drops a little before amusement pulls my mouth into a smile.

"You're a dick," I say in Italian, and he winks at me.

"Just to you." I shake my head, leaning it back to let out a sigh.

"Remember who's teaching you Italian for free," I remind him while he plays down his first card, making it my turn.

"Remember who's not beating you up for doing unthinkable things to their little sister," he replies, shutting me up for good.

Touché, I think to myself before smirking at my cards.

Chapter 38

Valentina

It's been a few days since everything happened, and things have slowly been settling. Since all four of my favorite guys wanted to celebrate my news, we decided to go for a round of bowling.

Cameron holds my hand the entire walk to where we get our shoes and pay for the lane. He's been quiet, something obviously weighing heavy on his mind, but he continues to bring a smile to his face whenever I look at him.

Adrian, James, and Gabriel follow behind us, discussing something about the new tires for this season. I wrap my arms around one of Cameron's and lean my head against his shoulder.

"Would you like to tell me what's bothering you?" I ask, earning an inquiring yet amused expression from him. His blue eyes pierce into mine before he lets out a small sigh.

"You know me too well," he complains with his thick Australian accent before nudging my head with his nose. I smile to myself as I wait for an explanation. "I dunno where to start," he says, but I don't rush him. "I'm in love with my friend. His name is Elijah, and we've known each other for a couple of years now. I don't know whether I should tell him or if I should just pretend I don't have any feelings. I've been fighting with myself for weeks, Valentina. What would you do in my place?"

I'm about to encourage him to go for it, to tell Elijah exactly how he feels because I think it's what I would do, but it's not. I'm not that forward nor that brave.

"I probably wouldn't tell him but only because I don't have the guts. If you're sure he's the one you want, that you're in love with him, then you should tell him. Don't put yourself in the same position as me because it only overcomplicates things. If I'd been honest with Gabriel from the start, and vice versa, we wouldn't have wasted our time," I explain, and Cameron stops dead in his tracks.

Adrian runs into him because, as always, he isn't looking where he is going. He barely holds himself up on Cameron's shoulders before we all burst into laughter.

"Sorry, mate," Cameron says, but Adrian is crying-laughing now.

James and Gabriel go ahead already to get a lane, but my brother takes another moment to compose himself.

"It's all good. Sorry I ran into you, but, Jesus, you're built like a fucking wall. Nice," Adrian compliments our friend before squeezing his shoulders and arms with an approving nod. "You know, Elijah would be an idiot to shoot you down." A big smile spreads over Adrian's lips before he blushes. "I overheard your conversation a little. Your voice is very loud and firm," Adrian says, but Cameron doesn't seem to mind him knowing.

"Well, let's hope he doesn't shoot me down." He nudges my brother's side but then takes my hand again. "Thank you for the advice. I knew you would understand," Cameron says, addressing me, and I wink at him.

"Go ahead, you can call me wise," I joke, and he bows before me.

"Oh yes, wise Ms. Romana, you are the greatest of them all." He shakes his head while laughing, and I drag him closer again as we continue walking. "So, you and Gabriel? Since when? How did I miss that? I'm usually very good at spotting these things," Cameron complains, and I chuckle.

"I don't know what Gabriel and I are, so maybe that's why your radar is off," I suggest, but he shakes his head.

"No, my radar easily spots two people horny for each other," he explains, earning him an attack from my elbow to his ribs. It's soft enough to barely move him. "I mean, I knew he had feelings for you, but that you have the hots for him is a surprise. After all, he's been moping over you for a while." *Moping...* I almost laugh. "Did he tell you about the time he let me convince him to get a tattoo on his ass because he got drunk when he found out you slept with someone else?" he asks, and I squeeze his arm while swallowing a chuckle.

"You're evil for that, you know," I remind him, but he brushes my comment off with a shrug of his shoulders.

"Hey, it's a cool tattoo." Even though he's right, I shake my head once again. "So, are you two dating now or..." He trails off, but I have no idea how to answer his question.

"I'm going to start training at the academy soon while he has to work, so I don't know where that leaves us," I admit to myself and him.

This is a conversation I should have with Gabriel first, but I also didn't expect this realization to sink in right now.

"He's crazy about you, Val. Gabriel will take you any and every way he possibly can."

Cameron kisses the side of my head before we speak to the woman at the counter, telling her which shoe sizes we need. Gabriel hands me mine as soon as I try to talk, smiling before shifting his attention back to the person handing out the equipment.

"Alright, darling, ready to lose against me?" James asks, and I raise both eyebrows in response.

"The last time I lost against you was when—when I—" I cut off abruptly, touching my chin as if I was thinking. "Never mind, I've never lost against you," I tease, making him frown while he tries to think of a time he won.

"Fine, then today will be the first of many. You'll see, you will all see," he announces to the rest of our group, but they give him a confused look. James clears his throat, and I stretch my lips into a straight line to keep my amusement at bay.

"Sure we will," I reply and pat his shoulder, but he takes advantage of that vulnerable position and attacks my sides, tickling me until I squeal.

I run away from him and to our lane.

Adrian and Gabriel are the first to join me, smiling at each other as they discuss who will win tonight. All of us are very competitive, especially Adrian and me. We don't handle losing well.

"Come on, Gabriel, we all know I'm the best. This will be an easy win for me," Adrian says, and I look up at the ceiling, rolling my eyes while I beg karma to make him lose after that comment.

"Actually, I think we all know Val will beat us without even breaking a sweat," Gabriel replies, and a blush heats up my cheeks.

I can feel his eyes on me as I tie my shoes, making me shake my head with a smile. We agreed to keep whatever it is we have on the down-low, at least until we have had the inevitable conversation of *what are we?*

I love him, and he cares about me, but it doesn't uncomplicate things as much as I'd like. My career comes first, and now more than ever, it will require most of my time. It's not fair to ask him to have half a relationship. The thought makes my chest sting, but I push it away to focus on tonight.

"Love, do you need a refresher course on how to hold a bowling ball?" James teases as he steps in front of me and brings me back to reality. My eyes shift to his face while a wicked grin dances onto my lips.

"You would be the best person to teach me about balls considering you were single most of your teenage years, wouldn't you?" I tease, and Gabriel and Adrian burst out into laughter. James' eyes widen and his mouth falls open.

"What did I miss?" Cameron asks when he finds my brother and Gabriel hunched over, and James still searching for a witty comeback.

"I taught James a lesson on how not to speak to a woman," I explain before winking at my best friend and walking over to the ball rack, grabbing one that looks like the universe.

Everyone watches me as I throw it down the lane, and it speeds toward the pins. Impatience combines with the hope to start off strong, which I do. All pins drop, earning me the first strike of the night. I jump up from excitement but straighten out my back and dress to pretend as if that was easy, no big deal.

All four of them have the same slightly annoyed, mostly impressed expression on their faces when I sit down to watch them have their turn.

Gabriel goes next and gets a spare. He smiles at me when he walks back, and I pat the space next to me, wanting him to be close. His arm wraps around me as he sits down, pulling me against his side. My eyes fixate on Adrian, whose first throw is so horrible, his ball lands in the gutter.

"I'm just warming up!" he defends when I laugh, and I raise my hands in mock surrender.

"You look stunning in that dress, mon tournesol," Gabriel compliments and runs his fingers over the soft cotton material. My heart does a few somersaults, unable to contain its excitement.

"'My sunflower,' huh?" I ask because last time I didn't, and it's been gnawing at me.

"The beauty you find in sunflowers is the one I see in you every time I look at you. They're your favorite, and you're mine," he explains without hesitation. I forget how to breathe.

"I'm your favorite flower, Mother Gothel?" I joke, and he gives me a small chuckle before placing his fingers under my chin to lift my face to his.

"You're my favorite everything, chérie."

He kisses my forehead but then brings his attention to Cameron as he throws his bowling ball. I lean my head against his shoulder, his familiar mahogany scent filling my nose.

Dammit, he needs to stop saying all the right things at all the right times.

There is only one round left. Adrian somehow managed to catch up, and we're head to head now. Gabriel, James, and Cameron haven't done well compared to us Romanas, but that's no surprise. My brother and I are too competitive to lose in a game we've been playing since we could walk.

I grab the bowling ball for the last time this round, glaring at my brother before moving toward the lane.

"Come on, chérie, you got this," Gabriel cheers followed by James and Cameron.

"Is no one on my side?" my brother complains while warmth spreads through my chest from their support. "So, when Val and I race against each other in the future, you'll be on her side too?" Adrian asks, and I turn to see him faking a pained expression.

"Most definitely," all three of our friends reply, and he lets out a laugh.

"Well, then that makes four of us. Go, Val!" he yells and claps, and I turn back around to throw my bowling ball.

I manage to get a spare with another throw, and my very last one is a strike. Adrian playfully rolls his eyes when I walk past him.

"Be careful. I wouldn't want you to trip over your big elephant feet and then use that as an excuse for losing," I tease, and he goes into attack mode. Adrian pulls me into the air just to drop me back on the ground and run like an idiot to the ball rack.

His first throw is a strike, which is why I grab Gabriel's arm and hold on tight. I'll never hear the end of it if Adrian wins tonight. My brother gives me a smug smile, but when he throws once more, he only knocks down a single pin. He doesn't manage to get a spare either, handing me the win.

"Oh yeah!"

My voice is louder than I intended for it to be, but my friends start celebrating with me, patting my back, or, in Gabriel's case, kissing my cheek. Adrian pretends to be deeply wounded by his loss before hugging me.

If happiness could be described as one single moment, this one would come very close for me.

Chapter 39

Gabriel

There is nothing I hate more in the world than this god-forsaken graveyard. I come here seven times a year, but it never gets easier. My heart doesn't get used to the squeezing from pain, and my lungs always burn from my uneven breaths. Still, I come here on every date tattooed on my hip because it's the closest I can get to people I've lost.

I wish there was another way for me to feel connected to them again.

"Hi, Max," I say as I settle down in front of my late best friend's gravestone.

My hands start to shake while I get ready to talk to him like I always do when I'm here. The first time, it felt weird because I knew he couldn't hear me, none of them can, but it's gotten easier over time. Valentina told me once, "You're not speaking for them to listen. You're speaking for yourself to process and heal." That was the first day I realized I couldn't be without her again, the day I understood just how in love I am.

"The season is going alright so far. I managed to win the first race, but then only came in fifth in the second one. James is currently leading the championship, which you know how I feel about," I say and let out a laugh.

James fucking Landon.

"But I'm going to keep pushing, don't worry." It's as much of a reassurance for him as it is for me.

"Excuse me, I don't mean to bother, but my granddaughter fell and I don't have a tissue to clean the wound. Do you perhaps have one for me?" an elderly man asks, and I stand up to reach into my back pocket.

"Of course. Here," I say and offer him a whole pack. "I hope she's okay," I add, and he smiles at me.

"She will be," he replies.

The man walks away, and my eyes shift to the gravestone across from Maxime's. The name *Josue Beau Romana* is written on it, and I sink back down to where I was before. Next to his stone is another with the name *Esmèe Rolande-Romana*.

How have I never noticed that Valentina's grandparents are buried right across from Maxime?

I always knew our fates were entangled, but this takes it to another level.

"Aunt Domi and Aunt Nicolette are doing well, they're almost back from vacation. Jean is much better than the last time we talked. He's worked through his grief. You'd be very proud of him," I say, focusing on my best friend. "I wish you were here. I have so many questions to ask you," I admit and rub my face with my hands. "I've made mistakes with Valentina, but I'm trying to be better. I'd do anything for her, for her happiness. And yet, I can't shake my fear of losing her. She's the only person I want a future with, so I know I have to let it go. For Valentina's sake, my paranoia needs to turn into devotion. I won't turn away from her anymore. I can't feed into the fear when both of us know mere friendship isn't going to be enough."

My rant comes to an abrupt end when I remember to breathe. A laugh I don't mean escapes me before I can hold it back.

"I need you, Maxime, to tell me everything will work out in the end. I need you to assure me I've experienced enough loss. I need you to be here, not wherever you are!" I say, feeling the pain in my chest taking over.

Tears shoot into my eyes, but I can't stop them.

"Fuck, when will this get easier? When am I going to stop bawling my eyes out because you're gone? I can't change it, so why the hell am I crying?" I ask, fighting the urge to throw grass like a little child. "I love my job. I love racing, but I will hate it forever for taking you from me."

I lift my hands to his name as the pain finally rolls down my cheeks. No other place can bring tears to my eyes. They turn into sobs until I break down completely, no longer fighting my feelings.

"I miss you," is the last thing I say before my heart falls into that all too familiar black hole in my chest, numbing my body to prevent it from feeling the same pain my soul and heart are experiencing.

This will never get easier, will it?

Chapter 40

Valentina

"I HOPE I WILL still get to see you occasionally," Evangelin says after I tell her my big news. I give her a small hug, the comfort of it running through me in waves.

"Spending time with you and in your shop always makes me very happy. I hope you know I will come and help out as much as I can," I promise with a smile that reaches my heart.

I don't think I will ever get used to the thought of joining the Velocità Rossa Driver Academy in a week. The third race of the year will be the last one I'm attending for the foreseeable future, which makes me sadder than I'd like to admit. Then again, I've never been so excited for the next chapter of my life.

"You need to focus on your career now, belle, don't worry about *Rush* or me. We'll be fine," she assures me, her flawless French smooth in my ears.

She wipes away a tear I hadn't noticed leaving me.

"Don't be sad, Valentina. Adrian and Carlos are best friends now so we'll spend lots of time together," Evangelin says and points at her husband and my brother on the couch, talking about Adrian's performance in Bahrain.

Every time the former world champion speaks, my brother's face lights up. He's happy to have someone to look up to in his life again, a role model who acts as a father figure.

"You're right. You're always right," I reply, making her cheeks turn a wonderful pinkish color.

"Yes, I am. Now, tell me, do you know who will be training with you at the academy?" she asks, and I pull my phone out of my pocket to check.

"They sent me an e-mail this morning with the list of names. I haven't checked it yet," I explain before reading the names to her. "Oh, yes! There is another woman," I blurt out when I read "Luciana Sanchez, she/her." I smile. "The rest of the drivers are all men. Haru Satō, Pedro Angeles... No, oh God, no, no, no," I say when I read the last name on the list. "This is a fucking joke. Please, tell me this is a joke," I croak out before apologizing to Evangelin.

My vulgar language caught her off-guard, I could tell by the way her eyes went wide, but she seems more confused than anything.

"What's wrong?" I cover my face with my hands and groan into them.

"You know the prince of Monaco? The younger one, not the one next in line for the throne?" I ask, and she gives me a small nod.

"Yes, Christian Crovetto. I've heard of him." My heart beats rapidly from the image of his face as it pops into my head. "Why? Is he on the list?"

It's my turn to nod then.

"He was my rival when we were children, and he always, and I mean *always*, tried to cheat. Christian didn't like losing to 'a weak girl,'" I explain, raising my fingers to show I'm quoting his disgusting words. "I can't believe I'm going to have to train with him. I hate him. Besides his inability to lose, he's a spoiled brat, and a royal one at that," I complain and drop onto the chair in her kitchen.

Evangelin clicks her tongue before handing me a glass of water.

"Then you need to show him who the fuck you are and that you're not to be messed with," she replies, causing me to almost spit out the sip I took. This woman will never cease to amaze me.

"He's never had a chance against me anyway," I eventually tell her, earning me a proud smile from my friend.

I stare down at my phone once more, wondering why the hell I've been punished like this. Out of all the race car drivers in the world, it had to be the most arrogant one, my nemesis, the guy I despise the most in the world.

This is bullshit.

My eyes scan the list one more time just to make sure I'm not mistaken, which, unfortunately, I'm not. I shake my head before my attention drifts to the date in the corner of the e-mail. It stands out to me for some reason, and when I check Gabriel's and my chat, I realize he hasn't texted me back all day.

A light bulb goes off in my head before I jump out of the chair.

"Evangelin, I'm so sorry. I know we're supposed to have lunch, but I have to go," I tell her with a rushed tone, but she assures me it's fine.

I let Adrian know where I'm going, but Carlos isn't ready for him to leave yet, so he decides to stay. My brother throws me the keys to the car, and I run toward it.

I can't believe I forgot!

James holds my hand as Grandfather talks about the kind of man his son was. Tears stream down my face, and Adrian sits beside me, his own falling down his cheeks. I want to take his hand, but I know he needs to hold onto Dad's cap with both of his.

James' thumb rubs circles on my skin, and I try my best to listen to Grandpa. Still, my eyes drift to the coffin he had to choose to bury his only son in, and I cry even harder. My friend's arm slides across my shoulders until he can pull me close and press a kiss to the top of my head. He is only three years older than I am, but he is much taller, which is why he can easily reach it.

Adrian stands up to move to the front so he can talk about our father.

"I know all of you are expecting a beautiful speech, but I can't give you one. It's too difficult for me to do." He takes a break to wipe his eyes. "I loved my father very much. He introduced me to a life full of excitement, and I won't ever have the chance to thank him for it. But I will race for you, Dad. Val and I will both continue to race for you. We know how much it meant to you that we continue this legacy, and we will. Even in death, we will make you proud."

Adrian turns to our father's coffin, places the cap on top of it, and walks back toward where I'm sitting. He takes my hand in his, and James lets go of me so Adrian can pull me close. With both of them holding onto me, I know I'm going to be okay.

"Goodbye, Daddy," I whisper as they lift his coffin into the ground.

I'm never going to see him again. He's gone, and I barely spent any time with him. I wish he hadn't prioritized his work. I wish he would have realized what was more important: his children.

Now, he will never have the chance.

Chapter 41

Valentina

THE FLOWERS IN MY shaking hand are heavy. With slow steps, I make my way down the path that leads to Maxime Thomas' gravestone.

When I met Gabriel, Maxime was still alive and healthy. He died in an accident in his Formula One car. It flipped ten times before landing upside down, with no halo on top to protect him. I was at that race, and it was horrible. None of the drivers left the hospital and neither did I until the doctor came out and gave everyone the news no one wanted to hear. I'd never seen Gabriel break down like he did that day. Losing Maxime was like losing a sibling, a mentor, his moral compass.

When I finally reach Gabriel, he doesn't hear me, and I do my best not to scare him. I hear sobs leaving his mouth, the tears welling up in my eyes entirely out of my control. I love him too much not to feel his pain.

My hand moves to his neck, but he doesn't even flinch. All he does is look up at me with his tear-stained face. I squat down on the ground next to him and place the flowers in front of the gravestone that reads:

Maxime Arthur Thomas

Friend, Son, Formula One Driver

"I miss him so much," Gabriel says, and I wipe away his tears with the back of my hand.

"I know, baby," I reply softly, and before I can move another muscle, Gabriel pulls me into his lap and wraps his arms around my body.

Another sob escapes him, and he hugs me tighter. We sit on the ground for a while, giving Gabriel time to calm down.

"You can't ever die, chérie. I could never live in a world without you in it." I lean back, place my lips on his briefly, and then slide my hands on each side of his face.

"I'm not going anywhere. I'm sorry I didn't remember earlier." Gabriel's gaze shifts from my lips to my eyes.

"Don't apologize, and don't ever stop taking care of yourself. You're—you're—" He cuts off, and more tears fall from his eyes.

"I know," I say.

I'm not supposed to disappear, not like everyone else he's ever cared for. Seeing him like this, heartbroken and vulnerable, makes me want to take all of his pain and put it on myself.

The redness in his green-brown eyes makes my heart thump rapidly against my ribcage. It's hard for me to understand how so much pain could be focused on one person. I put my thumb on his bottom lip and the rest of my fingers on his cheek.

"I know it hurts, but you have to remember one thing: you are strong, you can do this," I tell him, and his full lips form a straight line. "You are talented and wonderful, and I am so proud of you. I am proud of the man you are, the driver you have become, the friend you've always been, the whatever-you-are-to-me you are."

We both laugh a little, and I go back to building him up.

"Having you in my life has brought me so much joy, happiness, and love. Yes, it may have brought me heartache too, but from that pain, you have taught me how to be stronger, more independent, and most importantly, you've taught me how to love someone in a messy and exciting way." His eyes fixate on my lips as I smile at him.

"Let's go," he says and stands back up on his feet.

Gabriel holds his hands out for me, and I slide both of mine into his. He helps me up, and his lips find mine before he leads me away from the one place that is strong enough to drag him down.

Gabriel and I go back to his home and spend most of the day cuddling on his bed, watching movies on his laptop. We decided to watch all the Marvel movies in chronological order, and he got snacks for us. He rubs my back and plays with my hair for most of the first film, and by the time we reach the second one, I get up and take off my jacket. Gabriel is watching me closely with love in his eyes but doesn't say anything.

During moments like these, I wish I could crawl into his mind to know everything he's thinking and feeling.

After another hour, I feel his fingers on my chin, and he lifts my head so my gaze meets his. His lips press onto mine, but this kiss feels different. It feels more honest, more meaningful than all of our other ones. It isn't rushed, and it's not suppressing any feelings between us.

"Gabriel! Aunt Nicolette and Aunt Domi are back, and they brought a surprise," Jean screams, and Gabriel groans.

I lean back from the kiss, but Gabriel guides me closer so he can capture my lips again. A giggle escapes my throat as I push away from him. It sounded like Jean was excited, which means whatever the surprise is, it has to be good.

"Go, I'll be waiting here," I say, but he frowns at me.

"No, you're coming with me, and you're going to meet my aunts," he replies, and my heart skips a beat.

I'm meeting his aunts, now, at this very moment.

I swallow hard, and Gabriel flashes me a grin, revealing his perfect dimples. It calms me in an instant.

We walk down the stairs while Gabriel laces his fingers through mine, trying to comfort me to the best of his ability. I take a deep breath, and by the time we reach the bottom of the staircase, a genuine smile is on my face.

He leads me into the kitchen, and surely enough, Domi, Nicolette, and Jean are all standing there, smiling at each other. Nicolette, a tall, beautiful woman with long, red hair, light skin, and light brown eyes walks up to us to wrap her arms around Gabriel.

"We're having a baby," the woman says in perfect French, causing a smile to break out across my face. She turns to me with a warm expression. "Valentina, it's nice to finally meet you," she says before hugging me. "I'm Nicolette." She didn't have to introduce herself since I've seen videos and pictures of her. It does, however, surprise me that she knows exactly who I am.

"It's nice to meet you too. Congratulations," I tell her.

"Thank you, beauté."

Nicolette steps away, and I look at Domi, yet another gorgeous woman. She is a bit shorter compared to her wife and her curves are to die for. Her brown, coily hair complements her brown eyes, and her pinched nose highlights her full lips. Domi introduces herself as well, and afterward, I move over to give Jean a hug.

I find out Domi is the one who is carrying their baby and that the couple has been trying to get pregnant for a year now. Finally, the artificial insemination worked and Domi got pregnant.

For the rest of the evening, I get to know Gabriel's aunts. Nicolette is Gabriel's father's sister, and she met Domi when they were sixteen years old. Eight years later, they got married, and four years after that, they started to try and have a baby. Nicolette is very open with me, she shares her stories and asks questions in return.

And as much as I'm enjoying this, getting to know the women who raised two of my favorite people, this is an intimate moment. I feel like I'm intruding, which is why I decide it's time for me to leave.

"I have to go," I whisper into Gabriel's ear, and he takes my hand to lead me from the living room, up the stairs to his bedroom. He shuts the door, and I put my hands on his chest when he comes close to me again. "What's going on?"

"Don't leave," he says.

"I think Domi and Nicolette want to spend some time alone with you and Jean," I tell him, but he frowns at me.

"Stay," he begs when I step back, and I don't have the strength to say no again.

"What will we do if I stay?" I ask, smiling a little as he leans down to press a kiss to my cheek.

"I want you to pick out a book so I can read it to you while you lie on my chest." Gabriel's dimples appear with his smile as I nod.

I make my way over to his bookshelf, studying the row of books. A few novels I've been meaning to read stand out to me, and I turn to him.

"You've read them all?" I ask, pointing at the second-hand books. Gabriel rubs the back of his neck, a shy smile playing on his face.

"I may have bought them for you," he admits before sitting up and staring at me. "I remembered you telling me about them, so I added them to my collection a few days ago," he adds, and I shake my head in disbelief, shifting my gaze back to the shelf.

"You, Gabriel Biancheri, are something else entirely," I say, and the sound of his chuckle fills the room.

"Only for you."

We get ready for bed before he pulls his shirt over my head, and I inhale the mahogany scent coming off it, *Gabriel's scent*. An unfamiliar, heartwarming smile spreads over my lips. It feels like... it feels like every piece magically falls into place.

"God, I never understood it, not until now," he mutters to himself, but I hear him anyway. He doesn't need to explain because I get it. I didn't understand it either until this second. "I want you to wear my shirts from now on," he admits with a playful yet firm expression.

"Okay, but then you gotta wear mine too," I reply, and he frowns at me.

"Please, you would feel awful when you'd see how much better I'd pull your clothes off." I swat his arm, and he chuckles.

He takes my shirt from today and slides it over his head. It fits him perfectly, and I pout when I realize how good he looks. *At least he would look stupid in my crop tops, right? Ugh, who am I kidding? He'd look gorgeous.*

"Screw you," I say, and he laughs. I join him because his laughter is contagious.

We spent the rest of the night stealing looks until my eyes close and I fall asleep in his arms, listening to his soft voice as he reads to me.

Chapter 42

Valentina

"How dare you?" Gabriel's voice echoes through the whole house, and I shoot up in bed. Panic settles in my chest, and I pull on my shorts before I run down the stairs. "Are you fucking kidding me? Are you?" When I reach the living room, I see Gabriel and Jean meters apart, yelling at each other in French.

"Come on, Gabriel, you're way too immature to see her as anything other than something to conquer. You probably want to fuck her just to be able to say you did it. You're too messed up to ever take her more seriously than that." Gabriel takes a step back. "Valentina is way too good for you, and she will realize it soon enough, hopefully before you screw her and leave her."

I don't know how they got here, to this point in their conversation, but I get more worried by the second. Gabriel's breathing is heavy, and his hands are balled into fists.

"You really shouldn't have said that," he says. I step between them and put my hands on Gabriel's naked torso, which seems hotter than it should be.

"Gabriel, stop," I say, pleading with him.

His eyes shift from his brother to me, and all anger leaves him. His hands open up, and confusion settles on his face.

"Yeah, calm down, man. Listen to your conquest," Jean says from behind me, and anger returns to Gabriel's handsome features.

"Let me handle this," I beg, and Gabriel finds my eyes again.

He looks back at his brother, groans loudly, and leaves the room. I touch my lips with my fingers, thinking about what I'm going to say to Jean. When I finally figure it out, I turn around and look at the boy I thought was better than this.

"What happened?" It's best I don't insult or yell at him. Simply talking to him is my plan for now.

"Things got out of hand, Gabriel started yelling. I screamed back, we got to a point we shouldn't have gotten to, but what can you expect? Gabriel has always had a problem controlling his emotions."

"You know what, Jean, that's enough. I know he's your brother, but my relationship with him is none of your goddamn business. What did you think would happen when you called me a conquest, huh?" I defend the man I love, and Jean rolls his eyes.

My hand darts out before it hits his shoulder, hard enough to serve as a warning but too soft to hurt him.

"You're my friend, but you're acting like a dick. Gabriel has done nothing but treat me like the queen of the world." Jean stays quiet, clearly ashamed now. "If you ever doubt his intentions again when you have no idea what's going on, remember this: it's none of your fucking concern." I leave him standing there without saying another word, too bothered by his behavior.

The summer sun hits my eyes the second I leave the house in my search for Gabriel, and I lift my arm to be able to see.

"Chérie," he says from behind me, and I spin around to face him.

A sad expression decorates his face, and I take three strides so his body can envelop mine.

"I'm sorry, he was pushing all of my buttons, and I always get so angry with him." His body tenses again, and I run my fingers over his back to calm him down. He relaxes under my touch. "I don't know why," he admits.

I place my hands on each side of his face.

"Siblings. You love them, but sometimes, you just want to punch them. That's why I count down out loud with Adrian when he pisses me off," I explain, and Gabriel chuckles.

"Maybe I should start doing that as well." He brushes his nose against mine, an exhausted sigh slipping past his lips. "You're not a conquest to me, mon tournesol. You're the person I care about most in the world, nothing less. You know that, right?" he asks, and I put my palms on each side of his neck.

"I know." His hands move onto my hips, pulling me against his chest. "But I don't know what to do," I finally admit, and he lifts his eyebrows in surprise.

"About what, chérie?"

"About us. Things are about to get very complicated with me traveling to Italy for training and you around the world for races. We're not dating, so I know I shouldn't be this scared of what being apart will do to us, but—" Gabriel cuts me off with a firm kiss.

"I'm yours, Valentina Esmèe Cèlia Romana, all yours. No matter how you want me, I belong to you and you alone. I'll fly to Italy as much as you need me to, hell, I'll move there," he says, making a little laugh escape me, but he grabs my face to make me refocus. "You know how I feel about you, and I know how you feel about me. We will make it work," he says, and a blush settles on my cheeks, heating them up.

"I'm yours," I whisper in response, and he picks me up to lift me into the air.

"No more running away?" he asks, and I shake my head.

"No more. I want this, I want us."

Gabriel kisses me all over the face, making me giggle uncontrollably. It's taken us long enough to get here, and I hope more than anything that this pessimistic feeling in my stomach will be proven wrong. I don't doubt his feelings for me or mine for him, but life has a way of finding ways to hurt us when we expect it least.

Please, don't hurt us.

Chapter 43

Gabriel

My team and I are doing our routine track walk with Adrian's team right behind us. Someone, and I wish I knew who, thought it would be a good idea to give him and his performance coach scooters. They've been battling each other for the last two kilometers, always interrupting my team when we try to talk about basics and strategies.

"Focus, would you?" I call out in French when he zooms past me for the fifth time.

"Fuck off, would you?" he yells back, and I flip him off when he turns around to roll back to his team.

He blows me a kiss, and I think about stealing the scooter from him both because he's distracting and because he makes it look like a lot of fun.

"Gabriel, watch this curb at the end of turn twelve, okay?" Tomasso, my strategist, says, pulling me out of my thoughts. I assure him I will, making a plan in my head to try out different ways to avoid it during free practice tomorrow.

"Watch out!" Adrian warns as he speeds down the straight again, this time with Leonard by his side instead of his performance coach.

Surprise settles in my chest as I watch the Brit race against my teammate on the little scooter. Leonard takes his job more seriously than any of us, never getting distracted in any way, shape, or form. This side of him, the playful one, is something only Adrian brings out. They have a special bond I wish I knew more about. Out of all the drivers, Leonard only chooses to be himself around my teammate. It tugs on my curiosity, but it's none of my business, so I don't ask.

When we get back to the pit box, Valentina is talking to one of the engineers, smiling while telling him a story. He laughs at whatever it is, bending over to let it out. No one, and I mean absolutely no one, should be as good-hearted as her. The way she speaks to everyone, managing to brighten up their days is something I've never seen before.

Then, her eyes drift to mine, her smile no longer directed at anyone other than me.

Fuck, she adores me. She's all mine.

"How was the walk?" she asks when I'm in front of her, but I capture her lips with mine before answering.

A little giggle escapes her, warming everything inside of me. My day might be long and tiring, but a single kiss from Valentina is like a shot of espresso.

"Good, except Adrian forgot how to be a grown-up for the entire duration of it," I explain loud enough for my teammate to hear.

"I'm sorry I know how to have fun. You should try it once in a while," he says and places his hands on his car to check something his engineer is pointing at.

"Riding scooters is not the kind of riding I prefer either," Val chimes in, knocking the air out of my lungs. I fucking love it when she's dirty.

"Now that sounds like fun," I reply, guiding her against my chest by placing my hands on the small of her back and applying the slightest amount of pressure.

She gives me a naughty smirk, licking her lips before speaking again. A little move like that, and my cock pushes against my tight jeans, my body begging me to find a private room with her.

"Yeah, horseback riding is my favorite," she whispers before kissing my jaw and attempting to walk away.

I manage to take her hand, spinning her around once and then bringing her against my torso again. Val is smiling from ear to ear, fully aware of the effect her words and actions have on me.

"You drive me crazy," I whisper in French and let go in case she wants to leave again, but she doesn't. She presses her hands against my stomach, biting her bottom lip.

"I know," she replies and steps back. "What are you going to do about it?" she challenges, and I'm about to throw her over my shoulder when Tomasso drags my attention away from Val. A knowing smile spreads over her face while I'm forced to focus on my job again.

By the time I'm done discussing technical things with my strategist, Valentina has fallen into conversation with Adrian and Daniel, his performance coach. I sit down on the chair in my box, taking out my sketchbook to try and capture how beautiful she looks. It's impossible, but I always have a lot of fun taking a shot at it anyway.

"I can't believe you two are dating. I should buy her a pair of glasses," Cameron says, and I shake my head with a chuckle.

"Did you just come here to insult me?" I ask, and he crosses his arms in front of his chest, staring down at my drawing. I tilt my sketchbook toward him so he can see better.

"Why else would I be here?" he teases with a smile so contagious, I can't help but return it.

"Asshole," I mumble, and he lets out a laugh. Cameron squats down in front of me, his phone in his hand as he spins it around, a nervous habit of his. "What's going on?" I ask, putting my notebook and pencil away to focus on him.

"My team found a problem with the engine. I dunno if it's fixable until Saturday," he explains, and I give him a comforting look.

"They will, don't worry. You know how hard our teams work. They're incredible and deserve a little more faith from you," I almost scold, and he looks up at me with furrowed brows.

"Valentina really did a number on you. You never used to be so positive. It's frightening," he says, and I give his knee a nudge.

"Don't be an ass," I say, helping him stay upright and laughing with him.

"An arse? Me? I'd never be one," he replies, and I give him a playful frown.

"You made me get a tattoo on my butt cheek when I was drunk! I think that counts," I defend with amusement in my voice.

"First of all, we were both drunk and, secondly, can you imagine how stupidly in love you were with Val to get so drunk because you were pining over her? And, now, you're dating her," he points out, and the corners of my mouth lift before I can stop them.

"It hasn't changed how much I care for her, only that I get to prove it to her now," I say and grab my sketchbook again, my attention shifting to Valentina. She grins at Adrian, who is obviously joking around, like always.

"Don't fuck it up, mate. There will never be anyone that can compare to Val, and, if you break her heart, I will destroy you," he says and stands up.

"I'm pretty sure Adrian should have that talk with me," I tease, but Cameron doesn't even crack a smile.

"There's nothing I wouldn't do for her, Gabriel. You're my best friend, but so is Val."

"You have full permission to destroy me if I mess things up," I say, and he gives my head a pat, shaking it from side to side.

"I hope it'll never come to that."

Neither do I.

Chapter 44

Valentina

I'm sitting in Adrian's box, praying the start will be just as good as the Qualifying. My brother got pole yesterday with Gabriel in second, Kyle Hughes in third, James in fourth, and Jonathan Kent in fifth. Eduardo, who I haven't spoken to since I ended things, is in sixth, right in front of Cameron and Leonard.

All of the drivers are lined up on the grid, waiting for the green light to take the formation lap. They need to warm up their tires to have more grip and charge their cars' batteries before the start. Meanwhile, the nervous feeling in my chest is spreading until it's everywhere, and I can't sit still anymore.

The lights go out, and Adrian gets a great start, but not as good as Gabriel, who pushes past him and moves into the first position. Kyle and Jonathan crash into each other and fall out in the first corner. Thankfully, it's not a bad crash and both drivers make it out without an injury. Their cars, however, are wrecked. I know the Grenzenlos team is probably cursing and screaming right now, but my full attention is on the small screens.

"Oh my God, everyone! Look who it is! Valentina Romana," a familiar voice says, sounding more condescending and sarcastic than anyone I've ever met.

I turn my head and almost lose my composure. I don't reply nor do I let him know how surprised I am to see him here. I keep it all inside as my mind screams at the universe for bringing this man back into my life.

"How've you been, beautiful?" Christian Crovetto asks next, making terrible shivers run down my spine.

"I was great," I start and then look him up and down, placing a disgusted expression on my face. "Now I wish I was anywhere else in the world," I go on, focusing on the screens again.

"Don't be like that. I'm very happy we get to see each other," the prince says, but I roll my eyes.

"Well, then that makes one of us." The hatred I have for this royal brat is beyond any I've ever felt.

"Come on, Tina, don't give me the cold shoulder. I've missed you," he says and takes a step toward me, still keeping enough distance so I can't "accidentally" kick him in the shin. Not that I would, considering he's a royal and I'd get arrested for touching any of his white-blonde bleached hairs.

"It's Valentina to you, Christian," I remind him because I don't like his nickname for me, I never have.

"Then it's 'Your Royal Highness' to you," he replies, and I shake my head. He's already pissing me off, and we've barely spoken three words. *How am I going to make it an entire season in one academy with him?*

"Isn't there someone else you can blind with your box-dyed hair, *Your Royal Highness*?" I ask, annoyed, and his brown eyes go wide. Amusement sparkles in them as he crosses his trained arms in front of his chest.

"There is no one better than you," he says, and I'm barely able to keep my palm from connecting with my forehead.

The rest of the fifty-six laps in the Spanish Grand Prix, the third race of the season, goes by but slowly so. Luckily, Christian leaves me alone for the most part.

Adrian and Gabriel are a couple of seconds apart now, and I watch James, who is battling with his teammate. Eduardo attempts to fight James' overtake, but my best friend's tires are younger, allowing him to move back into third place. Cameron somehow is up in fifth, and I'm hoping he will remain there.

After the longest hour and a half of my life, Gabriel wins the race, Adrian comes in second, James third, Eduardo fifth, and Cameron sixth. I walk outside with the crowd of people and wait for the three most important men in my life to drive their cars to the first, second, and third-place signs.

The first one to come is James, then Adrian, and lastly Gabriel. They all get out of their cars, and my brother walks over to where I'm standing with the rest of his crew to give all of us a hug. James moves to his team but also comes to high-five me.

Meanwhile, Gabriel is getting out of his car and pulling his helmet off. He walks over to his engineers and mechanics, giving them hugs to celebrate. When he spots me on Adrian's side, he jogs over and grabs my face to plant his lips on mine.

It's a short kiss, a sweet one, that makes my body tingle. A blush settles on my cheeks, and I put my fingers to my lips as soon as he steps back. Gabriel brings a heartwarming, happy smile to his face, and I can't help but return it. I hardly ever get to see him this joyful.

He walks away to talk to the man who is patiently waiting for him to do the post-race interview.

"Congratulations, Gabriel Biancheri," Günther Willhelm, a famous Formula One driver who has been retired for thirty years, says and pats my boyfriend's shoulder. Gabriel nods, his smile never fading. "You had good pace, a well-planned strategy, and this is your second win of the season."

"Yes, we had great pace overall this weekend, and although the tires lost grip toward the end, we made it over the finish line in one piece, and a one-two for the team, which is always a success."

They continue talking until Günther moves on to interview a disappointed Adrian. He's hiding his feelings better than I would have expected, but I see right through him, just like he would me.

My eyes drift over to Gabriel, who is now talking to James. When he catches me, he winks, and I melt. I feel like a fan in a crowd, catching the attention of a celebrity. No, I feel like I just grabbed the attention of the most handsome man I've ever met, and he winked at me, making my body react in all kinds of ways.

When the interviewer is done, all three boys whisper something to each other before they turn around to, not very subtly, blow a kiss at me. My face turns a bright red before I let out a small laugh.

My silly boys...

They move onto the podium, and, soon, my home country's anthem plays through the speakers. Then follows the Italian one with everyone from the Velocità Rossa team singing along.

A wave of jealousy temporarily takes over my body when I think about how much I want to win a Grand Prix and stand on that podium. I push all those thoughts and every jealous feeling to the back of my mind to focus on how proud I am of Gabriel, Adrian, and James.

Each one of them receives their own trophy, then they take out the champagne and start spraying it around, a routine after every race.

The celebration is over soon, and I get pulled back inside by the crowd. I'm trying to find a way out of the cheering Velocità Rossa team, but I'm struggling. Luckily, I feel a hand wrap around my wrist, and seconds later, I'm standing in front of Gabriel inside an empty room.

His mouth finds mine before I can even say a word. He tastes like champagne and happiness. All I can think about is how addicting his full lips feel as they claim mine.

When he releases me, I have to hold onto his arms for support.

"That kiss just keeps going," I say when I can't stop my head from spinning. Gabriel chuckles, so I bring my eyes to his. "Congratulations on your win," I add, and he grins at me, flashing me his stunning dimples.

"Thank you, chérie," he whispers before he presses another kiss to my lips.

"So, where are we going to celebrate?" He purses his lips, and my mind drifts.

I don't know what he has planned, but I'd much rather take the celebrations back to our hotel. We finally have time to be alone, and I want to take advantage of it, to feel his hands all over my body. To have him study me while I memorize all of him. I want to touch him, make him moan my name over and over...

"Just a bar downtown," he replies, but I give him a confused look.

"What?" I ask, not remembering my question from before.

"You asked where we are going to celebrate, and I told you a bar downtown, but if you prefer, we could also celebrate alone," he offers and presses his body against mine.

"Aren't you exhausted?" His hands drop to my ass before he grabs it, making an involuntary gasp escape me.

"Yes, but never too exhausted to make you come over and over..." He trails off and lowers his head to my neck, nuzzling it to make me giggle.

"Okay, stop, you have to shower." He steps back, his bottom lip between his teeth.

"You don't want me all hot and sweaty?" he asks, and I bite the inside of my cheek before I respond.

"Not if that sweat doesn't come from us fucking all night long." A proud smile spreads over his lips, and I can't help the one on my face.

"You're so hot," he simply replies and smacks my ass. "You're also unbelievably beautiful, do you know that?" he asks, and I click my tongue.

"Tell me something I don't know, mon amour," I reply, and he lifts my chin to grab my entire attention. His eyes sparkle at the way I just addressed him.

"It doesn't matter how many times I look at you, you'll always have my heart racing," he says and gives me a peck on the lips.

With one more kiss, he disappears from the room, probably taking a shower.

"I finally understand how you got into the academy. Your brother couldn't help you so you snatched yourself the other Velocità Rossa driver. Glad he could get you a spot," Christian says from behind me.

I have no explanation for why my entire world comes crashing down on me from the thought or why tears sting my eyes. *What if the only reason they recruited me was because of Gabriel? Or Adrian?*

Anger consumes me as I turn to Christian Crovetto. It laces hatred into my next words.

"Says the prince of Monaco, who merely had to snap his fingers to get a spot," I start and keep walking until I'm in his face. "I have worked harder than you've ever had to because society was built for *you*, for privileged white boys that treat women like incompetent, baby-making objects. Let me tell you something and listen closely now: you're nothing special. You may have a title, more money than you could possibly need, and an attitude problem, but you're nothing compared to me. I come from a family of racers, it runs in my blood. It fuels me, and I will have you choking on my fucking dust this season, *Your Highness*," I spit the last two words, but this man is smiling at me the entire time I speak.

"I'd rather have you choking on my dick, Tina," he replies, and it's my turn to smile then.

"I can't choke on something that doesn't exist." Amusement leaves his face as I take a step back. "Sexually harass me again, and I won't be the one you'll have to deal with, the FIA will be." I walk away and back into the private room Gabriel and I were in earlier.

My knees cave in until I'm on the floor, my hands shaking as they cover my mouth to keep my sobs at bay.

I'm terrified he's right, that I wasn't enough and needed both Adrian and Gabriel to get into the academy.

I hope Christian is wrong because my confidence has begun to fade, and it won't return if there's truth behind his speculations.

Chapter 45

Valentina

Time passes. I'm not sure how much, but my phone rings after a while, pulling me from my panic-filled trance. My brother's name flashes on my screen, but I hit the decline button. I don't want to speak to him. Doubts have taken over my mind, and he will drag them out of me if I talk to him.

No part of me is ready to deal with the answers to my questions, but someone steps into the room moments later.

"What happened, ma chérie?" Gabriel asks as he kneels down in front of me. He's wearing his team shirt and long black jeans now. His hair is messy yet sexy, as always.

He's too gorgeous for his own good.

"Nothing," I lie, but my eyes shift from his face, and the tears I've been suppressing threaten to roll down my cheeks. "Did you have something to do with me getting accepted into the VRDA?" I say although it's the last question I want to be asking right now. Gabriel furrows his brows, confused about where this is coming from all of a sudden.

"What do you mean?" That's not a "no."

"Did you do anything that could have tipped the scales in my favor?" I clarify, but he shakes his head.

"I didn't do anything, it was all you, mon tournesol." Relief washes over me, and I take his hand to squeeze it. "The only thing I did was tell Colin Reiner you'd make a great addition to the team, but it was during a casual conversation we were having."

My heart stops for a brief moment before I drop his hand again and lean away from him.

"You did what?" I stand up to put more distance between us.

Panic washes over his face, settling in his eyes.

"I did nothing! He was already considering you, and I merely advocated. I promise all I did was tell him how talented you are," Gabriel assures me, but pain stings my chest now.

"Oh my God, Christian was right. You helped me get a spot."

Nausea bubbles up in my throat. I raise my hands when he tries to approach me, signaling for him not to get closer.

"Christian? Christian Crovetto? You're letting the royal with a walnut-sized brain get to you?" he asks, and the laugh that escapes me is out of my control. "Come on, chérie. Telling Colin you deserve a spot doesn't change the fact that you've earned this all by yourself. Unfortunately, this sport is all about connections, and I know everyone you'll be working with because I have worked with them before."

Grandfather used to tell me the same thing.

"I tell everybody you deserve a chance, even the lady at the coffee shop yesterday. She looked at me like I was crazy," he explains, making me laugh even more.

The tears finally drop while I close the distance between us.

"Please, don't let *His Royal Disgustingness* influence you. Adrian and I had nothing to do with your success. Christian wants to believe we did because he has a tiny, misogynistic brain. It can't process the fact that a woman is better than him," Gabriel explains, and I fling my arms around his neck.

"I'm sorry for getting so upset," I mumble, leaning my head against his chest, but he steps away quickly.

"You're apologizing now?" he asks before swearing in French and grabbing my face. "You're not the one who has to apologize. *His Nothingness* has to," my boyfriend tells me, and I chuckle at his name-calling.

"You're going to come up with all sorts of names for him, aren't you?" Gabriel gives me an easy smile, revealing his dimples.

"It comes naturally with a guy like him," he replies, and I nod.

"Agreed. After I told him to choke on my dust this season he told me he'd rather have me choke on his penis." A wave of disgust makes me shudder while Gabriel's eyes fill with fury.

"He said what?!" My brother's familiar voice fills my ears, and I turn around to find him in the doorframe, anger all over his face. "Okay, I've had it. I've hated that weasel from the day he became your rival, but this just took it too far. Give me a second while I go crush him like the bug he is," Adrian says, but my words stop him dead in his tracks.

"And deny me the pleasure of doing it myself through racing? Come on now, Adrian." He hesitates but then pushes his protective big brother side away to let his best friend one take charge.

"Fine, but if he says something along those lines again, I will kick him in his royal jewels," he replies, and I grab his arm to squeeze it reassuringly.

He's never doubted my ability to handle situations like these, but, when it comes to protecting me, there is hardly a line he won't cross.

Cameron, James, Adrian, Gabriel and I decide to go to a restaurant. Leonard is the last to show, but, for some reason, he takes the empty seat beside mine. I give him a smile as he sits down, and, for the first time since I've met him, he somewhat returns it.

I can't linger on the moment too long when Cameron and my brother get into a heated discussion about who would be able to convince James to pierce his ears. I'm not sure how they even got here, but by the time dessert comes around, they finally settle on Cameron being the only one in our friendship group that can get us to do anything. Gabriel settles the debate when he tells them about his tattoo.

James almost chokes on his beer and Adrian's eyes are close to popping out of his head. I chuckle as they start bombarding him with more questions, but a soft touch on my arm shifts my attention to the owner of it.

"I know we haven't gotten along well, and that's mostly my fault, but I wanted to tell you how happy I am for you. I've been watching your career and your struggle for a while, and it's about damn time you got your shot," Leonard says, his brown eyes staring into mine.

"Thank you," I reply because I'm not quite sure what else to say. He's never been this open toward me, but I have a feeling that's the case for most people.

"But I also want to warn you. A lot of people will hate you for pursuing this dream, no matter what you do. They don't care how hard you work or about your talent. They will hate you because of who you are, and then add the fact that you are faster and stronger than most, it will make them furious. You're going to need an even thicker skin if you want to succeed," he says, and I nod, finally understanding him for the first time.

Leonard was the first black man to join a Formula One team. He's experienced discrimination and racism for the entirety of his career, and he's worried about me, a woman, joining a competitive driver academy.

"If you need anything, just know, I'm always here," he promises and takes my hand. "I make a pretty good mentor if I do say so myself." I bring a real smile to my face, my uneven heartbeat calming now.

"I couldn't ask for a better one, Leonard." He gives my hand one last squeeze before turning to my brother and starting a conversation.

My eyes drift to each of my friends, a sad feeling creeping into my chest as I think about how much I will miss traveling with them. Gabriel lifts his thumb to my face, running it over my bottom lip and leaning toward me.

"Soon, you'll travel around the world for your own races, ma chérie," he says, accurately reading why my mood has changed. "Until then, each and every one of us will do whatever we can to make you proud, especially me and that elephant-footed brother of yours." A small chuckle leaves me while he traces the shape of my mouth. "Mon tournesol," he mumbles more to himself than to me, and I lift my finger to push one of his curls out of his face.

"Mon soleil," I reply, making his face light up.

He is my sun, the one that brightens up my life and helps me grow, and I can't believe he's mine.

Chapter 46

Gabriel

JEAN HAS BEEN AVOIDING me since our fight a week ago, hiding in his room whenever I get home from work.

As the big brother and the one who can't stand it when something's wrong between us, it's my job to make things right. I go upstairs, knocking on his door and waiting for permission to come in.

"Anyone but Gabriel may enter," he calls out, and I laugh as I step into the room anyway. If he wants to be a dick, fine, but I'm going to figure out what his problem is. "I thought I was clear, jerk, get out. I don't want to talk to you," he says while I lean against the doorframe, crossing my arms in front of my chest.

"What's your problem?" I ask. I don't understand how we went from brothers to enemies.

"You're my problem. Now, leave, I have schoolwork to do," he says. I walk over to him, grab his folders, and storm out of the door.

If there's one thing that will make him spend the day with me, it's a threat to his homework. He takes it very seriously.

"Gabriel, give it back! I'm not playing around," he yells at me from his room.

"Come with me, and you'll get it back," I say, but he groans so loudly, it vibrates through the whole house. "Don't be like that. I want to show you something. You'll like it," I promise, and move to where my Velocità Rossa is.

I get in, throw his folder on the backseat, and wait for him to stop pouting. Moments pass, but, eventually, he rips my door open and drops into the passenger seat.

"If you slam the door shut, I will tie you to the back of the car and make you walk," I warn because it's the only materialistic thing besides my books that means anything to me.

"Yeah, yeah, you don't have to threaten me," he says, but we both know he would have slammed the door if I hadn't. "Where are you taking me?" he asks.

"You'll see," I reply, pulling onto the street that leads to a secret path where Jean and I used to hike to a lookout point. We haven't been here since Dad died, which is probably why he doesn't remember it until we get out of the car.

"You think taking a walk is going to fix anything between us?" he spits as I shut my door.

"Fix what? You starting a fight with me about my intentions with Val? You ignoring and avoiding me for reasons you don't care to share with me?" I ask, but he storms down the path toward the most beautiful view, besides Valentina, I've ever seen. The view of my home country.

"We're broken, Gabriel. We can't love women like Valentina in the way they deserve. That's why I got mad at you! You're living in denial, and someone had to wake you up!" he yells as soon as I approach him.

Suddenly, everything makes sense to me.

"Who is she?" I ask, sitting down on the bench near the railing at the edge. Jean turns to me, surprise on his face.

"How did you—" He cuts off, closing his eyes and shaking his head. "I met her at university. Her name is Raegan, and I like her. I really like her, but, every time I get close to her, I panic. I run the other way, terrified of my feelings. I don't want to fall in love, but I'm afraid that's out of my hands whenever I'm with her. So, I mess it up, unwilling to let her get too close, even after she admitted how deeply she cares for me," he rants, and I take a deep breath, nodding along to his words.

I pat the seat next to me, and Jean sits down, his head dropping between his arms.

"I'm scared," he says, his words muffled because his mouth is turned away from me.

"You know, I only started dating my ex a few years ago because I knew she'd never have the ability to break my heart. She was safe. Don't get me wrong, I did care about her, but I didn't love her just like she didn't love me. We were using each other as distractions."

He raises his head, listening to every word and waiting to hear exactly what he needs to right now.

"I've been in love with Valentina for a long time, but I was scared of my feelings, just like you are now. Let me tell you something important, something I wish I'd known before:

running away is useless. She'll consume you either way, but you'll hurt both of you if you try to fight it. Don't do that, don't be that stupid," I say, and he lets out a harsh laugh.

"It doesn't change the fact that we're fucked up, Gabriel! How could we ever be the kind of men they deserve? How can we put them first if we're terrified of getting hurt? I can't feel any more pain. Is love really going to stop me from putting myself first when it comes down to it?" I can't help but smile at his question.

"I think you underestimate how powerful it is."

I stare at the ocean, searching for the right words to describe my feelings.

"It can swallow you whole until all you do is breathe for her. Valentina has consumed me, and I'd do anything for her, shield her from all the bad things in the world with my life. Yes, we've been hurt a lot, and I didn't think I was good enough for her either, but I wanted to be, so I try my best every day. That's how you become the right man," I explain, and Jean covers his face with his hands, groaning against them.

"I'm scared," he repeats, so I slide my hand onto his shoulder.

"But that's what makes you feel alive. You can't hide from life, and I don't want you to. Allow yourself to be a little vulnerable, not as recklessly as me, but, still, at least a little," I say with a laugh that he returns.

"I'm sorry for being a dick to you. I guess I was struggling with all of this and let it out on you," he replies, and I get up again, stretching on the spot.

"I'm not upset with you, Jean. I'm glad we've worked everything out and get to move on from this."

He stands up too, wrapping his arms around me.

"Alright, let's go home. Domi and Nicolette wanted to have a family dinner tonight," I remind him, and we make our way back to the car, leaving our fight on the bench at our former favorite spot.

Chapter 47

Valentina

In two days, I will be on a plane to Maranello. Adrian has been preparing me mentally for what I can expect, but he's only scared me this far.

Gabriel and I haven't spent any time together since we came back from Spain a few days ago. He's been busy with training and family responsibilities, but I, annoyingly enough, miss him a lot. I asked if he had time yesterday, but Domi had already requested for him to go to an ultrasound appointment with her.

I sit up in bed, stretching and putting on Gabriel's shirt, which I should probably return. My legs are sore as I make my way down the stairs, and I have to stop halfway to laugh through the pain. Maybe I'm pushing myself too hard, but knowing I'll be training with Christian Crovetto is enough motivation to drive me past my limits.

I eventually make it to the bottom of the staircase, walking toward my kitchen, when my heart skips a beat. Gabriel is singing and dancing along to *From Angels to Devils*, his favorite band.

"What are you doing here?" I ask, a smile creeping onto my face when he spins around.

A grin that reveals his dimples dances onto his face, heating up his cheeks. I caught him off-guard, but he doesn't seem embarrassed, merely amused.

"I'm here to make you breakfast and spend the day with you," he replies. "I make the best waffles. Trust me, Jean asks me to make them at least ten times a month," he jokes, and I laugh as I make my way to the high chair at the kitchen island.

"Well, don't oversell them. You like to make something seem really good, but it often is very disappointing. You know, like *some things,*" I tease, so he cocks a brow.

"If we measure disappointment by the number of times you've fallen apart under my touch, I must be the most disappointing man on the planet." My mouth drops, and he gives me a naughty smirk. "You're not the only one who can play this game." Excitement heats up my face because I'm too turned on to hide how his words affect me.

"I'm happy you're here," I admit as he walks over to the fridge.

"There is no place I'd rather be, ma chérie."

His gaze drops from my eyes to my lips as his teeth capture his bottom one between them, making my body ache for him. His eyes drop to the shirt covering my body, a satisfied little smirk slipping onto his features before he goes back to cooking.

I watch Gabriel's muscles as they flex with every movement of his. There must be a little bit of drool dripping from my mouth because I'm fantasizing about all the different things we could do, the way his body would feel between my legs.

"Valeeentttinnnaaaa," he sings, waving his hand in front of my face.

"What?" I ask, stunned he said my name like that.

"I've been asking if you want strawberries on your waffles for the past two minutes."

"Oh," I say, a small smile creeping onto my lips. "Yes, I would love some." He grins. "Okay then."

Gabriel gets back to his waffles, and I distract myself by setting the table.

I walk over to where he is, taking a freshly washed and cut strawberry before popping it into my mouth. Gabriel watches me closely, his gaze stuck on my lips. I run my tongue over my bottom one, making a muscle in his jaw tick.

"Stop," he says, but I merely give him an innocent look.

"I'm not doing anything," I defend. He shakes his head.

"Trust me, you are doing something."

I love having the same effect on him as he has on me, especially when he points it out.

"Oh, how's Domi?" I say and reflexively smack his stomach when I realize I haven't asked about his pregnant aunt yet. It's a soft slap, but, of course, he makes a big deal out of it.

"Oh man, go get the emergency kit. I think you might have broken a rib." He bends over, breathing heavily. I frown at him, and he straightens out his back again, smiling like an idiot.

"You're so weird," I tell him, but he shrugs.

"That's who I am, and we're dating, so that also makes you weird."

I give him a confused expression, waiting for an explanation, but he doesn't give me one. All he gives me is a sexy smirk.

I forget what we were talking about almost instantly.

"Was my point so strong it made you speechless?"

"Just finish breakfast, would you?" I tease, and he laughs.

"Yes, dear," he replies as if we're some married couple.

Gabriel's waffles are as delicious as he promised them to be. They're fluffy, full of flavor, and the strawberries go well with the vanilla taste. He's sitting directly next to me at the table, which is why it's hard for me to concentrate on anything other than his face. Luckily, I can play it off, pretending I'm just listening to him talk.

I pick up the last piece of my waffle with my fingers and place it in my mouth. Syrup drips from them, catching his attention. He takes my hand in his, lifts it to his lips, and then my index finger disappears into his mouth. I press my legs together when my most sensitive area starts to tingle from his hot mouth on my skin.

A whimper escapes my throat before I can help myself. He smiles before letting go of my index finger and doing the same to my middle one. His eyes are focused on mine, studying my reaction.

"You like that?" he asks when he lowers my hand again. I nod, unable to speak or calm my body. "How about this?" he continues, his lips brushing over the back of my hand, then my arm until he can't reach further, and gets up to put his lips on my neck.

His right hand settles on my left cheek, his thumb tilting my head so he can have better access to my throat. My body is on fire.

"Let's go take a shower," I say, and he follows me without hesitation.

I lift Gabriel's shirt over my head and let it fall down to the ground. I'm about to slide down my pants when his hand covers mine and his other moves to my hip.

"Let me," he whispers into my ear.

Gabriel guides my hair to the side before he trails kisses down my neck, shoulder, and back. He tugs down my pants and underwear in one swift movement. There are shivers all over my body.

He turns on the water while I do my best to control my need to be close to him. When he gets underdressed, my eyes linger on his moon tattoo. He spins around before my eyes are satisfied, so I focus on the dates on his hip instead, admiring the simple, black ink.

A faint scar catches my attention then. It runs down the outside of his left thigh.

"How'd you get that?" I ask, so his eyes follow my finger as I trail it along the mark.

"I don't lie to you, so I won't give you the excuse story I give most people, but I'm not ready to share this with anyone. I accidentally told Adrian once, but I don't think I can do it again at the moment. Is that okay?" he asks, and I bring my attention to his face.

"Of course. I understand."

As curious as I am, I would never be upset about something like this. If he's not ready now, he might be someday, just like me. There are things he doesn't know that I'm not ready to share, like my life with Aunt Carolina...

Gabriel pulls me under the water, letting it run over our heads and pressing his lips to mine. His fingers slide over my hard nipples, making my body beg for more.

"I could spend all day in the shower with you," he admits, and I let out a small laugh as my hands run through his wet hair.

"Eventually, you'd have to go home, train, race, and all that kind of stuff," I remind him.

"But I'd come right back, and I'd stay as long as you want me to."

I think about his offer for a second. I would love for him to be here twenty-four hours a day, but I also need some time to myself, and I know he needs it too. Not to mention, there are responsibilities I have to take care of... *like helping out Evangelin in her store!* Damn, I forgot she asked for my help today.

"What is it?" Either my facial expressions give me away, or this man knows me too well.

"I told Evangelin I would help her out today. Saturday is always her busiest day of the week," I explain. Gabriel bites the inside of his cheek, clearly thinking about what to do.

Without being able to help myself, I reach out and touch his cheek. His expression softens, and his thumb brushes over my left nipple. It's so soft and intimate, my body shudders.

"We'll go, and I'll finally meet the woman I've heard so much about," he assures me, and I smile brightly at him. "But first, let's clean you up. I wouldn't want Evangelin to have to endure the smell coming off you." My mouth drops, and I swat his arm. Of course, he's laughing at his own joke, just like he always does.

"For that rude joke, no shower sex," I retaliate, and all amusement leaves him.

"Don't do that to me, chérie," he begs, but I simply shrug.

"Shouldn't have said I stink," I reply, and Gabriel lets out a short laugh. It's a punishment for both of us, but I want to make him sweat a little.

"Fine, have it your way," he mumbles and picks up my loofah. He's putting soap all over it before he turns to me and starts washing my body.

"I'm more than capable of doing that myself," I say, making him frown once more.

"You want to rob me of every pleasure, don't you? Should I close my eyes, too?" he complains before pressing them shut and reaching out to touch me, pretending he can't see anything. His hands move all over my face, and I burst into laughter.

"Fine. Wash me then."

A content grin covers his face, and I shake my head in disbelief. Gabriel picks up my shampoo before looking at my hair. He puts some in, realizes it's not enough, adds more, and then groans.

"Jesus, chérie, I think I might need the whole bottle," he says. "My hair needs a fifth of what yours needs." I laugh at his words.

Gabriel keeps applying the shampoo to my curly, thick hair, and I enjoy the head massage he gives me. His fingers are gentle, careful. He's doing his best not to get stuck on any knots in my hair. Meanwhile, I haven't found a way to stop smiling.

"An hour later, and I have finally finished washing your hair," he teases, and I roll my eyes, not keeping the grin off my face.

When he turns me around, I see he also has shampoo in his hair. I love the way it sticks out all over the place.

"What?" he asks when he notices me staring.

"You're cute," I reply, his hand reaching for his head.

"My hair is always messy, I don't see how this is different," he jokes, and I nod.

"It's not. It's always sexy." He cocks an eyebrow, his fingers snaking around my wrists to guide me against his chest.

"Are you flirting with me?" he asks, but his lips are barely a centimeter from mine, making it impossible for my brain to focus on finding words.

"Maybe," I say with a breathless chuckle.

Gabriel brushes his mouth over my cheek and jaw before letting out a muffled moan when his hard cock presses against my stomach.

"Hmmm, I see," he adds and releases my wrists, taking a step back. My body has been lit on fire and not even the water in the shower can extinguish it.

Without another word, he starts washing out the shampoo in my hair, then his. My head is still spinning, trying to catch up with what just happened and figure out why it was so hot.

I turn off the water, and Gabriel gets towels for us. He places one around his lower body, quickly dries his hair, and then wraps one around me.

"Oh man, this is going to take another hour, isn't it?"

"Yes, now, dry my hair."

"As you wish, *Lady Valentina*." I almost burst into laughter.

Gabriel does as he is told, but it only takes a few minutes until it doesn't drip as much.

He takes my hand and leads me into my room. My heart is racing in my chest, and I don't have the power to calm my body. I sit down on the edge of my bed, and Gabriel kneels down in front of me, his hands sliding onto my naked thighs.

"You're the only one I'll ever kneel for," he says, his lips brushing over my thigh. I roll my head, a satisfied moan leaving me. "I want to taste you. May I?" The words send shivers down my spine. Everything starts to tingle as excitement runs through my veins.

"We don't have a lot of time," I reply, but his burning gaze excites me more.

"I only need a minute," he assures me, and my breathing hitches. "I want you to come all over my tongue." *Fuck.*

"Please," is the only thing I manage to say. His finger rubs over my clit, and I realize he's right. It won't take him long.

Gabriel smirks, his eyes on mine as he spreads my legs. He pulls my towel off and moves between my thighs, his lips firmly claiming mine. His tongue slips into my mouth, and I let out a small moan when his index finger runs over my swollen clit again.

"I'm yours," he mumbles between kisses.

I want to say it back, but my mind is preoccupied with how good his finger feels. All my voice does is form a moaning sound.

"You're mine," he says, making his way down and placing kisses all over my upper body.

"With everything I am."

He guides my legs over his shoulders before pulling me closer to the edge of the bed in one swift movement. A gasp leaves me as anticipation continues to grow with each second. His lips brush over the inside of my thighs, tracing my stretch marks.

"So soft, so perfect," he mumbles, and I smile to myself.

Gabriel looks up at me right before he presses his lips to my most sensitive area. My eyes flutter shut and my head falls back on the bed. He starts off with a simple kiss on my clit, but then his tongue takes over. I can't hold back the noises of pleasure that continue to leave my lips.

With every sound, his movements pick up speed. His wet, hot tongue feels euphoric, but when he slips a finger inside me and creates a perfect combination of friction and pressure, I have to grab the sheets for support.

"Oh fuck, Gabriel," I moan, my hips pushing off the bed, but he presses them back down.

His lips wrap around my clit, tugging on it and making my eyes roll into the back of my head. I slide my hands into his hair, holding on tight as his mouth brings a new kind of pleasure to my entire body.

I can feel it all the way in my toes, making them curl.

His tongue slips inside of me before it swipes over my aching clit again, bringing tension to my stomach. Gabriel keeps going while I scream for him.

My orgasm blindsides me, originating in my stomach and moving to my chest where my heart pumps it through my veins. I buck my hips, trying to savor this feeling of pleasure for as long as I can while my mind drifts back to its familiar high.

Gabriel presses a kiss to my stomach before he lies down next to me. I don't even notice I'm covering my face until Gabriel removes my hand. He presses a kiss to the back of it and then places it on his naked chest, letting me feel the way his heart is racing for me.

"Didn't even need the full minute," he says, making a breathless laugh escape me.

No, he most certainly did not.

Chapter 48

Valentina

My heart rate skyrockets before we step into Evangelin's store. I need both of them to get along, and I'm afraid of how she will react when she sees Gabriel. So far, there's been something off when I talked about him, and, even though I don't know what it is, it makes me worry.

The handsome man next to me grabs my hand, clearly also nervous. As soon as I feel his fingers intertwine with mine, I relax.

"Are you okay?" The words leave my lips and catch his attention. His gorgeous face is making all kinds of worried expressions. "She's going to love you," I assure him and pull our hands to my mouth, pressing a kiss to his. "Just behave yourself," I say, but he frowns at me.

Before we can both panic and overthink things any more, I open the door to *Rush* and lead Gabriel inside. No one is at the store yet, and Evangelin is hanging clothes on the racks. When she sees us, a beautiful grin spreads over her tired face.

"It's a pleasure to meet you, Gabriel." She holds out her hand for him, and he takes it, a polite smile on his face.

"The pleasure is all mine," he says, and it warms my heart. It's riveting to hear the French words fall off his lips. Evangelin nods at him before bringing her attention to me.

"You should be getting ready to leave for Italy," she scolds, and I give her half a frown.

"I'm not leaving you alone on the busiest day of the week." She takes my hand in hers and squeezes it. "And I've brought reinforcements. Gabriel is going to help us," I assure her.

"Thank you for everything you do for me and my store. I've been trying to hire someone to help out, but I've been struggling."

The small woman in front of me is about to cry when she catches herself and starts explaining to Gabriel what he could do to be useful. Meanwhile, I set up everything by the cash register.

As soon as the first customer walks in, Evangelin moves to greet them. The person asks her for a couple articles of clothing, and I cash them out soon after. More and more people come and, within an hour, the store is full.

Every now and then, I look over at Gabriel, who is doing much better than I would have expected. He's helping mostly men, although a lot of women walk over to him, asking for his help. I'm a bit worried about what they're asking him because his face is a deep red.

Luckily, the queue decreases soon enough, and I walk over to release Gabriel from a middle-aged woman, who's clearly asking him questions he seems unsure how to answer.

"I bet your girlfriend appreciates your great fashion sense," the woman says in English, which surprises me, but also doesn't distract me from the task at hand. Her fingers lift to his arm, and she squeezes it. His eyes find my face, and I see relief wash over him.

"Yes, I do," I reply, making the woman turn around. "I would also appreciate it if you would not touch my boyfriend without his consent."

The woman drops her hand, embarrassment in her gaze. She mumbles a quick "sorry" before she moves away and toward Evangelin. I bring my focus to Gabriel, whose smile is bigger than ever before.

"Are you okay?"

"More than," he replies. "You have no idea how long I've been waiting for you to call me that." His lips find mine before I can reply. It's a short kiss, but it still makes my knees weak. "I'm going to get some coffee." I don't even have to tell him my order, he knows my favorite drink. He gives me another brief kiss before walking over to Evangelin.

The store is almost completely empty when Gabriel leaves, and I check the time. My legs are already tired from standing for the past four hours. I sit down on the chair next to the cash, and Evangelin comes up to me, her grin making me nervous. I attempt to get up so she can sit, but she pushes me down onto the chair again.

"Gabriel is very sweet," she says, and, suddenly, her grin is contagious. "I'm glad the two of you have figured everything out. He seems to make you happy."

"He does, he makes me happy," I admit, smiling to myself. I hide my face behind my hands, a blush settling on my cheeks.

"Your love story has just begun. There are going to be many more ups and downs, and you have to realize relationships take work. You can't give up after every fight, but you also can't let things pile up. Communicate and make sure you always talk about things that bother you. If you don't, you might end up getting sick of each other. Carlos and I have been at a point before where we weren't communicating, and we broke up. It took us one messy year to find our way back to each other. So, remember, communication is very important," she says, and I nod.

"Thank you. I don't know what I would do without you and your wisdom," I admit, and she blushes.

"Stop it," she says, and I laugh a little. "Are you ready to start training?" Evangelin asks next, making me feel nervous again.

"I've been ready since my grandfather took me on my first run."

Gabriel steps back through the door, a tray with three coffees in his hand. He presses a kiss to the top of my head before we all fall into a casual conversation. He asks Evangelin about Carlos and her shop. She happily tells her story, and I decide to look around the store.

I scan the racks, a dress catching my eye. It's an evening gown with the most unique pattern of flowers that stretches from the bottom all the way across the chest area in one line. The rest of it is white, highlighting the different colors of the floral pattern. It has a boat neck, and the more I study it, the fancier I realize it is.

The price tag makes my heart skip a beat. It's more expensive than any other piece of clothing I have ever bought. It goes against my nature to carry it toward Evangelin, but I push past the feeling.

"Excuse me, ma'am, I would like to purchase this dress," I say, and she frowns at me.

"Since you called me 'ma'am,' the price of it just doubled," she jokes, and I chuckle. "Just take it, dear, you've done so much for me, you deserve it." I shake my head.

"No, I don't help you because I hope to get free clothes out of this. I help you because you're my friend. Now, I'd like to pay with my credit card," I inform her, and she sighs loudly.

"Okay, four hundred euros is your total," Evangelin says, and Gabriel's eyes widen.

"Let me pay," he offers, but I shake my head.

"No," I say, making him frown.

"Chérie, this is nothing for me, but you need to save your money."

I ignore his comment, digging around in my wallet to get my card. His hand slips around my wrist, stopping my movements.

"Let me pay, please. It's a selfish request, really. I like buying you things, especially dresses I will rip off your body," he goes on, whispering the last sentence.

I stretch my lips into a thin smile, but the blush on my cheeks reveals how much I like the image he has planted in my mind. Gabriel smirks, satisfied he's on the verge of convincing me.

"No," I repeat, firmer this time.

"Fine. I won't rip it off you then," he says, and, for a brief moment, I think about letting him pay just so he will.

I shake my head and insert the card, ignoring his upset expression. Grandpa and Dad have left me money, more than enough to live on until I earn my own. I hate spending any of it on something other than a necessity, but if I don't buy it now, Gabriel will.

"You can wear the dress to the Velocità Rossa unveiling event of their new sports car. Adrian and I have to attend it next week," Gabriel says as soon as we leave the store. "Would you like to go with me? As my date?" he says, and I bite the inside of my cheek.

"I would love to. Just to clarify, does that mean you are going to pick me up, drive me there, make me feel amazing the whole night?" He chuckles but also nods. "I never went to prom or any dance," I admit, and he squeezes my hand, which has been resting in his ever since we started walking.

"Neither did I." He steps in front of me to stop me from going any further. "I will give you the full experience," he says, his hands grabbing my hips and pulling me close to him. I focus on his bottom lip, which is tucked between his teeth.

"Oh, and what is the full experience?" I ask, desperate for more information.

His eyes drift from my face, and he touches his tongue to the roof of his mouth.

"It's in Rome, so I can pick you up in Maranello and we can drive there. We will probably stay in the same room so I'll be able to take you to the event and spend the whole night trying to find a way to touch you inappropriately without anyone noticing." I smile and my head drops, but he lifts it again, forcing me to make eye contact. "Then, I will take you back to the hotel room and make love to you all night long." His eyes fixate on my lips. My whole body tingles with excitement as I imagine it. "Not being able to touch you constantly today has been driving me wild, but thank you for bringing me. I loved meeting Evangelin, she's great."

He got along with her, and they like each other. A weight lifts off my shoulders, and after today, I'm sure I was just imagining the weird expression on Evangelin's face the first time she saw him. Gabriel's grip tightens on my hips, bringing me back into the moment.

"You make me really happy," he says.

"And you me, mon soleil," I tell him, making a smile spread over his full lips, exposing his gorgeous dimples. I lift my hand to his face, my index finger touching the one on his left cheek. "I love those damn dimples of yours," I admit, a blush settling on his cheeks.

"I love the ones on your lower back," he replies, and it's my turn to blush.

I had no idea I had them, but the fact that he likes them makes me adore them, too.

"Let's go home, ma chérie." The way he says the word "home" sounds right. I don't know what it is, but I push the ridiculous feeling to the back of my mind.

It's not time for that... *yet*.

Chapter 49

Gabriel

"I fucking hate board game night. Who suggested we play Monopoly?" Adrian asks, and I cover my mouth to keep from chuckling.

"You did, dumbass," Valentina responds, and everyone at the table starts laughing. He glares at her, but it fades the longer he listens to her laughter.

Cameron stares down at his phone, a serious look on his usually happy face.

"Is it your Mom again?" I ask, and he looks up at me, placing his index finger on his mouth to remind me he doesn't want anyone, especially Val, to know.

Cameron sees himself as the only person in her life who isn't a burden, that relieves some of the pressure and tension. He doesn't want her to know his mother keeps disappearing. Not because he thinks she wouldn't understand, I don't believe anyone would assume that about Valentina. He simply hates the thought of making her worry.

His mom shows up every once in a while, but only to tell Cameron everything is his fault because he left to focus on his career. Maybe part of him believes her and that's why he doesn't tell Val; he doesn't want her to think he's as bad as her father was. In reality, he still takes care of his family as much as he can, providing them with anything and everything they could ever ask for. Since his father left to start a new life with his secretary, all the family responsibilities somehow fell onto his shoulders.

"She came home and screamed at my sister so, nothing new," he whispers while James and Leonard celebrate Adrian having to go to jail. "It's alright, don't worry, mate." I place my hand on his shoulder and give it a reassuring squeeze.

"Twice in a row? Fuck this game!" Adrian complains, and Cameron finally smiles again.

"You should just stay in there at this point," he tells my teammate, who flips him off. The Australian grins before taking the dice to roll them and going straight into jail with Adrian.

"Shut up!" Adrian says before bursting into laughter. Cameron slaps his forehead with the palm of his hand and then shakes his head.

"I'll never hear the end of it now," he replies as Valentina brings his figurine to jail.

She takes my hand in hers, guiding it onto her lap where I grab her thigh. Val clears her throat quietly, pressing her legs together as I squeeze harder. A smirk slips onto my face, and I run my thumb in circles near the inside of her thigh. She shifts in her seat, removing my fingers to grab my hand between both of hers.

"*Per favore, basta*," she says when I try to slide them up. I cock a brow and smile.

"Oh, you speak Italian now?" I challenge.

"*Solo un poco*," she replies, using her Spanish to help her out and making me smile.

"I'll teach you," I promise in English, and she grins at me.

"I should learn if I hope to drive for Velocità Rossa one day," she explains. I lean toward her to press a kiss to her lips. She tastes sweet, like the piece of watermelon she ate a moment ago.

"Yes, you should, chérie." Because one day, she will drive for them, and they adore the drivers who learn Italian for their team. It's why Adrian is taking lessons from me and the reason I studied it in school. I'll have Valentina fluent by the time she's part of the F1 team.

"Okay, this is getting ridiculous now. I'm spending all of my fucking money just to get out of jail," Adrian says, interrupting my thoughts.

Cameron is crying from laughter, and Leonard is patting my teammate's back as comfort. James, on the other hand, is watching Val closely as she throws the dice and buys yet another property. When he notices me catching his dreamy look, he shifts his gaze to the board. *God, I fucking hate him.*

My arms have been wrapped around Valentina's body for a long time now, unable to let go and watch her drive away in the taxi. I want to go with her to Maranello, support her because I know how nervous she is, but Hector put his foot down. He told me to go to

Silverstone and stop getting distracted, to put my job first. When I told Val about it, she agreed with my performance coach in a heartbeat.

"I'll miss you," I say and lean back to kiss her. My tongue slips into her mouth, and I have to hold back the sigh bubbling up in my throat when Valentina lets out a little moan. "Fuck my job," I say breathlessly, my hands moving to her ass to guide her against my chest.

"I don't want to see that!" Adrian calls out from the taxi, and I lift my fingers to the small of her back where I know *her* dimples are. She steps on her tiptoes to plant her lips on my jaw.

"We'll see each other sooner than later, you'll see," I assure both of us because we still haven't found a way to let go. "And whatever you do, please, be careful, mon tournesol. If anything happens to you, I—" I cut off because she runs her thumb over my bottom lip.

"I'm not the one racing in an F1 car this weekend," she replies, and I cock an eyebrow.

"No, but you're going to be in the same room as Christian, which is even more dangerous," I remind her, and she lets out a small laugh.

"Yes, for him." Valentina steps on her tiptoes to press one last kiss to my lips and then moves back, being the stronger one out of the two of us. "Please, be safe," she says as I dig my hands into my pockets.

"You too, chérie," I reply as she gets into the taxi and drives off into her new life.

Chapter 50

Valentina

"Would you stop that?" I hiss at Adrian when he eats his fifth cracker, making the loudest crunching noises I've ever heard. This is not the first time today I've complained about something he's doing, which is, for some reason, bothering me all the way down to my bones.

"Okay, to summarize: I can't eat, drink, or breathe in your presence anymore. I'm going to sit over there now," Adrian says and attempts to get up, but I drag him back into his seat.

We're waiting for Colin Reiner to welcome the new and returning drivers. My brother insisted on coming along when he saw how nervous I was this morning. I asked him to travel to Maranello with me, and he assured me he could stay a day before flying to Silverstone for the fourth race of the season. James and Gabriel are already there, getting ready for the weekend despite their offer to join us here too.

"I'm sorry, it's not fair of me to act like this. Thank you for being here, but can you munch on those a little more quietly?" I ask, and he shakes his head with a chuckle.

Adrian fishes around in his pocket for a moment before taking out his phone and earphones. He places one bud in my ear and the other in his, playing a list of my favorite songs to calm me. It works like a charm, and I even take the cracker he hands me.

"Hello, everyone, thank you for waiting. It's a pleasure to have you all here, ahead of this exciting new chapter of your life," Mr. Reiner says, his attention drifting to Adrian. I notice Christian didn't bother showing up at the same moment he walks through the door.

"You're late, Mr. Crovetto," Mr. Reiner scolds, but the brat simply sits down at the back of the room.

"My bad. Had this annoying blonde in my room who just wouldn't stop talking," he replies, and I shake my head. Mr. Reiner's eyes go wide, and Adrian sits up to face the prince.

"If you already find yourself annoying, how do you think we feel?" my brother asks, and everyone in the room bursts into laughter.

"That's enough, Mr. Romana, thank you. And Mr. Crovetto, if you could refrain from sharing your personal life with us, it would be greatly appreciated." The *Royal Dickhead*, a nickname I'm sure Gabriel will come up with too, leans back in his chair and balances it on two legs, smiling at the man in charge.

"What are you going to do about it?" Christian asks, challenging *Colin Reiner*.

"Me? Nothing. But they will," he replies before someone pushes the brat's chair back on all four feet. "Drivers, meet Andrea Russo. They will be your instructor." Andrea is staring at Christian, their arms now crossed in front of their chest.

"You may be a royal in Monaco, but here you are a trainee. You listen to *me* and obey my commands. Piss me off, and I'll have your royal ass kicked out of the academy before you can say the word 'sorry.' Understood?" Christian offers them a single nod, and I grin from ear to ear. "Glad to see we're on the same page then," they add and give his shoulder a squeeze. "You may call me Andrea unless you get on my nerves, then it's Boss Russo to you. I will be your instructor, coach, and, if I do this right, friend for the duration of the season."

They make their way to the front where Mr. Reiner is standing, a content expression on their young face. Andrea can't be older than mid-thirties, their hair is cut into a bob, and the brown color compliments their tanned skin and brown eyes.

"You can leave now. I'm in good hands," I say to Adrian, who keeps checking the time on his phone.

"Are you sure?" he asks, and I lean over to kiss his cheek.

"I love you. Please, be safe this weekend." He assures me he will be before walking toward the exit.

I watch him shoot a deathly glare at Christian, who even leans away out of fear. Adrian looks over his shoulder to wink at me, and I mouth a "thank you," although the biggest thank you should go to Andrea. I doubt Christian ever got put in his place as hard as he was just now.

"Training will include workouts, simulator time, mental preparation, and more I won't bore you with right now. You will be assessed every single day for the ultimate end goal: getting you a spot in your desired field." Andrea grabs a chair, settling down on it as they address us. "I'll be brutally honest with those of you hoping it will happen like this," they say and snap their fingers. "Currently, there is one open position in Formula Three. We'll have to make the hard decision in a few weeks to pick one of you. I know you don't all want to race in Formula Three. As I understand, we only have two candidates interested," Andrea says. I hold my breath.

Please, don't let it be him, please, not him. Anyone but Christian.

"Ms. Romana and Mr. Crovetto."

"Fuck," I say, louder than I intended, but only the person in front of me hears it. They turn around, and I realize it's Luciana Sanchez.

"Yeah, I get it. I wouldn't want to be up against him either," she says with a thick Spanish accent, and I let out a breathy laugh.

"I've been battling against that royal douchebag since I was a kid," I explain, and she gives me a sympathetic smile.

"Don't worry, his behavior has gotten him kicked out of three other academies. This one won't be different."

A strange feeling in my gut tells me it will be because I'm here. Christian Crovetto was put on this Earth to torture me, *why else would all of this be happening?*

"I'm Luciana, but I prefer Lucie," she says and holds out her hand for me to shake.

"Valentina but call me Val, everyone except *His Highness* does." Sensing that I was speaking about him, he waves his fingers at me. "I've never wanted to punch someone so much," I say through gritted teeth, making Lucie laugh.

"I will help you keep your distance from him."

Our attention drifts back to Andrea.

"Okay, everyone, let's go. I'd like to show you around the Velocità Rossa headquarters."

We follow behind them through hallways with photographs of former drivers. Andrea brings us to where the rows of old Velocità Rossa F1 cars are. The last time I was here, my father had taken Adrian and me. I tried to touch one of them, earning me a furious lecture from my father. He even smacked my hand away in the moment, and I remember Adrian "blowing the pain into the stars" before holding it the entire way back to our car.

I refocus on the cars, yet again fascinated by how much they have evolved. My feet bring me to the one my father drove during the year of his championship title, making a sad feeling spread through my chest.

"Your father's?" Andrea interrupts my thoughts, and I force a smile at them.

"Yes, it was," I reply and step back. My attention drifts further up the line toward Grandfather's car. "That one was my grandpa's," I say. They give my arm a comforting squeeze.

"When I was younger, I always cheered for your father. He made me realize I wanted to become a race car driver," they explain, and I nod absentmindedly.

"That makes two of us." And neither one of us had gotten any help from him.

We stroll toward the cases of trophies next, past the row of helmets and portraits of Velocità Rossa drivers. Gabriel's catches my attention, and I smile at his handsome face, the dimples causing warmth to spread through my chest.

Someone beside me makes a vomiting sound.

"The love in your eyes is revolting," he says while my gaze stays on my boyfriend.

"Revolting is exactly what I think when I look at you," I reply, and Andrea lets out a single laugh before catching themself and telling us to follow them again.

The tour continues past a room with desks where Andrea tells us we will be learning how to analyze data and come up with strategies for races. It ends at the fitness and wellness floor. There are a dozen treadmills, bench presses, weight and neck training stations.

"Alright, everyone. That's it for today. I will see you tomorrow, bright and early for training," Andrea announces while handing out the schedule for the week, and all nine of us make our way back downstairs toward the exit.

My eyes study the paper to see we will be training for a little over a week straight, from Wednesday to Thursday, and then we have off until Tuesday the week after. It's a strange schedule, but I have a feeling Gabriel is responsible for it. I have time to go with him to the car unveiling event next week, which makes this a little too convenient. The chances of Andrea making this schedule to perfectly fit my plans are slim to none. I shake my head when I realize it was definitely Gabriel who requested it to be this way.

I turn around as I walk out the door to study the red color of the building. The horse, *Champion*, will stare right down at me like a guardian angel whenever I move through the doors of the headquarters. I'd like to think it's a representation of my father and grandfather, a way for them to stay with me everywhere I go in this chapter of my life.

"Val, hold up!" Lucie calls out, and I turn around to look into her brown eyes.

"What's up?" I ask as she hooks her arm through mine.

"Do you want to have dinner tonight by any chance? Haru and I want to go out," she says, and I smile at the short man walking next to her. He has somewhat long, black hair and warm brown eyes.

"I'd love to. Meet you in the lobby at seven?"

They both nod as we walk toward the *Maranello Suite Hotel* where we're all staying.

I have a great time at dinner. Haru is one of the most caring guys I've ever met, and Lucie is hilarious. She has me laughing through most of the meal while he finds new ways to ask me about my life. I return them, trying to get to know them better.

Haru shares that he was born in Japan but has moved all over the world for his father's job. From Singapore to Australia and now Italy, he's seen almost everything there is to see. Lucie, on the other hand, was born and raised in Spain to Venezuelan parents, who have always supported her dream of becoming a NASCAR driver. Haru is training to be an IndyCar driver. They both hope the Velocità Rossa Academy will prepare them for what's to come.

By the time we're done and have paid, it's eleven o'clock. We're all exhausted and ready to get enough sleep to do well tomorrow, especially me. I need to rest so I can beat the smug smile off Christian's face. If he thinks I won't do anything and everything to get that seat, he's gravely mistaken.

I fall into bed, checking my phone one last time to see if anyone's texted me. The biggest smile spreads across my face when I read Leonard's name on my screen, asking if I have a second to talk.

"Hi, Valentina, how was your first day?" he asks as soon as he picks up my call. I smile from ear to ear at his behavior.

"Good, how are you?"

Leonard briefly tells me about his busy day before asking me all sorts of questions about how they welcomed me at the academy. He even lets me rant about stupid Christian Crovetto, listening patiently and giving me tips afterward on ways to avoid him. It's sweet, but I also know my rival. He won't stop bothering me until I do something stupid like letting it affect my performance.

We hang up just in time for Gabriel's name to flash on my screen from an incoming text message.

Gabriel: Hi, chérie. I hope you had a great first day. Can't wait to hear all about it. I'll see you in my dreams. Bonne nuit, mon tournesol. I miss you.

It shouldn't be possible for me to fall more in love with him because of one text message, yet, here I am, grinning at my damn phone screen.

Val: Bonne nuit, mon soleil. I miss you more.

I don't expect him to respond, so when my phone lights up once more, my heart does a somersault.

Gabriel: Not possible.

Yeah, it is.

Chapter 51

Gabriel

"Get off your phone and focus, mate," Adrian says, and I turn it off, bringing my attention to Lincoln Nash, one of the Klein Racing drivers this season.

It's his birthday tonight, and all of the twenty drivers were invited to dinner. The Alfa Adrenalina drivers, Robert Lin and Felix Stark, had to leave early, something I wish I could have done too. However, Adrian told me to stay put.

The Spark, Grenzenlos, Aerodinámica, Hawke, Carousel, Tempête, Zeitgeist, and us Velocità Rossa teammates all sing 'Happy Birthday' as the waiter brings out the dessert with candles for Lincoln to blow out. He's a nice guy, but I'd rather be anywhere other than at his party right now. I hardly know him nor do I want to talk to anyone. I'm tired and miss Val. Today was her first day, and I want nothing more than to listen to her tell me all about it.

Leonard and Cameron are next to me, discussing the weather forecast for this weekend. I turn to them, my interest piqued now.

"It's supposed to rain?" I ask, earning me a cock of a brow from the Brit.

"Don't you do your homework?" he asks, obviously amused. I give him a playful frown, but he's right, I should have prepared myself better.

"Yeah, Gabriel, don't you do your homework?" Cameron scolds and I let out an annoyed laugh. He might be my best friend, but he's also the biggest pain in my ass.

"Excuse me, I was trying to have a conversation with Leonard," I reply, and the Australian bends at the waist to let out a low laugh.

"I think someone's a bit tipsy," Leonard says, patting Cameron's back.

"Gabriel Biancheri! What's with the serious expression?" Eduardo interrupts as he stumbles over to where Adrian, Cameron, Leonard, and I are standing. He's also tipsy, and I'm not in the fucking mood.

"If he touches me, I'll lose it," I whisper to my teammate a second before Eduardo wraps his arm around my shoulders.

Adrian presses his lips together, trying to keep from laughing. My hands ball into fists as. We weren't close before he and Val went out, and we sure as hell aren't now.

"You should lighten up a little. You're kind of bringing the mood down," the Spaniard goes on, and I shoot Adrian a look that says "Get him off me before I break his nose."

"Alright, Eduardo, let's get some water in you. You have to sober up for tomorrow," my teammate chimes in, and I mouth a "thank you" when he pulls the Hawke driver off me.

"Remind me to never piss you off," Cameron says from next to me.

"Why?" I ask, humor now spreading over his face.

"Because when you dislike someone, they become your nemesis," he explains, making me let out a laugh that reaches my chest.

"Well, I don't hate many people, so that's fine, right?" Cameron grabs my shoulder, trying to hide his amusement.

"Let's just hope not too many other people do something to Val you don't approve of," he replies, our attention drifting to my teammate as he pushes Eduardo down in his chair.

"Stay," he commands, and the Spaniard gives him a sad look as Adrian walks away.

"That's the last time I help you. Eduardo was about to tell me his favorite sex position, and that's not an image I need in my head," Adrian says as soon as he's next to me again. Cameron and I chuckle in response, earning us a glare from the tall man. "Fuck off, you wouldn't have wanted that either! The only people who should tell me what they like in bed are the ones I have sex with," he goes on, and, as if on cue, a blonde woman turns to him, clearly having overheard his statement.

"Would it be of interest to you to know mine?" she asks, and Adrian licks his lips, offering her an easy smirk.

"Most definitely," he replies, and she takes his hand, pulling him to her table.

"Does that mean I get to leave now too?" I call after him, but he doesn't even turn to me while raising his thumb into the air. I shake my head, shifting my gaze to Cameron's and Leonard's faces. They're full of disbelief.

"How? Just, how?" Leonard asks, and I let out a small laugh.

"I don't know. Maybe it's his face. He looks a lot like Val, which means he's gorgeous and can enchant anyone," I say before almost laughing at myself. I swoon over my girl way too often.

"God, you're wrapped around her finger like no one I've ever met before," Cameron says, and I cock a challenging eyebrow.

"Is that so? How's Elijah, huh?" I ask, and his cheeks go red in an instant.

"I thought you were leaving," he says with a laugh, and I pat his back before assuring him I will.

As much as I care about him and like spending time with him, I'm done with the evening.

Chapter 52

Valentina

"You can do it, little champion, push!" Grandpa yells, and I hold my head in the same straining position, working all of the muscles in my neck. "And, relax," he says, and I let out the groan I've been holding back. "Well done!" He pats me on the shoulder while I try to catch my breath. "The new karting league champion is only improving. The other racers better watch out because you're going to triumph over all of them soon enough." I take the bottle of water he hands me and beam up at him.

"Adrian better watch out then," I tease, and my brother winks at me from the other side of the room where he is lifting weights.

He hardly speaks when we train. Grandfather mostly focuses on me, trusting Adrian to know what he's doing now that he drives in F3. It's my dream to get to where my big brother is.

Grandfather looks between us before settling down on the bench, a serious expression on his tired face.

"I need to speak to you both about something," he starts, and, by his tone, I can tell this won't be good. Adrian and I sit down on the floor in front of him. "It's been a few weeks now since your father passed away, and it's time I told you what he put into his will," he goes on, and I swallow hard when tears fill his eyes. My grandfather has never cried in front of us, ever. "He wants you to move in with your mother's sister, Carolina." My heart splits into a million pieces.

"No. I want to stay with you. I don't want to leave you," I beg, tears rolling down my cheeks. Adrian takes my hand, but his attention is on Grandpa.

"Monaco is our home. Why are you making us leave? What about my career? What about Val's?" my brother asks, and I nod as if to say 'See, you can't send us away'.

"There is nothing I can do. I tried to fight it, get custody to keep you here, but Carolina accepted. I've tried everything, my loves. I'm so sorry, but you can come to visit. Adrian, you

will travel back and forth as much as you need for races. It will work, don't worry." This doesn't make either of us feel better. "We'll see each other, I promise." I cry harder then, wrapping my arms around his neck to hold onto him, this life, for as long as I can.

"I don't want to be apart from you," I sob as he wraps his arms around me.

We're all he has left in the world and vice versa. Aunt Carolina means nothing to us. We don't know her, and I don't want to either, not if it means leaving Grandpa all alone in this big house. This isn't fair.

Haven't we lost enough?

No one is at the academy when I arrive the next morning. My fear of showing up late anywhere combined with my inability to sleep when I'm nervous woke me up very early. I tug on my yoga pants a few times and then fix the Velocità Rossa shirt they gave us in the welcome bag yesterday. It's for working out, but I'm a bit scared I'll be the only one wearing it.

"Valentina, you're early," Andrea says, their Italian accent even thicker in the mornings.

"Yes, I'm sorry. I have a habit of showing up too early in order not to be late," I explain. They smile at my tomato-red cheeks before signaling for me to go with them.

"Personally, I appreciate punctuality. Rather show up before than too late, like Mr. Crovetto," they reply and step in front of me. For some reason, I feel comfortable around Andrea. "Don't tell him I said that. I have a feeling he'll tell his father about it, and I'd still like to visit Monaco in the summer." I let out a small laugh before assuring them I will keep my lips sealed. "Come with me. I would like to show you something."

I follow with hesitation because we're walking downstairs to the cars again. Andrea leads me to my father's, pointing at something written on a faded sticker inside. *For Adrian and my little champion*. My heart sinks into my stomach.

"I saw it after you left yesterday. I thought you'd like to see it too."

"I did, thank you," I manage to croak out, but I'm trying my best to hide how deeply this both hurts and heals me. Dad wasn't the best father, but he loved us. If only he could have shown it before he passed away.

"May I?" I ask, gesturing toward the car.

"Sure, but it stays between us." I give them a small nod, my hand gliding over the metal.

The feeling brings me right back to the first time Dad took me to his garage as a child. There is nothing I'd love more than to forgive him for what he's put Adrian and me through. Yet, knowing he took us from Grandpa will prevent me from ever reaching forgiveness.

"What, so because her daddy was the driver, she gets to touch the car?"

It's too early for me to deal with Christian's horrible personality, especially because I'm vulnerable right now. I raise all of my walls and drop my hand, straightening out my back.

"Careful, Andrea," I say and point at the floor where the royal is standing. Christian's eyes follow where I'm gesturing toward as I say, "Don't slip on the slime he's leaving behind."

Andrea sucks in a sharp breath as they try not to laugh. I'm definitely enjoying that they seem to be on my side. When I walk past Christian, I pretend to lose balance a little, as if I'm the one who "slipped."

"Might have to put up a sign." The words are meant for Andrea, but my eyes are on his.

"We both know, in reality, you're actually into me, and it scares you," he replies, smirking. My body cringes from disgust.

"Not even if you were the last living, breathing *thing* in the *universe*."

"Okay, enough you two. Let's take this energy and put it into our morning run, yes?" Andrea asks, but I don't break eye contact yet.

Christian is at least a head bigger than me, which is irritating when I'm trying to be intimidating. His smile makes me want to tackle him to the ground. It says "I've gotten everything I've ever wanted, never experienced any real pain, and have no human decency."

"After you, *Tina*." *Don't kick him in the balls. Don't do it. He's a royal. You'll get arrested*. I fake a smile instead.

"I hope you trip on your horrible personality and land on your face, asshole," I reply in Spanish because it's the only other language I'm fluent in that he doesn't understand.

As planned, his smile fades. There's nothing better than wiping the arrogance off his face.

Training starts soon after everyone arrives. Haru and Lucie each give me a hug when they see me. We stay in a group of three for the run since it's untimed for today, simply to test our endurance. Andrea wants to make it a game. Whoever can go the longest gets to train in the simulator first. The rest will have to do analysis work.

Haru and Lucie keep talking as we do the same lap over and over, which is probably why they are the first two to give up and sit at the side. Christian goes at a much slower tempo, almost walking while the rest of us keep a good pace.

According to my watch, it's been almost an hour by the time only Christian and I are left. Naturally, he has to start matching my speed to stay next to me then.

"Give up, Tina. You won't win today and you won't get the seat either. You're just a little girl, nothing more," he says, but his voice is strained and reveals how exhausted he is.

"Ah, yes, the sexism, very original, Christopher," I reply, and he gives me a confused look when I use a wrong name to address him. If he can't say my real one, I won't use his either.

"Alright, you two! Sprint to me, whoever is first, wins!" Andrea says, but Christian's reaction time is slower than mine.

I get enough of a headstart to make it to our instructor long before he does. Andrea lifts their hand for me, and I high-five them.

"Nice job, Romana," they say, and I feel happiness take over.

Like the little baby he is, Christian goes to complain about it not being fair because those weren't the original instructions and rules.

"It's all about training your mind to react, Christian. You have a lot to learn from Valentina." This makes him ball his hands into fists.

"It wasn't fair!" I roll my eyes at him.

"Someone get him a bottle, for Christ's sake," Lucie chimes in, and Haru falls over from laughter.

"How sweet. You got yourself an admirer. Girls supporting girls, *woohoo*." His voice is condescending, disgusted. Christian truly is the definition of "sexist."

"Do us a favor and crack a book, Christiano, preferably one on feminism," I spit, but he walks away without saying another word.

"Well then, the rest of you, follow me. Your day has just begun," Andrea announces, making everyone but me groan.

They might be tired, but I've never felt more awake.

Chapter 53

Gabriel

It feels strange to stand with all the drivers, listening to the English anthem without seeing Valentina's nervous face somewhere in the crowd around us. I miss the stupid smile that spreads over my face when she tries to give me a reassuring one, pretending like she isn't almost peeing her pants from nervosity.

Adrian gives me a nudge in the ribs, reminding me to pay attention and be respectful after my shoulders fall. I straighten out my back and place my hands behind me, listening to the young woman in front of us sing her heart out.

"What the hell is going on with you? Where is your head?" my teammate asks as we make our way back to our cars on the grid.

I got pole yesterday, but he's in third place behind Kyle Hughes. After what happened two races ago, the Grenzenlos driver being responsible for Adrian's DNF, I can tell this will be a tense battle for second place. I hope it will give me space to create a gap.

I need this win today.

"Hello? Jesus, it's like talking to a wall," Adrian says with a slight laugh, and I force my attention to him.

"Sorry, mate, I'm just in my head." I've been distracted today, but I can't drive like this. My mind needs to be with me in the car, not with Valentina at the academy.

"Get out of it then. I don't want you to drive into me," he says and winks at me, but I don't find that funny at all.

Maxime was distracted, he was in his head that day, and it cost him his life. It's the reason why I shut everything off when I get into the car. It's also the reason why I'm so glad Val works tirelessly to always be in balance when she races. If she ever got distracted for any reason, it would put her in great danger. The thought makes me shudder. I wish she was here right now. I need a hug after going to the dark place in my mind. *Fuck, I miss her so much...*

I'm about to walk away when Adrian grabs me by the shoulders and spins me back around to him.

"Hey, I miss her too. It's okay to," he assures me, and I sigh.

"It's annoying how you always see through me," I say because Adrian has this way of sensing whatever is wrong, even though I hardly ever share intimate details about my life with him.

"Well, it annoys me how in love you are with my sister, but here we are," he says, and I raise both my eyebrows.

"What, why?" Adrian drops his hands from my shoulders to cross his arms in front of his chest.

"You're my teammate, Gabriel, but you're also my biggest rival. The fact that my sister and you are dating isn't exactly ideal." It isn't ideal for either of us, but this wasn't a choice I made deliberately to mess with his head, or mine for that matter. If anything, it's Val's fault for being so damn perfect for me.

"I know, but whether or not I'm dating her doesn't influence the inevitable. I'm going to win the championship this year," I say with a smile, which he returns.

"At least you'll have Val's shoulder to cry on when I wipe the floor with you," he replies, and we shake hands, both of us chuckling. "Fair race," he says, and I give him a slight nod.

"Always."

We're the last ones to get into our cars. Hector hands me my helmet before making sure I have everything I need. My team works to get the car ready for the race, running last-minute diagnostics and checking the tires. I try to get comfortable in the car and force myself into my zone, ready for battle when it comes to it.

Soon, we're given the green light to take our formation lap, and I do my best to calm my nerves. This is my job, I'm used to them, but that doesn't mean I don't get nervous. If I would be able to turn that part off, I'd start questioning my sanity.

"Okay, Gabriel, remember: strategy A. Strategy A," my strategist's voice fills my ears, and I take another deep breath.

Strategy A means staying ahead, creating a gap, and playing off what the others are doing when it comes to pitstops. The last thing we need is an undercut if Grenzenlos pits earlier than us.

"Are we expecting rain?" I ask when the clouds above me turn a dark shade of grey.

"Negative. No rain on our radar," Tomasso assures me as I drive back to my place on the grid.

Adrian is behind me while Kyle moves next to me, staying slightly back. I watch the lights, taking a long, deep breath and letting it out as they go on. Then, they turn off, and I slam my foot on the gas, pressing the right buttons at the same time.

I manage to stay ahead, but Adrian is in second place already, fighting me for first. I have no idea how he managed to start this well, but I can't linger on it. I have to focus on keeping my place, which is exactly what I do.

Chapter 54

Valentina

The past week has been the most exhausting one, physically and mentally, I have ever experienced. Christian and I bickering has drained me emotionally too, and I'm ready for Gabriel to come and pick me up today.

We've spoken every day, especially on Sunday after he won the fourth race of the season. He's been strong in these few Grands Prix, proving he deserves the Velocità Rossa seat more than anyone else but Adrian, who came in second place. James had an engine failure toward the end, and I spent a good ten minutes reminding him he did everything right and the next race will be better.

Being away from home and everyone I care about makes me homesick. As happy as I am to have been given this opportunity and found new friends, I miss how things were. I miss my brother's humor, James' warmth, and Gabriel's love. They try their best to give me as much of it as they can through the phone, but it'll never compare. That's why I'm more than giddy to pack my luggage and rush outside to wait for the man I love.

To my surprise, he's already here, leaning against a bright red Velocità Rossa he must have been given by the team. I drop everything and run toward him, joy spreading through me. Gabriel catches me with ease, holding me as close to him as humanly possible.

"Ma chérie," he says softly, letting me hear how much he's missed me. I pull back, my palms moving to his cheeks. He smiles, revealing his dimples, which I trace with my thumbs. "Hi," Gabriel adds, but I don't respond. I press my lips to his, needing to feel his kiss after over a week of being apart. His tongue slips into my mouth, making me moan from happiness and pleasure. He moves on to my cheek, jaw, then neck, where he nuzzles his face and inhales.

"I've missed you," he says against my sensitive skin. *I'm finally home.*

"Oh yeah? What did you miss?" I tease, and he steps back.

"You. Your face. Your scent. Your body..." Gabriel trails off and grabs my hips to guide me against his chest. His green-brown eyes stare into mine as his fingers slip onto my ass. "Next time, I'll find a way for us not to be apart for this long. I don't like it." A chuckle vibrates off my chest, my hands sliding under his shirt to feel his muscles.

"Neither do I." I lean my forehead against his, my heart slowly calming from the excitement of being in his arms.

"Let's go, we have a long way ahead of us," he reminds me before kissing me one last time and opening my car door.

Gabriel and I talk a lot for the first hour of the drive, trying to catch up on what we've missed in each other's lives. Even though we spoke every day, there are little things we want to share. Eventually, silence fills the car, so he connects my phone through Bluetooth, telling me to play whatever I want. I shuffle random songs from my liked playlist before turning my head to look at him. The bandana he put on is keeping his hair in place, his curls draping over the red fabric. I can't help myself as I lift my phone to take a picture of him and set it as my lock screen. He looks so beautiful, and I love how happy he is.

We arrive at a traffic light, and Grabriel hits the brakes a little too hard, the notebook he carries around with him everywhere falling into my foot space. It opened, a sketch of me standing in the Velocità Rossa box, looking at the screens, drawn on the page. Before I look further, I close the book so I can place it back in the cupholder where it was before.

"You can look through it. It's mostly you anyway," he says, and my mouth drops.

"But isn't this like your diary?" He smiles, his eyes never shifting from the road.

"I'm not ashamed to show you what is going on inside my head."

My fingers run over the black, rough cover of the notebook, and I smile before I even reopen it. On the first page is a drawing of his Formula One car, and I scan it, admiring the detailed sketch. The next page has a wolf on it, which I know is his favorite animal.

The following ten pages are drawings of me either sleeping at the airport, doing yoga, lying on the beach, smiling, crying, laughing, or every other emotion I have ever shown him. Each drawing is so damn beautiful, and all of them have one interesting thing in common: I'm wearing a necklace with an F1 car and the number seven on it... *his number.*

I'm pretty sure I've forgotten how to breathe because, eventually, I silently gasp for air. I reach for Gabriel's hand and take it in mine, squeezing it. He lifts our intertwined hands to press a kiss to the back of mine while I skip through the empty pages and find another drawing on the last one. I don't recognize the woman in it.

"What's wrong, ma chérie?" he asks, but I'm too stuck on studying her features to respond.

She has straight, long, red hair and green eyes, the only two features in color, along with full lips and, unlike mine, a slim face.

"Valentina," he says. "Talk to me." I don't say anything to him. He pulls over on the side of the road, and I turn my head as soon as he parks. "What did I do?" His eyes are pleading with me now, and I swallow hard. I show him the page of his notebook that has my throat dry.

"Who is she?"

The answer terrifies me. There are no other girls in this book, only me, and all of a sudden I notice this woman, more beautiful than any other I've ever seen.

"Her name is Harlow. We slept together a few months ago after you went on your date with Eduardo," he explains while I nod along to his words. "It was a one-time thing, chérie, a distraction. I have no intention of ever seeing her again," he explains, his hand reaching out to touch my cheek. I let him, even though there is something about this that still bothers me.

"Why did you draw her if she was just a one-time thing, a distraction?" My voice is filled with pain, and he flinches when he hears it.

"Chérie, I can explain," he starts, but hearing those words makes me realize I don't want to hear what he has to say right now.

"Don't, I just need a minute." Without a doubt, I'm being irrational. I should be listening to him, and I shouldn't be reacting like this.

"But I can—"

"Don't, just please, don't," I interrupt him and turn my head so I don't have to look at his defeated expression.

"I'm yours, baby, you have me, one hundred percent. I'll explain when you're ready, but I don't want you to question that, ever," he says, and I close my eyes in response.

He starts the car again and drives to the hotel. He checks us into our hotel room while I try to understand his desire to draw someone he slept with and then keep it after.

We take the elevator to an antiquely decorated room. The colors on the walls are light pink and cream, and the couch in front of the television matches it. The bed is huge, and I wish my thoughts would move in the right direction.

Gabriel puts his bag on the chair on the far side of the bedroom. I sit on the couch and don't talk to him for quite some time. When he settles down opposite me, I can't control my feelings anymore. I've been quiet, thinking about what it could possibly mean for long enough.

"Why did you draw her?" I ask, and his eyes drop to the floor. "You slept with her, you drew her, and you kept the drawing? Why?"

"I drew her because I hoped it'd take my mind off you. I tried everything and it was just another way for me to deal with the fact that I'm never going to be good enough for you. You went on a date with Eduardo, and I was hurt." This only irritates me more.

"So, it's my fault?" I ask with a raised voice and stand up. He gets up too.

"No, fuck no, that's not what I'm trying to say, I'm trying to explain!" he says, his hands lifting to point at absolutely nothing in front of him.

"If she's still in there, maybe you do have some sort of feelings for her!" I don't know why I'm yelling, but it frustrates him.

"*Pour l'amour de Dieu, Valentina, je suis amoureux de toi!*" he says, his voice raised as he tells me he's in love with me for the first time. "I tried to get you out of my head by sketching her, but you can see I wasn't into it by looking at it. The drawing is horrible, it's ugly, it's nothing compared to the ones of you. I forgot it's even there, that is how meaningless it was." He's out of breath, and I tug on the hem of my shirt. "I know how much this must be bothering you, trust me. I am so sorry she is still in there, but you know what?"

He takes the notebook into his hands, goes to the page of *her*, and rips it out before he tears it apart and throws the shreds all over the room.

"I love *you*, I need *you*, I want *you*." Gabriel walks over to me, puts his hands on my hips, and shakes them while he is talking.

"I don't want you to draw other girls you slept with," I mumble. He puts his forehead against mine.

"I never will again. I don't enjoy drawing anyone else," he admits and chuckles, relief settling over both of us. "I want to draw you, all of you."

I pull back so I can look at his handsome features. My hands cup his face, the stubble of his beard rough against my soft skin, and teasingly press my lips to his. He groans in response, making me grin. I lean away, leaving us both wanting more, then remove my clothes, pull my hair out of my ponytail, and lie down on the bed.

"You want all of me?" I ask, and he nods. He seems to be in a trance as he looks my naked body up and down. "Then draw all of me," I say, but he shakes his head.

"Not here. I want a big canvas for you."

"Well, I'm naked, so either draw me or fuck me," I offer, and he rips his shirt over his head before he moves between my legs, claiming my lips.

His tongue slides into my mouth, and I moan into his. He lets his hands roam my body and swiftly runs his fingers over my clit, playing with it. My hips push off the bed so I can press my sensitive area against his finger.

"I love you so much," I blurt out, and his movements come to an abrupt stop as he leans back to look into my eyes.

"Say it again," he begs, both of us smiling like we just won the lottery.

"I love you, Gabriel Matteo Biancheri, with my entire heart and soul." He attacks my face with kisses, and I giggle underneath him.

"I love you," he repeats over and over again, his lips eventually capturing mine again. I'm sighing against them when he pulls back with wide eyes. "Shit, we have to go in twenty minutes," he says, lifting me up and off the bed.

He leads us to the shower, but I assure him I already took one this morning. He barely acknowledges my response before jumping in by himself.

"Fuck," he repeats every once in a while as he washes, and I can't help but laugh.

He's done within minutes, rushing past me and toward his suitcase. I finish my makeup in record time. It's simple, mostly brown tones that highlight my unique eyes. The dress I bought from Evangelin fits my body snuggly, showing off my curves. The white high heels match the dress with the flower pattern well.

When Gabriel notices me, his eyes fixate on my face, then my body.

"You look..." He doesn't finish the sentence, simply walks over to where I am and puts his hands on my hips, his favorite way to drag my body against his. "Let's ditch the event. I can think of a thousand better things to do." I laugh a little as he presses his lips to mine, stopping my laughter.

"Let's go."

Chapter 55

Valentina

My knees are shaking as I sit next to Gabriel in the rental car. He's driving us to the unveiling event, and I can't help the nervous feeling in my stomach. We're going to be seen and photographed together, and everyone is going to make a big deal of it. I'm his teammate's sister. Drama is going to encircle us, and there will be no way of stopping it.

My thoughts are spiraling. The only thing bringing me back to reality is Gabriel's hand as it wraps around mine. When he gives it a gentle squeeze, I finally let out the breath I've been holding. Gabriel knows I'm terrified, but he doesn't point it out. All he does is comfort me.

I focus on how handsome he looks in his tuxedo and forget all about the rest of the world. He always looks mouth-watering—I've never seen him dressed in something that didn't highlight how sexy he is—but he looks especially attractive in this outfit.

It would be so easy to rip his tuxedo off him, crawl across the middle console, and ride him right here in the car.

I catch myself, smile, and turn my head in the other direction. If I keep staring at him, I might actually go through with it.

Gabriel and I arrive at the event minutes later. We take a deep breath at the same time before laughing. He leads me to a carpet surrounded by paparazzi, and, as soon as we step onto it, clicking noises from the cameras and screaming photographers fill my ears, blinding us with their flashes.

My boyfriend brings me to the middle of the carpet and snakes his arm around my waist, clearly used to all of this attention. I try my best to give them the most beautiful smile I can muster, but the one that follows after Gabriel presses his lips to my temple is the most genuine one I could ever bring to my face.

"You're doing amazing," he encourages, squeezing my side.

I look up at him and he stares down at me until we're grinning at each other. The rest of the world vanishes for a moment as I get lost in his eyes.

As we walk away, Gabriel whispers sweet things into my ear. I bite my bottom lip and turn my head, and he kisses it without hesitation. People are screaming at us, but I can't understand a single thing. I'm too overwhelmed by the lights, the cameras, and the handsome man next to me to understand anything. We finish strolling down the carpet, and when we're finally out of sight, I relax my face.

"God, my cheeks are burning. I don't think I've ever had to smile that much," I tell Gabriel, and he laughs before leaning down to press a longer kiss to my lips.

He's especially affectionate tonight, and I'm enjoying every second. He pulls back but presses another quick kiss to my cheek before we walk into the large hall. A server, probably Gabriel's age, leads us to our table. Once we're sat, Gabriel leans to the side and puts his hand in mine. I set my other one on top of our intertwined fingers and rest them in my lap. His other hand lifts to trace my lips for a moment while he tells me he's driving the car onto the stage later, one of the highest honors at events like these.

"Hello, hello, hello." I don't even have to turn around to know that voice belongs to Adrian. I get up to greet him while James walks up behind him, making me press my lips together to keep from laughing.

"Hi, love," he says and kisses my cheek.

His dark blue suit brings out his eyes while Adrian is dressed in all black to make his green-blue-brown ones stand out.

"Couldn't find anyone besides James who wanted to be your date, huh?" I ask my brother, and he chuckles as he sits down.

"I needed a hot date, and he offered. How could I have turned him down?" Adrian replies, and I laugh. His expression turns serious then. "I mean it. I'm asking you how so I don't have to take him next time," he teases, earning him a slap to the arm from James.

"I dressed up for you in this uncomfortable suit, and this is how you thank me?" Adrian gives him an evil smile, but our best friend returns it. "You know what? I'm going to cock-block you all night for that comment." Adrian leans toward him and glares.

"You. Wouldn't. Dare." My brother hisses every word, but James gives him a wicked grin.

Gabriel covers his mouth with his fist as he places his elbow on the table to lean forward. He's trying his best to stay quiet but squeezes my hand to let me know how difficult it is.

The waitress from before returns a while after my brother and best friend stopped arguing, and her attention instantly drifts to Adrian. Her hand moves onto his shoulder as she asks him what he'd like to drink. Naturally, James answers before my brother even has the chance to swallow the big gulp of water he just took.

"He will have a glass of warm milk and a bib, you know, in case he has another spit-up accident," James says, whispering the last half of the sentence. Adrian spits out some of his water from surprise, and our best friend goes to clean it from his face. "See, it's already happening. Please, hurry," he says, so the waitress leaves without hesitation.

"You know, the more women you turn off me, the more desirable you'll start looking," he warns, and James shakes his head.

"Fine, I'll stop," he replies and lifts his arms in surrender.

Mindy, our waitress, returns with a few napkins for Adrian before stepping next to him and offering a flirtatious smile.

"May I clean you up, Mr. Romana?" she asks, and he smirks at her.

"Only if I get to buy you a drink after tonight's event," he says, and she starts wiping away imaginary droplets of water from his shirt and thighs.

She drops her number into his lap before disappearing again. Meanwhile, Gabriel is shaking his head and drawing a sunflower onto the napkin before handing it to me with a kiss. He finds all of this amusing, but James has steam coming out of his ears.

"It's not fucking fair. You make a fool of yourself and get a date! How does that even work?" James complains, but my brother merely shrugs.

"With a face like mine, I could be sitting here in a tinfoil suit and still manage to make everyone fall in love with me," he replies, and I smack my forehead with the palm of my hand.

Luckily, the event starts soon after. Giuseppe Camilleri, the current CEO of Velocità Rossa, approaches the microphone and gives a long speech, welcoming everyone and giving an introduction speech.

Gabriel kisses me when he has to leave to drive the car, and I smile the whole time he's on stage.

He switches between English and Italian, and I don't ever want him to stop talking. It's either his accent or the fact he's speaking Italian that makes my body crazy in all of the best ways.

Adrian joins Gabriel on the stage while I'm sitting with James, watching two of the most important people in my life stand up there, talking about their careers and achievements. I'm so proud of them.

When they finally finish, they walk back to our table. Gabriel kisses the top of my head before he sits down next to me and places his hand back where it belongs.

The rest of the evening goes by painfully slowly, but I enjoy spending time with my three favorite guys and getting to know the people Adrian and Gabriel work with. My boyfriend eventually starts playing with my curly hair, twisting it around his index finger.

"Let's go, ma chérie?" Gabriel says and brings me back to reality.

"I thought you'd never ask," I respond with a naughty smirk.

We say goodbye to the people I've been introduced to, Adrian, and James before Gabriel leads me back to our car.

"Tired?" he asks me when we're almost back at the hotel.

"Not even in the slightest," I admit.

My body has been waiting for us to get back since we left six hours ago. My mind has been running wild, and those thoughts are only strengthened when his eyes trail over me.

"Me neither," he says, his voice low and raspy.

His hand moves to my leg and his index finger starts tracing circles. Shivers run down my spine, but I stop his hand when it moves up and toward my ache. I need his fingers to be as far away from there as possible, otherwise, we won't make it back to the hotel room before I rip his suit off.

CHAPTER 56

Valentina

GABRIEL'S HAND IS WRAPPED around mine as I lead him through our hotel room door. We stop in front of the bed before he spins me around in his arms. My heart races in anticipation, unable to calm itself as his fingers move to my sides and glide toward my breasts. I guide his head to me, pressing my lips to his and stepping out of my heels.

"You taste so sweet," he says before slamming his mouth back onto mine to get another taste. A moan vibrates off him and through me, exciting every cell in my body.

Gabriel drops onto the bed, dragging me with him until I straddle his lap. I massage his tongue with mine until I feel his cock pressing against my aching clit. My hips rock back and forth, desperate for friction to ease the unbearable tension.

"Oh God," I moan as pleasure rolls through me, and Gabriel smirks.

"You certainly make me feel like one, ma chérie," he replies before flipping us over so I'm on my back.

Gabriel stands up again, removing his blazer before unbuttoning his shirt. His muscular torso makes my mouth water as my fingertips reach out to run over his abs. He lowers himself down on me, his fingers wrapping around the fabric of my dress, pulling it over my head in one swift movement. Everywhere his touch grazes my skin, shivers appear.

Once the dress is completely off, Gabriel places a soft kiss on my neck and fire ignites all around the area. My underwear is the only thing covering me now, but it's still too much, especially when he cups my breasts.

"Take it off," I demand, rolling my head when he pinches my hard nipples through the fabric. Gabriel's touch is soft as he unclasps my bra, tossing it to the side.

"You are my definition of perfection," he says as he brings his lips to my neck, merely brushing the skin there on his way to my left nipple. His teeth capture it before his hot mouth tugs on it.

"Fuck," I breathe. The combination of his hand squeezing my tit and his lips sucking the sensitive skin makes my eyes roll into the back of my head. "Please," I beg, but I'm unsure what for. *For him to undress? Undress me? Release me from this intolerable build-up?*

"I know, baby, lie back," he says, sensing I need all of the above as he slides down his pants, keeping his boxers on for now. He removes my panties and slides between my legs again.

A low moan leaves my throat when he sucks on my right nipple, and I let my head fall backward onto the mattress. Our bodies feel close but the stupid fabric of his underwear is in the way. My hands reach for the waistband of his boxers, and I tease him by running my index finger along the line of hair that leads from his naval to his cock. I need him to feel the same amount of aching, the same shivers that run down my spine.

Gabriel pulls away with a groan, and even though I know he's only doing it to remove his underwear, I want to complain. The loss of his touch drives me crazy, and I almost sigh when his mouth moves back onto my skin. He pins me down on the bed and slips his tongue into my mouth until I moan.

"Put on a condom," I say, breathless and impatient.

Gabriel leans away from me again, almost breaking skin contact entirely when his hands leave my body. The only parts of him touching me are his legs. I look at him to see what he's doing and find him staring at my body, his eyes shifting up and down. His dick makes me ache even more, but I'm worried about his serious expression.

"What's wrong?" I ask him, his gaze drifting to mine.

"Are you sure you're ready? I don't want you to feel pressured," he admits, his voice low and quiet, and I sit up in bed.

"I've been ready for a while. Don't make me wait any longer," I reply, taking his hand in mine. "You mean more to me than I'll ever understand, and having sex with you is going to be a whole new experience, one I've craved for a long time. I've never wanted this as much as I do with you." His heart jumps into his eyes at my words.

"I love you," he says and kisses me softly.

He moves off the bed to get a condom from his pants, handing it to me a second later and watching as I rip open the small package. Gabriel's cock is a lot bigger than anyone I've ever been with, which adds to both my nervousness and excitement.

I carefully slide the condom down his length, making him suck in a sharp breath as my fingers roam over his erection. I lean back once I'm done and satisfied with my work, looking at Gabriel, who is watching me. The smile on my face seems to be contagious because he returns it.

His hands slide back onto my breasts, squeezing them before he pinches my nipples again. My back arches to get closer to him, desperation seeping out of me in the form of a whimper. One of his fingers trails all the way down to my clit, running over the swollen area while a satisfied smirk settles on his lips.

"I'm yours, mon tournesol," he says, aligning his cock with my dripping entrance.

"And I'm yours, mon soleil," I reply as he places his hands on my angled legs, one of them sliding onto my lower abdomen.

"You are so, so beautiful, baby," he says before he slowly slips inside of me, causing an uncontrollable gasp to escape both of us.

Having him this close to me is the sweetest feeling, and I never want it to end. Gabriel seems to feel the same way because, for a brief moment, he doesn't move. I pull his head down and place a kiss on his lips as we lock eyes. My hips lift slightly to animate him to do the same, and he complies with a little smile.

Every movement feels better than the one before, and I want more, no, *need* more of him. His scent, the skin contact, and his kisses threaten to overwhelm me, but my moans allow me to relieve some of the build-up. My chest is on fire and every time he touches me, the feeling intensifies. I feel whole in a completely new way, in an addictive way.

My brain can't form a coherent thought anymore, but I don't mind. His thrusts are deep then shallow, hard then soft, fast and slow. The switches have my head spinning and my body consumed with pleasure. I'm a moaning mess underneath him as our movements harmonize and my nails dig into his arms. Whenever he speeds up, my body naturally adjusts to his rhythm as if we're two pieces of the same machine.

"You feel so good, chérie, so fucking good," he whispers into my ear before he nibbles on my lobe. He pushes my legs further apart, going deeper than before.

"Shit," I breathe because Gabriel has me feeling a type of way I've never experienced. I've had sex, but it never felt like this. Nothing has ever felt this fulfilling.

The friction between us loads me with energy as he manages to push against the perfect spot inside of me with almost every thrust. The tension in my stomach escalates, and I hold onto his arms for support. I wrap my legs around his hips, letting him go deeper and faster. His mouth moves back onto my nipples, his pumps never losing pace. The build-up brings me closer and closer to my release, which I know Gabriel senses when he presses down on my stomach again, going even faster.

"Gabriel," I scream and arch my back off the bed as the orgasm finally takes over my body, making it tremble.

My nails dig into his biceps as my breasts press against his torso. Gabriel continues his movements until he spills into the condom, his legs shaking and his arms barely holding him up, moaning so loudly, the sound fills the entire room. He stays on top of me for a bit longer while I run my hands through his messy, curly hair.

"I love you," I tell him, and he pushes off the bed again to kiss me.

"I love you so much." I smile at him as he pulls out of me. It feels weird, like part of me is missing now that he's gone, but I push the feeling away, too busy bringing his mouth back onto mine.

A couple hours and a few condoms later, we're both sweating and smiling. Gabriel leads me to the bathroom, kissing my shoulder and neck before walking over to the bathtub. He turns on the water while I find a bottle called "bubble bath" next to the sink.

Gabriel pulls me toward the bathtub, helping me in so the warm water can envelop my tired muscles. I'm between his legs then, my back pressing against his front.

"Have you ever thought about marriage and children?" Gabriel asks after a while of silence, and my heart skips a beat. He kisses my cheek as his fingers run over my stomach.

"I've been so busy fighting for my dream and dealing with life's curveballs, I haven't had a moment to think about marriage," I admit and feel him nod behind me. My eyes meet his as I turn my head. "But every moment with you allows me to breathe, to take a break from all of the pressure I constantly put on myself." I stop, grinning at a realization floating into my head. "You are my pitstop," I say, and he smiles.

"A moment of pause in the otherwise exhausting battle we call life where we get to recharge?" he asks, and I nod because it perfectly describes what I meant. "You are my pitstop too, chérie."

His lips brush over mine, and I realize something that scares me all the way down to my bones. I can't imagine getting married to anyone but him. When I picture my future, it's us, and that terrifies me.

"Have you thought about marriage?" I ask, too curious if he feels the same way I do.

"Every day that I see you or speak to you," he replies, and I sink further into his arms. "I'd love to marry and start a family with you in the future, I have for a while, and if that is what you want, too, I'd be a very happy man," Gabriel says, and I close my eyes in response.

"How can you be so sure this is what you want?" His touch moves to my lower stomach, his hands running over my stretch marks there.

"Because in my short twenty-one, almost two, years, I've gone through hell seven different times. I barely have any family left, and you know what makes me hopeful? My career does, it makes me so damn happy I get to live my dream. The fact that one day I am going to be holding the championship trophy and I am going to make everyone proud does. But you know what else?" he asks, tilting my head to the side again to look into my eyes. "You, ma chérie, you make me beyond happy. So, yes, we're still young, but I have known what I've wanted for a long time." A tear drops down my cheek as he smiles at me. "We've got time, there is no rush. Maybe you'll change your mind about me, maybe something will fall into our path and separate us. There is no knowing what the future holds, but I am dying to find out with you."

"So am I."

I lean my head back and against his shoulder, savoring every easy breath I get to take in his presence.

"Oh man, do you know what I just realized? I'd be marrying the weirdest guy on planet Earth. You know, considering how cheesy you are and the fact that you laugh at your own jokes. Not to mention, you always lose at least one sock when you do laundry," I say, but he starts tickling me for being mean.

I giggle and scream, begging to be released.

"Okay, but who doesn't?" he asks and laughs out loud. "I'd be Mr. I'm-a-little-too-competitive, so we're even," he teases. I cock a brow.

"You love how competitive I am!" I defend, and he chuckles against my back.

"And you love it when I laugh at my own jokes because you always join me," he points out. I can't contain my laughter anymore.

"Yeah, you're right. We're perfectly flawed for one another," I reply, and he kisses my cheek.

"For one another only."

Chapter 57

Valentina

"Chérie, wake up," Gabriel whispers, the pad of his thumb running over my cheek.

I smile, enjoying the way the electricity courses through my body from where his skin grazes mine. The mahogany scent coming off him almost makes me sigh. It doesn't matter how many times he touches me or how many times we kiss, it always affects me in the same way.

Even though I'm awake, I pretend to be asleep so I can hear him say my pet name again and feel his finger on my face for a little longer.

"I know you're awake," he says, so I bite the inside of my cheek to keep from laughing. "Are you going to make me kiss you?" he asks, and before I can help myself, I nod. "I knew you were awake." I open my eyes and giggle, pulling his head down so I can press my lips against his. I taste the mint from his toothpaste when his tongue slides into my mouth, making me moan.

"Good morning." My voice is raspy and hardly audible. He chuckles, his hand moving from my face to my arm to my hip. "What time is it?" A yawn escapes me, but I cover my mouth, lifting my arms to stretch a moment later.

"Six-thirty," he replies. I shove his arm away, an annoyed expression settling on my face.

"Why the hell are you waking me up at six-thirty in the morning?"

Gabriel rolls onto his stomach to laugh into his pillow. I want to stay mad, but he's being too cute and it causes a grin to spread over my features.

"Don't be an ass," I complain, but I'm also a bit distracted by the way his back muscles flex as he lifts off the bed. He faces me, my eyes drifting to his messy hair, which, as usual, makes him look a ridiculous kind of sexy.

"So, why did you wake me up so early? And how come you've already finished getting ready?" Gabriel pulls me upright, his hands cupping my face.

"We are driving back to Maranello because my team has asked me to test drive the new Velocità Rossa sports car, and I convinced them to let you too." A bright smile covers my lips as I crawl on top of him, straddling his lap.

"I'm going to drive it around the track?" I ask, and he gives me a nod. "Oh no, but that also means I'll be sitting next to you while you drive, right?"

"Yes, of course. That's how it works," he replies and chuckles, an unsure smile on his face. "Why?"

"I'm going to be terrified when you're the one behind the wheel!" I tease. He touches the tip of his tongue to the roof of his mouth, and I hold back my laughter.

"Oh really?" he asks, his hands grabbing my ass and squeezing it, making me forget my own name. "Terrified, huh?" His hands move under my breasts, teasing me.

"Yes, maybe you should let me go first so I can teach you how to properly race. You could use a few pointers." My palms move to each side of his neck, my gaze holding his as he lowers himself onto my body.

"Maybe I'll cancel, and we'll stay here where I can fuck that attitude right out of you," he says, his dirty words surprising me as much as they excite my body. "Go, get ready. We have to leave in half an hour," he demands with a slap on my ass, and I sigh before I move off his lap.

"Tease," I groan and walk into the bathroom.

It doesn't take me long to brush my hair and teeth and apply some light makeup. I put on my black jeans and a tight, purple, long-sleeved shirt. My hair falls loosely down my back, my natural curls more defined today than usual.

"You look absolutely breathtaking," Gabriel says when his eyes shift from his phone to me. "Thank you," Gabriel adds, so I give him a confused furrow of my brows.

"For what?"

"For making me the luckiest man in the world by being mine."

Gabriel has this way of saying all the right things at the perfect times, and I hate it. I hate it because it makes me fall more in love with him. I hate it because I adore how romantic he is all the time. To anyone else, Gabriel is this confident man, who isn't corny, but with me, he's wonderfully vulnerable. He blushes, he gets shy, and he lets me in. He's still that confident guy, but he also chooses to be himself with me.

"I love you," I say because nothing else would sound right.

"Every time you say it, my heart jumps in my chest." He smiles to himself for the swiftest second.

"Well, I do. I love you," I repeat and walk over to where he's sitting, placing both of my hands on each side of his face. I adore the way his soft skin contrasts his gruff stubble.

"I love you, ma chérie."

The sunlight illuminates the *Fiorano* track, making everything look vibrant. I enjoy how peaceful it is with almost no one here. It's so silent compared to race weekends where thousands of people are running around, but I enjoy both ways.

Gabriel takes my hand, leading me toward where his team is waiting for us along with a beautiful red and black Velocità Rossa. He talks to his team before holding up two helmets that have his F1 helmet design. The number seven is on either side, and black, white, and red stripes make up the rest of it. It's quite simple, but not everybody can come up with a design like mine.

He hands me the headgear and puts on his when I notice he's biting the inside of his cheek. There's something he wants to tell me but doesn't know how to.

"Spit it out," I say, and he stares at me, shock on his face.

"How did you know?"

"Because when something bothers you, you avoid eye contact, stare at the ground, your eyebrows furrow, and you bite the inside of your cheek. You always do that, every single time," I say, and he shakes his head as if he can't believe how well I know him.

"My publicist says we have to film us driving so they can post it online. It has to do with the fact that we need to generate more popularity and get more followers. It will benefit the sport and the team," he explains, and I nod.

Even though the drivers are doing their best to create more buzz, there's still a lot of work to be done. A young Velocità Rossa driver doing hot laps with a young female racer who is his girlfriend and his teammate's sister would invite a more diverse group to watch.

"Are you alright with that? If not, we could—"

"I'm very okay with it. Now, let's do this. We'll entertain the world when I'm behind the wheel by showing them a Velocità Rossa driver peeing his pants," I joke, and he smiles at me.

"Thank you." I don't know what he's thanking me for, but I don't press. "We have to ask each other a couple of questions while we drive. They are going to be about Formula One and racing, and it's supposed to help our followers get to know us." He's being very technical with me right now, which makes me grin.

We get into the car, and I buckle up. I'm getting a little nervous, but excitement has mostly taken over now. I've never driven in a car like this with Gabriel, but I trust him.

A tall, dark-haired man hands me a paper full of questions, and I read over them. He sits down in the driver's seat and puts his seatbelt on as well. I smile at him, and he returns it, showing me his dimples. My eyes drift to the cameras and to the team working on the car while we wait for them to give us the green light. My heart starts beating faster in my chest, and I'm convinced Gabriel feels the same way.

"Are you nervous?" I ask him after his team leaves and tells us we can go.

"More than," he admits and takes a deep, strained, and shaky breath.

"Are you okay to drive?" He tilts his head to look at me, smiling a little.

"Yes, I'm fine. I've just never had so much to lose when I drive."

My head falls back against the headrest, the helmet hitting the patting. I place my thumb on his lips, and Gabriel purses them against my finger.

"Okay, ready?" he asks, breaking the silence, and I nod.

He steps on the gas, making me scream in joy. He's going fast, and my heart stops and goes with each corner, each straight. The adrenaline that shoots through my veins is heaven.

"Have you always known you wanted to be a Formula One driver?" I ask, reading the first question aloud. I have to cover my eyes with my hands when he drifts in the corner.

"Yes, ever since my dad took me karting for the first time, I knew this is what I wanted to do. Luckily, I had great opportunities, and my family fought with me every step of the way," he replies, and I smile.

"How many Grands Prix have you started in?"

"Sixty-two."

He takes another corner in the same aggressive way as before, and I search for something to hold onto, careful not to swear on camera.

"Okay, you're doing that on purpose now," I say and he chuckles. He drives over one of the curbs, and my head bobs from side to side. "Gabriel!" I complain and laugh at the same time.

"I'll be more careful, baby." He avoids the next curb by far, keeping his promise.

"How do you feel about driving for Velocità Rossa?" I continue.

"It's a once-in-a-lifetime opportunity, and I'm thankful I've been given it. I hope to race with them for many more seasons."

We get back to the start and finish line, but he drives past it to go for another round so I can ask him the remaining questions. We laugh and talk about his career until we arrive at the garage again, and I take a deep breath to calm my heart rate.

"Your turn," he says before we switch seats.

Gabriel gives me time to familiarize myself with the car before I slam my foot on the gas.

"Alright, get used to the track first before speeding around it," he says and chuckles. I do as I'm told, although I know it well from the walks we took at the academy. "First question," he yells over the roaring of the engine as we speed down the straight of the start and finish line. "Are you trying to kill me?" he asks when I take the curb a little too hard.

"Is that the question?" I reply with a laugh.

"It's my question!" he says and holds onto the door when I drift into the next corner.

"Fine, I'll go easy on you, you big baby," I say and go as slow as he did for me. "Ask me the real question, would you?" Gabriel shoots me an amused grin.

"When did you first realize that Gabriel Biancheri is the hottest guy you'll ever meet?" I shake my head, taking the curb on purpose this time to make him bounce in his seat.

"When I saw your di—" He cuts me off.

"Hey, woah, chérie!" he warns, but I'm confused now. "Cameras are rolling," Gabriel says, and I burst into laughter.

"*Dimples*, Gabriel, when I first saw your *dimples*." His face turns a bright red shade.

"Oh, shit. Well, whoever looks through this footage later is going to have a laugh." I have to do my best to stay focused on the road ahead of us, but it's difficult to keep my amusement at bay. "First question," Gabriel repeats. "How long have you been interested in racing?" I hit the brakes in the corner only to press down on the gas again as we rush down the straight.

"Almost fourteen years now." Gabriel then asks me about my journey and experiences.

By the time I've completed about three laps, we're done with the questions, and I drive the car back into the pitlane. Gabriel turns to me after we take our helmets off and brings his lips to mine, but, for the sake of not being inappropriate in front of the cameras, he leans back sooner than either of us wants.

"That was fun," he says.

We get out of the car, and Gabriel starts talking to his team in Italian. My body reacts in all sorts of ways because he sounds too sexy to keep it in check.

"I love it when you speak Italian," I swoon once he's done, and he laughs a little.

"Ti amo," he says. He kisses me before he wraps his arms around me.

"I might actually vomit." Christian's voice fills my ears, and Gabriel tenses instantly. "Valentina Romana, always complaining about the unfair treatment she's received in this sport when she gets everything handed to her on a silver platter." Gabriel is about to step past me and, most likely, punch Christian in the face for his comment, but I hold him back.

"You call being kicked out of Formula Three for no reason getting things handed to me? What about getting turned down by every other driver academy? And everyone else who had the power to help me succeed in this sport? I've been turned away and pushed out of racing my entire life. What did you have to do, *Your Royal Highness*? Beg Daddy to make it happen and then get kicked out of every academy because of your own actions?" Christian takes a step toward me then, but Gabriel moves me behind him.

"Oh, look, how sweet. Your boyfriend's protecting you," the brat says, and Gabriel smiles.

He moves closer to the prince. "When I'm not here, Val will deal with you, but as long as I'm in your presence, it'd be wise for you to fear me. She *might* hold back from punching you, but I won't." I've never seen him this angry, but I can tell he's as sick of Christian as I am.

"Are you threatening me?" the prince asks, but Gabriel merely continues to smile.

"No, I'm warning you, *Your Royal Highness*, simply giving some free advice." He moves away from my rival, taking my hand and leading me inside to get some breakfast. "I can't wait for the day when he hears that you got the seat instead of him," Gabriel says and kisses my temple.

Neither can I.

Chapter 58

Gabriel

"Guillaume, look at our son! He looks so professional," my mom says as I settle down in my F4 car, getting ready for the first race of the season.

This is an important day in my career, but I'm not as nervous as I thought I'd be. My parents have a way of calming me. They say it's magic, but I know better. I know it's love.

"Take a picture. No, take a dozen. I always want to remember this moment," she adds, and my father stands in front of me, pulling out his little camera to do as she wants.

"How many is enough?" he asks her with a grin, and she pinches him in the arm. He laughs at her, pulling her close to press a kiss on her lips.

"Ewww," Jean says from next to me, and I shake my head in amusement. He thinks they're disgusting, but I can't wait for the day I have that with someone.

"Yeah, yeah, come here," Mom says, holding her hands out for Jean and lifting him into the air to attack his face with kisses.

I smile at them before my team pulls my attention to them, reminding me of everything I have to do for the start.

"Don't forget to breathe," Maxime chimes in, and I look up at my best friend, whose brown eyes stare into mine. "Your power lies in your breath, Gabri. Focus on it, control it, use it," he says, and I give him a nod to let him know I'm paying attention to his words. "Don't get distracted. It can be deadly," he warns, and I let out a deep breath.

"Don't scare him," my father scolds, but Maxime is right to remind me. It's important. "We have to go now, Gabriel, but you got this, son. We're proud of you, no matter what," my father tells me, tapping the front of my car and grabbing Jean by the hand.

"We love you, Gabriel," Mom adds, blowing me a kiss for good luck like she always does. I 'catch' it, placing it on top of my helmet so it stays with me for the duration of the race.

"Don't crash," Jean reminds me, and I assure him I will do my best to stay away from the other drivers and the barriers. He gives me a thumbs up with his stubby, short finger, and I can't help but smile. Maxime gives me a wink and walks away with them.

Man, I have the best family in the world.

I stare at the photograph of my mom, the one I keep in my wallet along with the ones of my father, grandparents, and Maxime. Today is the last day Valentina and I get to be together before I have to fly back to Monaco. It's also one of the hardest days of the year, but I'm not planning on telling her that. We should be enjoying our time with each other, and I have to stop looking at my mom's photo. It won't bring her back, nothing will, and studying the picture will only make me sadder. I was hoping it would make me feel connected to her, but it's only ripped open old wounds so far.

Val's hands slip over my shoulders before she starts massaging my sore neck. I don't remember a time in my life when it hasn't been, which she knows. It's also why she always tries to knead out the knots there.

"She's beautiful," Valentina says, rubbing them out one at a time.

"She was." I turn to hand her the photo, and she takes it from me, settling down on the bed to study it.

"You have her eyes," she points out and looks at me to reveal she's smiling.

I reach out to touch her cheek, running my thumb over her soft skin. Her light eyes watch me as she lifts her hand to cover mine. A tsunami of comfort collides with the pain in my chest, easing the hurt inside of me.

"I miss her more than anyone. We had a special bond, and I'd give anything to feel close to her again," I admit to someone else for the first time in my life.

I pull Val onto my lap when a sad look spreads over her features, and she places her palms on each side of my neck.

"Don't worry, chérie, I'm fine. I just miss her, that's all," I assure her to wipe the concern off her face, but she frowns even more.

"I don't like it when you lie to me about your feelings. It's okay not to be okay, Gabriel, don't hide from me," she says, leaning her forehead against mine.

"It hurts, especially today because it would have been her fiftieth birthday," I say, and Valentina's eyes go wide from surprise. She leans away, her hands remaining on my throat, sending warmth through me.

"Why didn't you tell me? I would have prepared something to celebrate her life," she states, and a genuine smile creeps onto my face as I guide her against me by her hips.

"Do you do that for your late family?" I ask, and she wiggles from side to side, a shy look in her eyes.

"No," she lies, her voice cracking from deceit. "Okay, yes, I do, but I've never told anyone, not even Adrian, so you need to keep this to yourself, which I know you will because I trust you, but—" Val cuts off when she realizes she hasn't stopped to end that sentence. "Sorry," she mumbles, embarrassment turning her cheeks a wonderful shade of red.

"What do you do to celebrate their lives?" I ask to shift her attention away from her rant and back to the sweet thing she was trying to tell me about before.

"I buy their favorite flowers, food, and drink, and then watch the sunset while eating and listening to music that reminds me of them," she explains while her thumb trails over my bottom lip, watching my reaction to see what I think of her tradition.

"Just when I thought you couldn't get more beautiful, here you are, showing me another piece of you to fall in love with," I say, and she places her lips on mine, smiling.

"Alright, let's go get her favorite things," Val announces, trying to move off my lap, but I hold her in place for a moment, not ready to let go when I'm mesmerized by her big heart for the millionth time since I've met her.

"Kiss me," I beg, but she tilts her head with a curious smile.

"I thought we were past asking each other that," she says, and I lick my lips, biting down on the bottom one to keep from smiling.

"I plan on those two words to be the last I'll ever say, right after 'I love you,'" I reply, and she gives me the small eye-roll that always comes with my cheesy words. I squeeze her perfectly round ass, forcing her to focus on me. "Kiss me," I repeat, and Valentina lowers her mouth to mine, our breaths intertwining.

"Always," she whispers before kissing me, the watermelon taste from her lip balm making me groan against her. She always tastes so good. "Let's go," she says against my mouth and slides off my lap to grab her purse.

We make our way to a local supermarket to buy two bottles of lemon iced tea, some bread with mortadella, and a bouquet of tulips, all of Mom's favorites. Valentina holds my hand as she skips and dances through the store with me, finding new ways to bring a smile to my face.

I miss Mom and everyone else I've lost, but this woman, this perfect human I get to call mine, eases all the pain I've ever felt and still endure. Val makes life worth living, and I don't ever want to lose her.

I drive us back to the headquarters where we walk toward the track, sitting down on one of the grandstands just in time to watch the sunset. Valentina hands me a sandwich and bottle, grabbing the others for herself. She takes a big bite, and, for a moment, I'm too lost in her to start eating myself.

"Here, you can play her favorite songs, if you'd like," she says with a full mouth, which she's covering with one hand as the other gives me her phone.

I notice a playlist named "Gabriel's favorites," bringing a smile to my face. My fingers tap on the screen, searching for a few songs to play that remind me of my mom.

"I'm going to miss you a lot when I go back tomorrow," I say after a while of silence between us. The music in the background is quiet so I can still have a conversation with her.

Val turns to me, a forced smile on her lips.

"I know, and I'll miss you, but we'll see each other soon, mon soleil. We always do," she promises, and I move toward her, pulling her between my legs and kissing her cheek. "I love you," Val says, leaning into me so I can completely wrap my arms around her.

"I love you, mon tournesol," I reply, nuzzling my face in the crook of her neck to inhale her sweet scent. "More than I'll ever understand."

Chapter 59

Valentina

My simulator times have been strong, a lot more so than Christian's. I have him beat in endurance too, and analysis, which has always been easy for me. However, he's physically stronger than I am, at least for the moment. Over the past few years, I haven't focused as much on lifting weights as I have on every other category. Seeing Christian do better in it is infuriating, especially because he keeps bothering me about it.

"Finally, Tina, you have all the proof you need to see you're weaker than me," he said yesterday after Andrea told us our results. I rolled my eyes. "Now, what does that show you?" he challenged me.

"It shows me you suck at analysis, considering you came to this conclusion by looking at one data point, Sebastian," I replied, pissing him off.

There is something that crosses his face every time I use a wrong name for him, and I'm convinced it's a combination of anger and disappointment. Meanwhile, victory floods through me whenever I manage to knock the arrogance off his lips.

Today, Andrea is taking us to *Extrema Kart*, a Go-Kart race track near the academy. Christian has been uncharacteristically quiet all morning, but I enjoy the peace. Lucie and Haru try to tell me a story about what they did last weekend, but I only understand half of it because they keep laughing. He shoots her a longing look after a while, which she doesn't seem to notice. No one does, except me. I see the way he smiles at Lucie as she beams at the chaotic time they had at the track during our time off.

It's been days since Gabriel left to go back to Monaco for work and family responsibilities. The last time I saw Adrian and James was at the event four days ago, and I miss them a lot. We text and call, but it's never going to be the same: James and Gabriel just barging into my house, and Adrian always being home after training.

"Alright, everyone, here are the rules for today. Ready?" Andrea asks, and we all answer with a "Yes, Boss!" "Have fun, okay? You've been working hard enough this week. Take a break," they add, and everyone cheers, except Christian. He's been frowning the entire time.

The others and I move over to where the karts and helmets are, but Andrea calls me over to them. Christian is already standing beside them, a brooding frown on his thin lips.

"I have some news. This morning, I got a call from Lorenzo Mattia, the Velocità Rossa F1 team principal," they start, and I hold my breath. "He said one of you can go to Baku for the fifth race and gather some experience working with the team." I take an involuntary step back, a nervous feeling spreading through my chest now. "I want you to take today's race to prove to me you're worthy of this opportunity, okay?" they ask, and both of us nod.

Andrea gives me a serious look, reminding me Christian is willing to do anything to win, and that I should be careful.

"I'm going to grind you to dust," Christian whispers in my ear as we make our way back over to the karts.

"You never have before," I reply when all of a sudden, he places his leg in front of mine, tripping me. I lose balance, but, luckily, Lucie and Haru were watching the whole thing and catch me before I fall to the ground.

"Don't fucking underestimate me," Christian warns in French to ensure I'm the only one who understands him. *Asshole.*

"Are you alright?" Lucie asks, but I assure her I'm fine, the anger I feel for Christian fueling me now. My body was tired from training before, but adrenaline replaces exhaustion. He can't win, I won't let him.

Andrea reminds us one last time to have fun and be safe before we get to drive around the track to get a feel for it. Then, we do a mock Qualifying to find out who will start where. Everyone simply takes one lap, and Andrea stops our time. Haru is fastest overall with me in second, Christian in third, Lucie in fourth, and the rest of the guys taking up places five to nine.

Our instructor stands at the side with a green flag in their hand, waving it when we're allowed to finally start. My reaction time is slightly better than Haru's, allowing me to overtake him in the first corner. I speed down the straight, breaking late to give me more of an advantage, but Christian is right behind me.

This race is only supposed to be two laps so that we can have careless fun afterward, but they are the longest laps of my life.

At the start of the second one, Christian bumps into the back of my kart, and I barely manage to keep it from swerving off the track. This gives him an advantage, allowing him to pull up next to me. I push ahead again, but he slams against me even harder than before.

My kart gets shoved into the barriers and off-track until I'm on a grass area where I'm thrown from it before it flips over itself. A stinging pain shoots through my left hand as I roll away from the vehicle. I distantly hear someone screaming my name, but my ears are ringing from hitting my head and helmet on the ground.

"Valentina," the voice repeats, and I identify it to be Andrea's. They appear in front of me, a first-aid kit in their grasp. My hand starts to throb, and I lift my right one to hold onto it.

"Can you take your helmet off?" I attempt to, but pain shoots through my left thumb.

I shake my head, and they remove it for me, the ringing finally stopping now that the pressure on my head is gone.

"What happened?" is the next question Andrea asks, and I look into their brown eyes.

"Christian, he—uhm, he—" I cut off, the shock confusing my mind.

"Did he push you off track?" I manage to nod before Andrea says something in Italian I don't understand. It sounds like swear words. "It's okay, Valentina, you're okay. I have some medical training in cases of emergency. May I check you for injury?" they ask, and I thank them.

Andrea puts pressure on every part of my legs, watching my reaction to see if anything hurts. They move on to my ribs and neck, but everything else is fine. The only thing bothering me is my left wrist.

"Nothing's broken, just bruised. It should heal in a few days," they assure me, and I offer yet another nod.

"I'm sorry about this. I tried to keep control of the kart, but he hit it so hard, I had no choice," I explain when my brain clears up. Andrea grabs me by the shoulders then.

"This was not your fault. I'm so happy you're okay, Valentina, and I'm the one who is sorry. I didn't think he would go this far to win the Baku opportunity," they say, but I give them a comforting smile.

"Don't worry, he would have done this whether you had told us about it or not," I reply while they wrap my wrist and hand in a dressing to keep it in place.

"Can you stand?" I try to, but the shock hasn't worn off completely, and my legs give out from shaking. "Okay, it's alright. Take your time."

This isn't my first crash, but it was a lot scarier than any other I've been in. After a few more moments, I manage to walk back to the main area to sit down. Andrea gets an ice pack for me and a bottle of water so I can take some painkillers.

As soon as the other drivers return, Andrea storms toward them, grabbing Christian by the collar and dragging him out of his kart. They throw him on the grass area before the prince has any time to react.

"Are you proud of yourself? You could have cost Valentina her life!" A wave of fear spreads through my chest at the thought.

"I won, so, yes, I'm very proud," he replies, and my fear is replaced by disgust.

"You're an arrogant, spoiled, childish boy, and, let me assure you, it won't get you far in my academy," they spit, and Christian stands up to step in front of them.

"It's not your academy, it's Mr. Reiner's. He is in charge, not you," he replies, as smug as always.

"Trust me, child, it's *my* academy. What I say goes, and you're no longer going to be a part of it anymore." Christian grabs them by the arm, making Andrea's eyes go wide.

"It was an accident. How will you prove it wasn't?" he asks, but our instructor realizes he's right.

They can't prove it, and neither can I. It'd be my word against Christian's, and, speaking from experience, people tend to believe the royal and *man* over anyone else.

"Pull that shit again, and I won't need proof." Andrea moves him out of the way before walking back over to me. They squat down, a sincere apologetic expression on their face. "I wish there was something I could do," they say.

"I know, don't worry. It'll be fine. He won't do anything again if he hopes to stay in the academy," I reply, trying to convince myself and Andrea. In reality, I have no idea what Christian is willing to do.

"Congratulations, Valentina, you have just earned yourself the opportunity to fly to Baku and work with the Velocità Rossa F1 team," Andrea announces to everyone, and my rival turns abruptly, anger all over his face.

"But she didn't even finish the race!" he complains, balling his hands into fists. Andrea raises themself and turns to scowl at him.

"I said to get this opportunity, you have to show you're worthy of it. That did *not* mean you had to finish first or at all. Valentina drove a clean race and suffered from your immaturity. She is worthy, you are not," Andrea replies, their voice firm.

Christian storms off without saying another word. Satisfaction spreads through my chest, and excitement settles in my heart. I will get to spend an entire weekend gathering experiences with an F1 team. On top of that, I will get to be with my favorite people in the world. At least something good came from Christian's immaturity.

"Go home to Monaco, Valentina, rest, and pack for Baku. I'll see you when you return," they say, and I let out a deep breath. Tears almost shoot into my eyes at the thought of finally going home.

It's been too long.

"It's okay, little champion, you're okay," Grandpa assures me as I hold my pinky and cry from pain.

He took us karting for the last time before we have to move, and one of the other people here accidentally bumped into me.

"Let me see," he says, inspecting the damage, even though both of us know I'm not crying because of my stupid finger.

"It hurts," I lie to cover up the fact that I'm weeping because this will be the last time in a while we get to be together.

"Val? Are you okay?" Adrian's voice appears from behind. He squats down in front of me too, wiping my tears and checking my face for injury. "What happened?" he asks Grandpa.

"Someone accidentally hit her kart, and she hurt her finger on the wheel," he explains, and I nod.

"Who? I'll make them apologize," Adrian replies and stands up, but Grandfather places his hand on his arm to keep him here.

"Don't worry, Valentina is going to be just fine." My grandpa catches my tears with the back of his fingers and smiles. "When we Romanas crash, we keep pushing with our heads

held high. The pain will fade, but the experience will stay forever. You'll learn from it, grow from it, and, ultimately, benefit from it. Okay?"

"Okay," I reply and smile back. "It doesn't hurt anymore," I assure both of them because Adrian is still looking at me with concern.

I move my finger to prove I'm not lying, and they each give me a proud look when I raise my head high.

"No one can ever take that strength away from you, little champion."

He's right because I won't let them.

Chapter 60

Valentina

I didn't let anyone know I was coming home, not even Adrian. All I told Gabriel was to please go to my room and find a ring I'd lost. He didn't understand but agreed to go anyway, no questions asked. This man is wrapped around my finger, just like I am around his.

Adrian told me he'd only be back home in the evening, which gives Gabriel and me enough time to catch up on the time we've been apart.

The taxi driver gives me a strange look when I place the money on his middle console as soon as he parks and hurry out of the car. I run toward my front door, dropping my backpack in the foyer and sprinting up the stairs.

Gabriel is already in my bedroom, his attention on his phone before he lifts it to his ear. Mine starts ringing then, and his eyes shift to me as I hit the answer button.

"I'm finally home," I say into the speaker, and he throws his phone onto the bed, opening his arms for me. I jump into them, wrapping my limbs around his body.

"So am I," he whispers against my neck.

I slide my fingers into his hair and grin. This is pure happiness. Being in his arms and feeling his body pressed against mine is my personal heaven.

Gabriel drops me onto my feet before capturing my lips with his, letting me know how much he missed me by the way he sighs against my mouth.

"What are you doing here?" he asks, his gaze shifting to my bruised wrist. "Who did this to you?" Anger and concern slip across his face, settling in his green-brown eyes.

"I took the curb wrong when we were karting, and—" Gabriel cuts me off.

"It was the royal dickhead, wasn't it?" I have no intention of telling him how terrifying the crash truly was, but I answer his question with a nod. "How?" My face is between his hands, his thumb tracing my bottom lip.

Although his touch is soft, I know he's angry. He's probably never been this angry, and I understand perfectly. If he came home with even the slightest scratch on his body because of someone else, I would be furious with whoever hurt him.

"It was a karting accident, but it's okay, don't worry. It already feels a lot better," I assure him and step back to drop onto my bed.

"Chérie, it's not okay. At least tell me you gave back harder than he dished out," he replies, getting frustrated with me now.

"Not a scratch on him, you want to know why?" I ask, and he crosses his arms in front of his chest.

It momentarily distracts me, his muscles and veins sticking out from under his rolled-up long-sleeved shirt.

"Tell me," he replies in French, and I smile.

"Because I'm better than him. I don't resort to violence, and I never will. The seat will be mine because I'm the one who follows all the rules."

My answer doesn't satisfy him one bit so I slide my shirt over my head and crooked my finger, signaling for him to come closer.

"Get your sweet ass over here and fuck me until I can't walk anymore, Gabriel." He runs his tongue over his bottom lip before biting down on it.

"You want it harder today, chérie?" he asks, lifting his shirt over his head and moving toward me.

"Yes," I admit while he places his hands on each side of me on the mattress.

"You want me to flip you onto your chest, pull you in by the hips, and fuck you from behind?" I swallow hard when his face is merely a few centimeters from mine, my heart racing.

"Yes." I bring my lips to his, barely brushing them.

My hand moves to his bulge so I can palm him through his jeans. His confident composure fades ever so slightly, and I smirk at the control my touch has over him.

"Just watch the wrist," I say with a challenging smile, and he brings it to his mouth, pressing a kiss to the dressing.

"I'll be gentle with it," he assures me as he places it on my lap again. "Have you ever had rough sex?" he asks, pushing my curls out of my face to grab it and tilt it upward to him.

"No, have you?" Gabriel gives me a sad smile.

"You can't make love if you're not in love. Before you, that was the only type of sex I had," he replies, and I hold my breath as he guides my lips back to his. "Say 'tournesol' if it gets too much for you, and I will stop immediately," he says, and I can see in his eyes that he doesn't want to overstep any boundaries.

But I need this. I want him to be rough with me, to fuck me like never before. He's been careful so far, almost as if I'd break if he pushed harder. I'm not easily broken, and we both crave this, I can see it in his eyes.

"Fuck me hard," I say before his lips crash onto mine.

Chapter 61

Gabriel

Valentina's tongue slips into my mouth, making a groan leave me. She smiles like she always does when I let her know how much I'm under her control. I do my best not to chuckle at her proud grin and focus. Val wants it rough, and I'm going to give my woman everything she desires, starting by removing those tight yoga pants that hug her ass way too perfectly. She watches me as I bring them to her ankles, my eyes shifting to her drenched panties. *Fuck*.

"Did I not tell you to be rough?" she asks, and I cock an eyebrow.

"You don't like it when I tease you?" I challenge, smirking at her as I run the tips of my fingers up her thighs, watching goosebumps appear in their wake. She's just as horny for me as I am for her, and I love it.

"Why am I even still in my underwear?" Valentina challenges back.

I narrow my eyes slightly, tilting my head as my gaze drops back to her panties. I want them gone, *need* them so far away from her body, it makes me ache. But I love teasing her. I love watching her squirm a little as I run my hands over the sensitive skin near her pussy. My index finger slips down the curve between her thigh and mound, and if I go a bit lower… *there it is*. Her whole body trembles from my touch.

"Patience, chérie," I whisper, running my fingers over the smooth skin on her stomach now. "I need you wet for me, for my cock," I say, but she lets out a whimper of complaint.

"I already am," she says, and I lean my head down.

"Not enough."

My mouth trails kisses and bites along the inside of her leg, making her press her soft thighs against my ears. She's trying to ease her ache, but I won't let her. That's my job.

"A little longer," I say, leaving wet kisses along the same curve I traced a moment ago.

Val moans, making my already hard cock unbearably so. It's begging me to hurry up, to slip inside of her, but my brain is still in charge, and it's focusing on her hard nipples right now. They're still covered by her bra, irritating me.

"Arch your back for me, baby," I command, and she does as she's told. "That's my girl," I praise as I remove the ridiculous fabric, which does nothing to contain her breasts.

Once they're free from their containment, I don't waste a single second. I wrap my mouth around her left nipple, sucking so hard, she cries out from pleasure instantly.

"Fuck," she groans, her hand moving onto my arm.

Her nails dig into my bicep as I massage her tit, flicking my tongue over the ache I created a moment ago. Valentina rolls her hips against me, trying to bring my throbbing groin against her swollen clit.

"Not yet," I say and push her hips down, moving over to her right nipple and paying the same attention to it. God, she tastes so sweet, like candy. I need more of her, need my mouth to be everywhere on her body at once.

I curl my fingers around the thin waistband of her thong and rip it off her body. Valentina gasps, but I don't give her mind time to linger on the broken fabric before I press my mouth to her swollen clit, groaning against it.

"Gabriel," she moans, and it takes all of my willpower to pull away again.

I'm not nearly done tasting her, but that's not what Val wants right now. She wants me to be rough, and I've teased her for long enough. Not to mention, I'm going to go crazy if her walls aren't wrapped around me soon.

I stand up straight, taking in the sight of her completely naked in front of me, her curves perfectly on display. My already hard dick press against my jeans, and I suck in another sharp breath. My thumbs trail over her hard nipples, circling them until she rolls her head from pleasure. I place a soft slap on her left one, trying to see how she reacts first before I keep going.

"Shit," she gasps, biting her bottom lip. "That felt..." Val trails off, a satisfied, little moan leaving her. Fuck, that sound gets under my skin, lighting me on fire.

"I know, baby," I reply before kissing her.

Desire takes over completely, and I pull Val close to me by her ankles, flipping her around until she's on her stomach.

"Oh," she says and giggles.

My fingers move to her hips, guiding her ass upward and toward my throbbing groin. I run my palms over her skin before slapping her right ass cheek and leaning down to flick my tongue over the ache. She bucks against me, a soft moan leaving her.

"You like that, chérie?" I ask, repeating the same action again, this time on the left side.

"Fuck," she whimpers, grinding her ass against my cock again. "Please, Gabriel, no more teasing," she begs while I rub my hands over her round ass, squeezing and kneading it until I'm satisfied. "Please," Val repeats when I don't move, and I'm ready to hand her the fucking world, heaven, and hell.

I unzip my pants and slide them down just enough for my erection to be free of the uncomfortable containment. A sharp groan leaves me as I roll the condom down my aching cock, the need to fill her taking over.

I trail my hand down her spine, watching goosebumps spread over her skin everywhere my fingers touch. I keep going until I reach the back of her neck, guiding her into an upright position.

"I'm fucking you from behind, ma chérie, so I need you to do something for me," I start and bring my index finger to her clit, rubbing tight circles that make her moan.

"Anything," she replies, grabbing my hand to keep it right where it is on her pussy.

"Keep saying my name. Remember whose dick is pleasuring you, baby." Valentina nods, more moans leaving her as she grinds herself against me.

I spread her legs wider, replacing my finger with my cock and gliding it back and forth. She's so wet for me, it almost makes me explode right then and there.

"Gabriel!" she screams, and I smirk to myself. *Fuck, I need to hear it again.*

I align myself with her entrance, anticipation spreading through me like wildfire. The thrill of being with Val takes over, and I slam into her, holding her against my chest while she moans my name again.

My lips brush over the shell of her ear before I bite down on the lobe, making her tense. The feeling of her wrapped around my cock lights me on fire everywhere. Every inch of me is burning from the heat she's responsible for, and it's weighing heavy on me in the best way possible. *God, she feels too fucking good.*

"You were made for me," I whisper into her ear, moving on to suck on her soft spot.

A whimper escapes her lips as I cup her breasts and squeeze her hard, perfect nipples.

"And you for me," she replies, breathless and in pleasure.

"Yes, I was, only for you."

I guide her chest back onto the mattress, keeping her ass in place to stay inside her without moving for a moment longer. Then, once Val has spread out her arms and tilted her head to the side, I slide back out, thrusting inside harder than I ever have before. She grips the sheets, repeating my name over and over as I create a friction that makes us weak. This position allows me to go deeper, something both of us are enjoying. I slap her ass again, her body trembling.

"Merde," she moans, and I can't help the smirk on my face.

I'm pleasuring her to the point where she switches to her mother tongue. The thought makes me go harder and faster, smacking her ass every once in a while to hear that same whimpering-surprised sound again. It surprises her that she likes it so much.

"You look so good wrapped around my cock like this, chérie," I say, slamming inside of her with another hard thrust.

The orgasm builds in my erection, slowly spreading through me, letting me know I'm close, *way too fucking close*. I push it down, for now, focusing on getting Val to her personal heaven before I let mine take over completely. My body is consumed by pleasure, thriving off it now like it would adrenaline.

"Gabriel, I'm gonna—fuck—oh fuck," she says in French, and I lift her up once more so my chest presses against her back.

"I know, ma chérie. I've got you," I say, my movements never stopping.

Val falls apart, her body shaking from the orgasm as she screams for me. I keep pushing inside of her, my own moans filling the room. She turns her head to me, claiming my lips with hers and sending me straight over the edge she brought me to in the first place. My whole body tenses as the build-up in my cock finally releases, my thrusts slowing as it pulsates, and I finally spill into the condom inside of her.

For the briefest moment, I feel invincible as my whole body is consumed by the feeling of relief. Relief both because the tension has dissolved within me and because Valentina is mine in the same way I am hers.

My fingers slip over her hips before I trace her stretch marks, trying to memorize their pattern on her soft skin. They're one of my favorite features of hers.

When she breaks our connection, I shove the desire to frown at the loss of contact aside and smile instead because her happy grin is everything to me. The way we fit together reminds me of a single gap on a bookshelf and the perfect-sized book to slide into the void.

Nothing compares to the rush of emotions I feel when Valentina and I are together like this, nothing but the rush of racing. Those are the two best feelings in the world for me, and I never want to give either of them up.

"I love you, mon tournesol," I blurt out, and she beams up at me.

"I love you more, mon soleil," she replies, but I shake my head.

"Would you really like to start an argument about that right now?" I challenge, and she chuckles, her full, plump lips pulling into a smirk.

"No, I'd rather make out a little more," Valentina says, her eyes bluer today than ever. Usually, the green color comes through more, in the sun the brown, but never the blue, not like this. "How about this? I love you *the same.*" I give her a satisfied nod.

"I like that," I admit and lean down to bring my lips to hers again.

There is no doubt in my mind that she was made for me and I for her in every way possible. I truly am the luckiest man alive.

Chapter 62

Valentina

Gabriel is fast asleep on my bed when I get up to get some water. He needs a nap after we've been having sex for the past couple of hours, and I need to see if Adrian is home. I haven't spoken to him since yesterday morning, and we haven't seen each other in over a week.

I try to be as quiet as possible while I make my way downstairs and find Adrian sitting on the couch, watching television. He ignores my presence, pretending I'm not there even as I sit down next to him. I grab the remote from the table and press pause on his movie.

"I'm watching that," he complains in French, and I realize something is wrong. Adrian doesn't speak to me in French.

"What's going on?" I ask him in English.

"You want to know?" I nod, and he sits up on the couch. "Okay, well, my sister had a horrible karting crash yesterday, and she hasn't taken the time to speak to me once because she was busy with her boyfriend." My eyes go wide.

"How do you know about the accident?" I ask, and he takes a sip of his water, rolling his eyes.

"Andrea called me because they were worried about Christian's behavior, which doesn't fucking matter right now. I come home today, see your luggage, and think to myself 'Wow, I actually get to spend time with my sister today.' I hope you can understand how upset I was when I had to leave the house because you were fucking my teammate."

His words hurt me, and I wish he'd stop, but I also understand why he's upset.

"You have been distant, barely talking to me. I feel like soon, you're going to be cheering for him instead of me. I'm still your family, Val, and as selfish as it sounds, I would appreciate it if every now and then you would think of me first!" Maybe if he'd approached it differently and told me in a calm tone instead of yelling, I wouldn't be angry.

"You know what, Adrian? That's bullshit. I came here to spend time with all of you, and I thought you were training today so I called Gabriel. I truly am sorry you came home early and had to hear that, but I'm not sorry I finally have a life."

He cocks both of his brows, waiting for my explanation.

"In LA, all I did was stay at home every single day, train, and do homework, but I want more. I have Evangelin, James, Gabriel, you, and my shot at making it into F1. It's hard to juggle, and I'm sorry about this morning, but I just want to experience things with Gabriel, things I have only dreamed of. I was hoping you would understand."

I can't believe he started a fight. It's as if no one wants me to stay happy for more than a day because someone always has to swoop in and ruin my good mood. It's ridiculous.

"Whatever, Val. You can fly out with Gabriel tomorrow. You can stay in his room, and you can cheer for him. Baku is one of his favorite races anyway. After all, maybe he'll be the world champion this year, and you can celebrate everything with him. Go for it, Valentina, live your life, forget about your brother, who has always taken care of you."

That's not fair. He's acting like I've forgotten about him when he's the one who barely has time for me too.

"How could you treat me like this when I'm the one who has always protected you?" he adds, and I lose it.

"Yeah, you protected me so well, Aunt Carolina abused me for years without you knowing!" The words leave my mouth before I can stop myself.

This is never how I wanted to tell him about that, but I couldn't help myself. The anger overwhelmed me. That's always what I do wrong, I throw things around without thinking about them. Adrian's eyes are wide open and so is his mouth.

"She what?" he asks, but I'm too surprised to talk.

I cannot believe I blurted this out to win a goddamn argument.

"I'm going to kill her!" he yells, but I'm still sitting on the couch, unable to move or speak. "I can't believe this, I can't believe this," he repeats over and over again.

I cover my face with my right hand and let out a sigh.

"How did she hurt you? You know what? Never mind. I'm going to kill her," he says before he storms off, and I get up to run after him.

"Adrian, please don't leave!" He's gone before I can catch up with him, and I sink to the floor by the entrance of my home.

"Chérie?" I lift my head to look in the direction of Gabriel's voice.

My brain is trying to process everything that just happened as he settles down next to me on the ground. I take his hand in mine. We sit in complete silence for a couple of minutes until he opens his mouth.

"Do you want to talk about it?" I nod, and Gabriel gets up again, pulling me with him. "I'm going to get you some ice cream. My mom used to say ice cream never fixes any problems, but it tastes so good, it will make you temporarily forget about how bad everything else is," he says as we walk into the kitchen.

"I've never heard words I relate to more," I reply, and he chuckles.

Once the ice cream is placed in front of me, I take the spoon and bring some of it to my mouth. Gabriel watches me closely, unsure of what I need from him.

"I said something to Adrian I shouldn't have told him in such a sensitive moment." Even saying it out loud makes me mad. "I told him about what our aunt did to me," I explain, and pain flashes over Gabriel's face.

"I heard that part. I want you to know you don't have to open up to me, but you can. If you want to cry, ball your eyes out, if you want to scream, do it until you lose your voice. You have every right, and all I want to do is make you comfortable to finally talk to someone about it," he assures me, and I give him half a smile.

I take a deep breath and relax my facial muscles, which are twitching in response to my forced expression.

"I've never told anyone, except James, who found out on his own," I start, my hands shaking now. Gabriel takes them in his, pressing soft kisses to the backs of them. "She didn't hit me often to make sure Adrian wouldn't find out, but it started soon after we moved in with her."

Tears shoot into my eyes, and I wish I could stop them. I don't want the mention of this story to bring me pain, but it's part of who I am. I need to speak about this if I ever want to move on.

"It was easy for her to hurt me, to try and force me into being someone she could accept. Naturally, she could never accept any version of me." I pause, unsure where to keep going.

"It's okay, take your time. You don't have to rush this," he assures me as I bring my legs to my chest on the chair.

"I don't know why Dad decided we should move in with my mother's sister and not stay with Grandpa, but what could we do after his death? Grandpa tried to fight it, but

Aunt Carolina had already accepted. To this day, I can't understand why she wanted us if she hated me," I say, but Gabriel gives me a look that tells me he has a suspicion.

"She wanted the money you came with, chérie," he replies, and I stare at something behind him. He's probably right. "Why didn't you tell Adrian?" His question is genuine as he tries to understand this dark time of my life.

"Telling anyone about Carolina was never an option. Adrian would have only tried to take me out of the house, meaning he would have had to give up his career, and he wouldn't have been able to keep me anyway. I thought about telling him everything and asking him to move back to Monaco so that we could live with our grandfather, but then Grandpa died."

I pause for another brief second before I'm able to speak. Gabriel squeezes my hand reassuringly, his eyes focused on my face.

"Nothing I ever did pleased that awful woman, and every single time I wasn't who she wanted me to be, I paid for it. She only stopped because James threatened her, and she knew better than to lay a finger on me after." I take another deep breath and watch a tear roll down Gabriel's cheek.

"Sorry, I'm sorry," he quickly apologizes. "Just the thought of you going through that, I can't even begin to describe how it makes me feel. I wish I'd known, I could have done something to help you," he says, and I squeeze his hand.

"I know, but what happened, happened. It will never leave me, and I will never be able to forget how weak and helpless I felt. It's easier for me to talk about now than it was a while ago. The only reason why I haven't is because I know Adrian would blame himself for not knowing and protecting me. That's why I am so angry it came out now and in the way it did. It's not fair, and I'm sure he's punching a wall somewhere." Tears stream down my face, blurring my vision. Guilt settles deep in my chest.

"You're allowed to let it come out in any way you want, chérie." He drops his head onto our intertwined hands and lets out a deep breath. I look down at my ice cream, pushing the bowl away when I see all of it has melted.

"Let's go to bed. We need to wake up early to catch our flight."

There is nothing I can do about Adrian right now. I know he needs time to process this. I also know he's probably at James', so I call my best friend. He picks up after one ring.

"Val, thank God, I was just about to call you. Adrian is crying on my sofa, saying he's the worst person on the planet. What the fuck happened?" More guilt washes over me in an instant.

"I told him about Aunt Carolina during a heated argument," I admit, shame in my voice.

"Okay, I'll handle it. Go lie down and rest, I'll talk to him." He hangs up a second later.

Gabriel and I walk upstairs. He sits down next to me on my bed, tucking one of my curls behind my ear. He presses his lips to mine before he crawls back on the mattress and wraps the blanket around himself. His eyes close, and he starts snoring, which I know he's faking. Gabriel only snores very lightly sometimes, not this aggressively. It makes me chuckle.

I lie down next to him and remove my pants, pain shooting through my wrist.

"Oh, wait, take this," he says, pulling his shirt off his body. "Put this on."

"What if I don't want to wear your old shirt," I ask, and he frowns at me.

"Until I replace it with something more meaningful, please do."

I switch shirts, making a content smile spread across his face. Gabriel's mahogany scent fills my nose, and I let out a sigh. I put my head on his muscular chest, making sure my wrist is resting in a good position at my side.

"When you asked me if I've ever thought about marriage and children, I only told you I haven't had the time to think about marriage," I start, and he kisses the top of my head.

"I remember," he says, pressing another kiss to the same spot.

"I have thought about having children," I admit, silence filling the room again.

"Do you want any?" Gabriel asks, making my breathing hitch.

"I didn't. With one mother abandoning me, and the other mother figure in my life being an abuser, I always thought I should never be one. I thought there was no way I could be a good mom, but ever since I met Evangelin and experienced the love of a mother figure, it feels different. I feel different." I look up at him, and he smiles down at me.

"She helped you realize you're neither of those horrible women," he says.

"Yes, she did. One day, I'll make a good parent, whether it is to a baby or a dog or a fish."

"You'll be the best mother in the world because of your experiences. You'll be everything you never had, and they will be the happiest children in the world," he replies, and I push myself up to kiss his jaw. "Of course, until they reach their teenage and adult years, and all their friends will have a crush on you." I laugh at his comment, but he takes my face in his hand, forcing my eyes to his. "And then they'll hate me because I'll be living the dream of calling you my wife every day of my life." He kisses me, and I let that fantasy play out in my head.

"Twenty-one, almost twenty-two, and you're already done searching the world for someone else?" I challenge, but he doesn't find it one bit amusing.

"I've been done since I first laid my eyes on you, mon tournesol."

"So have I." He kisses me again, and again, and then one more time. "Do you remember what happened the day we met?" I ask, and his attention drifts to me.

"Like it was yesterday, *Lady Valentina*," he replies, and embarrassment heats up my cheeks.

"You had me breathless from day one, Gabriel," I admit, and he takes my face between his hands.

"And you'll have me breathless until the last." His lips connect with mine, and I smile against them. He tastes like home, and I'll never get enough.

I wish this moment wasn't tainted by the fight between my brother and me.

I have to find a way to fix this.

Chapter 63

Valentina

We're in Baku for the fifth race of the season. Adrian hasn't spoken to me in days, but Gabriel has done his best to distract me. He took me sightseeing yesterday and when we got back to our hotel room, we took a shower together before I lay down on his chest while he read to me. It made my heart beat a little easier, even if it's still a brick in my chest, reminding me of my brother.

Leonard and I have been sitting at the table in one of the empty conference rooms, looking over my simulator times and other results. Ever since I started at the driver academy, we've become better friends than I would have ever imagined. He texts me at least twice a week to make sure I'm doing alright, and, whenever we both have time, he calls me to discuss my performance. It's usually longer conversations, moving from racing topics to anything else I need to get off my chest, like stupid Christian Crovetto's behavior. I also attempt to get to know him better, but he keeps his personal life private from me. He'll occasionally share how his workout routine is going, but never how his partner or family members are doing.

Gabriel is still working, and Adrian and James have avoided me all day. I pretend like it doesn't bother me so they don't worry if they see me, but it hurts. Fighting with my brother hurts. Having my best friend hardly communicate with me hurts.

"What do you struggle with the most in the simulator? Staying focused or endurance?" Leonard asks, staring at the paper with my results.

His question pulls me back out of my thoughts, and I look into his comforting brown eyes. There's something about having Leonard as a mentor that completes my life. After Grandfather died, I never thought there would be anyone who'd fill that position again. Adrian is someone I could have imagined taking the spot, but I think he didn't want to "replace" Grandpa.

Leonard doesn't look at it that way. He merely wants to be for me what Carlos has become for Adrian over the past few months.

"I struggle the most with controlling my nerves before I sit down. Then, once I start, everything's fine, but I'm scared it will influence my results when it matters most," I explain, and Leonard leans toward me, a hint of a smile on his usually serious face.

"I know you'd like to control everything, Val, but nerves are one thing we can't. You may get used to them, but they will be there either way. They remind you that you care," he says, and I tug on a loose thread from my pants.

"I don't like that I can't control them." *Or anything else really.*

Leonard chuckles, his full lips pulling back to reveal his set of white, straight teeth. I've never focused on this man long enough to appreciate how handsome he is, but since we've been spending more time together, I can't help but notice it.

"Listen, if your biggest struggle is how nervous you get, you'll be fine. You may not be able to overcome it, but you can use your breath to ease the effects. Deep breaths will slow your heart rate, allow your mind to focus on something else, and bring much-needed oxygen to your brain. Okay?" he asks, poking my leg when I shake my head. "Come on, you know I'm right."

"I don't think there's been a time when you haven't been, which is the annoying part," I say, and a genuine laugh falls from his lips. *I made Leonard Tick laugh...*

"You flatter me, maybe a little too much. I should go call my big brother. He has a way of humbling me," Leonard jokes, and it's my turn to laugh then. "Anyway, to get back to the serious topic, how is your neck strengthening going? You told me you struggle with it," he says, switching the subject to get back to business.

"It's been going great. Your tips have really helped me," I reply.

Leonard and I talk for a while longer, discussing everything about my time at the academy, excluding Christian because I don't feel like giving that asshole any attention today.

Eventually, he gives my shoulder a squeeze and leaves to get some rest before tomorrow. I text Gabriel to see if he's ready to go back to the hotel yet, but he lets me know he'll need a little longer to take care of something.

Cameron, on the other hand, is sleeping in his garage while his engineers work on the car. Seeing an evil opportunity, I creep toward him, trying to be as quiet as possible. His mouth is slightly opened, letting his snores rip free.

I take out my phone, capturing this innocent and hilarious moment. A tap on the shoulder pulls me from my concentration trance, and I look over my shoulder to see Leni, Cameron's performance coach, holding something up for me.

"Here, put this on. It'll scare him," she says with a mischievous grin, and I take the mask from her. It's a photo of my brother mid-sneeze, and I almost fall over from laughter. I place the elastic band around my head, forcing myself to keep it together while leaning toward Cameron until my face is merely a few centimeters from his, Leni filming us now.

"Cameron, it's Adrian, wakey wakey," I say with a soft voice.

He moves his head a bit, crossing his arms in front of his chest as his mouth parts wider.

"Cameron, wake up, mate. I need to tell you something," I whisper, running the back of my index finger over his cheek. His eyes flutter open before they go wide and he screams. It's *the* most high-pitched sound I've ever heard in my life, so I cover my ears to spare them.

"Oh, you're so dead," Cameron calls out when I lift the mask off my face. I run away screaming, but he catches me, holding me against him. He places his mouth on my shoulder, blowing air against it to make a farting noise and send awful shivers down my spine.

"You're pranking me now? Mean," he complains but joins my amusement with a chuckle. I burst into laughter, but he doesn't release me yet.

"I'm sorry," I squeal. "I won't do it again," I promise, and he lets go of me, spinning me around so I can see his amused grin. *Damn, I love this man.*

"Do you have any idea how terrifying it is to wake up to your brother's face?" he asks. The mention of my brother temporarily sends a sting through me.

"I'm sorry," I repeat, and he wipes away the tears of laughter that escaped my eye.

"Don't worry, I will get my revenge someday," he says, and my eyes widen, but he doesn't say anything more as his arm wraps around my shoulders. "Have you eaten yet?" Cameron asks, pulling me closer to press a kiss to the top of my head.

"Not yet. I was waiting for Gabriel, but he seems to be busy," I say as I check my phone for a message but find nothing.

"Then I'm taking you to dinner. You can text him to join us when he's done, but it's late enough already, and you need to eat." I don't even try to argue with him as he leads me out of his garage and toward his rental car. On our way to the restaurant, I text Gabriel to let him know where we're going.

Gabriel: I don't think I'll make it to dinner, but enjoy. I will see you at the hotel, ma chérie. Je t'aime.

I smile at my phone before answering.

Valentina: I love you the same.

Chapter 64

Gabriel

"Listen, Adrian, you either start talking to me or I'm leaving because I want to get back to Val. I haven't seen her all day," I say, and he finally lifts his head from between his arms to look at me. Half an hour ago, he walked into my private room, sat down against the wall, and has stayed quiet ever since.

"I want to talk to you, isn't that weird? I feel this need to share how I'm feeling with you because you love my sister more than anyone, except James and me," he says, and I do my best not to roll my eyes at the mention of his best friend. *Fucking James.* "Why is that? I hate that," Adrian says, forcing my attention away from my dislike of James.

"You hate that you want to talk to me?" I ask with a small smile, settling down on the floor in front of him. Adrian watches me like a hawk, uncertain how to answer my question. Then, he almost screams.

"Yes!" he blurts out, and I can't help but chuckle. "We weren't close before you started dating Val, but now? We've spent so much time together, bonded for some inexplicable reason, that I want you to tell me I'm not the worst brother in the world. I don't rely on other people, but I want you to reassure me now, and I fucking despise it."

"Would you like to know why, in this particular case, you feel most comfortable talking to me?" My words surprise him, grabbing his full attention. "James hid the truth from you, and you're too ashamed to face Valentina. I'm the only one who knows what happened that you don't mind looking at right now," I explain, and he nods absentmindedly as I speak. I can't imagine what he's going through, all the blame he's putting on himself.

"As much as I'd like that to be the sole reason, I think it's also because I trust you, and I don't trust many people." Neither do I, which is why we get along so well.

Silence fills the room for a moment before he breaks it again.

"Am I the worst brother in the world?" he asks, but I shake my head without hesitation.

"No, you're not. Adrian, protecting Val has been your number one priority from the day she was born, and you thought she was in safe hands with Carolina. You couldn't have known unless she gave you a reason to doubt that safety," I say, tears welling up in his eyes.

"I never saw any mark or bruise. When I was home, Carolina was... almost kind. And, Val, she kept it from me so well, I never suspected anything. But that's the problem! I should have, Gabriel. I should have known, I should have protected her!" he says, throwing his hands around to argue with me or himself, I'm not quite sure.

"I know hearing Val was abused for years was one of the hardest things you've ever had to hear, but you need to stop putting all of this on yourself. The only person to blame is Carolina. You are still the best brother anyone could ask for, but, right now, you need to get it together for the one person that matters the most: Val." He gives me a confused look, so I decide to elaborate. "She's miserable. She hates herself for the way all of this came out, and you need to get over your shit and assure her everything's alright. Unless you'd prefer it if she continued to feel horrible about it," I challenge, and a smile slips onto his face.

"Tough love? That's not really your thing," he says, watching me stand up and hold out my hand for him.

"Well, you're breaking the heart of the woman I love. I'll become anything to make her stop hurting," I reply, and he allows me to help him off the ground.

"You're right. I'm being selfish. I just don't know how to face her," he admits, dropping his head backward to suck in a sharp breath.

I grab him by the shoulders, forcing him to listen closely to my next words.

"Val is not angry with you. She does *not* blame you, she never has. No part of her holds you responsible. All Valentina wants is for you to get back to where you were before. It's as simple as that." His head bobs up and down, showing me he's paying attention. "She's ready, but it's up to you to forgive yourself now. Don't hold onto something that isn't your fault, Adrian. It will break you," I remind him, waiting for a response this time.

"I hate you for saying all the right things," he replies, and I let out a short laugh.

"Well, someone has to, and if your best friend can't, I'll always be here," I say, but he laughs at the way I roll my eyes when I mention James.

"You really don't like him, do you?" Adrian asks, smiling at my disgusted look.

"Fucking hate him is more like it," I admit without shame, and my teammate starts laughing.

"Yeah, I would too if I were you, considering he's been in love with her far longer than you have." It shouldn't piss me off, but it does.

"He's still in love with her?" I ask, resisting the urge to ball my hands into fists. I'd very much like to destroy that asshole.

Adrian's eyes go wide then, panicking when he sees how bothered I am by his insinuation.

"Well, I'm not sure, he never told me he was to begin with, but it's hard not to notice. I spent my whole childhood watching him look at her in the same hopelessly in love way. He'd probably say he isn't, not anymore, but a love like that, does it ever truly fade?"

Yeah, I'm going to punch the fucking wall if we keep talking about James' feelings.

"We better stop discussing this. I'd rather not get kicked out of Formula One for knocking out one of the Hawke drivers," I say and straighten out my back.

It's not jealousy that makes me angry. Val is mine as much as I am hers. I trust her and know she'd never leave me for her best friend, but it makes me mad that James still thinks he'll end up with her.

He needs to back off before I stop trying my best for Valentina.

"Good idea," Adrian chimes in and leads me out of the room, both of us ready to get some rest.

I can't wait for mon tournesol to fall asleep in my arms.

Chapter 65

Valentina

Adrian's been avoiding me, but at least James gives me updates every few hours, letting me know he's alright, merely processing. I've been keeping busy with Gabriel's team, trying to learn as much as I possibly can. It's only Friday, but they have taught me more about F1 strategy in the two days I've been working with them than I have learned in my entire life.

I twist the infinity band on my left ring finger, the one Adrian gave me as I step out of the garage with Tomasso, Gabriel's race engineer, as he shares more information with me.

"Valentina," I hear Adrian say from behind me, and within seconds, tears fall down my cheek.

Before he said my name, before I heard his voice, I had no idea how deeply I was hurting. I turn around and run into his arms. He wraps his around my back, and I fling mine around his neck. His familiar scent fills my nose, and I cry even more.

"I'm so sorry I put you through this. I should have never walked away, that wasn't fair, and I should have talked to you about it. I'm sorry I just left." I want to tell him it's okay, but I can't find my voice.

Adrian pulls back from the hug, and I can see even he shed a tear.

"I hate not talking to you," I say, and he laughs a little.

"Yeah, I missed your mean comments and big heart too." It's my turn to laugh then. "Are you going to tell me everything?" he asks. I nod as he wipes away the tear that rolled down his cheek earlier. I wipe away my own.

I spend an hour explaining to Adrian what Carolina did, how I hid it from him, why I did it, and why it's taken me this long to tell him about it. The whole time I'm talking, Adrian tries his best to keep eye contact with me, but I can tell it's hard for him.

My eyes must show the pain I felt every day I was living with her, but there is nothing I can do to change it. It's burned into my body, just like it is into who I am. With every story, every slap, he flinches, his knuckles turning whiter. I can't imagine what he must be thinking right now, how he must be feeling.

When I'm done sharing, he looks off into the distance, thinking about how to respond after my long, horrifying story. I wouldn't know what to say either if he told me something like this. I would be so angry with the person who ever dared to harm him, which is exactly what his face is telling me. There is anger and sadness carved into his features.

I reach out to take his hand, and he lets me comfort him.

"It's not your fault. You are not responsible for what happened to me. I need you to understand that you didn't fail me," I say, causing the corners of his mouth to drop and more tears to escape his eyes. He covers his face with his hands, and I get up from the chair I've been sitting in to hug him.

"I am so sorry," he cries, and my heart breaks into a million pieces. I never wanted to make him feel this way.

We hug for what feels like an eternity, but at least when I step back, he isn't crying anymore, and neither am I.

"Are we okay?" he asks, and I shake my head.

"No, I think you have to buy me a bucket of ice cream first." I laugh, and so does he.

"You know, I always knew Gabriel and you were connected, but this is just another area in your lives you have in common. It's crazy," Adrian says, and I furrow both of my brows.

"What are you talking about?" I ask because I'm lost. My brother looks at me with confusion all over his face.

"A fucked up sibling of a parent that made your lives miserable," he goes on, but I'm about to slap him for being vague.

"Adrian, either tell me the whole story or let it go. I don't have the energy to play guessing games," I complain, and my brother sits up straight, clearing his throat before explaining his comment.

"Gabriel had an uncle, but he shut him out of his life a long time ago," Adrian says, but I shake my head and shrug. He's never told me anything about his uncle. "He's the reason why Gabriel almost didn't get to be a Formula One driver. He was drunk and driving Gabriel home from school. Gabriel was fourteen at the time, and they got into a terrible crash. Denis, his uncle, drove into another car, killing the other driver and severely injuring everyone involved. It took Gabriel almost an entire year to be able to walk normally again. That's why he has a scar on his leg." I recall the first time I saw it in the shower, a frown now settling on my face. "Anyway, after that, Denis went to jail and now he's in rehab, and Gabriel hasn't spoken to him since."

The thought of my boyfriend going through that breaks my heart all over again. Adrian looks at someone behind me, panic crossing his face.

"Damn, I've got to go do an interview, Val. I'll see you later," my brother says and jumps up, pressing a kiss to the top of my head and going back to work.

Chapter 66

Valentina

It's race day for Adrian and James, and I'm sitting next to my grandfather, watching the tiny screens in the loud pit box. My fingernails start to look appealing when I feel nervosity settle in my chest. I know it would help the feeling in the pit of my stomach, but I also know better than to bite my nails. Grandpa hates it when I do that.

"Come, little champion, we will watch from the sidelines."

Grandpa leads me outside, and I follow him to an area where we can watch the track. The only thing separating us from it is a big, steel fence. Every time one of the Formula Two cars races by, the loud noise makes my ears ring in the best way. I can't wait to sit in one of those myself.

"We're so close," I say, excitement coursing through me. It's always the same when we go outside. I feel exhilarated.

"That look on your face is exactly why I keep bringing you here," he replies, and I know what he means.

I'm in awe and completely mesmerized. The speed, the fans, the excitement, and the nerves are everything I need. Grandfather flew me out to Italy for this race, despite Aunt Carolina's objections.

The screeching of tires and a loud crashing sound grab my attention, and I watch as Juan Marquez and Oliver Jackson spin into the barricades, too close to where I'm standing. I am paralyzed with shock and fear. Every muscle in my body has turned to stone.

I continue to watch the cars for any signs of hope the drivers are okay. Except for the occasional bird chirping, everyone has forgotten how to make a sound, and I'm convinced no one else is breathing either.

"What is going on?" I finally ask after moments pass without anyone speaking.

Grandpa puts his hand on my shoulder and squeezes it. He is on the phone with someone, and I wait impatiently for more information.

"One of the drivers got out of the car safely, but the other one is unconscious."

More minutes pass until an hour is over, and then another one follows. Juan Marquez has been brought to the hospital, and Oliver Jackson is safe in his pit box. I'm sitting with Adrian, James, and Grandpa, waiting to hear about a change in Marquez's condition.

James holds my hand and squeezes it gently every once in a while. We are all praying Juan is going to be okay, although it didn't look good when they pulled him from the car.

Adrian's phone eventually rings, but he is too nervous to answer it. Grandpa takes it, and I try to listen for an update.

"He didn't make it out of surgery," he says once he hangs up. "Juan died from his injuries."

Today is the first day I truly realize how dangerous racing is.

Today, my respect for the sport has doubled, and I will never stop fearing the consequences that come with it.

I love it, but I will do my best to never lose sight of this danger again.

A loud bang makes me jump up in bed, and I watch Gabriel struggle to pick up the water bottle he dropped. When he sees me awake, an apologetic expression covers his face.

"I'm so sorry, chérie. I was trying to be careful, but I had a dizzy spell," he says, and I rub my eyes to wake up. Gabriel sits at the foot of the bed and pulls down his pants. "Go back to sleep," he whispers, but I smile at him.

"It's okay. How was the rest of your day?" I ask him.

"It was good. I got a lot of work done."

Gabriel smiles at me before he pulls his shirt over his head. He smells it before walking over to his suitcase and pulling out another one. However, he doesn't put it on; he simply hands it to me. My eyes drop to my chest, and I remove the tank top I'm wearing. His shirt fits me perfectly, and I'm surprised it smells like him even though he hasn't worn it yet.

"How was your day?" he asks me when he comes back out of the bathroom and lies down next to me. Before I answer, he brings his lips to mine, and I sigh when I taste the mint from his toothpaste.

"Hi," he says, making me grin at him.

"Hi," I reply. "My day was good. I made up with Adrian." I go on, and he listens closely while playing with a strand of my hair. My eyes drop to the side of his thigh, and I fixate on the faded scar that runs down from the middle to his knee. I trail my fingers along the skin there, thinking about what my brother told me earlier.

"Adrian told you," he says. "I can see it in your eyes." My gaze shifts away from him, but he places his fingers under my chin to bring my attention back to him.

"Are you mad?" I ask before Gabriel leans down to press a swift kiss to my lips.

"No. I never asked him to keep it a secret." He shifts around a little to get closer to me. "I hate my uncle, and I wish he never appeared in my life. His irresponsible behavior almost ruined my career." I wait for him to tell me more, but I don't know if he will. My hand moves to his cheek, and he closes his eyes in response to my touch. "I almost lost the ability to walk because of him." His eyelids flutter shut as he takes a deep breath. "I can't talk about it more, chérie, not yet," he says, and I smile at him.

"I'm sorry," I reply, and he kisses me again.

"Don't apologize." He runs his hand over my thigh, sending shivers down my spine.

We talk a little more before I fall asleep on his chest.

Gabriel is ahead, leading since lap fifty. Adrian is less than a second behind him. They're racing, battling each other for first place. I can't take my eyes off the screen. I can't even decide which one of them I want to win. It's a problem, and it's exactly what Adrian accused me of, but I love them both, and I would be happy for either of them.

After another two laps, Adrian is right next to Gabriel, their wheels almost touching. I need to look away, but I can't. My heart is stuttering in my chest.

Adrian cuts it closer and closer until there is no more space for Gabriel to drive on the track. My brother pushes him off, causing his car to flip and crash into the barrier. I don't know how to react, but I'm convinced a scream leaves my throat. I cover my mouth with my hands and watch the paramedics as they pull his lifeless body out of the car.

"He's gone," Hector says as he wraps his arms around me to hold me up. "He's gone," he repeats, and, this time, I'm sure screams leave me because I can't stop.

I'm sobbing and crying, and I can't comprehend what is happening.

No, God, no, no, no, not him, not him...

Chapter 67

Valentina

"Valentina, wake up, baby," Gabriel's voice fills my ears, and I shoot up in bed, my eyes opening and my heart beating too hard against my ribcage.

My gaze fixates on the half-naked man in front of me, and only when I see his full lips and green-brown eyes do I manage to calm my body.

"You're shaking, chérie. Did you have a nightmare?" All I can do is wrap my arms around his neck and sob. I've had a dream like this twice before. One was about losing James, the other about Adrian.

"You died, and there was nothing I could do about it." I put my fingers on his torso as he takes my curly hair into his hands so he can drag it over my shoulder and let it rain down my back.

"You know, my dad used to say if someone dreams about your death, you'll live longer in real life. So, thank you." He chuckles softly, and I drop my head against his naked chest. His skin is hot, and the steady beat of his heart calms my body. "I'm sorry you had a bad dream. I just closed my eyes when you started moving around, and then you screamed," he says, and I lean away once again.

"I'm so sorry, Gabriel. I don't know what brought this on, or even why tonight, but I guess dreams are just as uncontrollable as..." I try to think of a good comparison, but my mind goes blank.

"My love for you," he finishes my sentence, and I roll my eyes. I run my fingers over his left nipple, and he tucks his bottom lip between his teeth.

"God, that was incredibly cheesy. I think we need to break up."

His jaw drops, but he smiles at me and wraps his arms around my stomach, flipping me onto my back.

His mouth claims mine, kissing me until I feel his cock growing hard against my leg.

"Cheesy, huh?"

"One kiss and you're done?" I challenge, and he shakes his head.

"Does this feel like I'm done to you?" He rubs his cock against my leg, kisses me firmly again, and cups my breasts. A moan leaves both of us, but they are dulled by his lips on mine.

"More," I say before he kisses me again.

"And this," he goes on, guiding my shorts down, spreading my legs, and pressing his tongue against my aching clit.

My hands move to his hair, and I tighten my grip, making him groan. The vibration makes my back arch off the bed, and Gabriel's hands slip onto my hips to hold me down. His name leaves my lips while he drags my body closer to his mouth.

It leaves my skin, and I am about to complain when he replaces his tongue with his thumb and uses it to trace circles. My head is spinning, my skin is on fire, and I scream when he adds two fingers and pushes them inside of me.

"Oh God," I say, unable to keep the sounds of pleasures to myself.

The friction is heavenly, and the circles make me dizzy from pleasure. His lips move to my lower stomach while his fingers keep playing with me until I fall apart under his touch and cover my face with a pillow as I come down from my high. I press my legs together, enjoying all of the sweet after-effects of the orgasm.

It's fascinating how alive he makes me feel. It's like every cell in my body gets its own heartbeat, and they dance with every touch from Gabriel.

He pulls the pillow from my face, revealing my smirk.

"Don't look at me like that. I'm already aching."

"Let me help you with that, Monsieur Biancheri."

I remove his shirt from my chest, letting my breasts bounce free. His eyes close as his head falls backward against the pillow and he lets out a loud groan.

"I don't understand," he says, confusion washing over me. "It's not fair, you know." He sits up in bed and puts his hands on my face, then drops them to my breasts. "No one should have a body like yours," he says as his eyes focus on my lips.

"Why?" I ask, a little distracted by the way his big hands are cupping my breasts.

"Because every centimeter of you is absolutely and otherworldly beautiful," he says, making my heart stumble all over itself.

I lean forward until our lips are a centimeter apart. My right hand moves down to his boxers, and I tease him by rubbing my thumb up and down on his cock. He moans, but I cut him off by bringing my lips to his.

"Tell me what you want," I whisper, and he opens his mouth. No words come out, only groans of pleasure. "Tell me," I say, but he doesn't answer.

I remove my thumb, and he opens his eyes to look at me. I love that I made him speechless, but I need to know what he wants.

"That pretty mouth around me, if you're ready," he admits, and I smirk at him.

"I've been ready for a while now." I place a kiss to the soft spot on his neck. His head falls to the side, and I suck on the already purple mark there. For a brief moment, I wonder if anyone saw it today, the possessive side of me hoping they all did.

I kiss his neck for a minute longer until I get off his lap and kneel down in front of him. Gabriel gets up, pulls his boxers down, and sits on the edge of the bed, in front of me. The thought of taking all of him in my mouth makes me anxious. *I won't be able to, will I?*

"You're so big," I say, and he puts his index finger under my chin, lifting my head to get me to look at him.

"Go slow, and let your hands do what they do best on the part that doesn't fit in your mouth."

I nod, put my hands on his thighs, take a small breath, and sit up so I can press my lips against his again. I feel like I need some more time to prepare, even if I've been ready to do this for weeks.

His hands cup my face, his tongue massaging mine. It's like he knows I need another moment and doesn't mind giving me as much time as I need.

I lean away and trace kisses down his body until I reach the line of hair that leads to his cock. I lick up his torso one more time, making him moan, his hand slipping into my hair. He's under my complete control, which excites every cell in my body. With another deep breath, I move down to his cock and press a kiss to the head of his penis.

"Mhmm," he says. Hearing him motivates me to go further.

I run my tongue down his cock, switching between licking him and sucking until he moans loudly.

"Yeah, just like that," he groans.

I look up at him and see his eyes are closed and lips slightly parted. My focus goes back to pleasuring him, and he grabs a handful of my hair, tugging. This is so unfamiliar to me, but at the same time, I like it. I like pleasuring him this way, to hear him moan my name.

"You're doing so well for me, chérie," he praises, so I go a bit faster.

His hands grip the edge of the bed while I take him all the way down my throat until my gag reflex sets in, then lean back again. I repeat the same thing when he starts to let out little moans for me.

"Fuuuuuuck, Val, I'm gonna—" He cuts off, but I keep going until I feel his warm liquid shoot down my throat. Gabriel's legs shake, and I give him a proud smile.

"Hmmm," I say as I stand up and straddle his lap. He pulls my mouth to his, kissing me fiercer than ever before.

"You didn't have to swallow, you never do." I lick my lips before I answer.

"I know, but I wanted to," I whisper in a seductive voice, and he falls onto the mattress.

"You can't say those things to me, otherwise I'll be proposing sooner than either of us is ready for," he jokes, and I lean forward until my lips are a centimeter from his.

"You mean things like how fucking good it felt to have you come in my mouth?" I ask, so he flips us over so I'm the one on my back.

"Yes, things like that," he says, indecisiveness on his face. I can tell he wants to keep going, but he needs to rest. Tomorrow is Qualifying, and he has to be fit for it.

"I love you," I tell him, taking away the sexual tension and making a soft expression cover his face.

"I love you the same, mon tournesol."

Chapter 68

Valentina

"Come on, Adrian," I whisper, my hands shaking and my legs bouncing up and down.

I hate watching him struggle in seventh place, but there is nothing he could have done. Eduardo pushed him off the track in the first corner and by the time he rejoined the others, he was in eighteenth place. He's been making his way back up while Gabriel occupies the second position, fighting Kyle for first. I keep watching Adrian, and I smile when he shoots past James and holds up his pinkie.

"Why is Adrian showing James his pinkie?" someone asks next to me.

I don't tell them. That story is too personal, and if anyone knew, it could be trouble for both of them. But I can't help that stupid grin on my face when I replay the memory of the pinkie incident in my head.

It happened about fourteen years ago, and it was one of the funniest things I've ever witnessed. I remember it as if it happened yesterday, even though I was so young.

It was on a Saturday, and Grandpa took Adrian, James, and me karting. I was racing against my brother and best friend for a little while, and I remember winning every race against them. Eventually, I had to go to the bathroom, which meant Grandpa went with me, leaving the two idiots alone on the track.

When we came back, Adrian had driven into James, and our friend broke his pinkie. I don't know how or why it happened, but I also know a couple of children like them didn't have common sense. Grandpa took James to the hospital where he had to get his pinkie in a cast and couldn't move it for an entire month.

From that moment on, Adrian started teasing James about it. Soon, because they were young and not allowed to show each other the middle finger, they chose to use their pinkies instead.

My eyes focus on the screen again, and my heart stops when I see Gabriel trying to move past Kyle. Their cars touch and Gabriel's front left tire gets a puncture, causing him to spin off the track. I gasp and groan when I see it. I can't believe he's out of the race now when he was so close to winning. Gabriel gets out of his car, and I sigh with relief when I see he's okay.

He's frustrated. I can see it in the way he kicks the dirt and puts his hands on his helmet. When they replay the incident, I notice Kyle didn't leave enough space for Gabriel and practically forced him off the track. That's why I'm glad when the FIA starts investigating the accident.

"You see this here, Valentina, this is what we deal with when a driver crashes," Tomasso, Gabriel's race engineer says, interrupting my thoughts.

I've been working with my boyfriend's team the entire weekend, studying their strategies, methods, and procedures. I listen to his explanation of the course of action they take.

Moments later, my boyfriend walks through the garage and toward me. I give him a confused look, but he merely grabs my hand and leads me into his private room, the one where he gets massaged after races.

He rips off his helmet and balaclava, throwing them to the side and closing the distance between us. His arms wrap around my chest, and I lift mine to hug him back, ignoring how sweaty he is.

"Are you sure I should be here?" I ask, and he pulls back to look at me.

Sweat drips down the side of his forehead, and I reach for the towel next to us to wipe it away. His eyes are glassy, making the green in them even more dominant.

"I want you right here and nowhere else," he replies, claiming my lips. "I need you." His arms wrap around me, holding me close for a very long time. I rub his back, comforting him to the best of my ability.

"You need to go out there. They are waiting for you," I remind him eventually, his arms tightening around me.

"I know," he says, pressing a kiss to my forehead.

"I'm sorry about your race. I know you were fighting really hard, but you know what, mon amour?" He smiles at me when I call him that like he always does. "I'm so proud of you, no matter if you win or lose. You are an incredible man, an amazing driver, and I know in the next race you are going to be on top again. I have absolutely no doubt."

"My pitstop," he mumbles, so I grin at him.

"Go and talk to your race engineer, look over the data and footage." His green eyes are focused on my face, his hands on my hips.

"This bossy side of you turns me on," he says, and I step on my tiptoes to press my lips to his.

"Go," I command, and he smirks at me.

His hands leave my skin, and, as he walks past me, I smack his ass. He turns around again, looks me up and down, and then disappears out of the room with the biggest grin on his face.

I walk back out just in time to see Adrian overtake Eduardo and finish in third place. I clutch my hands together in excitement and jump up and down.

"Yes," I whisper when I see James is in second place. He must have overtaken Adrian sometime during the race again, and Cameron is in fifth.

My happiness soon fades when I see Kyle didn't even get a penalty.

"What the fuck?" I say more to myself, but Gabriel's arms wrap around me from behind before he answers my unspoken question.

"I know, apparently it was a racing incident and nothing to investigate any further. Trust me, I'm just as angry as you. Well, probably not as angry. I mean there is steam coming out of your ears." I turn around and nudge his arm. "Hey, ouchie," he playfully complains but then smiles at me. "I'm going to go and be interviewed, but I'll see you later, ma chérie."

He kisses my cheek before I make my way outside to give my big brother a hug and celebrate with him. Adrian, James, and Kyle get out of their cars, and, unsurprisingly, while Kyle is being interviewed, James and Adrian hold up their pinkies to each other. They're laughing and talking until it is their turn.

Before they go up to the podium, James and Adrian come to hug their team and me.

After the celebrations, Tomasso and Hector do their best to give me a few more lessons on what a driver is meant to do after a race. I take notes, unwilling to forget even the smallest detail I've learned this weekend.

"Valentina," a familiar voice fills my ears, but I can't identify who it belongs to until I turn around.

Lorenzo Mattia, the boss of the Velocità Rossa team, approaches me, an approving smile on his face.

"How are you?" he asks and offers his hand for me to shake.

"Very well. Thank you so much for this opportunity, sir," I reply in Italian because I spent all weekend memorizing this sentence to impress him, which he seems to be.

"You're welcome," he states before switching back to English. "I must say, I am very impressed with you. There has hardly been a trainee as determined to learn as you. You've shown nothing but kindness to my team, and I will let Andrea know how well you've done," he says and squeezes my shoulder.

I'm about to respond when he starts a conversation with Tomasso instead.

"Come on," I hear Adrian say from beside me, taking my hand to lead me away from the team I don't ever want to leave.

I belong in this place, that has become more than clear to me over the past four days. There is nothing I won't do to get back here.

Chapter 69

Gabriel

Domi and Nicolette have been staring at my computer screen for the past few minutes, looking through the photos of the apartments I've chosen. They both have a sad look on their face, but we all know it's time I move out. The only reason I stayed was to make sure Jean was okay, and now he is.

I need my own space where Valentina and I can have privacy, where I can finally have that art studio I've always dreamed of. With the baby on the way, my aunts will need my room to convert into a nursery anyway.

"You sure this is what you want?" Domi asks, a tear slipping down her cheek. I wipe it away and take her hand in mine.

"I'm sorry it has to be now, but we all know it's for the best," I say, and Nicolette gives me a reassuring smile.

She's been on my ass to move out for a year now, telling me to live my life and stop worrying about everyone else. This will be easier for her than for Domi.

"But, what if we need you to help out with the baby? You won't be here," she points out, and I feel worse than I already did before when more tears stream down her face.

"I'll always be here, Domi," I promise, and she stands up to hug me.

"He's moving like ten minutes away from us, Dominique, it's not the end of the world," Nicolette says, earning herself a frown from her wife.

"He's my little racer," she says, and I smile at her.

She's called me that since I was ten years old when she met me for the first time at a karting race. *Damn... that was a long time ago.* The realization almost makes me shudder.

"It's going to be hard not to have him here when he isn't away winning Grands Prix." She settles down on her chair again, letting Nicolette hug her.

"I know, ma colombe, but he needs his space, and we can use his room for the baby," she says, kissing Domi's cheek and rubbing her stomach. "It'll be fine, don't worry," Nicolette adds with a smile that reveals how happy she is.

I shut my laptop and push it to the side, settling down in the seat across from them.

"Alright, baby names. What have you got so far?" I ask to change the subject.

Their faces light up, and we spend the next hour or so discussing what would fit best in our family. Eventually, Nicolette stands up to braid Domi's coily hair, something she's trying to get better at, and I make them a cup of tea.

"What about, if it's a boy, Maxime Guillaume," Domi suggests, and a pain shoots through my chest.

It's been a while since I've heard my father's name.

"If it's a girl, maybe we could name her Vivienne Lilliana," she goes on, and I fight the urge to walk away from this conversation.

Vivienne was my grandmother's name, and Lilliana was my mother's. What Domi is trying to do is wonderful and kind, but it rips my heart into several pieces. More pain crosses me, and I struggle to breathe.

"Those are perfect," I reply and get up, grabbing my phone to dial the number of the only person who can put my heart back together right now. "I have to get some work done, but I'll speak to you both later."

I kiss their cheeks before sprinting upstairs and shutting my bedroom door. The phone rings against my ear, but she picks up soon, her soft voice coming through the speaker.

"*Bonsoir, mon soleil. Est-ce que je te manques?*" she asks, and I enjoy the way the French falls from her lips.

"I do, I miss you more than anything," I reply, the grip on my phone tightening as I try to calm my heart.

It's getting more difficult to be apart from her, especially since the last time we were together was almost a week ago. I tried to visit her, but I had to do some photoshoots for the new sponsor my team got.

"I miss you the same, Gabriel, but I can hear there's something else bothering you. Do you want to tell me about it?" Valentina asks, and I realize for the millionth time I'm going to marry her.

One day, I will put a ring on her finger because she's the love of my life, and nothing will ever change my mind. I've known it for a while, longer than we've been dating, and even if I didn't want to admit it to myself before, I can no longer deny it.

"Domi and Nicolette were choosing baby names, and they decided on some that honor the family we've lost. I don't know why it hurt me." The control she has over me is dangerous. I'd never share this with anyone who isn't Val because it's too personal.

"I can't hear any names of the people I've lost without feeling pain. If I had to hear it every day... the thought would hurt me too," she says, and I sink to the floor, holding onto my knees while I listen to her soothing voice. "But I think it would also help me move on, in a way. The name would be given a different meaning, a happier one. It could be beautiful," Val adds, and I can sense the hint of a smile on her lips.

"When are you coming home?" I ask because I'm starting to feel homesick.

With my schedule, I won't be able to fly out and see her, but I'm hoping Valentina will be back in a few days.

"I don't know, mon amour. Andrea is pushing us past our limits since they have to decide who to give the spot to in a couple of weeks. Tomorrow we'll be setting our final simulator times, which they will use when they make the decision." Nervosity slips through in her voice, making it crack with the last word.

"You've been kicking Christian's ass for the last four weeks, ma chérie. You got this." And I have no doubt she does. The day he gets the seat over her is the day Adrian can walk past a mirror without fixing his hair and admiring himself.

"I hope so, but there are more categories I have to beat him in, one isn't enough," she reminds me, and I nod before realizing she can't see me.

"You were born to be an F1 driver, tournesol. One way or another, it will happen," I reply, and she sighs into the phone.

"Never stop dreaming with me, okay?" she asks, and I smile to myself, standing up and walking over to my bookshelf to look for something to distract my mind once she hangs up.

"It's not a dream, it'll be reality, and I need you to start believing it too," I say, almost scolding her.

Val laughs into the phone, the soft sound sending another wave of homesickness over me. My heart misses her, my head misses her, my entire existence *misses her.*

"I will believe it when it happens, not a moment before," she says, shutting down any further discussion on this subject. "Now, tell me, how is the apartment hunt going?" she asks, shifting our focus to a lighter topic.

"Pretty good. I've found a few places I like, but we need to see them together when you're back," I explain, grabbing one of the books I bought for Valentina.

"Why? You want to put me in different positions there and see if it looks good?" she teases, and I can't hold the chuckle back.

"Come on, baby, we both know you could make a dumpster an appealing place to live for me if you spread your legs on top of it," I reply, making her go silent for a brief moment.

"I'm going to ask Andrea when we next get the chance to go home. I hate this distance," she says, and I click my tongue in response.

"It won't be like that for much longer, you'll see."

My optimism is probably annoying her, but I can't turn it off anymore. Valentina is so close to getting everything she's worked for her entire life.

"I'm going to read one of your new books tonight," I say when she doesn't respond.

"Read it to me?" she asks, which is exactly what I was hoping she'd say. The only reason I picked it up was to hear this question.

"Always, chérie."

Chapter 70

Valentina

I've been nervous, but how I'm feeling right now takes it to another level. If my time is worse than Christian's, I'm going to struggle with my confidence in the rest of the categories too, which is what this test is about.

Am I capable of pushing everything aside to focus on the task ahead?

It's what my grandfather taught me to do, but I've never had this kind of pressure on my shoulders. I've never had it all come down to me fighting only against my rival, the person I despise the most in the entire universe.

"Is the always collected Tina nervous?" Christian asks as he steps into the room, his white-blonde hair even lighter today and his brown eyes full of amusement.

"You know, there is a processing time on the box. Maybe don't leave the dye in for *that* long next time. I wouldn't want your hair to fall out," I say, and he laughs at my comment.

"This hair cost me two thousand euros, sweetheart, it's not box-dyed, and you know it," he replies, but I give him a confused look.

"My bad. I underestimated how spoiled you truly are for the last time, *Your Royal Highness*," I spit, and he takes the seat next to mine.

I stand up immediately, trying to get as far away from him as possible. My body cringes from disgust every single time he comes close to it, and I need to stay in control right now. *Balance*. I have to find balance. I'm already struggling emotionally, I don't need him to throw me off physically because of his nausea-inflicting presence.

"How was Baku, by the way? Did you learn anything new? Like sucking off your boyfriend before the race?" He laughs at his "joke," but there's nothing funny about it.

His family would understand if I punched him in the face, right?

"You truly think that's all a woman is good for, don't you? Just attending to her man, making sure he has everything he needs, giving him head, and disregarding her own desires?"

"Not all women, just you." Christian gives me a wicked smile.

I won't let him succeed in his attempts to throw me off my game. He's trying to get under my skin, piss me off so anger will take over when I'm in the simulator.

"Although you're being very selfish with Gabriel at the moment. You're here all the time now when he needs you at his races. You're only focusing on your career, on what you need."

His words hit me hard, but not just because of Gabriel. They hit me because I know Adrian, James, Cameron, and Gabriel all miss me. It also doesn't help that I've been feeling selfish about this choice for a while, but Christian will not be the one to guilt-trip me. No one will.

"I may be selfish, but there's no question about you being a sexist, misogynistic asshole."

His eyes go wide for a moment before he composes himself again.

"Please, how much longer will you fight your attraction for me?" he asks.

"You disgust me, and I will never, ever be attracted to you, Christos."

He furrows his brows at the new name, just like he always does, and I almost smile.

"What's it with the fucking incorrect names? I'm not here calling you Valerie or some shit," he complains, and I turn away to hide how proud I am to have gotten in his head. "You will answer me when I speak to you," he demands, and my shoulders go stiff. "You're a citizen of Monaco, and I'm your prince. You will show me respect."

Don't beat him up. You'll get kicked out of the academy. Don't. It will ruin your career.

I turn around, curtsying before I raise my head.

"Burn in hell," I say in Spanish, frustrating him even more.

"You know what? I'm so done with you! You act like you're so special when I have been training to be a race car driver since I was two years old!" I cross my arms in front of my chest as he yells at me, yet again pretending to be better than me.

"And you've been a spoiled dick since birth. What's your fucking point?"

"I'm your prince!" he repeats as he steps toward me, but I roll my eyes.

He grabs my shoulders, but I slap his arms away with my hands, shoving him backward. Christian barely holds himself up, too surprised at my willingness to fight back.

"Touch me again, and I will do far worse than push you," I warn, but the shock on his face hasn't worn off entirely. "You're not my prince. You're nothing more to me than a rival that needs to be taught a lesson," I reply right as Andrea walks into the room. They look us up and down before clearing their throat.

"We're ready for you, Christos, uh, sorry, I mean Christian," they say, and the brat walks away without saying another word, anger making his shoulders vibrate. I laugh with Andrea, who turns to wink at me before disappearing into the simulator room.

I sit back down, more nervosity now washing through me. My phone rings and I notice a long message from my brother.

Adrian: I know you're nervous. I know you're scared you'll mess up, but you've got this. Out of the two of us, you've always been the more focused one. There's nothing you can't do. It's time they all found out, too. No matter what happens, know I'm the proudest brother in the world. You've come a long, difficult way, but it's all going to be worth it. I love you.

I text him back in time for Christian to walk out of the room, a smug smile on his face.

"There is no way you'll beat that time, Tina." He takes the seat next to mine again, and I get up to follow Andrea.

"Watch me, Christoph." His frown fuels my confidence.

Andrea tells me to settle down in the seat of the simulator, handing me the helmet and patting my shoulder to reassure me. I take a couple of seconds to calm my heart and prepare myself for what's to come.

Lorenzo Mattia, Colin Reiner, and Andrea are all watching me do this. I can*not* fuck this up. There's never been a more important moment in my life, and this is the ultimate test to see if I've got what it takes.

It's time I prove to them women deserve the same opportunities as men.

"Whenever you're ready," Mr. Mattia says, and I give him a slight nod.

They chose the Australian track, which almost makes me smile. I've been racing virtually on this one for years, longer than any other.

I take one last deep breath before the simulation starts, pressing down on the gas pedal as soon as the lights go out. I speed down the track, avoiding the curbs as much as I can, braking later than I probably should, and accelerating to the maximum as soon as I know a straight is coming. Everything is going well. Adrenaline courses through me, pushing me further than ever.

Too far.

I almost lose control of the car as I take the curb, but, somehow, it stays on track. It probably cost me a lot of time though, which momentarily distracts me. *Breathe, race, win*. My grandfather's voice echoes in my ears, so I push myself to focus.

I finish the lap, but I'm not shown my time. They instruct me to wait outside once I'm out of the simulator, and I do as I'm told, ignoring Christian's presence. After that horrible lap, I'm not up for another battle. I have to concentrate solely on not bursting into tears of disappointment.

Grandfather would scold me for losing my focus. He'd also give me a big hug and tell me everything will be alright, but I can only do one of those for myself right now.

A while later, Andrea and Lorenzo appear in the doorframe, serious expressions on their faces. The team principal takes a step toward us, a piece of paper in his hands. His body turns to Christian, his shoulders rising and falling in a steady motion.

"I heard about Valentina's karting 'accident,'" he starts, making air quotations around the word. My rival tenses. "We do not tolerate that behavior in our academy, let alone our Formula One team. Do you understand me?"

"I didn't do any—" He's cut off before he can finish lying.

"Do you understand me?" Lorenzo repeats, his voice firm and demanding now.

"Yes, sir," Christian says, and I almost pity him. His usual cold demeanor has vanished, a child-like one taking its place.

"Good. As for your results—" Lorenzo pauses, turning to me with a smile growing on his face. "Valentina was two-tenths faster." Christian's eyes go wide as he storms in front of Andrea.

"Which track did she get? She got an easier one, didn't she? You're taking pity on her because she's a girl!" Andrea wipes something off their face, and I realize he must have spat on them in his rage.

"If I were you, I'd sit my ass down before I drag you from the headquarters myself," they warn, but Christian shakes his head. "I really don't think you understand what it means for a person who isn't a cis-gender man in this sport. I'm done listening to someone who wasn't oppressed talk to me, *to us*, about fucking pity opportunities."

The prince suddenly becomes quiet as our instructor puts him in his place.

"Valentina had the same track as you, the same settings, and she even made a slight mistake in the tenth corner, but she was still faster. Let that speak for itself, *Your Highness.*"

I can barely hold back the smile that wants to light up my face. *I did well. I did better than him.* My legs vibrate, begging me to jump up and down from excitement. Somehow, I manage to stay grounded, at least for the moment.

"You can all suck my dick!" Christian says in French so the other two don't understand before he rushes out of the room.

My eyes go wide, but my attention shifts to Lorenzo Mattia, who is holding out his hand for me to shake.

"Well done, Valentina. I'm looking forward to seeing your next results," he says and leaves the room as well.

Andrea turns to me, and I finally let the tears of relief drop.

"You look like you could use a hug," they point out, and I nod before they wrap their arms around me, rubbing my back to comfort me. "I hope you know I will do everything I can to help you get that seat. You deserve it more than anyone I've ever taught here," they say, and I step back to show them my smile.

"I'm thankful for everything you've already done."

"You think I'd let you fight this royal brat by yourself? Never," they promise and give my shoulder one last squeeze. "Now, it's about time you got to go home. I'll see you in about a week," they say, and excitement fills my chest.

I finally get to see my family again.

Chapter 71

Valentina

Adrian and Gabriel are busy when I arrive in Monaco, which gives me time to find out what's been going on with my best friend.

I knock on James' door, who I haven't heard from in days, and wait impatiently for him to open it. I'm concerned; he's never ignored me like this. Adrian hasn't seen or spoken to him either, which is odd. Something's wrong, and I'm going to find out what it is.

When minutes pass, and there is no sign of life, I walk around his house down the path that leads to the pool area. The door that is usually unlocked is locked for the first time in years, and I groan as I climb over the gate. James is making this a lot more difficult than it needs to be.

I make my way toward the sliding doors leading into his living room and can't believe my eyes when I see James on his couch in front of his television. *Why didn't he open the door?*

I knock on the glass, and his head lifts up. That's when I get really worried. He hasn't shaved in days, there are empty beer bottles all around him, dark circles under his eyes, and even from far away, I can see they are flaming red. He's either been crying or not sleeping.

When he sees me, he rolls his eyes and focuses on his television again. I know he wants me to leave, but I'm too concerned. My fist keeps knocking on the glass.

"What the fuck do you want? Can't you see I want to be left alone?" He's yelling at me, but I don't think he's mad at me. "Leave me alone, Valentina. Just leave me alone."

He slams the door shut again, so I go back to knocking.

"Just go away," he tells me when he rips it open. This time, however, tears fall down his cheeks, and he's no longer furious.

"Let me in," I beg, and he nods, his head falling in defeat. I wrap my arms around his torso, ignoring how bad he smells. Beer and sweat.

"What happened?" I ask with a gentle, low voice. When he doesn't answer, I pull back and look at him. "Let me in," I repeat, but this time I mean it in a different way.

"I'm going to be a dad," he says and chokes on his own spit.

James covers his mouth with his hand before sinking to the ground, and I follow him. He's silent for a long time, and I rub the back of his hand with my thumb in an attempt to comfort him. My heart is racing in my chest as I try to process this new information.

"How—" I can't even finish phrasing the sentence before my voice cracks.

"About seven months ago, I was casually seeing this girl Annabel, and she came to my place on Thursday. She could not have been more pregnant, Val." He shakes his head, but I can't comprehend anything he's saying. "I even took a paternity test. I really am the father, there is no denying that." More tears roll down his cheek. "I'm twenty-three years old, I can't be a father! This isn't how it was supposed to happen. I'm supposed to fall in love with a girl, marry her, then think about expanding our family. This is not how it's supposed to go." James is yelling at me again, and I can't hold back the tears leaving my eyes.

I'm quiet for a while until I find words.

"I know it's not, but, James, you're going to be a dad. You're going to have a child that needs you. This baby is going to love you, and you don't have to do any of it alone. I'm right here by your side, Annabel is going to be there, and she is probably just as terrified as you are. And you have Adrian, your sister, and your parents. We're all here for you. But what you have to do is, well, first of all, you need to take a shower. You smell absolutely disgusting," I inform him, and he lets out a laugh he doesn't mean. "Then you gotta stop drinking because it's not going to make this go away. Afterward, you have to go talk to Annabel."

He nods, and I take his other hand in mine.

"I got you, James. You know that, but now, you have to meet me halfway."

I get up from the ground and hold out my hand for him. He takes it, so I help him up, too.

James tells me more about Annabel after he has finished showering and shaving. I find out she is from Monaco, has a sister, and didn't tell him she was pregnant for six months because she didn't want to ruin his life. I can't imagine what she must have gone through. Finding out she's having a baby at twenty-two, unsure whether or not to tell the father because he just started his career, and then doing it all by herself must be terrifying. Her parents live in England, and she only has her sister here.

I want to say I don't understand why she didn't tell James earlier, but I can't. Annabel must be scared, like James is. I am too, in a way, terrified *for* him.

I wipe my face with my hands. James is in the kitchen getting some water while I check my phone for any messages. I have three new ones, all from Gabriel.

Gabriel: I miss you.

Gabriel: I'm home now.

Gabriel: If you want, you can come to my place or I'll go to yours.

I shake my head and smile at my phone. It soon fades when I realize I can't go to his house. My first priority is to make sure James meets with Annabel and sorts this mess out.

Valentina: I miss you the same, but I have to take care of something, mon amour. I'll let you know when I'll be home.

Within seconds, Gabriel texts back.

Gabriel: If you need me, I'm here.

James walks back into the room with a glass of water for me.

"Will you come with me? I don't think I can do this by myself." I bite my bottom lip and think about his request for a brief moment.

"Sure," I say, and he gives me a small smile. Before I can overthink things any further, I get up from the couch and walk over to where his keys are.

Annabel knows we're coming, and it takes us ten long minutes, which are filled with silence, to get there.

"Come on," I tell James, who has been staring at her small home since we got here.

"I'm terrified," he whispers, so I put my hand on his.

"I know. You don't have to do this alone, I'm right here," I reassure him, and he places his head against his headrest while he studies my expression.

"I love you so much. You know that, right?"

"I know, and I love you. Now, let's face our fear, yeah?" Once again, he only nods.

We walk down the short path that leads to Annabel's house, and I knock on the door before James can change his mind.

I feel like throwing up. This is too much for one person to process as quickly as I'm trying to. I keep reminding myself of James' feelings, and I have to continue to prioritize them. If I focus on mine, I might actually throw up.

A beautiful, very pregnant woman opens the door for us. Annabel has long, brown hair, and round lips. She's breathtaking.

"James," she says when her brown eyes find him standing awkwardly next to me.

I wonder why my best friend was only casually seeing her, but that's a question for later when things have settled.

"Who are you?" she asks me, so I hold out my hand for her.

"I'm Valentina," I say because I'm not quite sure what else to tell her.

"It's nice to meet you. I'm sorry, I wasn't expecting someone else to join us, but please, come in. Make yourselves at home. I'll be right there, I just have to run to the bathroom. This baby seems to think my bladder is a trampoline," she jokes, and I smile at her.

She shoots James a quick grin before leaving the room.

"Maybe it's that pregnant glow, but she is gorgeous. And she seems very nice," I say to James, and he gives me a brief smile.

"Yeah, she is, I guess. I don't know. She isn't the one I thought I would end up having a baby with." He gives me a weird look, and I feel my heart skip a beat.

Oh.

"I had this whole dream in my head of how life was going to be, but now, everything is so messy," he replies, making me frown. For the first time in my life, he looks truly broken.

"I understand, I really do, James, but you gotta take a deep breath. This is reality, it's not a fantasy, and saying it's unfair won't change what's going on. Now, Annabel doesn't need any more stress. I'm sure she has enough as it is."

"Yeah, well, so have I. My life is fucking upside down, and I don't want it. I don't want any of it," he yells at me just as Annabel walks back into the room.

My best friend storms out of the house while Annabel is standing in the same spot, tears filling her eyes.

"I'm so sorry, Annabel, " I say and step toward her.

She waves away my apology and dabs her eyes with a tissue.

"Don't be silly. It's not your fault. I'm sorry for creating this mess. I never wanted to do this to him, which is why I didn't tell him to begin with. Deep down, I knew this would happen," she explains while I help her sit down on the couch. "Thank you." I smile at her.

"It takes two people to have sex, Annabel. This isn't your fault. Accidents happen. I'm just sorry James is reacting like this." I take a deep breath and look into her warm eyes. "I do understand why he is feeling this way, though." She nods and takes a sip of her water.

"So do I, but how can I make this easier for him? I'm not forcing him to be involved in this baby's life," she says. It's not her responsibility to make it easier for him.

"It's up to James now. There's nothing you can do."

After a while of Annabel and I talking about where she grew up and what she studied in university, James walks back into the room.

"Val, can you give us some time? You can take my car home," he tells me, but I pull his keys out of my pocket.

"I'll walk home. It's not far," I assure him, but he only nods absentmindedly.

He's not listening to me anymore, he's focused on the woman carrying their baby.

"It was nice to meet you. If you need anything, feel free to call me, you have my number." Annabel squeezes my arm and I hand James his keys.

He gives me a brief kiss on the top of my head before I leave.

Chapter 72

Valentina

For the first time in hours, I inhale, filling my lungs with as much oxygen as possible before letting out the breath through gritted teeth. I take my time walking home to be able to process everything that happened today.

James is going to be a father. He's going to have a child... I still can't believe it.

It takes me a moment to decide whether or not I want to see Gabriel or be alone right now. My body makes that choice for me when I walk past my house and toward Gabriel's.

My feet start to move faster with every step until I find myself running down the street. I won't be able to tell him about today, it isn't my secret to share, but I really need to be with him.

My fist connects with the front door, and seconds later, Jean opens it for me.

"Val, what's wrong?" he asks, and I try to force a smile. His green eyes study my face.

"Where's Gabriel?" I don't want to make small talk with him. All I want to do is find my boyfriend and feel his arms wrapped around my tired body.

"He's upstairs."

I run past him and to Gabriel's room. I don't bother knocking on his door either. When I step in, he's lying on the bed with a notebook and pencil in his hands. His eyes lift from the drawing, panic settling in them when he sees me.

"Chérie?" he says and gets up. I let his arms give me the comfort I crave. A sigh slips past my lips, but I don't try to stop it either. My pitstop. I can finally breathe again.

"What happened?" His mahogany scent fills my nose, making me sigh.

"I can't tell you," I reply, so he pulls back to look at me.

"Are you sure? Maybe I can help you." I smile at him.

"It's not my story to tell, and to be honest, mon soleil, I just want to be with you right now." Although I can see the curiosity burning in his eyes, he loves me enough to drop it. He simply nods, kisses me on my lips, and leads me to his bed.

"Okay, so I bought a canvas today, and I was thinking about drawing you on it." My eyes go wide, and I stop moving.

"Naked?" I ask him, and he smiles.

"Naked, clothed, whatever you want," he responds, and as much as I try to hide my smile, I can't.

"Where would we hang it? We can't just put it in your room. Jean and your aunts will see it. And we can't hang it in my room because of Adrian and Mrs. Beaumont." Gabriel nods and puts on his thinking face: biting the inside of his cheek and staring at the wall.

"The only solution I can think of is buying our own house," he says, and, just like expected, my heart skips several beats.

"We've only been dating a few weeks!" I laugh, but he doesn't.

"I've waited long enough," he says. I walk over to him to put my hands on his cheeks.

"Listen closely, Gabriel. We've only been dating for a couple of months, we can't buy a house. I know we've known each other a lot longer, but still! Are you crazy?" My voice is gentle, which is why he smiles.

"Yeah, crazy about you, about us, about our future," he says, so I let out a short laugh.

"We're not ready for that, and you know it." Gabriel frowns, but I run my thumbs over his thick eyebrows. He closes his eyes in response and pulls his bottom lip between his teeth. I let go of him and guide the dress I'm wearing over my head. "However, I am ready to get naked for you," I tell him, and his eyes linger on my breasts as his hands lift to them.

"To get drawn or to fuck?" My body reacts to his words instantly, the familiar ache returning between my legs.

"Both offers are extremely tempting," I respond and put my index finger under my chin as if I'm contemplating which of his suggestions to take. "I'd say first draw me, and if you do a good job, maybe we can move on to the next part." He closes the distance between us to nibble on my neck and make me giggle.

I get completely naked and lie down on the bed. Gabriel walks over to me and adjusts my position, my hair, and asks me to change my facial expression before he gets a thin fabric and covers my sex and breasts. This solves the problem of where we will hang it because it's no longer as inappropriate, at least no more than me in a bikini.

"Comfortable?" he asks, and I smile at him.

"For now, but I'm going to sit here for a while, so ask me again later."

Gabriel chuckles as he sets up the canvas on his artist's easel and starts drawing. I watch him with a genuine smile, and he grins at me when he catches me staring. Every now and then, we talk about something random, but he's mostly focused on the canvas in front of him.

It fascinates me how he goes from looking all concentrated and handsome to smiling at me and looking adorable.

Eventually, the hand on which my head is resting gets tired, but I ignore the uncomfortable feeling to continue focusing on Gabriel. He asks me a couple of times how I'm doing, and I continue to assure him I'm fine. He seems too happy for me to admit that my hand is asleep and I'm getting cold.

The more I watch him, the more I can't help but realize how far I've fallen. It's weird that I can't imagine my life without him anymore. He's become one of the few people I rely on. He's become the only other person apart from James and my family I have felt comfortable saying "I love you" to, and it means more than anyone could ever understand.

I need him because he gives me something I can't live without anymore. He gives me hope for a family, a beautiful life, love, and everything I could ever want in the future. I'm going to make my dream come true, and we'll travel the world together, winning races and continuing to explore this very new, very raw thing between us. I've never loved someone like I love him. I don't think I could ever stop. Our passions overlap. We fit so well together, it scares me a little. I fear no one will make me feel the same way he does. I fear he's the one for me, which may be my naïve almost nineteen-year-old brain talking.

Then again, I don't think it is. I've never met anyone who could make me feel so... complete. The holes in my chest have become more bearable, and although I miss the ones I've lost, thinking of them doesn't bring me this awful pain anymore.

"Okay, I think I'm finished with the sketch. I'll add the colors later," he says, and I grin.

"You think you'll remember everything about my body when I'm not here?" I ask while he studies his work.

"I have memorized everything about you, ma chérie. I'll be fine," he replies, sending warmth spread through me. "You are breathtaking," he mumbles at the canvas, and I smile at him.

He turns it for me to look at, and I forget how to breathe. Gabriel made me look like an angel. I stare back at him in awe.

"You like it?" he asks, and I tilt my head.

"I love it," I reply, making Gabriel smirk proudly. A few moments pass before I get a little impatient and remove the cloth. "Why are you so far away?" I ask him, and he cocks an eyebrow at me.

The dimples in his cheeks cause my insides to turn, and the way his smile changes into a sexy smirk makes my body ache. Gabriel removes his shirt, and I bite my lip in response as his muscles flex. He struts over to me, wasting no time before he pins me down on the bed.

"I crave you," he says before pressing a gentle kiss to my lips.

"I'm yours," I reply once he leans back to look at me again.

I free my hands from his grasp and put them on each side of his face, guiding it down to slide my tongue into his mouth. His hard cock presses against me through his thin sweatpants, and Gabriel rubs it in circles, making me moan.

"I want to try something," I say when he moves on to kiss my neck, sending a wave of shivers and fire over me.

"Anything," he whispers against my skin.

"Tie me up."

Gabriel freezes for a split second before lifting his head to study my face. He's trying to make sure he didn't misunderstand.

"I want to be under your complete control," I admit. He bites down on his full bottom lip.

The only place I'm willing to give up control is in the bedroom, something I'm convinced he's realized by now, too. Handing it over to him isn't something he's taking lightly.

"Are you sure?" I nod, waiting for him to do what I want him to.

He takes the same cloth that was covering me earlier and ties my hands together over my head. I'm so curious about how this is going to feel but also irritated he's still wearing his pants.

"Take off your clothes," I complain, and he grins at me.

"One second, baby," he replies and tightens the material around my wrists. A gasp leaves me as he pulls on each end, my lips pressing together to muffle the moan.

Once he's happy with his work, his hands roam over my breasts, exploring me. I push off the bed to get closer, body lighting on fire with every touch of his, every slow caress.

He runs his fingers all over me, teasing me. He glides one of them over my clit, only for the briefest second. I moan, rolling my hips to get more contact.

"You are so sexy," he says, and I bite my bottom lip.

Gabriel goes on to take off his clothes, removing them too slowly for my liking. As soon as he's naked, I smile victoriously, making him shake his head with a chuckle. My eyes fixate on his thick cock as he slides a condom on it, moving back between my legs when he's done.

As soon as he starts kissing me again, I feel a wave of adrenaline rush through my body. I would have never thought being tied up would make me feel this alive, this excited. The build-up sends a thrill through me, and I want more. My skin is on fire, my nipples painfully hard. His fingers run from my neck all the way down to my hips, goosebumps awakening in response.

Gabriel kisses my lips, my neck, and then my nipples. My back arches off the bed again, and I ball my hands into fists because that's all I can do while they are tied up. Not being able to touch him frustrates me, but my body is too distracted by the way he explores it to care.

He takes his time pleasuring every single sensitive area of mine, making it impossible to lie still. My legs try to find a way to press together, to ease the pressure even a little, but Gabriel's body is in the way.

I moan with every lick, nibble, and kiss he plants on me. The anticipation drives me crazy, especially when the head of his cock presses against my entrance, but he doesn't move. He stays there, taunting me.

My head screams for him to slide inside, to fill and complete me in every way, but he doesn't. His hands roam over my needy body, and I almost let out a complaining whine.

"Please," I beg, something I've been doing a lot with him recently, but I adore the way I don't have to be in control when we have sex.

In all the other parts of my life, I need to be on high alert and in charge, but not with Gabriel. He gives me what I need, no questions asked.

"A little bit longer, chérie," he says, his mouth dropping back onto my nipples.

A wave of pleasure courses through me, and I wish I could touch myself to ease the ache. I pull on the cloth as Gabriel runs his tongue down my body. He presses kisses to my hip bone, getting closer to where I crave his mouth the most.

"Gabriel," I moan, rolling my hips again, but he pushes me down on the bed.

The tension makes me dizzy, and I close my eyes while I wait for him to release me.

"You're so wet for me, chérie, always so wet," Gabriel says with satisfaction dripping from his words.

His fingers slip inside of me, curling at the perfect spot.

"So ready for my cock," he adds, thrusting his fingers inside again.

I'm already so close to falling apart that I whimper when he removes them. I open my eyes to see him move on top of me, kissing me until I forget my own name.

"Ready?" he asks, and I manage to nod before he slams inside of me.

I let all sounds of pleasure leave my lips, including one of relief. My hands tug on the cloth, looking for anything to hold onto while he slides back out and thrusts in again.

"I need you to stay quiet for me, baby, just this once," he says, and I breathe an "okay."

Gabriel creates a delicious rhythm, and the low groans that leave him only send more waves of pleasure through me. His hands bring my legs up to his shoulders, resting them there, his head between them while his cock slips deeper inside of me.

He drives into me harder and faster until the familiar tension builds in my stomach.

"You're so close, baby. I can feel it. Come for me, come all over my cock, chérie." His words shove me over the edge, but Gabriel keeps going, despite my legs shaking and my body getting overwhelmed by pleasure. I press my lips together to keep from screaming at the top of my lungs.

He's rubbing my clit between his thumb and index finger, sending another orgasm through my body, different but just as consuming.

"Oh God, Gabriel," I moan, and he smiles before bringing his lips to my leg.

He fucks into me even harder before his whole body trembles, his movements turning sloppy. Gabriel groans my name as his body shakes and shakes and shakes from the orgasm. With another moan, he slowly stops gliding in and out of me, lowering himself on top of me as he collapses from the after-effects. Sweat coats both of our foreheads, so we let out small laughs of pleasure. He kisses me all over the face, untying me at the same time.

"I'll be right back," he says and gives me one last kiss before disappearing into his bathroom. I take my now free hands, running them everywhere Gabriel touched me.

When he walks back out, he's wearing nothing but a smile that warms my insides. I open my arms for him, and he drops his body onto my chest, nuzzling his face into the crook of my neck. My legs wrap around his torso, trying to get him even closer to me.

My hands slip into his curly brown hair, tugging a little until I hear him chuckle on top of me. The sound vibrates through me until it reaches my toes and fingertips, leaving my body again with ease.

"I like this," he says. "I like this a lot," he adds, and a small laugh skips off my lips and into the silent room.

"Being naked?" I ask, and Gabriel raises his head, showing me his dimple-accessorized smile and green-brown eyes. Both are full of happiness.

"Being naked *with you*," he clarifies, pressing a kiss to my stomach after.

"I like it too," I admit, bringing my hands to his face and tracing his dimples. "I like everything with you."

"Oh God, that was incredibly cheesy, too much so even for me," he says and attempts to get up, but I keep him trapped between my legs.

Gabriel laughs from the bottom of his heart, and I join him, feeling lighter than ever.

Chapter 73
Gabriel

The doctor applies the usual gel to Domi's lower abdomen, and my aunt smiles from ear to ear, waiting impatiently to see her fetus. Nicolette grabs my hand, nervosity taking over for her as well. Jean is on the other side of the room, trying not to faint at the thought of a human growing inside of Domi. It's a good thing too because he's a fainter, and I don't think I'd catch him before he'd drop to the floor.

"How are we feeling?" Doctor Alvarez asks. Domi lets out a sharp breath.

She's not had the easiest of pregnancies this far with back pains, feeling extra sensitive everywhere, and nausea throughout the whole day. I've bought her more crackers and given her more backrubs in the past few weeks than I have for anyone in my entire life.

"Well, except for the fact that my morning sickness happens at any hour, I'm doing well," she says as the doctor runs the machine over her stomach.

My eyes shift to the screen just to see... absolutely nothing. I don't see anything at first, not until Doctor Alvarez points at the small bean that's going to grow into my cousin. The thought is as weird as it is beautiful at the same time.

"That's good. From what I can see here, everything looks great. The baby looks healthy." All four of us start smiling at the news.

For a split second, my mind drifts to the day Val and I will look at each other in the same loving, joyful way Domi and Nicolette are right now after hearing their child is healthy.

I shake my head, forcing the thought away to focus on my aunts, who are asking Jean and me what we'd like to do now.

"I have a date I don't want to be late for, but I'll see you tomorrow," I say, giving Nicolette and Domi a kiss on the cheek. Jean tells me he's fine, he doesn't need one, and I can't help but chuckle as I walk out of the room.

Valentina called me yesterday, telling me to put on something nice for dinner at her house. I decide on a white dress shirt and black pants, hoping it's fancy enough for her liking. The last thing I want is for Val to be disappointed because I didn't put enough effort into my appearance.

With my hair still dripping from the shower, I walk toward her home, excitement now filling my chest. Rose petals lead from the open gate toward the veranda where she's waiting for me in a long, red dress, the same color as my F1 car, and a smile that has my knees weak. Every curve of her body is highlighted in that damn outfit, and it takes everything out of me not to kneel before her.

"You're the most beautiful woman to have ever walked the Earth," I say as I approach the only person I want to spend the rest of my life with, pulling her against me by those hips that make my mouth drool.

"Ever?" she asks, amusement on her face as mine stays serious.

"Ever."

I wrap my lips around hers, needing to taste the watermelon flavor of her lip balm, which I've loved since the first time I kissed her. Her hands lift to my stomach, one of her favorite parts of my body, while I slide my tongue through her parted lips. My hands hold her face, a little moan leaving her, driving me crazy.

"The food's going to get cold," she says, breathless and quiet, when I move on to kiss her neck, feeling the soft skin against my mouth. "Gabriel," she half-warns, half-moans, and I step back with a smirk on my face.

Her cheeks have turned a warm shade of pink, and I bite my bottom lip in response to the thought that she's definitely horny for me right now.

"Where do you want me?" I ask, and Valentina flashes me one of those naughty grins, the ones that never fail to make me race more in love.

"For now, in that chair," she says, pointing to the one on my left.

I walk to the right one, pull it out, and wait for her to sit down to push it back against the table.

"Thank you." Her voice is soft, full of love, and I press a kiss to the top of her head.

I settle down on my chair, for the first time inhaling the aroma of the paella she made. Candles are on each side of the pot with more petals on the table.

"You look gorgeous," Val says, making my eyes lift to hers. "Thank you for dressing up. I thought it would be fun," she explains with a shy look, and I place my hand on top of hers, guiding it to my face where she traces my bottom lip with her thumb.

"It is. I just wish you would have let me help you cook or set all of this up," I complain, but she lets out a small laugh.

"That's not how it works, Monsieur Biancheri. I invited you on this date, so I get to organize everything." I shake my head, disbelief washing over me.

I've never had someone do anything like this for me...

"I'm the one that's supposed to spoil you," I counter, but that makes her frown.

"Says who?" she challenges, crossing her arms in front of her chest to push her breasts together and knock the air out of my chest. "Well, whoever it is, they can fuck off because I get to spoil you just as much as you do me," she says, placing some of the food onto my plate.

I watch her with fascination, unable to speak.

"Bon Appétit," Valentina adds before bringing a spoonful of her meal to her lips, a mischievous grin on her face again.

"Uh oh, what did you do?" I ask, trying her food too. Naturally, it's the best paella I've ever tasted.

"I got a tattoo today," she states, folding both of her lips between her teeth to keep from showing me any kind of emotion. I, on the other hand, must have a thousand of them wash over my face.

"You didn't," I say, too shocked to believe her. Val merely shrugs, putting another spoonful into her mouth. "Where?" I ask, needing more information. The thought of her having a tattoo excites me to my core.

"Hmm, I think you need to search and find it," she replies, leaning back in her chair and wiping her mouth with the serviette she put on her lap minutes ago.

A smile tugs on the corners of my mouth until it has set itself on my face.

"Will you give me a tip?" I ask, standing up to walk over to where she is.

Her chest starts rising and falling more abruptly as I drop to my knees in front of her, one of my favorite places in the world.

"It's in the same place as yours," she says, and I forget how to breathe. *Fuuuuck.*

One of her legs rests on top of the other as I run my fingers over her ankles, guiding them apart. The slit in her dress lets me trail my hand over her right thigh, and I lean forward to press a kiss to it. Goosebumps instantly cover the area around my lips, making me smile.

"You have to stand, baby, so I can see your tattoo," I say, but she takes my chin between her fingers to grab my full attention.

"It's not on my ass." *It's on her hip.* I don't think I'll survive that.

My heart races while I lift her dress by the slit until the tattoo is exposed to me, two little words written on her skin: *Bon Appétit*. I lick my lips, my mouth watering.

"Do you like it?" she asks, but all I manage to do is nod. "It's not meaningful at all, but I think it's hot," Val explains, and I reach out to trace the outside of the clear bandage.

"It's too sexy, ma chérie. I don't think I can resist what it's saying." She spreads her legs for me, and I bring one of them over my shoulder, her black panties exposed to me now. I lean forward, my fingers pushing the thin fabric—

"I've just had the weirdest day of my fucking life!" Adrian's voice comes from the gate area, and I jump up, putting distance between Val and me.

He appears on the veranda just as I fall back onto my chair, panic in his eyes.

"Shit, am I interrupting date night? I'm sorry." An awkward silence fills the room as he passes by us, stopping to inhale the smell of the food. "Can I take a plate?" he asks, and my sunflower clears her throat, forcing her head back to reality.

"Yeah, sure," she says, her eyes shifting to me as Adrian walks inside to grab a plate. "I guess we should eat first," she whispers, and I smile at her.

"We should, but let's hurry up. I crave dessert."

Chapter 74

Valentina

James has been cryptic for the past two days, only sending minimal texts to let me know he's okay and figuring things out. For the first time in the duration of our friendship, he's putting himself before what he thinks I may want, and I couldn't be prouder of him. I will give him as much space as he needs, and, once he's ready, I will be there for him in any and every way he needs me.

Gabriel and Adrian were asked to test out some of the changes the team has made to their cars, so we're all flying to Maranello together. I'm getting sick of traveling every week, but, at least with them by my side, it's more tolerable.

Gabriel keeps drawing me as I read the book we started almost a week ago. He turns his sketchbook whenever he finishes a drawing, a proud look on his handsome face. I give him a smile every time, and he goes back to sketching me again when I shift my position, careful not to put pressure on my new tattoo. It's been healing well so far.

"How many more do you want to create? There will be too much of me in your book," I say with amusement, but he frowns at me.

"There is no such thing as too much of you, Valentina, stop being silly," he scolds, and Adrian chuckles beside me.

"I hope I will never be that wrapped around someone's finger. I don't ever want to say garbage like that," my brother says, earning himself a smack on the arm from me. "Hey, what? Gabriel didn't use to be this way, this romantic. I'm scared it'll happen to me," he explains, and I cover my mouth to keep from laughing.

Gabriel leans forward in his chair because he's across from us and wants to make sure his teammate hears his next words clearly.

"It will, Adrian, and, when it does, I'll remind you of this moment," he promises, briefly wiggling his eyebrows at him. Gabriel winks at me and leans back in his chair, going back to drawing. My brother scoffs, and my boyfriend smiles. "You're going to fall in love so hard," my boyfriend adds, and I let out the laugh I was trying to suppress.

"You're both annoying. I'm going to find someone else to sit with," he complains, catching the gaze of a beautiful, curvy brunette across from him. She stares down at the seat beside her, inviting him to join her. "Whoever is in charge of my life, thank you," he says before walking toward her, a smirk on his lips.

I shake my head, my focus shifting back to Gabriel, who turns his sketchbook to show me a Formula One car with the number nine on it. Next to it, he drew me in a race suit with a helmet tucked between my hip and arm.

"I know, it's not that great, but it'll be better when I get to draw it from real life," he says and turns his sketchbook again to work on his art.

"You're the most talented artist I've ever met, Gabriel," I finally manage to croak out, and he notices the change in my emotions. He sits down next to me, taking my hand and placing a kiss on the back of it.

"It'll happen, I'll make sure of it, even if I have to give up my own seat to get you one," he says, and I lean away from him, surprise probably all over my face. His thumb traces my bottom lip as he smiles. "I'd do anything to see your dream come true, mon tournesol."

My eyes move to my brother, who's close enough to have heard this whole conversation. He mouths the words "me too," and I bring my gaze back to Gabriel's.

"It will happen. We will make sure of it."

"No, you won't, I won't let you. You can't be my savior in this, no matter how much you want to be. This is my fight, and I'll make it happen, just like I was taught."

Both of my Velocità Rossa drivers have been in the car, testing the new upgrades, for the past hour. Meanwhile, I've been talking to the strategists, engineers, and Lorenzo Mattia, trying to learn as much as I'm allowed to about the procedures. I watch an impressed look slip onto the team principal's face every time I add something to the conversation, like a suggestion about the front wing that could help them slightly increase their speed down a straight.

Grandpa taught me a lot about the workings of an F1 car, and I've been doing my best to study them as they evolve, something that seems to be earning me plus points with Lorenzo.

"You know, I remember the first time I ever saw you," he says as we're watching Adrian's lap time improve.

I turn to him, his smile contagious.

"You were this tall." He holds his hand a meter above the ground. "And you had this look of awe on your face that I hadn't, *haven't*, seen on many people, let alone little children," he goes on, staring off into the distance as he recalls the events of that day. "Your father told me afterward that you wanted to be a Formula One driver, and I remember telling him if you proved to me you had what it takes, I'd let you race for my team one day."

I have no idea how to respond, but I do my best to fight the tears of hope shooting into my eyes.

"Your Nonno and Papà were two of the best drivers in the history of racing. What they had in them, I see in you," he says, pointing at my heart.

All my life, I've been told the opposite by the men in charge. I've been told I lack the spirit of a racer, that I lacked what my family had. The tears stream down now because I can't stop them, I don't want to anymore. Lorenzo gives my shoulder a squeeze.

"*Avere fede.*" *Have faith.*

"*Sempre*," I reply, and he gives me another proud smile before walking away.

"It's going to rain," someone else says in Italian, and I'm impressed by how much I already understand. Gabriel is a great teacher.

Adrian is the first to return, his car already dripping from the sudden shower pouring down. He gets out and walks toward me, soaking wet. I try to run from him, but he catches me, lifts me into the air, and transfers the rain onto my clothes. Annoyance is replaced by pure joy, and laughter leaves me as he drops me on my feet again.

"If I have to suffer, so do you," he says, his words muffled because of his helmet. I nudge him in the ribs, but he doesn't even move a centimeter. "You should probably change. Your clothes are soaked," he points out, and I nudge him again, this time hard enough to make him bend over. "Yeah, I deserve that one." We both burst into laughter. Adrian walks away, probably to put on some dry clothes, but my eyes fixate on the rain.

"Is anyone driving right now?" I ask the man in charge of giving the green light for any driver to go on track.

"No. Why?" he replies, and I smile at him.

"Do you mind if I—" I cut off, simply pointing at the track.

He follows my finger before giving me a thumbs up and focusing on his screens again. I spot Gabriel getting out of his car, but I'm on a mission.

Warm drops of water hit my skin as soon as I step outside and make my way onto the track. I spin around once I'm at the start and finish line. My feet carry me around while I let the rain drench my dress. I can't explain the feeling of freedom spreading through me, the adrenaline coursing through my veins, but it comes close to the one racing brings me.

Music fills my ears then, and I shift my gaze to the speakers at the fence next to me. James Arthur's voice comes through them, and I spin once more. The moment I stop, Gabriel's arms are around me, guiding me to the music. I beam up at him, and he uses the opportunity to kiss me deeply.

"You hate dancing," I remind him as water soaks his hair. My hands lift to it, pushing it out of his beautiful face.

"With you, I'd dance anywhere, anytime, even in the pouring rain," he says, twisting me around once just to bring me against his chest.

An uncontrollable giggle leaves me, and he smiles in return. I can barely keep my eyes open as more water hits them, but it's worth it; everything up to this moment has been worth it.

"I'm the luckiest woman in the world because you fell in love with me," I say, blinking away the rain to watch his features soften.

"I didn't *fall*, ma chérie, I *raced*." He plants his lips on mine, smiling against my mouth before spinning me around one last time. "I always want to be the man you deserve."

"You are, mon soleil, always."

Gabriel kisses me again as the entire world around us blurs into nothing more than the noise of drops hitting asphalt.

Chapter 75

Gabriel

It's been three weeks since Adrian and I were in Maranello for testing. Being away from Valentina is still not easy, but I've been to see her a couple of times. Apart from that, I had to be away for an entire week for the race in Montreal and then another for the one in Texas.

I won the Canadian Grand Prix with Adrian in second, *fucking Eduardo* in third, and Kyle in fourth. It was a great race with important points for the whole team, and it also expanded my championship lead again. Adrian won his first race of the season in the U.S., with me in second place, Jonathan in third, and James in fourth.

I shouldn't get my hopes up because the season isn't even halfway done, but I can't stop myself from imagining how it'd feel to finally hold that trophy, carry the title any F1 driver dreams of having. I push the thought aside, not ready to let myself linger on that scenario yet.

Valentina has been kicking His Royal Grossness' ass in every category except strength. For some inexplicable reason, Christian is a lot stronger than her physically, but one category, especially that one, won't stand in Val's way of getting the Formula Three seat. It can't.

She's excelled at everything they have given her, the practical and the theoretical, analysis and racing itself. If they give him the seat instead of her, there will be no other explanation except that Christian is a royal and a man.

"Are you okay? You're in your head a lot today," Adrian says as he stares at me from across the room. We've just finished filming a video for our team to upload for the fans. I look outside the window at the Texas track, counting down the minutes until I can get on a plane and back to my sunflower.

"Would you hate me if I won the championship this year instead of you?" I ask, the question surprising both of us. Adrian shifts in his seat, the awkward silence creating a veil of tension that makes us both uncomfortable.

"No, I wouldn't hate you. We're teammates, and we've been friends for years. This sport is brutal, and if you are the one to win this year, then I'll be happy for you." He truly is the best guy I've ever met. "I'll snatch the title from you sooner or later if that happens," Adrian adds, and I let out a small laugh. "You're family, Gabriel, whether you want to be or not. I could never hate you unless you hurt my sister. That's where I draw the line," he warns, and I nod.

"I'd never hurt her, not if I can do something about it." Adrian leans back in his chair, caressing his temples. My answer bothers him.

"What if you don't have a choice? What if something happens, and you have the power to spare her more pain if you do something that hurts you more than it will her? Are you capable of putting Val first, always?" I want to answer him, tell him I'd give my heart and soul to her, for her, but Adrian lifts his hands to stop me. "You can't answer because you haven't had to make that decision. I hope you never will," he says, shutting me up for good.

I go back to staring out the window when Eduardo and James step into the room.

I can't catch a fucking break.

"What's up, lads? Why the serious expressions?" James asks, and I have the urge to punch him in his fucking face for being who he is.

Adrian would never doubt the Brit because James has been proving himself to my teammate their entire lives. He probably thinks his best friend would be perfect for his sister. *Great, now I'm nauseous.*

"Oh, so you're talking to me again? Why, thank you, Your Majesty, for blessing us with your presence," Adrian says, annoyance in his voice. I sit upright, surprised at this shift in the atmosphere. My senses go on high alert as I watch the situation in front of me unravel.

"I think you've lost your bloody mind, mate," James replies, shoving his hands into his pockets.

"*I* have lost *my* mind? You're the one who's been a dick to me for the past month, and now you come in here like everything's alright? What the hell?"

Eduardo steps away when Adrian gets in James' face, but both of us are ready to separate them if they need to be.

"Figuring shit out counts as being a dick now?" Adrian rolls his eyes.

"When your best friend ignores and avoids you for four weeks without an explanation, yes, it counts."

His words come from a place of hurt, even if he's letting anger work as the spokesperson at the moment. Yelling won't do anything but frustrate both of them.

I'm about to tell him to calm down when James throws something into the room that knocks the breath from my chest.

"Maybe your best friend is struggling with the fact that he's going to be a fucking father!" He sinks down on one of the chairs while my hand lifts to my mouth, subtly covering it to keep it shut.

"You what?" Adrian asks his tone soft.

James drops his head, and I signal for Eduardo and me to give them some privacy. He gives me a slight nod, and the last thing I see is my teammate's arms wrapping around his best friend.

"Could you imagine having a kid right now?" the Spaniard asks when we're out of the room, and I give him a look that I hope says "why-the-fuck-are-you-talking-to-me?"

We make our way downstairs toward the exit.

"What? I just mean I'm glad Valentina and I used protection. I couldn't imagine having a child right now." I stop dead in my tracks, anger making my shoulders vibrate. "What? Does it bother you she and I fucked?" he says, a smug smile on his face.

It takes everything in me not to punch him in his crooked white teeth. He's taken it too far now, but he knows it. This was his intention when he started speaking to me. Eduardo wanted to piss me off, and he has succeeded. Even though I'm not sure he's telling the truth—I thought all they did was kiss—doesn't stop the irritation from settling deep inside of me.

I'm pissed off now.

"Maybe if you'd done a better job, it would, but Val doesn't even remember you exist. That's how much of an impression you left." I walk past him, my shoulder hitting his.

"Sure, if that's what you need to tell yourself," Eduardo calls after me, but I'm done with this conversation.

He's a coward for saying all of this to my face without Val present. He knows she'd mess him up for everything that just came out of his mouth.

I'd hold her fucking purse and cheer as she did it too.

Chapter 76

Valentina

Today Andrea is going to announce who got the Formula Three seat. Haru and Lucie officially told me they're dating a week ago, which is why they're sitting across from me now, cuddling on the couch-like seating area. He presses a soft kiss to her lips, and she smiles against his. Such a simple action, but it makes me miss Gabriel with my entire being.

It's been a week since I've seen him, since I've felt his arms around me. What makes all of this worse is James has barely spoken to me and the last time I saw him was the day I found out about the baby.

Evangelin has been avoiding me too, but I don't have an explanation for that. Last we spoke, everything was fine. Maybe she's upset because I haven't gone to see her and *Rush* in a while. I'll have to check on her when I fly back tomorrow.

"I'll burn this place down if they don't give you the seat," Adrian says, ripping me out of my thoughts and bringing a smile to my face. He was the only one who could make it here today. Gabriel has sponsor meetings and James has an ultrasound to attend with Annabel.

"It's a possibility you might want to prepare yourself for," I suggest, but he frowns then.

"It cannot be, Valentina. What else do they expect of you? To not need a car and just run like you're The Flash or something?" he asks. I laugh at his analogy.

"I don't know. Just, don't get your hopes up, that's all I'm asking," I say, so he wraps his arm around my shoulder, pressing a kiss to my temple. He doesn't reply, merely holds me while we wait for Andrea to bring us the news I'm expecting.

"It's so cute how you bring your brother everywhere. He's such a good boy, always following you around," Christian says, interrupting the peaceful moment Adrian and I were trying to have.

"Careful, he attacks on my command," I warn, and Adrian starts growling next to me. The brat takes a step back, a disgusted expression on his face.

"You're both so fucking weird," he says, but walks away, looking over his shoulder with an expression that tells me he's making sure Adrian isn't coming after him. My brother and I burst into laughter as he raises his hand for a high-five that I give him without hesitation.

"Valentina, Christian, are you ready?" Andrea asks, and I shift my eyes to where they're standing. An unreadable expression lingers on their features, and fear consumes me.

My rival and I get up at the same time, moving over to where our instructor is. Adrian is right beside me like he has been for every moment leading up to this point, holding my hand.

"I want to let you both know you've done an exceptional job and no matter what I'm about to tell you, you should be proud of your performance." Their eyes are on me then shift to Christian throughout their speech.

"Whoever doesn't get accepted is allowed to stay in the academy and train for another opportunity, right?" The question leaves me before the words are processed in my head.

"Who gives a shit? Just tell Valentina I'm the one who got the seat," Christian chimes in, and my stomach turns upside down.

Andrea stares at the ground before taking a deep breath. Their eyes slip back to me, sadness in them now.

Realization dawns on me.

"I'm sorry, Valentina, I tried everything I could, but Mr. Mattia and Mr. Reiner were firm on their decision to have Christian race in Formula Three. I'm so sorry," they say, and I feel my head nod as everything inside of me goes numb.

"Hell yeah! I got the seat!" Christian celebrates as I sink into Adrian's arms, the shock sending my body into temporary paralysis.

"No, fuck this! How is that possible? Valentina outperformed that prick in every category but one!" Adrian fights for me, but I also regain my ability to speak.

"Do I get to stay in the academy?" I ask, but tears fill Andrea's eyes.

"No," they reply, so I nod again, my mouth turning into a desert as swallowing my own spit becomes impossible. "They don't want you to be a part of this academy anymore."

I can't listen to more, even though Adrian is arguing with Andrea now, demanding to have an answer they can't give him. I turn around, ready to run away from all of this when I see Gabriel in the doorframe.

His face is full of pain, letting me know he heard everything.

"Chérie," he says, his voice so soft, it shoves the tears out of my eyes and down my cheeks.

My body is frozen again because I'm not sure if I want to sprint into his arms, run from everything, or sink to the ground to let the darkness swallow me.

"It's okay, I've got you," he says in French, and I rush into his arms.

He wraps them around me, enveloping me as if to shield me from all the pain and hurt my heart is trying to process. I sob against his chest, breaking down as he caresses the back of my head.

"Adrian, Andrea is not the one who decided this. Focus on what's important, would you? We'll get answers later," Gabriel tells my brother before attempting to lead me out of the room.

"I told you I'd get the seat, belle. Don't take it personally. It's just how the world works, nothing you can do to change it, no matter how determined you are," Christian says.

"You know what, Christian? I may not have a dick to get me ahead in life, but at least I don't act like one either. I hope you have a successful, long career. May lots of disappointments come your way so you can produce a better personality," I reply and step out of the room.

My feet don't stop until I'm outside where I collapse onto the ground. Breathing, crying, *being*, it all hurts. I cover my mouth and let out a scream, unable to hold it back any longer.

I scream for my grandfather, who gave everything to make my dream come true.

I scream for my father, who raced for me, but I'll never be able to race for him.

I scream for Adrian, who yet again has to help me pick up the pieces.

I scream for Gabriel, who feels my pain just as deeply because our souls are intertwined.

They didn't even let me stay in the academy...

"Mon amour," Gabriel says from next to me. I don't know how long I've been in this position, crying over what I've lost, but my sobs have slowed, only shaking my body every few minutes. Tears still stream down my face, but they come as naturally as breathing now.

"We will get to the bottom of this, Val, I promise. There must be a reason why—"

"Please, stop. Please. I can't do this anymore, Adrian. This ripping pain in my chest, I can't take it. I can't fight anymore. Please, don't make me fight," I beg, treading closer to the dark hole in my mind I've been balancing around my whole life.

Adrian takes my face between his hands, forcing me to focus.

"You listen to me, little champion, you will race in a Formula One car. This academy? It means nothing! It was supposed to help you, and, now that it didn't, fuck that. We don't need them. Lorenzo Mattia might be my boss, but I will make his life a living hell for what he's taken from you today. We can't stop fighting now because you haven't made it to where you want to be yet. You're not alone in this, you'll never be. This is not the end of your story, Valentina, this is not where you give up on your dream," Adrian says, standing up and holding his hand out for me. "I won't let you, just like Grandpa and Dad wouldn't. Fight for them, fight for us, but, most importantly, keep fighting for yourself."

I slide my hand into his, unwilling to argue with him when he's so full of hope.

"Okay," is all I answer, but we both know it's done now. There is nothing more we can do. He'll figure this out while I do my best to walk in the opposite direction of the darkness.

"Whatever it takes," Gabriel adds, his hand cupping my face and wiping away the physical representation of my emotions. "Adrian is right. This is not the end. How could it be? Your story has hardly begun."

I lean toward my boyfriend, kissing his lips in an attempt to relieve some of the tension in my chest. It works for a brief moment until I pull back and reality sinks in again.

"I hate agreeing with anyone that isn't me, but Gabriel is right. Then again, he's recycling my words, so..." Adrian trails off with a shrug, and I let out a small, genuine laugh.

"Let's go home, as far away from this place as possible," I say, and they both give me a nod.

It's time I get back to Monaco and figure out what the hell I'm going to do with my life now that my last chance has been ripped from me.

Chapter 77

Gabriel

The rooms are too small, the windows barely let in any light, and the kitchen is a disaster. This is the third apartment my realtor has taken Valentina and me to, and all of them have looked better in the photos than in real life. I can't see myself living in any of the spaces we've seen, which is quite disappointing. We need our privacy, but none of them felt right.

I drop my head in response.

"Mon amour," Valentina says, her arms wrapping around me from behind. "We'll find one, don't worry," she assures me in French, sending a thrill through me. I love the way it falls off her lips.

"I know," I reply, running my hands over her arms before I guide her in front of me to capture her lips with mine. She smiles, kissing me a few times and then stepping back. The bags under her eyes break my heart, especially because they're not from crying.

They've appeared because she isn't sleeping. We've been spending our nights reading, but every time she closes her eyes, I feel her heart accelerate and then they open again.

"Listen, bébé, I had a feeling we wouldn't find something you'd be happy with today, so I got you this," she says, and I smile at the pet name before focusing on the ring-sized box she lifts up for me to take.

"Are you proposing?" I ask and cock an eyebrow. Her cheeks turn a bright red.

"No, it's way too early for that," she says with a small laugh, making me smile.

"Promise when it isn't, you'll let me propose. I want to be the one." Val lets out another little laugh, straightening out her back.

"We'll see," she simply replies, urging me to open the box. I do as I'm told, raising the lid to see a key sitting inside. "To my house. I discussed it with Adrian, and we both agreed it's time for you to have one. I want you to be comfortable in my home," she explains, stepping back and touching the tips of her fingers to her mouth while she waits for a reaction from me.

"Are you sure we're ready for this?" I know I am, but I want her to be, too.

"Gabriel, this is long overdue. My house, my grandfather's house, it's my safe place, but so are you. I want you to be able to feel at home there, too." I reach for her hips, her now healed tattoo no longer at risk of me applying too much pressure and hurting her.

"Wherever you are, I'll feel at home." She pretends like she hates my cheesy, corny words, but the corners of her mouth always stretch into a smile. She secretly loves it, which is why I never hold back from saying them out loud. "I'll still text and ask for permission before coming over. I won't just show up," I say, and Valentina chuckles, her hands lifting to my neck.

"I know, which is why I feel so comfortable giving you this." I'm about to kiss her again when my realtor interrupts us.

"Ready to go?" she asks, and I turn to the short woman.

"Yes, we're ready," I say, grabbing Val's hand and leading her toward the door. She needs to get some sleep, and I have to find a way to get her mind off what haunts her at night.

"I'm going to look for places with more windows and bigger rooms. Also one with a balcony that overlooks the ocean. How does that sound?" Kim, my realtor, says, and I thank her a few times. Valentina does so as well before we make our way to my car.

"What can I do to make you happy?" I ask my sunflower when she sits in the passenger seat, staring out of the window and getting lost in her thoughts.

She tilts her head to me, a tired smile on her face.

"You already have," she replies, closing her eyes as I place my hand on her thigh.

Val falls asleep before we even make it home, and I carry her to bed. I wrap the blanket around her, caressing her cheek for a moment. My heart beats a little more evenly now that she's getting the rest she needs.

"How is she?" Adrian's voice comes from behind me, but I signal for him to leave the room with me. I don't want to risk waking Val under any circumstance.

"She's sleeping now, which is an improvement." He nods, rubbing his face with his hand and revealing how tired and frustrated he is. "When's the last time you got any sleep?" I ask, but he shakes his head as if to dismiss my question.

"I got better things to do. I've been trying to contact Lorenzo Mattia, but he hasn't answered any of my calls, texts, or e-mails. I think he's scared to face me," he jokes, a yawn slipping past his lips.

The usual white in his eyes is fire red, and there are dark circles underneath them.

"Well, it's too late now, he won't get back to you at this hour. You, mate, need to rest. We all do," I remind him, and he gives me an agreeing wink.

"Yeah, you're right. I have to get up early. Daniel wants us to go for a run."

He rolls his eyes, giving my shoulder one last squeeze before disappearing into his bedroom. I walk into Val's, undressing and sliding under the blanket to get close to her. I hold her close to my chest, hoping that my proximity will transfer some of her pain onto me.

Chapter 78
Valentina

"Will it ever get easier?" I ask Grandfather, who raises his bushy, white eyebrow in confusion. "Getting turned away?" I add as he takes my hand while we walk away from the karting track where none of the talent scouts were interested in sponsoring me.

"Listen, little champion, success wouldn't exist without failure. Often, we need to learn how to fall before we can get up, do you understand?" he says, but I shake my head.

He's not making any sense to me.

"If everything was simply handed to you, you'd never know how to deal with rejection. Today is not something to cry over, it's something to grow from. You need to learn to be worthy of an F1 seat. In races, you won't always get the results you desire. It'll be difficult, disappointing, and frustrating, but you'll know how to deal with it better than anyone. It won't cloud your judgment during races, not like it would for people that never handled rejection." He leads me back to his car, but I stop before we reach it.

"But why don't they want to recruit me? I won the Karting Championship," I defend, and my grandfather grabs me by the shoulders, making sure I pay close attention to his next words.

"You are a girl, Valentina. They will always look at you like the weak one because of that. I tried to shield you for as long as I could, but you have to understand boys will get top priority. That's why Adrian is doing so well. He's just as talented as you, has gotten the same opportunities, and the scouts were interested as soon as he arrived at the same event we went to today. It's how the world works, which is why I'm trying my very best to help you change that, okay? We will make sure, together, that the mindsets of the people will no longer be closed off. You will be the change the world needs," he says. I nod.

"That's a big responsibility," I reply, and he gives me a proud smile.

"You don't have to do anything other than be yourself and keep on fighting. That's all you have to do," Grandfather assures me, and I grin at him.

I will do exactly as he said.
I will be the change.

I find myself wandering around the house, searching for something to occupy my time, but I do so in vain. Adrian and Gabriel are out with their coaches, and James is busy filming a commercial.

When I don't find anything, I decide to go for a run on the beach. I want to work out. It'll clear my head and keep me from overthinking what happened.

I jog for a long time, not stopping once to breathe or rest. The burning in my lungs is a nice distraction from the constant pain I've been feeling in my chest, so I keep going. My legs get tired long before my mind does, and, somehow, I end up in front of *Rush*.

I don't know how I got here, but I know why. *Evangelin.*

My feet are cemented to the ground, keeping me from walking into Evangelin's store. I watch her roam around in there, smiling at her customers. I've kept my distance from James and her because it doesn't feel real yet. I've spent my entire life working toward one specific goal, and I know as soon as she hears about what happened, reality will set in for me.

She spots me before I can walk away, waving me inside with a smile. After she's been avoiding me for the past few months, I'm relieved to see her face light up from my presence.

"Ma belle Valentina," she says and wraps her arms around me, hugging me tighter than ever before. "It's been too long. How are you?" Evangelin asks, and I feel her trying to pull away, but I hold her close while tears fill my eyes. "What's wrong?" She strokes my hair, making a sob leave me. "Alright, it's okay, dear. Sit down." I do as I'm told, my hands shaking.

I don't want to tell this story, share my failure with someone I never want to disappoint. Evangelin locks the door to ensure no one will bother us before sitting down with me.

"What happened? Tell me," she encourages with a warm smile as I wipe my tears.

"I didn't get the seat, and they kicked me out of the academy. My instructor, Andrea, had no idea why either. They just told me I couldn't be a part of it anymore," I explain, trying my best to be comprehensible. "This academy was my last hope, but it's over now. There is nothing left for me to do but find a new passion," I say, and silence fills the small boutique.

"I think you should get another passion anyway, whether you decide to give up or not." The way the words sound coming out of her mouth, "give up," bothers me.

"I didn't give up on my dream, *it* keeps giving up on *me*," I clarify, but she merely shrugs, moving over to a pile of clothes and folding them.

"I know it does. I know 'unfair' doesn't begin to cover what you've gone through in your life, but why would you let it win?" I run my hands over my face and sigh.

"Because I'm done. I'm done trying to achieve something that's never going to happen," I defend, so her blue eyes shift to me, skepticism dancing in them.

"Do you think your grandfather would want that?" I don't have words for the stinging spreading through my entire body, forcing tears back into my tired eyes. "I didn't have to know him to tell you this is the last thing he would have wanted for you," she adds.

"He thought I'd change the world, Evangelin, but how am I meant to do that when the world doesn't want to be changed?" I challenge, and she places her hands on her hips.

"You do it by setting an example! Demand answers. Don't allow them to take away what makes you unstoppable, and that is your ability to find positivity in the darkest times. If you can't do it for yourself, do it for all the little girls out there who share the same dream as you."

I forget how to breathe as I imagine my own daughter giving up on whatever dream she may have one day. The thought breaks my heart.

"Demand answers," Evangelin repeats as she finishes folding the last dress. "I'm not ready for you to lose faith in yourself, my child, not yet, not ever," she adds, and I give her one more hug.

"I love you," I blurt out before I can stop myself. "I should go," I say and step back, but she holds me close for another moment.

"I love you too, Valentina." My emotions overwhelm me, which is why I make my way back home.

A box, identical to the ones Gabriel sent me a while ago, sits on my doorstep, and I walk over to it with a smile. I rip the tape off, sitting down on the steps to study the contents. Just like the first one I've ever received, there is a drawing of me and a letter.

I pick up the art first, admiring how talented he is. The details and the pencil strokes are beyond incredible. He makes me look like an angel, simply lying on the beach. The way he drew my face, lips, lashes, and curly hair reminds me yet again he sees me in a way no one else does. He notices things I've never even seen in myself.

No one is ever going to look at me the way he does.

I pick up the letter and tear it open, my hands shaking now. My emotions are all over the place, and I don't know if I'm nervous to read his words or overwhelmingly excited.

Ma Chérie,

You and I know better than most how difficult life gets. We've experienced its cruelty more often than not, especially you, but I need you to remember one thing: you are a sunflower. You follow the sun's light wherever it goes, even when it seems to have disappeared right now, you never let that stop you. You stand in the pouring rain, finding happiness and growth in the water. Let this rainy time fuel you, not stop you. I'll forever be your sun, but you don't need me to tell you that. We all know I'd do anything to get rid of the thundering clouds above you. I know you ell enough to see this situation for what it truly is: your villain origin story.

I lower the letter for a moment to let out a laugh that reaches my heart.

I'm just teasing. We all know the world would have no chance if you became the villain, especially because you'd have three idiot sidekicks, who would carry backpacks with your weapons in them. Anyway, I think I got a little distracted in my attempt to remind you of the unforgiving strength lying beneath that warm s mile of yours. No one can take it from you, mon tournesol.

Je t'aime, chérie.

Only yours,
Gabriel

How could I have made someone like this fall in love with me?

I never have an answer that satisfies this question. I also don't have a justification that pleases the part of me that wants to keep fighting. It doesn't care about getting hurt. All it gives a damn about is doing what my supportive family keeps telling me to do: keep fucking going until I make it.

Chapter 79

Valentina

"What's this for?" James asks when he holds up the present I gave him.

"For being you." He's been having a hard time accepting this new part of his life, and I wanted to brighten up his day.

"I am pretty awesome," he says, and I cock an amused eyebrow. "Most of the time," he adds, and I continue to smile at him. His blue eyes stand out even more as the sun shines onto them, and his blonde hair seems thicker and curlier today.

"You are. I love you, James Oliver Landon. I don't remember much from before I met you, and I'm glad I don't. Life is better with you in it, and I hope this small gift is something that can show you how deeply I care about you."

A tear drops down my cheek, and I quickly wipe it away. I can tell James is about to cry too, which is why I point at the box, indicating for him to open it.

James opens the gift and pulls out the small canvas with a picture of him and me on the front. We're sitting at a table in a restaurant. It's a somewhat recent picture, but the reason I chose it is because it represents our relationship. James has whipped cream all over his face, I am laughing, and my hand is resting on top of his.

I ordered a bunch of canvases with pictures, a couple of Adrian in his Formula One car, some of my friends and me, and one for James. For Gabriel, I ordered a canvas of him holding his first trophy in Formula One. He looks so happy in it, it always warms my insides.

"Thank you. This is absolutely gorgeous," James says, and finally, a tear rolls down his cheek. "I love you," he says and flings his arms around my chest.

"Seriously, thank you for giving me this. I'm going to hang it in my bedroom," he informs me as soon as he sets me down. I grin at him and wipe under his eyes.

"I'm glad you like I—" He cuts me off.

"I don't like it, I bloody love it." James takes the canvas into his hands and stares at it for a couple of moments. He then puts it back down and stares at me.

"How are you feeling?" he asks, a worried expression on his face.

"I'm not okay," I admit but being able to say it actually feels like a weight lifting off my shoulders. "But what am I supposed to do about it? It'll be easier to just find something new to do with my life." James nods before he picks up his blue mug and sips the tea in it.

"If that's what you want," he says, and I shrug.

"I think so." *I have no idea.*

James wraps his hand around mine, picks it up, presses a small kiss to the back of it, and then puts our intertwined fingers back on the table.

"Where has my Valentina gone?" His question takes me aback, and for a second, I'm not sure I want to answer it.

"I don't know. I'm trying to get her back, but with every 'no,' she drifts further away." I look past James, taking a deep breath. "I don't want to be the one to lose every single time," I say, the last few words coming out in a whisper. James studies me before he nods.

"I know, darling, but you have to hold onto who you are, okay?" he asks, his gaze shifting to the canvas on the table in front of him.

"I'm not going anywhere, James, I promise." I wink at him, and he smiles in return. "Anyway, how's it going with you and Emma? Did you tell her about the baby?" I ask, desperately needing to change the subject.

My heart is aching in my chest, and I feel like throwing up when I talk about racing.

"Oh, yeah, well," he starts, and I frown. Something obviously went wrong between the two of them, which is weird since they only started dating a few weeks ago. "Turns out she doesn't like what I do for a living, and naturally, I can't be with someone who doesn't support what I do. You should've heard her, Val. 'That is way too dangerous.' 'You're just driving around in circles,'" he imitates her, and I start laughing. "She honestly said all of that to me with a straight face. You should have seen me run out of her house. I was faster than an F1 car." As I imagine it, I can't contain my laughter. James is not a sexy runner.

"I'm sorry it didn't work out," I tell him, wiping away the tears of laughter.

Another short laugh leaves my throat, and I look at him, the amusement still on my face. He gives me a brilliant smile, and I look at him, confused.

"What?"

"Nothing, I just adore that I can make you smile like this." I bring the most childish grin to my face.

"Like this?" I ask, pointing at my weird expression.

"Yup, like that," he teases and pokes my cheek. "Now, get out of here, I have to go train."

A playful frown spreads over my face, but I gather my stuff and kiss him on the cheek before leaving.

Being back home for good hurts a lot, but it also gives me the chance to find myself and be with the people I love. I spent the whole day yesterday with Adrian, the day before with Gabriel, and before that, I had time to myself. I have to be able to see the positive side of things, especially when the glass seems empty. *I'm just going to fill it with my tears*, I think and almost laugh at how ridiculous that thought is.

The afternoon sun feels like heaven, so I stop walking for a minute to take it all in. I'm sunbathing more often now that I'm home, and I love it. After another minute of enjoying the warmth of the sun, I keep making my way home. Gabriel and I agreed for him to stay at my place tonight, and he texted me an hour ago, letting me know he's already there. Giving him a key was a big step for us, but I adore the thought of him waiting for me at home.

I sprint up the stairs, all the way to my bedroom where he's lying at the foot of my bed, sketching something as he listens to music. His eyes light up when he sees the happiness on my face, and I jump onto the mattress next to him. Gabriel drops his notebook to pull me against him, tickling me until I giggle. His hands move to each side of my head as I look up at him.

"How was your day with James?" he asks and pushes a strand of hair from my face.

"I'm about to lose my fucking mind!" Adrian screams from downstairs, and Gabriel and I listen to him storm toward my door. "Are you two decent?" he asks, and I sit up with a groan.

"Yeah, come in," Gabriel says, and I cock an eyebrow.

"You're allowing people to come into *my* room now?" Gabriel lets out a small laugh.

"Sorry, chérie, I didn't know we're considering Adrian as people."

My brother interrupts my laughter as he drops down onto my mattress, like I did only a few minutes ago, steam almost coming out of his ears.

"I swear to God, I will strangle that man when I see him on Thursday!" Adrian blurts out without any context, his hands falling onto his chest. "All day I've been trying to reach him, but does he fucking answer? No! Of course not." He mumbles the last sentence.

With a smile, I shift around on my bed, placing his head in my lap and massaging it.

"Relax, Adrian, everything will be okay. Now, why don't you tell us what's weighing on your chest," I suggest, and he lets out a groan.

"Lorenzo Mattia is a pain in my ass. I've been trying to contact him all week to get some answers, but that coward is hiding from me," he explains, pouting like a little child.

"Just let it go, Adrian, there is no point fighting his decision." My brother shoots into an upward position to grab me by the shoulders.

"I understand you don't have the strength to keep fighting right now, but you have to let me at least try for you, okay? Let me try," he says, and I give him a small nod.

"You mean fail? Considering you can't get a hold of him," I joke, but he doesn't smile.

"I will, and when I do, hellfire is going to rain on him, mark my words!" Adrian announces before strutting out of the room like Hulk when he has to use the stairs instead of the elevator in *Endgame*.

"That brother of yours—" Gabriel cuts off, letting out a deep breath and shaking his head. "He's a lot of work," he adds, and we burst into laughter.

We keep going until we're both lying on our backs, staring at the ceiling of my room. Eventually, he turns my head toward him, bringing my lips closer to his mouth.

"Thank you for the canvas you sent me. It's beautiful," he says and presses a soft kiss to my lips. Everything inside of me somersaults and warms at this small gesture. "But I don't like that you spent money on me."

I kiss him again, ignoring his comment. I will do whatever I want with my money, especially to see his dimple-featured smile.

No price is too high to see it, none ever will be.

Chapter 80

Valentina

"Gabriel?" I whisper, but he doesn't wake up. "Amour?" I say a little louder, and his eyes flutter open. I put my hands on his face, and he gives me a sleepy smile.

"You look so beautiful," he tells me in French, and my heart skips a beat.

"Well, I did get ready so I could wake you, looking like the angel you think I am." I laugh, and he does too. It feels wonderfully strange to speak French with him.

"What time is it?" He sits up and slides his hand into my hair.

"It's six-thirty! *Ha!* How does that feel?" I ask and give him a victorious smile. He starts laughing and falls backward onto the bed, covering his face with both of his hands. "Okay, I'm kidding. It's eight-thirty. I would never wake you up that early." This only makes him laugh more.

"You're still holding a grudge? That was so long ago," he says as I crawl on top of him.

"I guess you could make me forget about it," I tease and put my hands on his naked chest. His rest on my thighs, and he bites his bottom lip with seduction in his eyes. "But that's not why I woke you," I admit in a whisper, and he smirks at me.

"Is that so?" he replies and chuckles ever so slightly. "Then tell me, why did you wake me? If it's not to have sex." I lean forward to press my lips to his but stop before they touch.

"I'm hungry, and I thought we could go out for breakfast." The smile he shows me with his dimples carved into his cheeks makes my heart ache.

"I'm hungry too, but I'd love breakfast in bed. I think a compromise would be to have both," he says, his fingers trailing up my skirt before they squeeze my legs. "One day, your beautifully thick thighs will be the death of me," he adds, and I lower myself to feel his morning wood against my aching clit.

"What would you like to have?" I ask, and Gabriel licks his lips. I run my hands over his naked torso, rolling my hips to create a friction that makes both of us moan.

"I want you to ride me, chérie, to use my cock and come all over it," he says, making me groan as I remove my shirt. "Keep the skirt on. It's so sexy."

I do as I'm told, earning me an approving smile. He pulls on the waistband just enough to expose my tattoo, smirking at it.

"Use me, baby," he says when I think about what to do. "Fuck me however you want," Gabriel adds, his fingers gliding further upward.

Confidence races through me as I lean down to trail kisses along his chest.

"Give me a condom," I command as I tug on the waistband of his boxers. He reaches into the nightstand, handing me one of the small foils.

"You're hot when you're bossy," he says, his eyes on me as I drag down his underwear.

"Is that why you're so hard for me," I reply, bringing my face closer to his as my hand wraps around his dick.

"Fuck, Val," he groans and pushes his head into the pillows when I start rubbing him in the way he loves.

"Mhmmm," I moan into his ear, and he tenses for a brief moment as the vibrations travel from my chest and through his.

"Please, I need to have you wrapped around me, chérie. No teasing," he begs, moaning again when I run his cock over my covered clit.

Gabriel reaches for my panties, pushing them to the side just enough to expose my pussy to him.

"Let me feel you." I roll the condom down his erection, too impatient to keep denying us both what we crave the most: each other.

Gabriel aligns himself with my entrance, the anticipation now spreading through me, settling in my chest and stomach in the form of butterflies. I sink down on his cock, both of us gasping in response to feeling whole again. My mind revels in the pleasure for a moment, unable to move until my needy body demands a release from the build-up that has us out of breath.

"You're always so goddamn wet for me, it makes me weak," he says as I reposition myself to start bouncing on him.

I take the opportunity to press a kiss to his lips before placing my hands on his pecs and pushing off him. I stop right before he'd slip out of me and slam back down.

"Fuck," we moan at the same time, and I keep going, keep repeating that simple movement to experience the same sweet pleasure over and over.

Gabriel swears in French, his fingers digging into my thighs and his eyes rolling into the back of his head.

"You're doing so well, baby," he praises, encouraging me and sending a thrill through me that settles in my lower abdomen. "Fuck, yes, keep going." He's breathless, but so am I.

Every time I come down, it feels like the feeling goes straight to my head, making me high. I never understood when people called their significant others a drug until I met Gabriel. He's mine, and I need more of him, as much as my body can take. I roll my hips and then bounce, grinding myself against his thumb when it lifts to my clit. My breasts jump with every move I make, and I notice Gabriel's eyes keep shifting between them and my face. I smile at him, slamming down harder now.

"Holy shit," he moans as I feel him tense under me, growing closer to his orgasm.

"Gabriel, fuck, I'm so close," I say, and he lifts my hips to thrust inside of me. He's desperate, going faster and deeper as I fall forward, my hands barely keeping me off his chest.

"Merde," he says while I become a moaning mess on top of him. His lips crash onto mine the same moment he slams inside of me, sending an orgasm through my body.

I start to tremble, shaking with pleasure as he spills into the condom and holds me close to him. Everything and everyone else disappears until there is nothing left in the world but us.

I sink onto his chest, listening to his accelerated heartbeat.

"Ma femme parfait," Gabriel whispers before kissing the top of my head.

He's still inside of me when I sit up again to show him the happy smile on my face. He reveals his, the green-brown eyes I fell in love with half-closed.

"I'll get ready, and we'll get some breakfast. Okay?" he asks, and his hands rub up and down my legs.

"Okay," I reply and kiss him again before getting off him.

Gabriel stands up, stretching his arms into the air. My mouth waters when I see his muscle flex, always on display for me. He turns around, and, when he catches me staring, he smirks. A blush settles on my cheeks.

When Gabriel walks out of the bathroom again, he's wearing a plain white shirt, light blue jeans, a bandana holding back his messy hair, and sunglasses hanging from his neckline. He looks absurdly attractive.

I make my way toward my purse, gathering everything I need.

"Ma chérie?" he asks, and my head shoots up. "What do you want to do for your birthday?"

My eyes go wide when I realize I'm going to turn nineteen in less than a week. I haven't even thought about my birthday. I've been so caught up in my messy, heartbreaking, and beautiful life, that I didn't notice how much time has passed.

"I want us to do something special. Maybe we can have a nice dinner with Adrian, Evangelin, Carlos, James, Jean, my aunts, Cameron and Elijah, maybe even Lucie, Andrea, and Haru. What do you think?" I smile at him and walk over to where he's standing.

"I think that's a really great idea," I say, and he beams at me.

"Okay, let me take care of everything. The only thing you have to do is be there." I let out a small laugh.

He gives me a quick peck, but I stand on my tiptoes when he pulls away just to give him another, longer kiss. I feel him grin against me. We've been kissing so much, my lips feel sore, but in the best way possible.

"What are we going to do for *your* birthday?" I ask, and he shrugs.

"I'm racing this year." Gabriel's birthday is five weeks after mine. "I'll probably be too tired to do anything," he says and lets out a short laugh.

"Well, hopefully not too tired," I reply and stand on my tiptoes once again to press my mouth to the soft spot just below his jaw.

"Never too tired for that," he assures me, and I chuckle.

Chapter 81

Valentina

Adrian and I have been sitting in front of his phone for the past half hour, waiting for the callback Lorenzo Mattia promised my brother. He's bouncing his legs up and down, his head between his arms. I've never seen him this nervous.

Out of the two of us, Adrian is the calm and collected one most of the time, but, right now, the roles are reversed. I know this call won't do anything, but he's clinging onto hope as if it's a drop of water in a desert.

"When will you let this go?" I ask after another long silence. My brother raises his head, anger on his features.

"The day you get an F1 seat," he replies, flinching toward his phone when the screen lights up. A groan leaves him because it's a message, not a call. "This man better call soon before I lose it." I stand up and move over to the seat next to him.

"You're going to break yourself fighting for me," I say, my voice soft as I take his hand. "Trust me, *I know*," I add, but he drops his face into his arms, resting them on the table next to the phone that won't ring.

"If you're going to be negative, please leave. I don't want that energy here." His words are muffled, but I hear them loud and clear, and they bother me.

"Pardon me for having lost my optimism," I spit and walk away from him.

"I get it, Val, I really do, but you can't—" I cut him off.

"You don't have the right to tell me what I can and cannot do, Adrian. You've been handed everything in your life. You never experienced the same rejection I have, so I don't expect you to understand how tiring it gets to live this part of my life," I scream, and he shakes his head.

"You're absolutely right. I have no idea. I've been by your side through it all, felt your pain as if it were my own, but I know I'll never truly understand. That's why I keep trying. You were taught to do your best by Dad and Grandpa, I was taught to do the same for you, okay? Now let me fucking do this because that's what they would have wanted, and it's what you need!"

Tears shoot into his eyes, making some sting mine as well.

"Please, Val, don't fight me on this. You've had the pressure of Grandfather's expectations on your shoulders your whole life, and the reason why getting rejected hurts you so much is because you see it as your failure. It's not. It's never been. The only failure you can put on yourself is giving up when I have the power to do something about what happened at the driver academy." Adrian sinks back onto his chair after he stood up to yell back at me. There are a lot of emotions surrounding us, but I'm hung up on his words.

"What if you can't do anything about it?" I ask, wiping away my tears.

"Then it's not you giving up anymore, Val. It's having done your best in a society that hates women who succeed, but it hasn't come to that yet, and I won't let it," he says, and I suck in an uneven, sharp breath.

"I don't want to stop fighting, I'm not ready to," I admit to him and myself. I'm not ready to stop.

A smile tugs on the corners of my brother's mouth.

"Good," he replies at the same time as our doorbell rings.

"Yoohoo, anyone home?" Christian's annoying voice comes from the gate area, and Adrian and I exchange a disgusted-confused look. "I can see you both," he says, and I storm toward him with determination.

Two bodyguards stand beside him, making me hesitate for a moment.

"Coward," I spit in French, and he whispers something to one of them. They step away as he brings his attention to my face. "What the hell do you want? You might be a royal, but I'm not obligated to let you inside my house," I bark, amusement sparkling in his eyes as soon as the words leave me.

"I love it when you deny me something, Tina. It's so hot," he says, and my body revolts.

"You disgust me," I respond, and he smiles.

"Yeah, yeah, you've said so before, but I just came here to talk. Please, may I come inside?" he asks a genuine, serious expression neutralizing his usually smug features.

"Rot in hell," I say and walk away, but his next words make me stop dead in my tracks.

"I'm sorry, Valentina, truly." That means nothing to me, but I'm surprised at his humanity. "The seat should have been yours," he goes on, and I turn around to see someone else get out of the limo.

It's the crown prince of Monaco, Thomas Crovetto, wearing a suit that's more expensive than anything I will ever own. He adjusts his tie as he steps out of the car, making his way toward the gate more gracefully than anyone else I've ever met. The light-blue color of his clothes complements his dark skin. He has piercing hazel eyes and full, round lips.

The princes are half-brothers, with Thomas being the son of the king's first wife and Christian being the son of his second. The two could not be more opposite from appearance all the way to behavior.

"Good afternoon, Ms. Romana. How are you?"

I don't know whether to curtsy or drop onto my knees, but no matter who society has deemed them to be, I don't kneel for any man. *Well, maybe just one...*

"I'd be much better if you removed your brother from my property, Your Highness, thank you," I reply, and Thomas gives me a smile I'm sure has made people fall in love with him in the past.

"Forgive us, we're simply here for my brother to take responsibility for what he's done to you in the past. For one, he should have never endangered your life during that karting incident a few weeks ago. I hope your wrist has healed well," he says, sincerity in his tone.

I look down at the faint bruise, which hasn't disappeared yet before crossing my arms in front of my chest.

"I appreciate the sentiment, but I don't want an apology. However, I'd love to never see His Royal Slimeness again," I say and almost slap my mouth when I realize in whose presence I am.

But Thomas assures me it's fine with a laugh, making me grin.

"She was doing that the whole time we were at the academy together," Christian complains, but there is something different about him with his big brother next to him. He seems... *almost childish?*

"Good, you deserve it. You're not better than Valentina or anyone else because of your title, Christian, and I'm glad she reminded you of that," Thomas says, and I give him a genuine smile.

"Would you like to have a cup of coffee or tea, Your Highness?" I ask, addressing Thomas and him alone.

He gives his brother a pat on the back before letting out a laugh.

"Go wait in the car, I'll be right there. George, crack the window for him, please," he yells the last sentence at one of the bodyguards, and I unlock the gate for him.

Thomas holds out his hand for me, and I slide mine into his, prepared to shake it. Instead, he lifts it to his mouth, pressing a kiss to the back of it.

"Pleasure to meet you in person. I've heard and seen a lot about you," he says, and, for some reason, a blush settles on my cheeks.

"It's an honor to meet you, Your Highness," I reply because I think it's the right thing to say. He drops my hand and waves my comment away.

"Call me Thomas. I don't like those titles, I'm not my brother."

"I know, that's why I invited you to stay for coffee," I explain, and he chuckles, his eyes staring into mine.

"I like you. You're not afraid to speak your mind in my presence. It's refreshing." He smiles again as he adds, "How would you like to join my team of advisors? I've been searching for someone like you," he says with an amused tone, and I give him a look of utter disbelief as we make our way to the terrace where Adrian is standing with a dropped jaw.

Panic settles in my chest, worry rising in my throat until a lump forms, preventing me from asking what happened. Adrian lowers his phone from his ear, dropping it onto the ground.

"I'm afraid Valentina will be too busy racing for the Alfa Adrenalina F1 team next year to work for you," my brother states, and I feel my heart drop into my stomach.

What?

Chapter 82

Valentina

"What are you talking about?" I ask, taking a step toward him with shaking hands. "Don't joke about this, Adrian," I beg, but he shakes his head, tears falling down his cheeks.

"I'm not, Val. Lorenzo Mattia is going to offer you a contract to be the test and reserve driver for Velocità Rossa for the rest of the season with a guaranteed spot in the Alfa Adrenalina team next year," my brother says, making everything around me spin.

"I should go. Congratulations, Valentina," Thomas interrupts, and I thank him, still trying to process what Adrian told me not even a minute ago.

"He's coming to your birthday party to bring the contract and tell you in person."

I sink to my knees because they are no longer capable of allowing me to stand. My whole body trembles as I try to let that information register.

"I did it?" I ask as my brother kneels down in front of me, more tears flowing down.

"Yes, little champion, you did it. You proved to him, Mr. Reiner, Andrea, and the whole Velocità Rossa team that you deserve a seat, and they listened. They saw you, and they've given you the chance to live your dream." I grab his hand, needing to feel him to know this isn't a dream. Sensing it, he pinches my palm, and I let out a gasp which turns into a sob.

"I did it." He nods, and, for the first time in my life, I fall apart out of happiness.

All of the pain has led up to this point of pure, raw joy, and no one will ever be able to take it away from me. I fling my arms around Adrian's neck, and his wrap around my back, hugging me tighter and with more emotion than ever before.

"Thank you for everything," I say when I've managed to calm down a little.

"I did nothing. This was all you, Val, all you," he replies, bringing me closer to his chest.

I bury my face in the crook of his neck, inhaling his comforting scent. All these years, all those people who told me I wasn't good enough, they all got me to where I am now, proving them fucking wrong.

"I have to call James and Gabriel, oh, and Evangelin. I want to tell them," I say, still crying because I've never felt this combination of relief, happiness, and victory before.

"You can call James and Evangelin tomorrow. For tonight, go to Gabriel, celebrate. I'll see you for your birthday party tomorrow," Adrian says, kissing my cheek and standing up to help me. "Go," he encourages when I hesitate.

I give his hand one last squeeze before grabbing my phone and sprinting all the way to Gabriel's house. My heart is racing from running and the excitement of my good news.

I knock on the door, waiting for anyone to open it for me. Domi does, a warm smile resting on her face.

"Valentina, it's so nice to see you. How are you, belle?" she asks, giving me a kiss on each cheek.

"I'm well, how are you? How is the baby?" I reply, her face lighting up at the mention of her unborn child.

"Everything is great, but I know you're probably here to see Gabriel. He's upstairs. Go ahead," she says, stepping out of the way to let me go past. I smile at her before rushing to his room and knocking on his door.

"Come in." Gabriel's voice is soft, and I hesitate. I know how he'll react. This will be a moment I'll never forget, another core memory to add to today, but I'm nervous anyway.

I open the door to reveal a painting Gabriel, who is dancing on the spot to his favorite song. His lips pull into a smile when he sees me, and I jump into his arms, my legs wrapping around him.

"What's going on?" he asks, his hands moving to the underside of my thighs to hold me up.

"I'm going to race for Alfa Adrenalina next year," I blurt out, and he drops me onto my feet, his hands moving to each side of my neck.

"Shut up! Oh my God!" he cheers, jumping up and down from excitement. He attacks my face with kisses before stepping back and shaking his head. "I don't even know what to do with myself, that's how happy I am," he admits, and I let out a small laugh as more tears fill my eyes. I don't care about them anymore. Today I get to cry as much as I want.

"Neither do I. It seems very surreal. Maybe I need to have the contract in my hands first," I say, and Gabriel shakes his head in disbelief and awe once more.

"It's not going to feel real until you have your number on the car and sit down in it for the first time," he replies, rubbing his face with his hands. "I can't believe this! I've never heard better news in my entire life. Fuck, I have to sit down," he says, and I chuckle at his behavior. "What do you want to do? We can pop a bottle of champagne and spray it all over ourselves to help you practice what happens on the podium," he suggests, but it's my turn to shake my head then, laughing as I do so.

"Honestly, mon soleil, I would love nothing more than cuddling up against you while you read me a good book," I say, and he stands up, walking toward me to kiss me.

"Get on the bed then," he whispers, and I run toward it, dropping on it with a dramatic motion and waiting for him to grab a book from his shelf. He lies down next to me, a pen in his other hand. "Tell me what you think, and I'll write it down in here," he says, and I place my head on his chest before we start annotating the book together.

This moment is my personal brand of happiness.

"Since it's already past midnight, Happy Birthday, ma chérie," he tells me right before he presses his lips to mine and lowers the book again. We've been reading for longer than I thought.

"Thank you," I say when I lean back, and he grins at me.

"Wait here," he commands and gets up from the bed.

A small box lies in his grasp when he walks back over to me.

"This is the first gift I have for you, but it's the most important one."

Gabriel hands me the box. Within it lies the same necklace I have seen countless times in his sketches. The number seven, his number, is carved into the charm. I have no idea what my face is doing. I try to smile, but I'm mesmerized by his gift. It's the most magnificent necklace I have ever seen.

"Val?" he asks after a moment of silence. My eyes lift from the jewelry to him.

"This is so beautiful," I say in a low voice and laugh at myself for being so emotional. I throw my arms around his neck.

"I haven't explained the meaning yet, hold on." I pull back and stare at him. "I guess in a way this is like a promise ring, but it's also not. It's more than just a stupid promise. The necklace is supposed to remind you that you're on my team. My Formula One career is my life, and you are my life. You wearing it is supposed to symbolize that all of it means nothing to me without you. I love you, Valentina Esmèe Cèlia Romana."

"I love you the same, Gabriel Matteo Biancheri." I take the necklace and put it on. Gabriel watches me, and I smile at him once it's securely fixed around my neck. "I will wear this with pride."

I wrap my fingers around the charm before I look at the man in front of me again. There is nothing but love in his eyes as he watches me bring it to my lips and press a kiss against it. Gabriel lifts his hand to touch my cheek, his thumb tracing my bottom lip.

"Tired?" he asks, and I nod.

It's been a long day, and tomorrow will be another. We both need some rest for the party he has planned and organized.

"Good night, mon tournesol," Gabriel whispers into my ear as he spoons me on his bed.

"Bonne nuit, mon soleil."

CHAPTER 83

Valentina

I WAKE UP TO the smell of coffee, Gabriel's famous waffles, and freshly cut fruit. My eyes open to find my boyfriend sitting in front of me with a tray of food and, thankfully, no shirt on his body. There are at least five gifts next to me on the bed.

"Happy Birthday. It's ten in the morning, I hope I didn't wake you too early," he says, and I let out a short laugh. God, he makes me sound so lazy. "I made you some breakfast, but before you eat, open your presents," he commands, but I shake my head.

"Before I open them and eat, I want to do something else."

I cock my brow, making Gabriel smirk at me. He puts the tray with the food on the nightstand, and I remove the blanket from my chest. His delicious body moves between my legs before his tongue enters my mouth. He kisses me like he'll never get enough, like he'll never need to come up for breath.

"Open your presents," he says a moment later, and I laugh.

I groan a "fine," and he hands me the first gift. It's an envelope, and I retrieve a single piece of paper that reads

'Andrea, Lucie, and Haru are coming to your party'

My jaw drops, and I look at Gabriel in disbelief. All of them told me they were busy and couldn't make it.

"They were trying to figure out a way to come before I contacted them. Andrea is particularly excited to see you, and I can't imagine how happy they will be when you tell them you're racing for Alfa next season," he says, and a wave of excitement courses through me.

"Thank you, mon amour. This has already made my day." The smile on his face is enchanting.

He leans over me to get the second present, and I take it from him with a grin. This one is much bigger, and I have to put it on my lap to open it. Inside the box is the most beautiful deep-red, silk dress. It has white flowers at the bottom and will reach just above my knees.

"It's for your party tonight," he explains, and I beam up at him.

"It's gorgeous. Thank you."

He hands me another box without wasting any time. This one is small, and inside of it lies a dried sunflower.

"It's from the first day I brought you to my room. Remember? When I had dozens of sunflowers?" he asks with a shy laugh while I pick up the dried flower.

"Baby," is all I can say.

He hands me another present. In it are fitting shoes to the dress.

"Where did you get the dress and shoes? They are stunning," I tell him, and he flashes me a mischievous smile.

"Evangelin and I picked them out for you. So, I can't take all the credit." He chuckles as I put my hand on his cheek. The stubble on it is rough against my skin. "Okay, last one," he says and hands me the biggest package of all of them. "I stole this idea from James, kind of," he admits, and I furrow my brows.

The all too familiar helmet I designed when I was a child lies inside the box, sucking the breath from my lungs. It's a full-sized one, not the small version that's on my desk in my room.

"At first, I got this because you are going to need your own helmet when you drive with me around the track like we did in Maranello, but now—" Gabriel cuts off, joy glistening in his green-brown eyes. "Now you get to wear it when you test drive, reserve drive, or next year." I swallow down the tears. It's starting to feel less surreal with this gift in my hands. I'm speechless as I look at the helmet covered in flowers. Everything is in its proper spot.

"I don't know what to say." We both let out a short laugh, and he wipes away the tears I'm no longer able to hold back. "This is freaking amazing." I put the helmet on. It fits my head perfectly. "I can't believe you did this," I say, but I can barely hear myself.

I get up from the bed and walk into the bathroom to look at myself. A warm feeling spreads through my chest at the sight in the mirror. The smile on my face gets even bigger.

I run back into Gabriel's room, put the helmet down on the bed, and kiss him to say thank you until I'm convinced it's enough.

"What do you want to do today?" he asks while we eat the breakfast he made.

"Uhmm," I say as I think about what to do, popping another piece of waffle into my mouth. Gabriel watches me with an amused expression, so I grin. "Maybe we can go mini-golfing," I tell him and clap my hands together in excitement. He chuckles and nods.

"All right. We'll go mini-golfing. We just have to be back by four because I've got some preparations to do." Gabriel leans forward and touches his lips to my forehead before he gets up.

I remind him I have to go home and change. He assures me he will come with me and disappears into his bathroom to get ready.

I wait for him on his bed while putting on my clothes from yesterday. Gabriel comes out again, completely naked. There is water dripping from his hair, his curls more defined when they're wet. My eyes fall to the moon tattoo on his ass cheek, and they linger there until I find the faint scar on the side of his thigh.

Gabriel and I walk to my house, and when Adrian sees me come through the door, he jumps up from the couch. He sings 'Happy Birthday' before hugging me and pulling me into the air. When he drops me back on my feet and leans away, tears glisten in his eyes.

"I'll give you your present later," he says, but I scold him with my eyes for spending money. He gives me a kiss on the cheek before telling me to take a shower because, according to him, I stink.

"It's my birthday, you have to be nice to me," I remind my brother, who rolls his eyes with a smile. I poke his stomach, which only makes him laugh. "We're going to play mini-golf, asshole. Are you going to be nice or should I not invite you?" I ask, and he straightens out his back until he stands before me like a soldier.

"Ma'am, yes, ma'am, I will behave," he promises. I shake my head at his silly behavior.

Gabriel stays downstairs with Adrian while I rush through my routine. After my shower, I put on a short, green dress that brings out my eyes. I leave off the makeup, too lazy and comfortable to bother.

My eyes shift to the necklace Gabriel gave me, but I doubt my reflection does it justice. I've never owned a jewelry piece as special and meaningful as this one.

When I step outside onto the veranda, Gabriel and Adrian are in a heated argument. I have no idea what it's about, but I see my boyfriend's hands balled into fists and my brother's face redder than a tomato. They're glaring at each other like they haven't been becoming close friends, as if they've been rivals this entire time.

"You are buying people now, is that what it is? You buy them so they prioritize you?"

"I am not *buying* anyone. They may prioritize me because I have more fucking points than you. How dare you accuse me of bribing the team?" Gabriel asks.

With every heartbeat, they get closer to each other.

"Hey, what's going on?" I say as I step between the two angry men.

There is one motivation that can calm down their fury, which is my safety. They might hit each other, but they'd die before anything happens to me.

"Your boyfriend's getting special treatment because he's been paying people," Adrian says, and Gabriel takes another step closer to the guy who is accusing him.

When his chest touches my arm, he takes a step back again.

"You got proof?" I challenge, and Adrian's expression changes.

"No," he admits, and I frown at him.

"Then what the hell are you doing? Why are you starting a fight with him, a fight you know neither of you will win?" I ask, and he looks at me with a guilty expression.

Gabriel's breathing is still heavy next to me, so I take his fist in my hand, and he opens it so I can put my palm against his.

"We are going mini-golfing. Will you be able to drop this and pick it back up tomorrow?" If it wasn't easy to tell how defeated Adrian was before, it definitely is now.

"I'm sorry, Val, but I don't want to be in his presence right now." A wave of sadness storms through me for a brief moment, but I shove it away.

"Fine, we'll see you later." Gabriel squeezes my hand, and we leave my brother standing by himself on the veranda.

I get the keys to the Mustang, and as soon as we leave my driveway, I turn to Gabriel.

"Why would he think you bribed the team?" I ask, needing more information.

"Because there have been a couple of meetings now where the strategists have favored me, but I don't have anything to do with it. I swear on us, and that is the highest swear I could ever make." I look at him again, sensing there is more he wants to say. "I know why they do it," he admits, and I cock an eyebrow, waiting for him to tell me. "They think I have the potential to win the championship this year, they think I'm faster than Adrian, stronger." I forget to breathe as soon as the words leave him. "I promise, I will talk to them—"

"Don't," I say, and, from the corner of my eye, I can see the confusion on his face. "If Adrian has a problem with the strategists, he has to talk to them. This isn't your problem, as noble as it would be. Adrian is a big boy." I look over my shoulder while I make a left turn. "You wanted to punch him, didn't you?" I ask curiosity in my voice. I'd like to think they're both mature enough to get upset without starting a physical fight, even if I hadn't shown up.

"I don't cheat, and he was questioning my integrity. So, yes, I wanted to punch him for doing so. He has this way of pushing my buttons." I park the car at the mini-golf spot.

The *Princess Antoinette Park* is where Grandpa used to take Adrian and me, and I have those memories stored securely in my mind. They've been packed away for a while, but now, they all come crashing to the front of my mind, filling me with nostalgia.

"He does have that ability," I joke, and we both laugh. "But please, don't hit my brother, ever. I'd have to kick your ass, and we both know I can," I say, and Gabriel licks his bottom lip in response, making a wave of shivers run down my spine.

"I'd take any punishment from you," he replies with a smirk. I touch my tongue to the roof of my mouth.

"Do you think you could handle a punishment from me?" I lean closer to him, teasing him with my hand as it glides up his leg and toward his crotch.

"Depends. How would you punish me? Spank me?" The smirk on his lips deepens, but I shake my head.

"No, that wouldn't be a punishment. You'd probably enjoy that." He gives me a shameless nod, bringing a smile to my lips. "Yeah, so I'd have to do something to drive you crazy." I think for a moment, getting closer to his lips and my fingers to his cock. "Maybe tie you to a chair and make you watch while I fuck myself," I say, noticing his breathing hitch.

"I guess I better not do it then," he says and clears his throat.

I peck his lips before I open my door and get out of the car, leaving him with that image.

The hot summer air almost instantly makes me sweat. It must be at least thirty degrees outside. I wrap my fingers around my new charm and enjoy how it feels in my hand.

"I knew the necklace would be much better than a ring," he mumbles when he stands next to me. I smile at the man who makes me the happiest woman in the world.

"It is," I say with pride.

Gabriel presses a kiss to my temple and wraps his arm around my shoulders, letting out a content "hmm" into my ear.

"But, don't worry, the ring will come," he says, and I let out a nervous laugh.

"Eventually," I remind him, and he rubs his nose against mine.

"Eventually," he whispers, returning my smile.

Chapter 84

Valentina

GABRIEL PAYS FOR THE round of eighteen holes, and the guy at the counter hands us two putters with an expression of awe. He knows who he's helping, so my boyfriend asks if he wants to take a photo. The man gives him a few excited nods. I take their picture before we go outside.

Gabriel hands me a golf ball and a putter, winking at me as he does it. I set it at the start line and move into position to hit it. The summer sun is hot on my skin, but I ignore it as I get ready to kick Gabriel's butt.

Naturally, while I position myself, I push my ass out a little more than necessary to mess with him. I swing my putter and the ball lands close to the hole, making me stick out my tongue at him. He shakes his head, his smile bright and his dimples deeply imprinted in his cheeks.

Gabriel hits his ball, and it rolls almost directly next to mine. However, he's closer than I am, which is why I go first and sink the ball on my second try. Somehow, it takes Gabriel three more until he succeeds, which I can't help but make fun of. I'm only joking, and he knows it, making him roll his eyes with amusement.

The next four holes are uneventful, but he's ahead when we arrive at the sixth one, so I have to find a better way to distract him. If he wins, he's going to brag about it for the next few weeks, and I am not going to let that happen.

I clear my throat before I start my distraction plan.

"Mon amour, did I tell you how hot you look today? Your legs, your arms, and your ass look fantastic in that outfit."

It does exactly what I want it to. Gabriel turns around with a surprised expression, but there's also something else on there. *Pride?*

"Man, I really love your tight—"

"Okay, chérie, we're in public."

I hold up my hands in mock surrender and mumble a "fine" before I let him get into position again. I get up and stand behind him, my hands covering his ass. He chuckles in response, but, for some reason, he doesn't make me stop and doesn't remove my hands.

"You're being very naughty," he tells me, and I grin.

"I know, but I also know you love it." He hits the ball, and, just as expected, it lands far away from the hole. "Too easy," I say more to myself than him, but he hears me anyway.

"Wait, does that mean you don't actually like my ass?" Gabriel pushes his bottom lip forward, and I laugh.

"Of course I do," I assure him, and he looks at me with a confused expression.

I don't think he believes my intentions to be pure, which they aren't. When I get a hole-in-one on my try, I jump up in disbelief and turn to Gabriel, who is shaking his head.

"Doesn't count," he says, and I let out half a laugh.

"Of course it does!" But Gabriel is shaking his head, his curls bouncing a bit from the movement.

"Nope, it can't. It's not fair," he explains, and I burst into laughter, jumping onto his back when he tries to walk away. He catches me, holding onto my legs. "Don't try to cheer me up when you're kicking my ass," he says, but I press my lips to his ear, whispering "sorry."

A couple of holes later, I'm barely ahead on the scorecard. I lie the ball on the line in front of me, for the fifteenth time, and position myself to hit the golf ball. Sweat drips down the left side of my face, and I wipe it away. It's getting hotter now, and I look over at Gabriel to see if we have any water left. He hands me the bottle, and I give it back to him once I have taken a few sips.

"Do you mind if I empty it?" he asks, and I shake my head.

Gabriel takes the bottle, and, not very subtly, pours the content all over his white shirt. It becomes see-through in an instant, the fabric clinging to his abs in the most delicious way. My heart forgets how to beat, and my head forgets how to breathe. No matter how many times I've seen him shirtless, his body never ceases to make mine ache.

"Oops," he says, but we both know it was no accident.

I clear my throat in an attempt to bring my head back to reality, and it works, somewhat. I force my full attention to the ball and hit it. It lands centimeters from the hole, and I turn back to look at my frantic boyfriend.

"What you gotta know is, mon soleil, I may love your body, but I also love winning." He bites his bottom lip and nods.

"You know what I love? That beautiful smile on your full lips. However, I'm going to win and wipe it off your face."

My mouth forms an O-shape, but then I giggle when he sticks out his tongue and puts on a concentrating face I have never seen before. It's cute and weird at the same time, his nose scrunched and his tongue pressing against his teeth.

"I got this. Watch me, baby." I'm a little disappointed when he misses the hole by at least two meters.

By the time we arrive at the last hole, Gabriel and I are head to head, and he ends up winning the game. My hand lifts to the necklace he gave me, and I smile to myself. I'm on his team. Whenever he succeeds at something, I'm going to be happy for him because that's how much I love him. If he fails, I will be upset. So, it's a good thing he won, otherwise I wouldn't have enjoyed my victory as much anyway.

At least that's what I keep telling myself to feel better.

Gabriel turns to me with his smile bright and sweet. I take two steps toward him, closing the unbearable distance, and put my hands on his hips. He places his on my neck and leans down to kiss me. I grin against his lips, and he kisses my cheek before pulling away.

I wrap my arms around him as he hugs me back just as tight. I could stay like this forever, but Gabriel has to get back to my house soon to start his preparations. Somehow, I manage to peel myself off him, frowning as I do. He smiles at my expression, running his thumb over my bottom lip.

"And you say I'm the clingy one," he says, causing me to grin from ear to ear.

I hand him the keys to my Mustang and let him take me home. For the first time in my life, no part of me feels like driving. I'd rather look out of the window and appreciate how breathtaking my home is. There are no clouds in the sky, all of the plants are in full bloom, and birds are chirping happily.

Then, I turn my head to admire Gabriel. The way his veins stick out on his arm as he drives, the way he bites the inside of his cheek as he concentrates on the road ahead of him, and the way his stubble complements his green-brown eyes make me swoon. I love his stubble, too. It's short, clean, and I think it fits his face very well. It was patchy when I first met him, but that was only because he was so young. Now that he's almost twenty-two, it's full and makes him look mature.

When we arrive home, Gabriel tells me to stay in my room and get ready until he's done and my guests have arrived. All of the presents he gave me this morning are on my bed, and I take out the helmet before placing it on the nightstand on the other side of where I sleep. My eyes drift to the mini one James gave me exactly one year ago.

I'm worried about my best friend. I've texted him a couple of times, but he won't answer any of the messages. Everything was fine, and now he's distant again. I hope he'll be at my party, but he hasn't even called to sing "Happy Birthday" like he does every year.

Before I can overthink things, I go into my bathroom and put on some makeup to match the silk dress Gabriel bought me. I slide it on, the material smooth against my skin. I'm not surprised my boyfriend chose a dress that highlights my breasts.

I let my mind freak out about the fact that Lorenzo Mattia will be at my house in less than an hour, contract in hand.

It's really happening.

I'm going to be a fucking F1 driver.

We did it, Grandpa.

Chapter 85

Valentina

"Ma chérie?" I'm stepping into my shoes when I see Gabriel leaning against my doorframe, admiring my appearance with his arms crossed in front of his chest and a smirk on his face.

"Haven't you ever heard of knocking? What if I was indecent?" He chuckles as he walks closer to me.

"Nothing I haven't seen before," he explains in such an arrogant and cocky way, I can't help the next words leaving my lips.

"What if I was touching myself?" I ask, and he bites his bottom lip.

"You would call me first because you know I'd take care of that for you." He's got an answer for everything, but I can't help but smile.

"Fine," I say, so he returns my smile.

"Now, I would love to continue this, but your guests are waiting for you downstairs." Nervosity settles in my stomach now. A lot of people are going to be there.

When I reach the bottom of the steps, I'm greeted by everyone. Each and every one of them comes up to say *Happy Birthday*. Evangelin hugs me and tells me how happy she is for the opportunity she heard I've received. Cameron introduces me to Elijah, a gorgeous dark-skinned man with brown eyes.

Lorenzo and his wife Maria come up to me, and I have a captivating conversation with both of them. The Velocità Rossa team principal informs me personally of his decision and offer before handing me a contract he demands I read as thoroughly as possible. I assure him I will, placing the papers on the stairs.

Domi and Nicolette grab my attention next.

The whole time I talk to them, or anyone, I can't help the bubble of sadness rising in my throat. I had a feeling James wasn't going to come, but I would have never expected him not to call.

"Valentina," Andrea says, walking up to me and wrapping their arms around me. "Lorenzo has informed me of his decision. I'm so proud of you!" I hug them back, happiness consuming me like it always does now at the mention of my success.

"Thank you for coming. I'm so happy to see you," I say, earning me a smile from them.

Lucie and Haru appear next to Andrea, grinning at each other like the two people in love they are. They shift their gazes to me eventually to make conversation.

"I hope you'll invite us to one of your races next year," Lucie says, her accent thick.

"Of course."

An arm wraps around my waist, pulling me against the owner's chest.

"I'm sorry, I can't help myself. You, in that dress, have me at your mercy," he whispers into my ear.

I smile while I attempt to listen to Haru tell me how things have been at the academy, but I keep getting distracted by Gabriel's warmth and mahogany scent. I only manage to nod every so often to show my attention is on Haru.

"You're kidding! Holy shit, Val!" I hear Cameron scream from beside me where he's speaking to my brother and Leonard.

He skips over to where I'm standing, picking me up and raising me into the air.

"I'm so fucking excited!" he yells, and I let out a joy-filled laugh that vibrates through the whole room. He drops me back onto my feet, making sure to be gentle, and presses a big, wet kiss on my cheek.

"Adrian told you?" I ask, giving my brother a teasing angry look. He shrugs, his smile bright and contagious.

"I'm sorry, I don't know what came over me, but I want to tell everyone," he says, rubbing the back of his neck in response.

I give him another scolding expression, but he merely chuckles.

"Hey, you're going to be the first woman racing in F1 for an entire season, Val. It's a big deal, and you should be very proud!" Adrian says, and everyone in the room starts applauding for me. My cheeks heat up in an instant, and I feel the urge to bury my face in my boyfriend's neck to hide from the attention.

"Let's pop some champagne, yeah?" Gabriel interrupts, bringing everyone's focus to him.

"Thank you," I whisper, and he leans down to kiss the bridge of my nose.

"I know my woman," he says, and I blush.

"I love you."

Before he can reply, my eyes drift from his face and land on James as he walks through the front door. I step out of my boyfriend's arms and rush over to my best friend so I can have his wrapped around me.

When he sees me, he lets out a long breath, and I watch relief wash over his face. He gives me a firm hug, his head resting on my shoulder.

"Happy Birthday," James mumbles.

"Thank you for coming." I pull back and put my hands on his shoulders.

"I'm sorry, things have been hectic, and I needed some time to figure everything out by myself. I shouldn't have gone MIA, forgive me," he says while I study his tired features.

"Don't apologize, I'm not upset." A sad smile spreads over his lips. "I have so many questions," I admit.

"Tomorrow, darling. Tonight, let's celebrate your birthday." I squeeze his shoulders before he hands me a present. "Read the card later," he says, and I nod.

I lead him inside the house. Leonard gives me a brief squeeze on the shoulder as I walk by him, congratulating me on my seat, which I told him about through text yesterday. At least he's one person besides Gabriel I got to tell myself.

My boyfriend walks up to us, handing the Brit a glass of champagne. I take Gabriel's hand, but he wraps his arm around my shoulders instead. He taps my collarbone, and I lift my hand, allowing him to take it and intertwine our fingers.

We make casual conversation until Gabriel makes us sit down to eat the catered meal. The decorations are wonderful. He placed sunflowers all over the rooms, there are banners with my name hung on almost every wall, and he picked out some brown and yellow tones for the table decorations to match the sunflowers.

"This is stunning," I say to Gabriel, who pulls out the chair for me and then pushes it back in when I've sat down.

"Anything for you, chérie," he replies before Lorenzo Mattia grabs my attention.

I love that my friends and family are all here to celebrate me, but whenever I turn my head, someone else is trying to make conversation. I'm convinced my social battery is going to run out long before the evening is over.

"I need you to read over the contract as soon as possible so we can get you ready to start working with the team in Austria for the next race," Lorenzo says, and I nod with more enthusiasm than is necessary.

"I will look over the contract with her tomorrow," James chimes in, and I realize Adrian must have told him too because I haven't had the chance yet.

I look at my brother, who immediately turns his head away from me to hide the guilty expression on his face.

"Big mouth," I call out in French, and Gabriel snickers next to me.

We both know my brother is the worst at keeping secrets out of everyone we know.

The food is delicious, and for dessert, Gabriel carries a three-tier chocolate cake over to me, candles burning on top. Everyone sings to me first in English, then in French. Gabriel kisses me after I blow out the candles before we all enjoy the cake.

After dinner, we scatter around the room.

"Do you know where Evangelin is?" I ask Carlos, and the former F1 champion gives me an unreadable expression.

"She went outside to get some air," he says, and I go there to check on her.

I would have never expected to find her like this.

Chapter 86

Valentina

"Evangelin?" I ask, and she attempts to wipe away her tears. My heart is aching in my chest because of how afraid I am of what's happening. Worry consumes me until nothing else remains.

"Oh, I'm sorry, Valentina. Just go back inside, belle." She doesn't know me if she thinks I am going to leave her by herself when she's crying.

"What's wrong?" I ask in French, and she lets out a sob.

"It's a long story." I place my hand on her shoulder and rub it to comfort her.

"Would talking about it make you feel better?" She looks off into the distance.

"I've never spoken to anyone about this," she starts, and I take her hand to lead her to the chairs on the veranda. "Gabriel is Carlos' grandson."

I swallow hard because I can't comprehend that sentence. At first, I think she's joking and I almost laugh, but then more tears flow out of her eyes, making me unable to breathe.

"Fifty-one years ago, a year after Carlos and I got married, he had an affair with an Italian woman. Nine months later, she had his child, but she gave her baby girl up, and only told Carlos about her years later."

Evangelin stops to let out a sob, and I can't bring myself to move. Her words have paralyzed me. This is not happening. She cannot be telling me the truth right now. I swallow again to get rid of the lump in my throat.

"I don't understand," I croak out when she doesn't continue the story.

"There was no way to find her, or at least that was what he thought. He didn't tell me about the affair for ten years and let me tell you, it took everything out of me to stay with him, to forgive and offer him a second chance. Then, a couple of years later, we found out about the baby. Sierra, the Italian woman, wrote Carlos a letter, but we never received a call or any other form of contact. We searched for years, only to find out Carlos' daughter had a brain aneurysm the summer before."

Gabriel's mom had a brain aneurysm. No, this cannot be happening.

"We also found out Carlos has two grandchildren, and one of them is a successful Formula One driver, just like he was. Carlos didn't have the strength to find out their address. The only name he got was 'Gabriel.'"

I get up from the chair I've been sitting in and try to find a way to start breathing again. I'm convinced I'm hyperventilating.

"Then you came into my life, and you told me about this gorgeous man you were in love with, but I would have never expected it would be *him*. Seeing Gabriel at the store that first time, I couldn't help how sad I felt."

The day she started crying after she saw him. Oh my God. I had a feeling something was off, but this? This is beyond anything I could have ever imagined.

"Everything I had suppressed over the years came crashing back, but I knew I had to get a grip. I care a lot about you, Valentina, and I wanted to make this work, but I can't anymore. It's painful seeing him." Evangelin lets out another sob. "Gabriel only exists because my husband didn't love me enough. Don't misunderstand me, I am so grateful he does because Gabriel is a wonderful young man, but seeing him and Jean *hurts* me."

I look at her with anger and compassion. The paradox is making my head spin, but I can't control my feelings. This is too much all at once.

"I care about you as well, but you know I can't keep this a secret. Gabriel and Jean have lost more people than you will ever understand, and I can't deny them the opportunity to know about their biological grandfather, to maybe have a chance to have some more family." I run my fingers through my curly hair, get stuck on seven different knots, and groan in frustration.

"You can't tell them," she mumbles, and I look at her, only with anger now.

"No, Carlos and you have to do that. I can't be the one, it wouldn't be right," I say, my emotions threatening to overwhelm me.

"Now?" she asks, and I sink onto the chair next to her.

"Please don't ask me to hide this from Gabriel. It will ruin our relationship, break the trust I have earned by never doing anything like you're asking of me right now. Gabriel would never forgive me," I explain, but she shakes her head. "Please, get your husband,

Jean, and Gabriel, and sit down with them. I am not keeping this from my family because that is what they are, *my family*."

Evangelin looks down at the table, tears still running down her cheeks, and I want to apologize for being so harsh.

"I'm sorry, Evangelin, I didn't mean for it to come out that way. It's not your fault. I just wish you would have warned me before dropping this huge bomb. You are asking too much of me, and you knew that when you started this story. And it's okay, just please, I love him too much to keep such a big secret," I say, and she stops crying. "Imagine keeping something like this from Carlos." Evangelin looks at me with a soft expression. "You wouldn't be able to, would you?" I ask, and she shakes her head.

"No, I couldn't do the same thing he did. It's too big of a betrayal." The small woman gets up from her seat and walks inside without saying another word to me.

A minute later, Gabriel, Jean, Carlos, and her step outside. I can't look at any of them.

"Chérie?" Gabriel asks, his voice soft and worried.

"I'm inside if you need me," I say and press a kiss to his cheek before making my way over to Adrian.

"Val?" my brother asks, so I look at him. "I'm sorry about this morning. I shouldn't have accused Gabriel of bribing people. I know he doesn't. I'm going to talk to the team."

I honestly don't give a shit about that problem anymore. All I can think about is how Gabriel and Jean must be feeling right now.

"All good, Adrian. Don't worry about it." He nods while I force a smile.

"You know I love you," he says to cheer me up.

"I love you, Adrian, no matter how stupid you act," I reply, giving him my full attention for the first time. He nudges my arm, making me grin. It doesn't feel right, which is why the corners of my mouth drop almost immediately.

"Love?" I spin around to look at James. "I have to go home, but open your present and read the letter. I'll see you tomorrow to go over the contract," he says, pressing a kiss to my cheek and leaving without waiting for a response from me.

Elijah and Cameron do so a few minutes later as well. Everyone else follows shortly after, leaving Adrian and me alone inside the house. Gabriel and Jean are still on the veranda with Evangelin and... *their grandfather*.

"What's on your mind?" Adrian asks, but I shake my head and smile at him.

I feel like throwing up or screaming, or anything to let out the frustration in my chest.

Finally, after what feels like an eternity, Gabriel and Jean walk through the veranda door. The younger brother has a smile on his face, but my eyes focus on Gabriel. He looks confused and shocked, but he doesn't say anything.

For one short second, he simply looks at me with too many emotions to identify and then moves upstairs toward my bedroom. I thank Jean for coming, but he's in his own world, probably dreaming about what's to come in the future. I'm glad he's happy about it, someone should be.

My feet bring me to the steps of the staircase, and I take two at a time to get to my room faster. I open the door to find Gabriel staring at the large canvas I got him. We hung it over my bed a few days ago, intending for it to stay there until he finds an apartment.

"Gabriel?" I ask softly, and he turns to me with tears running down his cheeks. They are bright red, and his eyes are bloodshot. Pain shoots through me when I see how devastated he is.

"Everything's upside down. I need time to think, to sort out my feelings." Another pain courses through me when I realize he doesn't want to stay with me.

"What can I do?" I ask as he looks at the canvas again.

"Nothing. You can't do anything." Gabriel walks over to me and places his hands on each side of my face. "I love you, ma chérie. Just give me some time." I want to throw a tantrum, tell him he can't leave, but he should never feel like he can't take some time for himself.

"I love you the same, mon amour. Please, please, text me or call me if you need me. I don't want you to leave, but I understand. Just don't think you're alone. I'm right here." Gabriel's eyes shed more tears, and he takes a deep breath before he envelops my lips with his and rushes out the door.

I can't imagine how he's feeling. His mom was adopted. He has a grandfather who is still alive and well, and maybe a grandmother out there somewhere. She might have more family, too. He could have twenty more blood relatives. This could be huge for him and Jean, even for Domi and Nicolette. Gabriel is in so much pain from losing almost everyone he's ever loved, and this news, it's not purely positive. His thoughts are probably spiraling right now... just like mine are.

What are the fucking chances Carlos Klein turns out to be Jean's and Gabriel's grandfather?

I want to scream at the top of my lungs. Nothing makes sense anymore, which is why I don't bother trying to figure it out. I remove my dress and makeup before lying in bed only wearing underwear. There is no energy left in my body to put on some clothes. My thoughts spiral down into one specific question.

He's going to come back to me, right?

I lie awake for a long time, unable to keep my mind off Gabriel and what he's going through right now. Every part of me longs to be with him, comfort him while he processes what he heard tonight.

A groan leaves me as I sit up in bed, sliding out of it to grab James' present and card. I open the envelope first, feeling my heart settle into a calm speed for the first time in hours.

Happy Birthday, my love.

I'm sorry I've been distant and haven't been the friend you deserve. If I'm being honest with both of us, I struggle to be in your presence now. You support me through it all, but you represent something to me that makes it difficult to look into your eyes.

Do you know what's harder though? Not seeing you. Not speaking to you. Avoiding you because of things that should stay in the past. I want to move forward, and I need you, darling. I need you more than anyone else in my life (don't tell Adrian I said that), and I'm sorry it has taken me so long to realize it.

Please, forgive me. You deserve better, and I will be just that.

I love you.

James

He was in love with me, imagined a life with me, and wanted to grow old with me. It was a fantasy, a hope even, he had since we were children. This baby turned everything upside down for him. It ripped the fantasy away, and now, I've become the representation he spoke of in the letter. I hate that. I hate how much pain I bring him without being able to do something to change it.

Maybe distance wasn't the worst idea, but neither of us wants that. We're happier when we're together.

My fingers wrap around the little gift he gave me, undoing the ribbons to open it. In it lies a keychain with a photo of Adrian, James, Gabriel, Cameron, and me. I smile to myself and grab the letter and gift, hugging it close to my body.

Finally, sleep consumes me, even if it's the most restless one I've ever had.

Chapter 87

Gabriel

I've never turned to alcohol to solve anything because I know it won't. I also know the consequences it will have on my body, but I don't give a shit right now. It numbs the overwhelming feelings in my mind, not that I could accurately name any of them. *Shock? Pain? Happiness? Fear?*

Shock definitely describes what my body is experiencing, but I'm not sure about pain and happiness. I am afraid, of what this will mean, of whether or not I can get my shit together and finally call the woman I love.

Valentina has been patient, giving me the space I asked her for when in reality all I want is to be with her, but not like this. Not when I'm fucked up and all over the place.

I should be excited about this like my brother is. I should be happy about having a shot at getting more family, but I'm not. *Why the hell am I not excited? What the fuck is wrong with me? Why can't I have the same reaction as Jean?*

Tears fall from my face, staining my shirt and the carpet.

"Gabriel, would you like some food?" Domi asks through my bedroom door, and I swallow the lump in my throat to speak.

"No, I'm fine," I reply, my voice cracking because I haven't heard it in days.

I've avoided everyone, loneliness camping in my chest, unwilling to leave me alone.

"If you change your mind, I will leave a plate for you in the oven," my wonderful aunt says before walking away again.

The urge to throw the bottle against my bookshelf is strong because it feels like my world has turned into one of those goddamn fiction novels that sit on there.

My phone vibrates and a message from Valentina lights up the screen. I think about ignoring it because whatever she said will make me break down more than I already have. It'll make me realize that, right now, I'm not the man she deserves.

I made a promise to Adrian and myself to always put her first, no matter what it means for my own feelings. I need her more than anything, but I'm a mess she doesn't deserve to deal with after getting the news of a lifetime only a few days ago.

Fuck, she's going to have everything she's ever wanted, and I'll drag her down. I'll distract her from the most important thing in our lives: her career. I can't do that. I *won't* do that.

Another message appears on my phone, this time it's one from Adrian. I know I can't hide from reality forever, even if I should, at least until I figure out what's going on in my head. My fingers tap my screen faster than my brain can react to stop them, and I read Valentina's message first.

Valentina: Hi, mon soleil. I don't mean to bother you, just checking in to see how you're doing. It's been a few days, and I wanted to remind you I'm a phone call away. You don't have to go through this alone if you don't want to. I know you don't want to bring any sort of negativity into my life, but I'm here to dance in the rain with you. Let me be your sun for a little.

I love you.

My heart is racing by the time I finish the sweetest message I have ever received. I shift my attention to Adrian's text, unable to let her words sink in completely yet.

Adrian: Hey, man. Just making sure you're doing alright. Val told me what's going on, and I want to let you know I'm here if you need anything. You can come vent to me anytime if you need to speak to someone who isn't Val. Maybe you don't want her to see you in a bad place or whatever, I don't know. Just remember I'm here for you too, for anything.

I think about calling him, asking him what the hell I'm supposed to do with myself now. Then again, he won't understand how I'm feeling nor will he tell me what I want to hear.

I'd need him to assure me I can go look for my family and stay with Valentina. I'd need him to make me feel okay about being the wrong man for his sister as I fall into darkness, and that would never happen.

If he were here, he'd tell me I have to let her go to protect her, at least until I figure everything out again.

Valentina deserves someone who isn't broken, who doesn't fall apart from hearing they have a chance to have more family. *But what is family? Is it blood?* I used to think so, but after meeting Adrian and Val, I've realized family is whoever makes you feel whole.

Then why the fuck do I want to find Sierra?

The answer pops into my head before I can stop it.

Because Sierra and Carlos are my mother's biological parents. I miss her more than anything, and if there is a chance I can feel connected to Mom again, I have to try.

Chapter 88

Valentina

Yesterday, James and I went over my revised contract, making sure everything was absolutely perfect before I signed it. Despite not knowing what's going on with Gabriel and constantly worrying, I could not stop smiling at my achievement.

Annabel showed up at James' too because they planned on going to her ultrasound appointment together. We talked for a little, and I even helped them come up with the perfect name for their baby: Damian Parker Rossi-Landon.

Leonard also messaged me yesterday, asking if he could come over to discuss something important. I haven't been feeling very social since my last interaction with Gabriel a couple of days ago, but whatever he wants to discuss sounded urgent over the phone.

After everything he's done, I didn't want to deny him the one favor he's asked of me, no matter how badly I want to be by myself to overthink. Then again, I like Leonard, and spending time with him always brightens up my day.

I place the biscuits I baked on a plate to bring outside onto the veranda, making a plan to prepare the coffee when Leonard arrives. He's perfectly on time, greeting me with a slight hug for the first time. His fresh scent fills my nose, and I smile at him.

"Thank you for seeing me on such short notice," he says as he settles down on the chair I point to, lifting a black folder onto my table.

A small smirk tugs at the corner of my mouth while I study his professional attitude.

"I feel like I'm in trouble," I tease, and he gives me a half-amused, half-challenging expression.

"Why? What have you done?" he replies. I raise my hands in mock surrender, leaning away from him to show my innocence. "Oh no, you've finally done it, haven't you? I know he can be annoying, but locking Adrian in the basement isn't the answer," Leonard says, and I burst into laughter.

"Please, I wouldn't put him in my basement. I'd lock him in James' so he'd take the fall for it," I reply, and the Brit gives me a chuckle while shaking his head. "Anyway, what's going on? How can I help you with whatever is in that folder?" I ask, and Leonard refocuses on business, his favorite subject to discuss with me.

He's been opening up more and more toward me, and I love that we've connected. I hope, one day, we can be good friends.

"Before I get into what's in this folder, I'd like to explain why I kept my distance from you in the past," he starts, and I swallow hard.

"You mean why you didn't like me?" I say to relieve some of the tension, but he frowns at my words.

"It's not that I didn't like you, Valentina. You were a constant reminder to me of what is wrong with the sport we love. You reminded me of what I went through, even if our experiences differ. We both had to fight harder than the rest of them, and I hated seeing you hide how much you struggled without being able to do something about it. It made the feelings of when I was a child and tried everything to get accepted by any teams resurface, but I couldn't do anything to help myself either. My father had to work three jobs to finance my dream, but we heard the word 'no' more often than I could keep count," he says.

I take a deep breath when I remember my body needs oxygen to function.

"Getting close to you wasn't an option, not until I knew how to help you. That's why I wanted to become your mentor. You needed someone who experienced something similar, someone who understood you." He opens the folder as he speaks, avoiding eye contact with me, which I'm grateful for. I'm convinced I'd cry if he looked at me.

"You were trying to find a way to help me get a seat?"

All this time I thought he didn't like me when he was fighting for me. *Man...* I'm the luckiest girl in the world to have a support system like no one else.

"Of course. I spoke to Mr. Reiner and sat down with him to analyze your times and compare them thoroughly with the rest of the drivers in line for the spot. I didn't stop until he listened because you, Valentina, have something inside of you that hardly anyone else has. You have the spirit of a true racer. You didn't give up," he says, and guilt spreads through my chest.

"I did give up. After they kicked me out of the VRDA, I didn't want to fight anymore. I argued with everyone because they didn't understand how tiring it is to be rejected all the time. I was ready to find something else, a new career," I admit, and Leonard lifts his gaze to mine, warmth settling in my cheeks from his comforting smile.

"But you weren't looking for anything else, were you?"

I think about the time between Christian getting the Formula Three seat and me getting the F1 one, but he's right. I said I'd have to find a new passion and couldn't bring myself to do anything else. I wasn't done fighting yet, even when I thought I was.

"I'll take that as a 'no,'" he says and hands me the folder, but I'm stuck on something else he brought up before.

"You were responsible for getting me that spot in the VRDA?" I ask, panic filling his eyes when he hears the disappointment in my voice.

"No, no, no, none of that! I sat down with *your* statistics, with *your* lap times, and proved to him you're worth taking a chance on. It's different for me, I'm already a Formula One driver with a good, reliable reputation. My word, my opinions, they matter to these people, but it doesn't change your talent. Don't you start doubting yourself," he scolds, pointing at me with a warning finger. I let out a small laugh and assure him I won't.

"Okay, tell me, what's this?" I ask, looking down at the pages in front of me.

"It's an idea I had, and I want you to be my partner," he says, and my heart momentarily forgets how to beat.

The title of the first page reads "Driver Academy for Kids Like Us."

"I want to open a race school for children that have been denied a chance because of who they are, where they come from, and what opportunities they've been given. I came from a low-income family and only had enough money to get into racing because my dad found someone who wanted to sponsor me. This school is going to be the place where talented children get the chance to prove themselves, and, based on their results, not the color of their skin or their gender, they will be judged. We'll need a lot of sponsors and partners in this endeavor, but I want your name to be right next to mine." I listen to him, scanning the page of the folder to see what sponsors he intends to have invest.

"This is a wonderful idea, Leonard, but who the hell would be crazy enough to invest in something without foreseeable profit?" I ask, and he leans forward on the table, ready to prove me wrong.

"In the long run, they'll make money from the drivers. Plus, nowadays, this sport attempts to pride itself on being diverse and inclusive. This is its way of actually *showing* it to the world."

I nod, still reading over his papers.

"I know it won't be easy, but I'd like to try and make a difference, and, like I said, I want you to be my partner."

He reaches for the folder, flipping it back to the first page and tapping the name.

"'For Kids Like Us,'" he says, and my heart sinks into my chest.

"I don't know how much time I can put into this academy with my career just taking off," I explain, but Leonard shakes his head at me.

"All I need from you is advice, strategy planning, and bagging investors. You're a force to be reckoned with, Val, and they will see that. You could be a key part of this school because you're the first woman to ever get a spot in Formula One. So, what do you say?"

I cock an eyebrow, staying silent to build suspense, but I already have an answer for him.

"Come on, Val, don't do that to me," he begs, and I can't help but smile at the side he's showing me.

"I would love nothing more than to be your partner on this," I say, standing up and holding out my hand for him to shake.

Instead, he walks around the table to wrap his arms around me.

"Thank you," Leonard says, and I hug him back, needing the comfort of it for more than one reason.

"Thank you for fighting for me."

Chapter 89

Valentina

It's been a while since I've seen my grandfather, and it's starting to hurt how much I miss him. Aunt Carolina has no sympathy for my homesickness, so I make sure not to show it in front of her. I don't want her to get angry with me.

"Val, I have a little surprise for you," Adrian says while I'm on my bed, trying to study. "Come with me," he adds, holding out his hand for me to take.

There is a serious look on his face, worrying me. It's a surprise, so it shouldn't be bad, but it looks like he just got the worst news of his life; his face is pale and his eyes are red.

"What's wrong?" I ask him as he wraps his fingers around mine.

Adrian stays quiet until we reach the bottom of the stairs. Grandfather sits on the couch in the living room, and I sprint over to where he is.

"Grandpa!" I call out, my arms wrapping around his neck.

"Hi, little champion," he says, hugging me back. "I'm sorry, this isn't going to be a happy visit, but I've been dragging it out for long enough. It's time we talked."

I hold my breath as he guides me down onto the couch next to him.

"I don't understand," I say, panic flooding my chest.

Grandfather's tired eyes fill with tears, and he lets out a heavy, shaky breath.

"I'm not going to be—" He cuts off, inhaling again to gather courage. "I'm not going to be around for much longer, Valentina. I'm going to see your Grandma soon."

Fear strikes through me.

"No, you're not. You're still healthy, you're not that old," I say, disbelief coming through as denial.

"I have lung cancer, sweetheart. I'm dying," he explains, but I shake my head.

"No, that can't be. You're not a smoker."

I don't know who I'm trying to reason with, his disease or him, but it's not fair. He can't leave me. There is so much we still have left to do. I haven't made it into Formula One yet! He needs to see me fulfill our dream. He cannot leave me!

"Listen to me. I know this is going to be very hard for you, but I need you to promise me you'll keep your heart. Don't shut it off, don't start pushing people away. Not everyone leaves, I promise."

I shake my head again, tears pouring down my cheeks.

"You need to let me go now, my children. You have to so you can keep focusing on your careers and stay in balance in all three categories. Do you remember?"

I nod, but I don't want to. I want to throw things, scream, and break down.

"Good, remember them. Don't let your emotions throw everything off balance. You have to let go, even if it's the worst pain you've ever felt. You have to let go because this is out of our control. There is nothing we can do to change it, but you can't let it tear you down from what's important, okay? Don't allow anyone to put themselves before your dream."

He turns to me, grabbing my face to make sure I pay close attention to him.

"One day, I hope you'll meet someone who will prioritize you and your career no matter what. That person will be the one for you. When you find them, and they show you how much they value your dream, don't shut them out of your heart."

I don't know why he's telling me any of this. I don't care about the future if he won't be in mine.

"There is a lot I have left to teach you, but I'm afraid I'm out of time."

It's been days since I've last seen or spoken to Gabriel. I've texted him a couple of times, and I've tried calling him, but he doesn't answer. Evangelin has tried contacting me, but I'm not ready to talk to her yet. James is busy with Annabel, and Adrian is training with his performance coach.

Lorenzo Mattia has finalized everything for me, and I will officially drive for Alfa Adrenalina next season. He's also told me I have to work almost every day of the three-week Formula One summer break to test drive the car. It's going to be busy, but I'm excited to get started.

After not knowing what to do with my free time, I decide to spend the whole day taking care of myself. First, I work out, then I go for a swim in my pool before taking a shower and putting on a face mask.

I pick up Gabriel's copy of *Die For Me* and continue reading from where I stopped months ago. My eyes go back to Gabriel's annotations, and they focus on a specific one.

If I ever got her, would I have the strength to leave her?

God, I hope he doesn't. I hope more than anything he will come back to me. Yet, with every day he doesn't talk to me, I grow more certain he's getting strong enough to leave me.

He's going to leave me, isn't he?

Of course he is, otherwise, he wouldn't be avoiding me.

It's been a while since Gabriel and I have gone more than a day without talking to each other. Not texting or calling him every day feels unnatural.

I distract myself by turning on a comedy show and removing my face mask. Adrian comes home from his workout, and I spend some time with him, desperate to get my mind off my own problems. He tells me he's prepared for Austria, and I let him know how proud I am.

Adrian is working harder than he ever has before.

After dinner, I go upstairs to be by myself for a little. My head has been spinning, thinking about Gabriel the whole time I was with Adrian, and I can't stand it.

A knock on my bedroom door startles me, but I don't even flinch.

"Come in," I say, wondering who it could possibly be.

When he walks through my door, I stop breathing.

"NO," I say louder than necessary, a tear rolling down his cheek. "Why did you knock? You explained to me you didn't have to knock any more, and I was okay with it. So, don't start knocking again," I beg the tears that leave my eyes full of pain.

"Valentina, please don't make this more difficult than it already is."

I get up from my bed, but I don't move closer.

"No, I am going to make this as hard as possible because you are about to destroy everything, and I want it to hurt you just as much as it is going to hurt me."

It's selfish, and I know it's wrong. I'm hoping he won't leave once he realizes it's so hard to say goodbye because he loves me more than anything else in the world.

"You don't think this is going to hurt? You think I haven't been battling with myself for the past four days? Baby, I love you so much, and doing this now is going to break me, but I have to. I haven't been treating you right since I found out Carlos is my grandfather, and I am not going to be right for you again until I find Sierra and the rest of her family... *my family.*" I sink down on the bed, trying to stay strong, but my bottom lip starts to tremble. "Please, don't do that."

"Then don't leave. You said I am your life, you gave me this necklace to remind me of that, and now you throw me away like I never meant anything to you," I yell at him. The tears falling from his eyes hurt me more than my own.

"I need to do this. I made a promise to put you first, and this is me doing that."

I nod and look at him with as much anger in my eyes as I can. My heart is shattering in my chest in a way I have never felt before.

"I don't care that you think you're still keeping it. You're not, and you're making me break mine, too." I'm yelling, which makes him take a step back. "Why can't you go out and search for your family with me by your side? Why do you have to leave me to do that?"

He walks over to me, but I get up to put more distance between us again.

"Because you need to focus on your career. You cannot be in your head, wondering about my feelings and picking up the pieces of my broken world! You need all of your attention on one task: preparing yourself to become an F1 driver. I cannot be the reason why you get hurt in the car or why your performance isn't at its best. Trust me, I know what happens when you lose balance in your mind. It fucks you over, and I will *not* do that to you. I won't lose you the same way I lost Maxime!" he yells and points at me, pieces falling into place in my mind. *Maxime...* "I love you too much, chérie, and that's why I have to do this. I won't be who you need me to be, and that's not fair. Your career has to come first, always," he whispers, and I look at him in disbelief.

I still cannot breathe, or think, and my heart is sending waves of fear through my bloodstream.

"You know what's messed up? That even though you're breaking up with me, I want you to find your family." I laugh at myself and watch pain shoot over his face. "I've lost many people too. So, I understand why you're doing this, but as the girl who is in love with you, I can't help but be angry at your reasoning. You are giving up on us as if we never meant anything to you to begin with."

I've never been more self-centered than I am at this moment, but I don't care. He's doing this to us, he's squeezing all of my organs, and he's making me want to throw up.

"I'm not giving up," he complains before he throws his hands into the air.

"Yes, you are." Gabriel sits down on my bed and drops his face into his hands.

"I'm doing this for you, for your career! Valentina, I love—"

"Stop," I interrupt him. "Stop saying that. If you really loved me, you wouldn't leave me." His head shoots up, and he shakes it at my response.

"Try to understand," he begs, and I let out a short laugh I don't mean.

"I do, I truly do, but let me put it this way. I love you, and I let you in. I never let anyone in, but I did with you, and you are ripping me apart from the inside out. So, as much as I understand it, I can't forgive you for this." He nods but doesn't look at me. I want to scream louder than I have ever before. Gabriel is doing this, he's letting go. "You walk out of that door and I will never be able to forgive you for this."

I put my hands on my hips because I'm trying to stand my ground. In reality, I want to lie down, curl up in a fetal position, and ball my goddamn eyes out.

"I hope you *will* be able to forgive me."

Gabriel stands in front of me, and I let him press a kiss on the top of my head. I can't help myself. Maybe I want to feel his lips on my skin one more time before I let anger consume me.

"I'm broken, mon tournesol, and I won't tear you down with me, not while you're finally getting everything you've ever wanted." I shake my head as he steps away from me.

"Everything I've ever wanted includes you, Gabriel. You spoke about marrying me, but now you're pushing me out of your life during your darkest time. You don't trust my love for you, which is the saddest part of it all," I say, and he rubs his tired face.

"No, chérie, I know you'd help me work through everything, but it would be at the expense of your career. Don't you understand that? You can't have a split mind right now. No Formula One driver has made it far if their head wasn't focused entirely on their success in the beginning stages, in the one you're in. Please, please, Valentina, you have to let me go," he explains, desperation all over the beautiful face I've studied more than anyone else's.

Some of my anger drifts as I stare at him.

"My grandfather warned me about you, but I never expected it to hurt like this," I admit, unwilling to hide my emotions from him.

"My mother warned me about you too. She said I'd fall in love with the strongest, most beautiful woman in the world."

Without looking back once or saying another word, he leaves my room and my life.

I can't help but hope it's just for now...

Read how Valentina and Gabriel's story continues in Chase: Part One & Two

Chase: Chapter One

Gabriel

I CLOSE THE DOOR behind me using all the strength my body has left, leaving my heart and soul with Valentina. She'll never forgive me for this. I'm choosing myself over her, but I have to. I have to do what's best for me to be everything she deserves. Since I found out Carlos Klein is my fucking grandfather, I've been the wrong man for her. Someone who drinks and wallows in pain and self-pity isn't the type of person Valentina deserves. My mess shouldn't become hers during the most important time of her life.

She's just been offered a seat in Formula One. Alfa Adrenalina saw her potential, and she'll be training the entire summer break to prepare herself for the rest of the season. The woman I love will be the first female F1 driver, but for now, she'll be the reserve driver for my team, Velocità Rossa, which is already a big responsibility. It's going to need her entire focus. I can't drag her into the dark space I've spiraled into. It's not fair. If I knew Val could be selfish, focus solely on herself, I wouldn't be leaving, but she's not that type of person. She loves me too much. And I love her more than anything or anyone else. Which is why I have to do this.

It's how I become the man she deserves again.

I straighten out my back, ignoring the tears streaming down my face as I walk down the stairs and the way my muscles try to fight against it. Every part of me is drawing me backward, back to Val, because I'm not whole without her. Half of me is her, just like half of her is me. We complete each other and walking away? It goes against my survival instinct.

"What the fuck did you just do?" *Shit.* Adrian's voice is full of anger and frustration, and I spin around to show him how horrible I look. His eyes widen at the sight of me. "Jesus, Gabriel. What happened?" he asks, and I let the tears drop down my face.

"I ripped my heart out and left it with her. That's what happened," I reply and attempt to leave again when his hand wraps around my elbow to stop me.

"Don't. Don't leave her like this, mate. You'll do more harm than good," he says gently and firmly, understanding my pain as well as trying to protect his sister from harm. If he could look inside the dark hole in my head, he'd know letting me leave is the best thing for her.

"Let me go," I say when his grip tightens around my arm.

"If you do this, there's no going back," Adrian warns me, and I know what he means. There will be no undoing the pain I've caused. Val will hate me. He will hate me. My only hope is that they loved me enough at one point to forgive me once I've put myself back together.

"If I don't do this, I will be putting Val's life in danger," I whisper-scream, ripping my arm free. This has gone on long enough. I have to get out of this house, the one that's somehow become more of a home to me than my childhood house, before Valentina hears us.

"Don't pretend you're doing this for her," Adrian replies, pissed at me now. Good. Maybe he will let me walk out the door if he's angry.

"I am. And you have to promise me you will do everything in your power to ensure she's focused when she tests the car, you hear me? Her mind needs to be in her head, not stuck on wherever I am. Do you understand me?" I ask, grabbing his shoulders as I speak to be certain he's hearing me. Nothing can happen to mon tournesol, especially not because of me.

"Val is my little sister, Gabriel, the most important person in my life. I will do whatever it takes to keep her safe," he says like I should already know this, and I do. It's one of the reasons I know I'm doing the right thing.

"So will I," I reply, leaving him standing in the middle of the entrance before walking outside and letting the hot summer sun burn my skin.

My lungs are constricting, preventing me from breathing. My heart feels like it has stopped beating, slowing my steps. My head is screaming, telling me what a horrible man I am and, at the same time, reminding me this is for the best.

God, I'm so fucked.

Acknowledgements

To all my readers, from the bottom of my heart, thank you.

About the Author

Bridget L. Rose is a half-German, half-Italian author, who was born and raised in Germany until the age of thirteen. She fell in love with books from a young age, and soon discovered her passion for writing as well. She likes to spend her free time with her family, reading a book, or writing one herself. She also adores the sport Formula One, which led her to write her Pitstop Series.

Books by Bridget L. Rose

The Pitstop Series

Jump-Start

The Inside of a Rainbow

Rush: Part One & Two

Chase: Part One & Two

From Angels to Devils Series

From Devils to Angels

Printed in Great Britain
by Amazon

40800889R00239